Hidden Beneath

Hidden Beneath

The Captivating Sequel to City of Dreams

By
Suzanne Burkett

First Edition

Illustrated by Pete Burkett

Published by Suzanne Burkett Incline Village, Nevada

ISBN-13: 979-8-9871346-1-0
Library of Congress Control Number: 2022919244
Hidden Beneath
The Captivating Sequel to City of Dreams

Contact:
Suzanne Burkett
PO Box 5656, Incline Village, NV 89450

This is a work of fiction. Characters, names, locations, places, and incidents are products of the author's imagination, or are used fictitiously. Any resemblance to actual persons, living or dead, business establishments, or events is entirely coincidental.

First Edition

For Sawyer and Paisley

Acknowledgements

With thanks to my readers who encouraged and supported me as they waited for this sequel to City of Dreams.
Thank you dear husband, Pete Burkett for your inspired cover illustration.
Thanks to Elaine Van Fossen Greynald for reading and discussing content and plot.
Much thanks to my Editor, Adele Brinkley

Table of Contents

Prologue

They were not holy men. As they roamed the ancient city, for like attracts like, the group of unfortunates grew. The first was a slender one who earned favor with his soft and comforting words. Others followed. They had adopted the garb of the revered monks. In so doing, they received favor from the prosperous inhabitants of their crowded city. But not for long. Soon, in only three full cycles of the moon, their secret became known. Two monks were caught in the home of a wealthy lord, carrying away his gold and silver. They were desperate men, liars all of them. "Duplicity is futile in a cluster of miscreants," the slender one told them.

No longer did the lords and ladies, mongers and drudges bestow favor upon them. These false brethren had taken advantage. They were not pious men, but lower than thieves. The citizens spat at their feet.

The men were wan and weak from wandering the steep streets of the seven hills that made up their city. Their bowls had gone unfilled for six days, and rain fell without hesitation. Their thin cloaks absorbed water and mud. Gathered in the ruins where they slept, the men examined their plunder and decided it was time to leave. On their final night, with silent skill and, under cover of the torrents, they robbed dozens of households.

In a splendid dawn, with heads bowed and arms folded over their cloaks to conceal satchels of provisions, the men walked in single file, the slender one leading them through the city gates.

They went in search of refuge from a growing civilization that they didn't understand, for each of these thirty-three men had suffered inexplicable and incomprehensible torment. As generations of people have done before, in many ways, they had unwittingly inflicted the repercussions of life upon themselves. Still, undeniably, their hearts bore bloody scars etched by physical pain, affliction, and unbearable loss. Their souls had become deadened by a broken fate and the anguish that pushes in with it.

The men walked so far and so long that their soft shoes fell away, and their feet bled, leaving a trail of hopeless footprints across the warm stones. Each man felt in his heart the punishment of his own misdeeds. Youthful aspirations, long since trampled, loitered at the cliff of their awareness and threatened to drag them down.

They walked along in moonlight and felt connected to the vastness above them. They stumbled through black nights of empty sky to find reward when the wind shoved the clouds away, and the stars danced so near, they held them in the palms of their hands.

But in the long, hot days, with only scraps of food left among them, they simply lost the desire to walk on. When the decision to end their journey became apparent, the grimy, exhausted men observed their surroundings. The land around was intimidating, but lush and welcoming with bushes full of shiny red berries. They crumpled upon the soft, damp banks of a river of dancing crystalline water so cold it made their feet tingle, and the tingling that spread throughout their bodies told them this was home.

One by one, they removed their cloaks to reveal the utensils and tools they had stolen from the never home. They created a hamlet at the edge of the river and agreed to share all that they'd brought and all that they would find. Their task became a strict ritual by which they lived. It began by clearing the land with sickle and shovel. In the dirt, they found their toil rewarded them with rectangular stones that became the foundation of their existence and their religion. Into these stones—gifts from the land they claimed as their own—they poured their pain. From deep within the solid stone, collected since the beginning of time, emerged an energy, a will to go on.

In the evenings, they sat upon the riverbank, their thoughts absorbed in the powerful current. Weeks crept by in comfortable silence, until, revived by toil, they began to share ideas once again. Thereupon, the thirty-three men adopted a new way of living based on the laws they observed in the nature surrounding them. The tall, slender monk said, "What is belief but religion and what is religion but what each man knows in his own heart to be true? We will survive."

Because they didn't understand what the vocation of monk truly meant, they focused on endurance. The men began to build their monastery where a new and separate way of life could flourish.

The day's labor commenced upon awakening and continued until hunger and thirst overtook them. They replenished themselves by drinking fresh, clear water that ran through their fingers and shimmered in the morning light, reflecting the colors of the earth like a prism in their grateful hands. At dusk, they lay down on straw mats to sleep like the dead.

The months passed in amiable silence, for none among them wished to discuss or remember the past. A few monks fell from the rickety bridge that they had strung across the river and were swept away by the fast-flowing water. Several were injured by the very tools and stones they labored with. Their skin suffered cuts, scrapes, lesions, and gaping wounds. They tended themselves with poultices of mud, plants, and beeswax. They took on the task of smeremongere and worked inside a lean-to making candles. The strongest endured the pulling, heaving, and levering of stones.

There was nothing to steal, and they could not receive alms, so they roamed the surrounding hills, observed, and gathered. They studied the movement of the water and marveled at its clarity. Some monks made wine, others bread, but none of them wanted to hunt. After the river swelled with the rain, they noticed fish flapping in a pool. When the water retreated, they gathered the fish in baskets.

For months, then years, and safely ensconced inside their hand-carved walls, the men collaborated. They forgot about the world they had left behind and the people who had damaged them. They kept to their rigid routine, day after day and year after year. They built square dwellings in a rectangle of protection with a spacious gathering room in the center. Outside of their sanctuary, they set to work connecting oblong stones to create the foundation of their monastery walls. Two monks sculpted three bells from lost-wax, bronze castings. They hoisted them to hang in the tall, timber-roofed belfry at one connecting corner of their enclosure. The echoing peal of bells renewed their faith in themselves.

In their harmonious world, nightfall was a hallowed event. The bells rang to remind the men working outside the walls to return before the gates were closed and barricaded by two massive wooden beams. Those left outside could not partake in the star catching ritual. On their long journey, the monks had learned the stars protected them from perils of the dark. After welcoming the guiding lights, the men lit candles until their walls glowed, and their shadows fluttered in relief.

Decades passed as they diligently built their monastery walls. Then, the disagreements began. How could they continue to build? There were only eleven monks left. They had no plan. They gathered in their sanctuary to discuss possible solutions. Wiser monks had passed away, taking their knowledge with them. Although pleased by the beauty of their walls, not one of them knew how to span the wide gap and construct the roof. The monks fell into bitter discussion, continuous arguing, and finally accusation.

Four monks set out to find help from the outside world. The seven who remained, having nothing else to do and doubting the return of the others with outsiders, continued to work. They couldn't go up, so they went down. They dug a cellar and kept digging and dug another cellar below that and pushed farther and deeper into the glittering earth. Each monk built his own passage to go in and out.

They kept their own counsel during the day and in the evenings walked together and showed each other the paths they'd created. They made doors from heavy wood and stained them green with the plant life surrounding them.

Nine years later, the four monks returned with slaves and masons.

To protect their monastery and guided by the wisdom of the slender one, the seven indrawn monks began diverting river water to create the loch and the moat in plain view of hundreds of men who had no idea what the cunning monks were doing. In their tireless digging, the monks had learned how to split the river into channels. On the surface, one could not be distinguished from the other.

The first, a powerful stream of clear water, travelled through a spiral crevice in the bedrock as it made its way through and beneath the monastery walls to the lower caverns where it tumbled melodiously into a deep stone pool. The second stream which passed through the meadow to mix with the marshes' mingling silt and foliage, which turned their moat a murky green. The newcomers covered their noses in dismay and revulsion.

For themselves, the seven had protected their stone walls and underground spring with ingenious deception. The seven monks, who were not monks, had found a secret and they had no intention of sharing it with anyone. They still had the inclination to steal, but now they sought knowledge. Cloaked in their mute disdain for outsiders, they prowled among the new masons, listening and learning. Luring the youngest and strongest with gifts, they succeeded in finishing the roof of their monastery.

When the monks first came to the City of Dreams, there was no city, only dreams.

Chapter 1

Wearing an oversized hooded cloak, the locksmith strolled along the crowded street as if he had no place to go. A man of such desirable skills, he did his best to keep his identity secret when among the public. Stepping deftly sideways, he stopped in front of the door. Slipping one rust-stained hand from inside his cloak and clutching his heavy satchel with the other, he lifted the triangular rapper hanging below the lion head and then let if fall. Inclining his head, he bent and listened as the key engaged the gear, the cylinder turned, and the door opened.

"I didn't call for you," Irene declared.

Pushing the heavy door fully open, Lucas placed his hand on Irene's shoulder and said, "I did."

"Whatever for?" Irene protested.

Lucas briefly closed his eyes, leaned over, and whispered in Irene's ear. "I want even more security." Beckoning the locksmith, Gacheru, to come through, he led Irene back toward the kitchen.

She stood in front of the simmering iron pot with her hands planted firmly on her hips, a stern but amused scowl on her face. "When did you decide to lock her in?"

"I'm not locking her in." Lucas swung around to nod to Gacheru to get on with his work. "I'm locking them out."

"Who? Our boarders?"

"No, no of course not. They now come in from the back door anyway."

"They do?"

"Um hmm," Lucas glanced around the kitchen and grabbed a chunk of bread from the sideboard.

"Since when?" She tapped her foot and coughed to cover a chuckle.

"Well, as you know, Irene, at the present time, all of our boarders are laborers and masons and the like, those working on the cathedral. They come through the back door. That's what they prefer. None of them are parlour sitters."

"So, you're changing a perfectly good lock to . . .?"

"No, I'm adding another lock to the lock that is already in place."

Irene shook her head, unwound her morning shawl, tossed it onto a ladderback chair, and picked up the iron kettle. "On the back door as well?" she took a seat with her cup of tea.

He nodded.

"I thought we were safe from Barrington and Dugald and their kind now. They're all dead, jailed, or banished. Is that not correct?"

"It's correct." Lucas braced his arms in the doorway and kept his eye on the locksmith.

"Does Alina know you're locking her in?"

"I'm not!"

Irene burst out laughing and spit her tea across the table. "That lass will be climbing out the window or going through the courtyard and over the garden wall. You can't lock her in."

"I have new locks for the courtyard doors and windows as well." He nodded and left her at the table as he went to oversee the locksmith.

She called after him, "Make sure I have a key to all these locks. And Carissa and Perina too. And Madam Trousdale and Nikolas, of course. And Ikarus and all the boarders. Oh, and don't forget Alina. She should have a key too lest you lock her out."

Lucas raked his hands through his hair as he swaggered back into the parlour. Gacheru had strayed into the courtyard where he stood at the threshold aimlessly opening and closing the garden door, his eyes fixated on the assortment of herbs and plants that sat on shelves and ledges. Their fine tendrils dangling like emerald filigree swayed slightly by a phantom breeze.

"What are you doing?" Lucas demanded.

"Oh, uh . . . you mentioned the courtyard door. Wall is tall . . ." His gaze drifted from the garden wall to stare blankly at Lucas.

Lucas moved closer. "I instructed you to begin with the front door."

"Just me thinking, Gacheru shifted his gaze from Lucas to scan the parlour. He leaned left to peer into the kitchen before turning his attention back to the copious assortment of greenery.

"Have you never seen plants before?"

Gacheru shook his head while mumbling incoherently. He hobbled back to the front door and rummaged through his satchel, dropping implements on the floor as he searched.

"Never mind. Forget about it," Lucas growled. "Collect your junk and get out of here." He opened the door and shoved the fumbling buffoon and his tangle of tools outside. After closing and locking the door, he glanced up the stairs and then retreated to the garden bench that had become his refuge.

Since her return to the boarding house a week ago, Alina had not yet come downstairs. He took her meals on a tray, and sometimes they sat in silence and ate. But mostly, after their first passionate night upon her return, she had slept. She had retreated to her initial shyness, and Lucas feared he knew why.

They had spent that first night guzzling wine and getting to know each other, entwined in the most intimate ways. He had tried to talk to her about his longing but could not formulate the proper words. He also had consumed much wine and felt foolhardy for presenting bottle after bottle. One thing for certainty, they had not become husband and wife in the true sense of being. But it was time. They could wait no longer. As he sat in the tranquility of the aromatic courtyard garden, he decided he'd better let her know that forthwith.

He sighed, and closed his eyes, remembering their passionate night. In front of the blazing fire, with trembling hands, Lucas and Alina had confirmed their love and desire. They explored each other with trembling hands and loving eyes. Desire replaced the fear and sorrow that had overtaken them in their time apart. They discovered the mystery of their yearning bodies as they laughed and sobbed, and released the burdens of a shared aching heart. She buried her face in his neck and he in the soft warmth of her tummy. Lucas wanted more than anything he had ever wished for to take Alina finally as his, but his terror of losing her again struck him with bridled restraint. Even though she consented with her eyes and her warm delicate hands, Lucas drew back and poured more wine. But in the whispered words of lovers, he promised they would become one in the most magnificent manner of any two living souls.

In the morning, Lucas awoke on the floor to see Alina clutching her sides and vomiting. When she'd finally emptied her stomach, he lifted her pale, shivering body and carried her into her room where he snuggled her into her coverlet.

Stroking her sweaty hair away from her eyes, he asked, "Irene?"

She winced and nodded her head.

It took all that day and half of the next for Alina to feel better and for Lucas to clean up the wine stains and food scraps strewn about his bedchamber floor.

* * *

Alina finished combing her hair and set the silver-handled brush on her dressing table. Brushing her own hair was a comfort now. She wondered how she could have let her maid Daria dote on her for so long. Her window was open, and the air smelled like summer. She must get out of the boarding house. Perhaps, she should just wander downstairs and invite Lucas to go out for a walk. But how could she after what she'd done. She'd made a complete fool of herself by retching into Lucas' wash basin and all over their clothes strewn about the floor. It had been a beautiful, enchanting, romantic evening, and then the next thing she remembered was herself, naked and shivering with vomit spewing from her clammy, trembling body. He had swaddled her in a soft blanket, but she could only beg him to take her to her own room and call for Irene. They both saw her as the helpless wreck that she was. She had yet to thank Irene for her teas and dry bread. How does one recover from such utter humiliation?

A gentle breeze ruffled her loose hair. That's it, she decided and yanked open her door only to find Lucas, poised with his hand in the air, ready to knock.

"Oh."

"Alina, my darling." Lucas clasped his hands together and exhaled. "Look at you, my gorgeous girl. You're feeling better?"

Despite her fluttering stomach, she smiled. "Yes, Lucas, I'm well."

"Shall we go for a walk? It's a fine day."

"Yes, please, let's go. I'm sorry, Lucas."

"About what?"

"Destroying your room with the contents of my stomach for one thing."

Lucas laughed. "Ah Alina, I so enjoy your sense of humor!"

"It's not a joke though." She scowled at the floorboards.

"Well, you said you wanted to behave like children together, so, we did."

"I'm sure it took days to clean the room." She blushed and covered her face.

Lucas took her by the hand. "Come on, let's get outside. We absolutely need to talk."

As Lucas pulled open the front door, Irene, wiping her hands on her apron, approached from the kitchen. She came through the parlour and took Alina's hand in hers. "Sweet girl, you are family. You need not hide anything."

Alina nodded as she fought back tears. Her lips trembled, but she could not speak.

"You see, Alina, tis true. You have nothing to hide, no matter where it comes from," Lucas said. He chuckled, as did Irene.

Alina allowed herself to giggle with them as she dabbed at her eyes. "I feel so witless."

"Most of us do," Irene said with a wink before she ambled back to the kitchen.

Outside, the warm, blossom-scented breeze boosted their mood. Alina wore a pale-yellow dress with white lace trim at the three-quarter sleeves and hem. Lucas, wearing his customary loose-sleeved white shirt and black trousers, folded her arm in his. "And here we start again," he stated as they melded out into the street. "Let's stop by the flower vendor."

Alina smiled in agreement. He noticed the shy uncertainty in her eyes, but it was mixed with joy and anticipation. She stood by while Lucas selected ten pink tulips. The woman waved to Alina, who gleamed in acknowledgement. Lucas held the bouquet in one hand and Alina's hand in the other as they turned toward the river.

Once seated upon the dry grass, he turned to Alina. "In case you are wondering, you are still a maiden," he blurted out.

She tittered and reached for the tulips. "I was wondering! I thought I should know, . . . but my goodness, what overtook me that night?"

Lucas held the tulips at arm's length and cleared his throat. "I did, and uh, well the wine got both of us, but honestly, we missed each other. You had been gone for weeks, Alina. I nearly died from grief that I would never see you again."

Alina's eyes widened and filled with tears. "Lucas, I've hurt you. Can you believe I didn't mean to?"

He brushed a loose curl away from her cheek. "Yes, I will always believe in you. That's plain truth, and I want you to believe in me. You can trust that a lot happened that night, but not everything." He took her chin in his hand and presented the flowers. "Alina. It's time now. You have to marry me."

"I . . . I . . . we will . . . soon, right?"

"More than soon. Let's hurry now. I swear you can be yourself and wander the city wearing brazen necklines and glittering rubies and I won't tell you what to do."

Her hand went to her throat. "Brazen."

"I will protect you though. And if that involves hiring Igmus and Rathbone to follow you, then so be it."

"Ahh, Lucas! I believe I may be safer on my own than with those two trailing me." She laughed, "I mean I know they are good friends to Nikolas, and they look after both of you."

Lucas chuckled. "Their bulky appearance is what scares vagabonds and thieves away, but don't let them frighten you. They will protect you as well, my love."

"Fine men they are indeed," Alina said, "but I don't need guards, Lucas."

He gazed at her with twinkling eyes. "Straightaway, we shall acquire the ring. Let's go now to the jeweller."

"No."

"Yes."

She giggled again. "Lucas, wait. You've reminded me." She lifted her skirt and took up a corner of her shift. Prying apart the secret pocket, she murmured, "Your gift." She pulled out the purple velvet pouch. Taking Lucas' hand, she placed it into his palm. "Open it."

Feeling the weight of it in his hand, he appeared perplexed and hesitated.

"Your wedding gift."

He beamed, pulled her to him, and planted a soft kiss on her silky mouth. Opening the ties on the pouch, he took out the gold pocket watch with hunter case and chain. He held it up to the sunlight. "It's magnificent, Alina. But it dismays me to think you had gone out to acquire this when Dugald grabbed you. I almost lost you forever."

"We didn't lose each other, though. My father was correct about you. He saw that we were meant to be together." She sighed and placed her hand upon Lucas' chest where he still carried the black lace veil.

He peered deep into her eyes. "I see you as you see me. From now on, nothing is ever wrong between us. We will persevere together. Thank you for this watch, Alina, but most of all, thank you for saying it is my wedding gift."

"I'm sorry I disappeared like that. I don't know what I was thinking." She gazed out across the wide green river. "I felt like a . . . I don't know, a different person."

Lucas waited, listening, never taking his hand from hers or his eyes from her melancholy face.

"You haven't even asked me why I ran to my father's house and didn't come home after Dugald and the monastery." She turned to him with wide wet eyes.

"You went there because you had a place to go. You missed your father. And you were angry with me," he replied softly.

Looking wistfully away, she nodded. "I suppose it could be that simple."

"Is there anything else you want to tell me? Other than I let you down?"

"No, but I think I let myself down. I didn't come to you . . ."

"And shout at me as you should have." Lucas stroked her back and sighed. He buried his hand in her hair and rubbed her skull.

"I was angry at everyone. Uncle Vasil for killing my father. My father for dying and leaving me alone. Were you angry when your mother died?"

"I was too young to feel anger. I was scared, terrified of the world that had suddenly become so vast and empty. I ran through Arcana and the City of Dreams and looked down upon myself as if from the eyes of a hawk. I imagined its wide wingspan dipping and soaring as it followed me. Most days, I wished it would snatch me up and drop me far out into a distant sea."

"Oh, Lucas."

"I think you know how that feels."

She nodded. "So, you . . ."

"I ran. I ran for years. In a way, I kept running until I met you."

Alina half smiled. "That's what I did too. I thought I was going home. Even though it was my father's house, there weren't any memories there for me. I hid from you, Lucas."

"Yes, you certainly did. You are clever and strong, and I'm glad of that. But as I said, from now on, we will proceed together. What else is on your mind, Alina?"

"Daria."

"Not who you thought she was."

"No! I can't comprehend her behavior. She lied and tricked me! We were practically sisters." Alina shook her head, imploring Lucas for insight.

He frowned. "A covetous woman after all. She didn't see you in the same manner. I am disappointed as well. I looked forward to you having her back in your life."

"She knew how heartbroken I felt. I watched Ikarus light lanterns from my window, and I cried and cried."

Lucas watched her every move, noticed each nuance in her voice, the tilt of her head, the ruffle of her skirt in the warm breeze. His heart pounded in relief that she sat beside him. The anguish of the lack of her still echoed in his heart. "How I yearned to hold you."

"And I you, Lucas."

He laughed. "No wonder we lost our minds the other night."

Mischief lit her eyes. "Other than throwing up, I would do it again."

"And we will!"

Lucas grabbed her, pulled her to him and covered her mouth with his.

When he finally let her go, she clasped her hands together and laughed. "Well, I see I didn't scare you off, what with all my spewing."

He winked. "Not possible."

"What do you think will happen to Daria now?"

Lucas stroked her hair. "That depends on you, my darling. What do you want to happen to her?"

Alina frowned and took a breath. "I want her gone."

"Full gone or shipped off after her appearance before the magistrate?"

"Shipped off."

Lucas brushed his hands together. "All right, that's settled. Let's stroll over to the dressmaker."

They held hands as they made their way through the lively streets. To shade their goods from the abundant spring sun, the outdoor vendors strung colorful canvas canopies over their stalls. Lucas weaved and ducked to avoid colliding with the abrupt corners. Window baskets spilled over with pink impatiens, red geranium, and tiny white, sweet alyssum.

Lucas and Alina were greeted by cheerful citizens who appeared pleased to see them together. Just as the dressmaker shop came into view, Alina stopped. She clutched Lucas' arm. "You never did explain how you heal yourself, Lucas."

Lucas scowled and glanced around. "No, I didn't," he mumbled.

Alina pouted.

Leaning closer he whispered, "It's not me."

"What's not you?"

"However, it happens, I don't do it. You see, I don't know, my love. If I knew, I would make sure it is the same with you."

Fear darkened her face, and she shuddered. Lucas wrapped his arm around her shoulders and led her to the shop door. "It's not a frightening thing. It's good, don't you agree? Let's see what cloth they have in here for you to choose. Our wedding day is all we need to think about now." As he pulled open the door, a bell chimed their arrival. Alina gazed up at Lucas with delight in her dazzling, summer green eyes.

Inside, five rows of tables held colorful bolts of cloth. Alina's hand fluttered to her throat when the shop girl approached. Lucas placed a delicate kiss on Alina's cheek and gazed into her eyes. "You need not hurry in here. Choose whatever you desire. And afterward, you can bring Irene and the ladies in to help you decide upon the design."

He handed Alina the bouquet of tulips and left her with the cherubic girl while he made his way to the back room to discuss plans with the shopkeeper. Nikolas had planned with the silk merchant, Julian, to distribute his cloth goods as well as wine. The man had no stomach for the sea and hoped to limit his trips back and forth from Ingleena to the City of Dreams.

When they returned to the boarding house, Irene and Madam Trousdale were sipping tea in the courtyard garden surrounded by the dangling greenery.

"Madam Trousdale, my dear Aunty Brigit, how charming to see you."

Brigit stood and clasped Lucas' hand. Still bewildered by the knowledge that she was his mother's sister, he peered at her from under hooded lids. Her eyes flashed through their assorted colors as she squeezed his hand, smoothed her blue, green, and purple layered skirts, and offered them tea.

Lucas gave Irene's shoulders a squeeze. "I'm glad to see you relaxing."

"I'm glad to see you two up and outside."

"We went to the river," Lucas said.

"And then the dressmaker." Alina beamed. Pleased that she had made the announcement, Lucas took her in his arms.

Irene clapped her hands together. "Wonderful! What did you choose?"

Alina glanced at Lucas and bit her lip. "I think I have chosen the cloth for my wedding dress, but I would appreciate your opinions."

"Of course, you would," Brigit declared. "When shall we go?"

Alina laughed. "Can we all go?" she asked directing her question to Irene. "Carissa and Perina as well?"

"Of course, my dear. Anytime you like. We will lock the doors and go!"

"I planted ivy at your father's house," Brigit declared.

"Ivy?" Lucas scratched the back of his neck. "The window needs repair."

"That's done. And the ivy is planted too. When it grows up to the second story windows, you can go back." Brigit nodded at Lucas and Alina who glanced at each other, puzzled.

"Ivy wards off evil spirits."

Pleased, Lucas said, "Thank you for taking care of that, Brigit." Then thinking for a moment, he asked, "How does it do that? I've heard this, but no one had ever said how the warding off occurs."

"The evil doers are punished with pain," Brigit explained.

Lucas nodded, wishing he hadn't asked. He feared she was about to launch into a lengthy and gruesome description. Giving Brigit a look, he said, "Good enough."

She smirked and poured the tea. He and Alina sat together on the stone bench and sipped their tea while the women chattered about the wedding plans and decided the garden was the perfect place. Lucas suggested they choose a day as soon as the dress was ready. Then, he excused himself and made his way to the harbour to seek out Nikolas.

Chapter 2

As Lucas absentmindedly meandered along the familiar route, he wondered about Alina's question; how had he healed himself? A question he had never cared to ask, he now found it too difficult to ponder on such a brilliant day, so he pushed it from his mind.

He noticed a shadow at the corner of his eye. Lucas stopped and spun around. The gray cat circled him and then rubbed against his legs. He reached down to scratch behind her ears. "Where are you off to today, old friend?" he murmured. The cat stretched and kneaded its forepaws into Lucas' trouser. Then, it dropped to all fours and trotted off down a dark alley close between three-story buildings. Curious about how the cat spent her days, Lucas followed.

The sudden dimness blinded him. He could only look ahead toward the bright light at the end of the windowless walls. A soft thumping against the cobbles told him the cat was running, so he ran too. He swayed and bumped the damp wall, steadying himself with one hand. He used the other to shield his eyes and peer up. The sky was still blue, but a shadow swept swiftly across the slot of daylight.

When they reached the end and emerged into the daylight of an abandoned courtyard, the gray cat sat licking a paw as if she wondered what had taken Lucas so long.

Another shadow caught his eye. A hawk soared above. It dipped one wing and dove toward them. Lucas lurched to protect the cat. The hawk glided to nearly eye level, then pitched away and climbed up and out of sight into the warm blue sky. The cat gawked at Lucas, whose head had begun to pound. "Flaming hell," he slurred as he gripped his forehead with both hands. The headache subsided. "Did you see that?" he asked the cat that twitched each eye independently and then turned and headed off, looking only once over her shoulder to see if Lucas was still there.

The tall tower stood in white contrast to the brilliant blue sky. He didn't want to approach the monastery right now. He took a breath, held it for several beats and then let it out slowly. The cat plunged into a low bramble of bushes that ran alongside the murky moat. Lucas crouched and followed, practically walking on his knees. Sharp brambles caught in his hair and tore his shirt. Drops of blood appeared and then disappeared.

When they emerged upon a circular spot of mud, the cat traversed the moat on a precarious fallen log. Lucas followed. Taking long, quick steps, he swore under his breath at the cat and himself for his ignorance. Once upon the other side, he swooped the cat up and held her above his head. "What game is this? Why have you led me here?" The cat squeezed her eyes shut and kicked her hind legs.

Setting her down in the tall grass, Lucas examined the monastery from this angle. He wasn't sure which way to turn to find the small door that he and Nikolas had gone through when they had searched for Alina. With hands on his hips, he observed the cat that rolled on its back in the grass. "Which way?" he asked. The cat sat up and began cleaning her face with her paw.

Lucas turned and trudged along the narrow stretch of grass that paralleled the high walls. There he came to another thicket where he waited for the cat that did not appear. Just as he decided to head back to the harbour and grab Nikolas for an ale, he glanced up and saw the hawk perched on the tower turret. He whistled for the cat, hoping it hid itself. Birds chirped within the brambles. The cat had most likely gone ahead of him. Lucas crawled through the brambles for what seemed like hours until they opened to a canopy of weeping mulberry trees. He quickly wove his way through the serpentine branches. His throat parched and his chest sweaty, he finally emerged onto a swath of soft green grass that made him think of Alina's eyes. But what he saw before him as he stood sent a shiver up and down his spine. Seven gravestones sat scattered like crooked teeth in the spongey grass.

* * *

When Nikolas finished his work at the harbour, he decided to go over to the boarding house and see what everyone was up to. Yesterday, Lucas was frustrated that Alina still wouldn't come out of her bedchamber. He went in through the kitchen door, and finding no one there, he passed through to the parlour. The three women seated in the garden noticed him and immediately stopped talking.

"Scuse me. I didn't mean to interrupt. Just looking for Lucas. Lovely to see you, Alina." He bowed slightly and turned to go up the stairs.

"He went to find you," Irene piped.

Brigit leapt up and swept into the parlour, her ebony hair flying in several different directions. She clutched Nikolas' forearm. "He's been gone awhile. Don't alarm them," she warned.

"Oh, yes, of course. I must have missed him. I've been wandering around the city all morning."

Irene and Alina gaped in silent concern.

"He'll be back soon," Brigit lied. Picking up some drawings from the table she said, "I'll take this design to the dressmaker on the way to my cottage. Enjoy the afternoon." she waved nonchalantly and followed Nikolas out the front door.

"What's going on?" he asked once they stood on the street.

"Lucas went over an hour ago to the harbour."

"I've been there all day, but I haven't seen him."

Brigit shook her head and her long mane rippled over her shoulders. "There's something wrong," she declared.

"Tsk. No, I'm sure Lucas is fine. He can take care of himself. You women need to stop fearing everything."

"We don't fear everything!" she hissed.

Nikolas laughed. "Well, *you* certainly don't. I'll go to the Blue Gate. He probably stopped there on his way to me." He grabbed Brigit by the back of her head and pulled her to him to plant an alluring kiss on her dark red lips. "Let's drink some wine together later." He laughed as he referred to their private joke about Lucas and Alina's drinking bout.

Brigit laughed with him. "I like how you think. Let's meet at the Blue Gate after a while." They turned and walked in opposite directions. After dropping off the drawings for Alina's wedding gown, Brigit thought Lucas was possibly ruminating by the river about the expectations of a married man. As much as he loved Alina, Brigit knew that Lucas had the wild blood of a wanderer running through his veins.

She stomped up and down the riverbank as if her angry steps would make him appear. "More people, more problems," she muttered to herself. Standing at the edge of the water, she inhaled the scent of water and linden flowers. She raised her arms to the sky. "Lu…cas," she hummed. Something sharp poked her. She reached for the claw ornament hanging around her neck, but it wasn't the claw that cut her. It was the hourglass. It had shattered. The sand ran down between her breasts. "Aghhh!" She tugged the cord from her neck and clutched the shattered time piece in her hand. A shadow passed over her and Brigit ran.

* * *

For several long moments, Lucas did not move. The solemnity of this secret cemetery transfixed him. Bees buzzed and hovered just above the lush grass. His eyes scanned the limestone monastery wall and then returned to the leaning gravestones. He could not read the letters inscribed in the stones. They seemed to be written backwards. But then one clearly caught his eye. He gasped as the letters became clear:

Linnea

Beloved

Lucas knelt before the stone. His hand shook as he ran it across the letters. His mother's grave, here? How could that be? Atop the grave, an iron cross had been set in the stone. And there, on top of the cross, Lucas noticed the distinct glitter of gold. A thin gold circular band.

"Your mother's wedding ring."

Lucas turned so quickly, he lost his balance and landed on his bottom in the soft grass. The bony figure of a monk stood before him. He was wearing his consuming cloak, but the hood had slid back, and Lucas could see his head, partially covered with patches of wispy, white hair. The eyes bottomless and dark, almost as black as his own, contrasted with the man's milky skin.

Scrambling to his feet, Lucas blurted out, "Are you real?"

"As real as you."

The monk laughed, and Lucas clutched his heart. "You are my father?" His voice came out unusually high.

"Yes, I am. I am Seppo. I am your father.

"You have a lot to explain," Lucas said.

"I am the one who decided upon your name." The monk took the ring from the top of Linnea's gravestone and reached for Lucas' hand.

Lucas pulled back but the monk's grip was firm and cold. He opened Lucas' clenched fist and placed the ring in his palm. "For now, take this."

Lucas closed his fingers around the ring. "Did she wear it?"

The monk nodded.

"Is she really buried here?"

"Yes, Lucas, your mother, my wife, is buried right here."

"She was your wife, then. How so? Did you kill her?"

"Yes, we were married. You already know how she died."

Lucas scratched his neck. "The farmers said they buried her."

"And I brought her home."

"What . . . what do you mean by that?"

"We brought her here and gave her a proper burial."

"We?"

"The other monks."

"Where are they?'

"Another time, Lucas. You best go on. They are looking for you." He crossed his arms dismissively.

Madam Trousdale burst through the brambled forest.

"Brigit!" Lucas nearly shouted, so relieved he was to see her.

Swooping past the monk, Brigit grabbed Lucas by the shirt and shook him. "There's no time to waste. The hourglass is broken!"

The long, twig like fingers of the monk, clutched Brigit's shoulder. "Be still."

Her eyes bulged. "Who is. . ." turning to Lucas. "Is this . . ." Glancing over Lucas' shoulder, Brigit saw for the first time the gravestones and Linnea's name. Her hair, purple now, shot straight up in the air as she collapsed at their feet.

"Oh, no," Lucas moaned as he knelt beside her.

Seppo seemed to float over to the monastery wall where he vanished for a moment. Seconds elapsed as the insects hummed and buzzed, and then the monk's gracile figure emerged from the ivy with cupped hands. Water shimmered in his palms. Seppo stepped over to Brigit and tossed the water directly into her face.

"Phewt!" She gulped, coughed, sat up, and struggled with trembling hands to calm her whirling hair. Lucas reached out to help her. She slapped his hand away. "I'm fine."

"You were not!"

"You don't know what you think you saw."

"I certainly do. You fainted! This is my mother's grave. And this is my father." Lucas turned to Seppo, but he was gone. "Brigit, did you see him?"

"Of course, I saw him. And I see Linnea's gravestone." On the ground beside her lay the hourglass, full and unbroken. She picked it up and shook her head, her hair black again, settled into its natural sheen. "Lucas it's all right. You are alive. The shatter was not for you. Go back to the living. Marry your girl. Let the dead care for themselves."

Lucas breathed in and out slowly. He brushed his hair back, moved to Linnea's stone, bent down, and placed his hands upon it. "I will return."

Brigit stood before the stone. "Your son is exceptional, Linny," she said and bowed her head.

Lucas waited on the path at the corner of the monastery. When Brigit approached, he wrapped her in his arms and squeezed tightly.

"Come on, Lucas. You have time for one whisky at the Blue Gate. Nikolas is waiting. Don't you dare tell anyone I fainted."

Lucas took Brigit by the hand and led her around the side of the building along the worn path. "How did you find me?" he asked as they ducked under the mulberry trees.

"Not this way. I don't remember. I was looking for you at the river when the hourglass broke. Then I found myself in the . . . the . . ."

"Secret cemetery."

"Yes. How did you end up here today, Lucas?"

"I followed the cat. I hope it's safe. There was a hawk."

They emerged at the makeshift bridge. "Go quickly," Lucas advised as he bounded across the log. Brigit crossed the log without so much of a quaver in her step. "The hourglass is not broken," he stated. "It's fully intact."

She clutched it and looked into his eyes, "Thankfully, it is."

Lucas took the tiny hourglass in his hand. He placed his other hand firmly upon her shoulder and searched her face, "Tell me the meaning of this hourglass."

She took it from him and said, "It's a miniature hourglass."

Lucas kept a firm hand upon her. "Why did it shatter, and whose time does it keep, mine or yours?"

"Both, for us and our kin, I realized. I always thought it was my time, but when we met, it started overturning, behaving oddly."

"Is that so."

"I wondered, and when Alina was missing, and you dying from a broken heart. It remained empty."

"Therefore, you hid it in your blouse."

"Yes, during that time, it was mostly empty. Sometimes one grain of sand appeared."

Lucas released his grip on her shoulder and stepped back. "Where did you get it?"

"It was made for my mother. It's all I have left from those years in the caravan."

"Who made it for her?"

"A wizard." She let the hourglass drop against her chest, patted it, picked up the claw pendant, and began absentmindedly pulling it through her hair.

"Oh, I see. A wizard."

Brigit narrowed her eyes. "Do you?"

"Do you?"

"I don't know. Sometimes, maybe." She peered off into the distant trees. "He was tall and smooth barked like a robust birch tree, but the other was gnarled with the peeling bark of a dying alder."

"Humans have skin, not bark."

"Did I say he was human?"

"No, you said he was a tree." Lucas frowned.

She tossed her hair over her shoulder. "The evil one was not quite human. The other was the chieftain, and he was good. He presented this hourglass to my mother when she and my father wed."

"So, what's wrong with that?"

She glared at Lucas. "Listen, I'm trying to tell you. There were two wizard men. One was good, the other was always sneaking around doing despicable things, waiting for people to let their guard down. He had the peeling bark. You're confusing me with all these questions. He was evil. The bad one was evil inside. That's all that matters."

"Yes, it's what lies in wait that matters." The two of them glanced around. Lucas spoke again softly this time. "Does something lie in wait for you, Brigit?"

She shielded her eyes and looked toward the hills. "Not only me. Ultimately, for all of us," she said.

"Yes, you're right. Not often you are," he grinned now. "But when is the unanswerable question. So, for you, from now on, I will keep a lookout for the wizard tree man. The evil one. Now, let's go back." He waited while Brigit finished combing her luxurious hair. "You've grown another claw. You have two claws now."

"Yes, two." She turned them around in her fingers and smiled. "I could gouge out a pair of eyes with these."

At the Blue Gate, Nikolas sat by the window drumming his fingers on the table. He'd been tending the same whisky for well over an hour. "At last," he exclaimed when Lucas and Brigit came through the door. He downed the dregs of his glass and motioned to the serving girl. "I didn't think I could hold out much longer. Where have you two been?"

Lucas sat and stared blankly until his whisky was placed in front of him. He drank it in one gulp and gestured for another. Brigit explained to Nikolas how the hourglass had shattered at the riverbank and how she came to find herself with Lucas. She lowered her voice to a barely audible whisper when she mentioned the secret cemetery.

"The hourglass is not broken now," Lucas said with relief.

"I didn't conjure it," Brigit said defensively.

"Why did you go to the monastery, Lucas?" Nik asked. "I would have gone with you."

"He followed the gray cat."

"I was on my way to you, Nik, when the cat came along and enticed me to follow. And there was a hawk as well." He swirled the whisky in the bottom of his glass.

"A hawk now also?" Nikolas gaped.

Lucas nodded. "All of this started, Madam Trousdale, after the first time I came to your cottage with Irene," Lucas said, staring at Brigit and pressing his lips together into a thin line.

"Don't blame me for your hallucinations."

"Why do the two of you bicker like husband and fish wife?" Nikolas interrupted.

Lucas shrugged. "She vexes me."

"And you, me."

Nik briefly clutched Lucas by the wrist. "What happened today, friend?"

"I'm being stalked by a hawk. Never mind about it. A memory from childhood still haunts me. Alina and I talked at great length. She has agreed to marry me." Lucas smiled and the three toasted, lightening the mood. Lucas slipped the gold ring that Seppo had given him from a small pocket in his trousers. "My father gave me this. My mother's wedding ring. The gray cat led me to this destiny today."

Nikolas whistled between his teeth. "Tell me about your father."

"He *is* that pale monk we saw, Nik. But he is not weak at all. His eyes, they are so dark and deep, they reflect back. His gaze is riveting. When I looked into his eyes, it was as if I were standing at the edge of the horizon, in the blackest moment before the first glimmer of dawn."

Nik began to smile, but Brigit said, "Even I felt unnerved."

Lucas nodded his head in agreement. "Sorry for leaving you waiting in the tavern, Nik." They all laughed now.

When they left the Blue Gate, Brigit turned toward the cottages. "I'll catch up with you later at the boarding house."

Once inside her cottage, Brigit drew the curtains and lit all the candles, murmuring to herself as she did so. She brewed a strong tea from several different herbs and stoked the fire before dropping into her chair beside the leaping flames. Only then did the tightness in her brow release. Relieved to be alone, she closed her eyes. The voices and thoughts of others were beginning to tire her. Having met Seppo, Linnea's husband, at last, confused her. Did she truly choose to go with that spidery creature of a man, or was she snatched away against her will? If only Linnea hadn't resided at the farm, she would not have met that creature. Dismayed, Brigit set down her cup, rested her head back against the wing-backed chair, and began to chant in a monotonic hum as she pondered potential potions to protect them all against Seppo.

* * *

Lucas and Nikolas cheerfully wove their way through the vibrant, blossoming streets. Nik explained as they went, "Julian will select the pure silk, wool, taffeta, damask, and velvet. He has spent enough time here in the City of Dreams to know what we need."

"Yes," Lucas agreed, "with the dressmaker and the patronage of the Boulevard citizens who prefer to utilize their own private seamstresses, it will be more than sufficient for legitimate business. And the wine, of course. Everyone wants that."

Alina and Carissa were tending the plants in the courtyard when the men entered the house. The first thing Lucas noticed was the gray cat sprawled across the garden wall flicking her tail. He studied its bright eyes, but the cat overlooked him. Alina set down a delicate green plant and went forward with concern etched upon her beautiful face. Lucas immediately felt dreadful for his long, unexplained absence.

He went to the sidebar and poured two goblets of wine. "Let's relax in this lovely garden," he said. Nik and Carissa ambled off to the kitchen mumbling about helping Irene prepare supper.

Beginning with the gray cat leading him down the dark alleyway, Lucas relayed to Alina the events of the afternoon. He told her every detail, including the hawk, the brambled mulberry trees, Seppo, the broken hourglass, and Brigit's appearance in the secret cemetery. She listened with rapt attention and gulped her wine when he described Linnea's gravestone. Finally, Lucas dug into his trouser pocket and brought out the gold ring that Seppo had given him. "Would you wear this, Alina?" he stammered. "Is it too ghostly for you?"

Her hand fluttered to her heart, "Ahh, it's splendid, Lucas. I'm not afraid. It's part of your mother. And you as well. I would be honored to wear it."

He smiled softly and held the ring up to her finger. "It appears it will fit perfectly."

"As your mother's dresses do."

Lucas smiled and nodded. "But we will wait until our wedding day to slip it on your finger." He cupped her chin in his palm and leaned over to kiss her soft lips with slow and passionate purpose.

When he released her, Alina blushingly announced that the dressmaker had sent word that her gown would be ready in eleven days.

Lucas took her hand and placed it over his heart. "That brings us to Saturday, the 10th day of June. A wonderful day for our betrothal ceremony. I will count the seconds with the beats of my heart."

"As will I," she concurred with shining eyes. "The days are already warm like summer."

Lucas kissed her fingertips one at a time. "A lifetime of beauty and passion awaits us."

Alina blushed. "Lucas, . . ."

"What is it, love?"

"In the secret cemetery, to whom do the additional gravestones belong?"

Lucas' hand fell to his lap. "Huh . . . I . . ."

Nikolas appeared in the threshold. "Excuse me for interrupting the lovebirds on the garden bench, but, Lucas, do you remember if Brigit said she would meet us here?"

Irene, standing on tiptoes, peeped over his shoulder and said, "She best show up. We have roast lamb, and she promised there will be exotic greens to celebrate your official engagement. Carissa and Perina are tired from their toil. They've been brining, chopping, and slicing all afternoon. They had to fetch a lad to deliver a cask of wine. Perhaps you two should trade in wines as well as textiles."

Lucas got up, crossed over to Irene, and gave her a gentle hug. "We intend to, Irene. Yes, Nik, Brigit said she'd meet us back here."

The front door flew open, slamming into the wall with a sharp crack. Alina jumped to her feet, and Irene scooted behind Lucas. They stood transfixed for a moment. Her twirling hair appeared first, blue-black and silver, shining like a mirror. "What are you all gawking at?"

Lucas leaned toward Nik and whispered, "How do you tolerate it? The wild hair and eyes changing color. One never knows what she'll do next."

Nik chortled and then murmured, "In many ways, she's a wild mare ripping across the uplands." And to Brigit he said, "Here you are. What are you lugging there?" Nik hefted a heavy black cauldron from Brigit who brushed tangled hair away from her face.

"The exotic greens have arrived," Lucas announced as Nikolas passed through to the kitchen.

"You'll thank me for this vital porry." Brigit slammed the door, but it bounced open, and Ikarus shambled in wearing a look of concern. "Is it all right that I join for supper before lighting the lanterns? It's best this time of year. We have light longer. I need not walk around hungry."

"Of course, Ik," Lucas waved him in. "As a permanent resident, you are always welcome for supper. We are celebrating again."

Alina stood beside Carissa and Perina and helped them fill the pewter wine goblets. "Please don't pour too much for me," she said.

"I won't ask where you've been, Lucas, but your shirt is torn and dirty," Irene remarked.

"Ah yes," he lifted a corner of his shirt and frowned. "I liked this one."

"It's a shame that you tore it in so many places." Irene poked her finger through one of the holes. "It can't be sewn. You'll look like a mumblecrust. I wonder what would cause so many rips."

Lucas laughed. "Come up with me while I grab a fresh shirt, Irene. I'll explain it all to you."

Irene sat at the end of the bed. He scrubbed his face and hands in the wash basin, pulled off the tattered shirt, and donned a dark gray one with gathered, full sleeves and loose laces at the chest. Irene listened with uncustomary silence as he retold the events of his encounter at the monastery. He changed into clean trousers. "Don't you have any questions, Irene?"

"I can't think of anything. I'm not surprised by much anymore."

"So then, now we see what digging in the past does for us."

She nodded.

"Never mind, Irene. The changing times are good for the most part, don't you agree?"

"I do." She smiled. "I've been drinking this wonderful tea that Mr. Pagett and Brigit concocted for me."

"Ah yes, the apothecary. When will he join us for supper?"

"He won't. I already told you that. He can stay in his little shop where he belongs."

They joined the others around the long table as Brigit explained the beneficial ingredients of her vegetable porry mash. "The pot is rarely empty all the way. I add things and replenish as I go. The chard is chopped and soaked for days. Then, I add the vine leeks, borache, orache, onions, and watercress with garlic, water, and wine, of course. I keep filling it up every day before it gets too low. Go ahead and dunk your bread in there too."

Ikarus looked perplexed. "Go on lad, don't be shy," Brigit said. "It was delicious last week and even better today." She gestured with her wooden ladle. He took a hearty spoonful, but promptly dribbled it back into his bowl.

"What do we do with it?" Alina whispered into Lucas' ear. Carissa passed the platter of meat, and Perina passed a small bowl of herbs to add to the porry. The two maids didn't add any porry to their bowls; instead, they whispered to each other about the wedding supper. Alina tilted her head to better hear them.

"Eat now or regret later," Brigit warned.

The table was silent for long minutes while they chewed and chewed. Swallowing hard, Lucas finally said, "We should send word of the wedding to Arcana for Bernard and Wentworth." They all raised their cups and toasted.

"I could ride out to Arcana," Ikarus offered.

Lucas frowned. "You? Alone?"

"I can do it, Lucas. I can take a mate to ride with me. I'd like to see the farm where Bernard and Wentworth live. They knew you a long time ago. It's where you grew up, isn't it, Lucas?"

"Yes, I did spend my early years in the country. It's a promising idea, Ik. I'll light the lanterns tomorrow night. You can ride to the farm and stay the night. Stop by the Grande Inn and tell Mr. Hartwinn to expect Alina and I in eleven days. We'll take my usual bedchamber. Nik, can you bring a couple of slow horses around for Ikarus and his companion?"

"Thank you, sir." Ikarus flashed his sky-blue eyes at Lucas and brushed his pale-yellow hair away from his face with both hands. His skin, in contrast, was as tanned as the furniture Lucas had noticed in Alina's house. The lad's lanky frame was filling out, and his arms showed the definition of lean muscles. So distracted by Alina, Lucas had barely noticed Ikarus in the past weeks. Now, he realized the pale trembling lad benefitted greatly from regular meals and a warm bed at night. With a twinge, he recalled his own hungry youth.

"Were you born in the City of Dreams, Ik?"

"Me? Oh no. No, I was born in the white winter of those far away, jagged-peaked mountains."

"Where's your family now?" Nikolas asked.

"Tsk, how rude. None of us have ever asked from whence you came, Ikarus. Please forgive us," Irene lamented.

Ikarus blushed. "I don't mind," he said and continued chewing.

"Where are your people now?" Brigit pressed.

"We brought our herd down."

"Herd?" Lucas leaned forward.

Ikarus nodded and took another bite.

"Herd of what?" Alina asked.

"Sheep."

"Ikarus, please stop eating for a moment. We want to know about you," Irene insisted.

Ikarus swallowed, gulped his wine, and then swiped his forearm across his mouth. "We brought some sheep to market. My sister and brother went back up. I stayed here." He picked up a chunk of bread.

"Why did you stay?" Irene asked.

Ikarus inhaled and hoped the questions would stop. He hadn't actually stayed on purpose. Everything after his arrival in the city had gone wrong, and then he was pickpocketed for the little money he had, his boots too. Even though he managed to steal the boots and coins back, he took a beating for it. That gave him the idea to possibly make some quick money. He only meant to linger a few extra weeks, but he'd been unlucky at pickpocketing. His idea of returning to the mountains a wealthy and respectable man faded in the realization that he wished he'd been able to return home with his sister and brother. He didn't possess the cunning of a thief. Fear of proving himself a fool kept him from leaving and making his way home alone. He remained because he had no choice. *They don't need to know that,* he thought, glancing at the friendly faces. "No reason. Believed I might like it here."

"Do you?" Lucas reached for Ikarus' pewter goblet to refill it.

Ikarus smiled, flushed, and mumbled "Starting to."

"And your sister and brother, they returned safely to your mountain home?" Irene seemed reluctant to drop the inquiry.

"I don't know," Ikarus said. Brushing his hands together over his plate, he stood to leave. "Appreciate the meal. Must get to the lanterns now. I'll leave for Arcana in the morning, Lucas. I know how to ride a fast horse."

No one spoke for several moments until Brigit cast a multi-colored gaze around the table. "There is more to his story. How long has he been here, Lucas?"

Lucas thought for a moment. "It's been a year that he's helped me, I think. Maybe longer even. I don't know."

"When you light the lanterns tomorrow, I want to go with you, Lucas," Alina said placing her hand on his arm.

"Sounds romantic," Irene remarked.

Carissa and Perina stood and began clearing the platters and bowls from the table. "We have some ideas on how to decorate the courtyard, Alina," Carissa said.

They all ambled into the courtyard garden chattering about where to place candles and which ledges could use some trailing greenery, where Alina and Lucas would stand in the center for the handfasting ceremony. "Let's invite the boarders who aren't working at the cathedral that day," Alina said. "But Lucas did you want to marry at Saint Sempre?"

"I had thought so, but perhaps not. There is much dust and noise from the renovations. Mostly, I don't want to wait."

"And it's too close to the monastery," Brigit muttered.

Lucas frowned at Brigit before turning to Alina. "We don't want to waste time waiting for the restorations to be completed. That could take years!"

Alina smiled up at him. "If you like, we will have our wedding right here," she said.

"It's settled then. We will visit Saint Sempre on our way to Arcana. The priests will bless us and in a while our babes as well."

Alina blushed and gazed down at her goblet. "I'll bring more wine."

"She's nervous," Irene said when Alina retreated to the parlour.

"Yes, she is. Perhaps we will retire now. Alina enjoys time to herself."

She returned with the wine. "And let's invite, the flower vendor. I'm afraid I don't even know her name, but she is part of our courtship. And Madam Van Dessen and the widow Keats, and Igmus and Rathbone too," she gushed.

"Indeed," Lucas rubbed his chin.

"Igmus and Rathbone it is!" Nikolas agreed. "I know where to find them."

Carissa and Perina giggled as they wrote notes in a small book.

"I'll invite Mister Pagett," Irene said rolling her eyes. Brigit caught Lucas' surprised expression and winked.

Alina set her wine goblet down without finishing it. "I'm so excited that I'm fatigued now. Thank you, everyone." And to Lucas, she asked, "Are you ready to end the day?"

He raised his eyebrows and smiled. Upstairs in Lucas' room the fire that he had set while changing his clothes blazed with warmth. The window was open as well, and the scented night air, combined with woodsmoke, gave the room a soothing redolence. Alina slipped under the coverlet wearing her lace shift. Lucas donned his sleeping trousers. They giggled at themselves as they snuggled close. "Are you happy with the selections of cloth for your gown?"

"Very much," she murmured sleepily.

"And the plans for the ceremony?" Alina didn't respond. Lucas sat up, "Alina?"

"Sure," she said as her eyelids fluttered, and she drifted off to sleep. He lay beside her waiting for sleep to come.

His mind kept drifting to Seppo. He wished he had never met the monk or man or whatever he was. His skin was snow white, but; Lucas couldn't help but notice blue lines beneath it. He feared if the monk removed his shirt, he would see the heart beating beneath that alabaster membrane. Or would he?

He turned on one side then the other, carefully, trying not to disturb Alina. Why did she fall asleep so quickly? He wanted to talk some more. Was she really pleased about the wedding plans? She was excited about the wedding feast it seemed. Had the ladies decided upon the menu? He'd forgotten to ask. He got up and kicked a log off the fire; its glow was too bright. He closed the window and lay down. In a moment, he got up and opened the window again hoping to hear the lark singing. It was all too much. Too soon. Why had he insisted they marry right away? She had fled once already. He wanted to hold her forever close to him, but maybe he should allow her more time.

Chapter 3

Lucas awoke to the sound of Alina splashing in the wash basin. "Oh," she tittered, "I was trying not to wake you. I have to meet the dressmaker."

Lucas sat up and reached out his hand to her. She came to him and brushed her lips against his forehead. "Let's have breakfast first," he said grasping her arm as she tried to pull away.

"I can't. I'm afraid I must go," she gushed. "It's such an exciting day isn't it, Lucas?" He nodded and released her arm. She grabbed her dress and flung open the door. "I'll finish dressing in my room."

Before Lucas could reply, she was gone. He must have slept, but he felt as if he had thrashed all night. He closed his eyes, hoping sleep would come. Something still nagged at the back of his mind. When he heard the front door slam, he leapt up and looked out the window in time to see Alina, Irene, Carissa, and Perina all walking in the direction of the dress shop. The wedding plans were moving forward. Abandoning his plan to eat something, he dressed and hurried through the kitchen and down the stone staircase into the cellar. At the end of the cellar, in a corner at the back of the house, he unlocked the door to the hidden vault where his and Alina's treasures were kept safely locked away. He opened a small chest and pulled out a heavy satchel of gems. On the way back through the kitchen, he placed the jewelry inside Irene's embroidered market sack. On the table sat half a loaf of bread, along with a plate of jam and butter. He tore off a chunk of bread, dipped it into the jam, and went out the back door.

* * *

When Nikolas awoke alone in Brigit's cottage, he noticed she had added a new assortment of colored glass bottles to her potion collection. Sitting up, he studied them wondering what they were intended to do. He pulled his hands through his tangled sand-colored hair. He'd been sweating; his hair was matted. She'd been more wild than usual last night.

He'd found himself utterly tangled in her long mane several times. It excited him when her hair turned a deep watery blue. They had drunk wine as he'd suggested. A heavy wine that Brigit had saved for them. She murmured strange words as she often did. When he asked her what they meant, she covered his ears with her palms and said, "They aren't meant for you." Her eyes glistened with gold specks as she ran her long cool fingers up and down his body. She stayed atop him and wouldn't allow him to take over.

Remembering all the rousing sensations, he laughed and flopped back onto the bed. He rolled over, hoping that wherever she'd gone that she'd be back soon. He loved her wild, untamed affections and wanted some more.

* * *

Lucas followed a reedy canal as he made his way over the decaying bridges of the rarely used, often flooded, back streets that led out of the City of Dreams. The officials had mostly given up on maintaining this area because the bridges crumbled as the foliage grew with such a fierce resolve that the various tubers and stalks ate their way through mortar and created tunnels in the stone supports. The day was so warm and his thoughts so scattered, he decided to sit on the wall and admire the swans that inhabited the area now that it lacked people. He leaned back on his elbows and watched a graceful pair float past him in serene silence. They moved their pure, white feathers and elegantly curved necks like a dance.

In just eleven days, he and Alina would be married. The late spring season had brought more changes in weeks than he'd imagined could occur in a lifetime. What had happened to her wish to behave like children, he wondered? Of course, they could do that after marriage. They would not move to her father's house soon, if ever, if she didn't care to. But the house was there waiting for her, and he felt the time would come when she would want to move in. For now, living in the boarding house with Irene, his beloved adopted mother, remained a comfort to him and he believed to Alina as well.

Alina hadn't mentioned a desire to return to her childhood home of Ingleena, but if she ever did, he doubted he could go. After attempting to sail there when she was missing, he worried that he could not board a ship without becoming ill again. For now, the wound above his heart remained healed. Without knowing how or why he healed himself, he might never know if he could leave the vicinity of the City of Dreams and Arcana.

He noticed one of the swans gazing in his direction and spoke to it. "Besides," he said, "we must keep the one we love close within our wingspan." He hoped Alina never wanted to go to Ingleena, for he could lose her there if she suddenly changed her mind about him. He couldn't go and didn't want to try.

Lucas sighed and settled into a stream of worrying thoughts. Did Alina realize they would never travel to Ingleena together? Why was she content to marry at the boarding house? They spent a lot of time there. Too much. On their wedding day, she was supposed to walk down the stairs to the garden courtyard, join him in marriage, and then have a wedding feast, all in the same cramped space. It wasn't all that cramped he knew, but suddenly, he felt like the walls of the boarding house were closing in and trapping him, them, inside.

The swans faced each other, ruffling and then lifting their wings. They grunted and hissed at each other. Each one flapped its wings, dipped its head under water, and then shook its body. The mating ritual, Lucas realized. He wished Alina were there to see it.

When the shadows lengthened and the swans drifted away, he placed his hands on his thighs, pushed himself up, and tossed the market sack over his shoulder. His own urgency to rush the wedding vexed him, and he had to do something about it now.

As he followed the crumbled path along the canal, Lucas noticed something disturbing in the distance. A mad woman approached. She dripped in marsh mud and stumbled, for she appeared burdened with two satchels; one was dripping down her layered skirt. Her hair was a stringy, brown tangle hanging all the way down to her waist. She was humming or chanting. He stopped and then began to back slowly away as to not attract her attention.

Just as he was about to swing left and dash over a bridge, the woman looked up. She halted him with her piercing blue eyes. Lucas couldn't move. It took him several moments to comprehend that he was staring into the face of Brigit. When his mind finally caught up with his eyes, he rushed forward. "My God, what has happened to you!?" he asked.

"What are you doing here?" she snarled and pushed him away with a muddy hand.

He gasped and stared and then shook his head. "You fell in."

"I did not. I'm gathering things." She set the satchels on the ground with a grunt. "Water makes it heavy."

"What do you have there?" Lucas poked his fingers inside the driest satchel.

"Leave it," she ordered.

"This is foxglove. What do you want that for?"

"Nothing. I need it. Get on. Where are you going?"

"Nowhere." He peeked in again despite her protests. "You also have belladonna and monkshood. What do you need all these poisonous plants for, Brigit?"

"How do you know what they are?"

Lucas chuckled. "Have you forgotten who you are talking to? My mother and I gathered plants. I know them."

She glowered. "Yes, well I do too. There is nothing for you to fret about, Lucas." She gave him a little shove. "Go on."

He grabbed for the saturated satchel. "What's in this one?"

"Just watercress. What are you doing out here?"

He folded his arms across his chest, "You did fall in."

"I went in. There's a difference." She narrowed her eyes, "What are you carrying in Irene's market sack?"

"Nothing." He gazed off into the distance in order to evade her prying eyes that had remained bright blue. She grabbed his forearm with her dirty hand. Lucas shook her off, knowing she was trying to read his thoughts. "Whatever you put in your pot of exotic greens was quite disgusting."

She laughed and stepped back, "Nonetheless you all managed to choke it down."

"Choke indeed. What are you brewing up now?"

"I know what's best. That's all you need to know, Lucas."

Raising his eyebrows, he smiled. "There's no reason to mention our encounter to anyone, is there, Brigit?"

"Everyone has secrets," she murmured.

"Don't walk into the city looking like that," he advised. "Rinse in the river first."

She offered a half smile. "I'll keep your secret too."

Lucas nodded, turned, and hurried across the final bridge. He wanted to glance back and see in which direction Brigit went, but he could feel her bottomless blue eyes boring into the back of his head. Why didn't her eyes change color today? And what was she doing collecting plants all the way out here? It was still difficult to imagine his lovely, calm mother growing up with Madam Trousdale. The woman was mad. She could be dangerous. He didn't know what to do about Brigit. They were blood after all. He should warn Nik about her strange tramping through the canals. His friend must be growing tired of her lunacy by now.

The bell tower of Saint Sempre came into view, and his thoughts quickly changed. He couldn't let the wedding ceremony go on as planned. He had to speak to the priest before it was too late.

Brigit watched Lucas until he disappeared among the trees. It looked like he turned toward the monastery. Too curious for his own good, just like his mother, and that's what had gotten her into trouble. She went off with that monk creature! She couldn't let Seppo seize Lucas as he had Linny. What drew them to that ancient man? Taking Lucas' advice, she huffed and headed toward the river. She didn't want to walk into the city as grimy as she was; a disheveled appearance might sully her reputation.

Nikolas, having finally gotten out of bed, drank a cup of tea and finished a loaf of warm bread. Just as he decided his elusive lady love would not return soon, she burst through the rickety door. Her wet and disheveled presence startled him. "What in . . ."

"Oh, you're here. Help me lay these plants out and hang to dry."

He titled his head, "Sure. You had to swim for them?" He started to embrace her and then changed his mind.

"In a way. The canals, you know." She opened the satchel and carefully placed the plants onto the table while Nik strung a strand of jute. When he finished, Brigit was removing her sopping clothes. He hesitated then began to unlace his shirt.

Shaking her head, she said, "I'm late. Can you help me dry my hair. Grab that linen. I was supposed to meet them at the dress shop."

Nikolas gathered her long hair and rubbed it vigorously between the folds of the large linen. When he leaned over and kissed the back of her neck, she turned and wrapped her arms around his waist. They held each other for a moment before she stood upright and shook her hair back.

"If you run, it will help dry it," he said.

"Yes, all right."

"Why did you need these plants first thing this morning?" he asked as he started hanging them.

"We can never be too careful."

"I suppose not." He lifted one shoulder and peered at her. "What are you worried about?"

Brigit bit her lip. "Nothing. I just think it's foolish to believe you're safe."

He went over to help her tie the laces on her shift. "I find it satisfying to believe so."

"Ah, Nikolas, I'll protect you," she said nodding toward the plants. "I'll protect all of us." She pulled a purple and yellow dress over her head.

Nik took her chin in his hand and gave her a long deep kiss. "See you later." He swatted her bottom as she turned to swirl out the door.

* * *

Alina stood with her arms outstretched while the tailor took measurements. The shop girl served tea and sweet buns to Irene, while Carissa and Perina held up bolts of cloth and imagined the gowns that they could make from them. When Brigit came through the door, her hair was smooth and flowing black again. "There you are!" Alina gushed. "I feared I had forgotten to ask you to join us!"

"All is well, sweet girl." Brigit took a seat beside Irene who patted her hand.

Alina said, "Will you help Carissa and Perina choose the flowers to braid into my hair, Brigit? You know which flowers will last the longest."

"I'm happy to help with anything. Anything you need." Brigit's eyes swirled through their colors.

The ladies left the dress shop and strolled over to La Tulipa Tavern where they sat outside in the garden and enjoyed peaches, cheese, and rose´ wine. Irene made a toast. "I feel as if both my daughter and son are marrying. And I don't even have any children," she said with a mixture of joy and sorrow. They all clasped hands as Irene offered a prayer, and Brigit added a few words that nobody understood. The gray cat darted out from under the table, and everyone laughed.

* * *

Feeling pleased after his visit with the priest at Saint Sempre and another stop at the monastery, Lucas allowed himself to relax and enjoy all the ado about the wedding. He smiled quietly to himself knowing things would not go as they planned, but in the end everyone would understand. He dressed in his work clothes and knocked on Alina's door. They still hadn't discussed how their living arrangements might change, but it didn't matter now. She opened the door and stepped into the hallway wearing a loose, worn-out gown.

Aghast, Lucas asked, "Where did that come from?"

"Ah," she smirked, "I came from Ingleena in this old thing. It once belonged to one of our maids. I wanted to travel unnoticed."

"Even that shabby dress could not hide your spirit, Alina!" Lucas took her hand and kissed it. "It's perfect for lighting lanterns."

"I'm glad. And it reminds me of how fortunate I am. I dreaded wearing this dress when I boarded the ship. I was embarrassed. I'm really not your sort of woman, you know, Lucas."

"I knew that from the start, my blessed girl."

In the kitchen, he unlocked the cupboard and handed Alina four hand lanterns. He placed spare candles into the pockets of her oversized dress. Grabbing the rest of his tools they went out the back door.

The sun had just slipped behind the buildings, leaving the street with the calm hush of a completed day. Citizens still walking about hurried their pace. "The best part is when darkness descends just enough to distort the shapes. The stars began to appear. And then we light the lanterns, and the world changes."

"It goes from spooky to cheerful," she said.

"I never thought of it that way," Lucas said as he reached his lighting stick up to the first lantern. "I suppose others see it that way also."

"That's why you're here."

"Alina, you make my heart race and trip over itself." He leaned the stick against the wall and cupped her chin in his hand. When she smiled up at him, he furrowed his brow and hoped his conversation with the priest didn't haunt him later.

It took much longer to light the lanterns than usual, but he enjoyed showing Alina how to aim the stick correctly and observing the illuminated joy that spread across her face. They stopped often to chat with the citizens who walked out at night. Alina asked if they should announce their wedding to everyone, but Lucas advised against it. The last thing they needed was the entire city to turn out on that day.

They went to the dark zone where she placed the hand lanterns. They had to be replaced often, for they disappeared almost nightly, sometimes found in a different location, but most often never seen again. Just as they finished and were ready to turn toward home, Lucas had an idea to spy on Brigit. He presented the idea to Alina as a prank, but in truth, he wanted to see how she spent her time on the evenings that she didn't join them for supper.

Without any light at all, he took Alina by the hand and led her along the narrow cobbles to the dirt path that led to Brigit's cottage. Alina whispered and giggled so much, he feared everyone in the cottages would come outside.

Once there, he remembered the days when the gold-jewelled box tormented his thoughts. Now, something else did: Brigit's strange behavior at the canal. The cottage glowed, and a plume of smoke rose from the chimney. The haphazard door was now repaired; Lucas wondered by whom. They circled the entire cottage before finding a curtain loose enough for them to peer inside.

Seated at the table, with her long hair hanging around her like a shroud, was Brigit. One candle was lit, and something was in a bowl in front of her. She was murmuring. Lucas, fearing his whim may have placed Alina in danger, clutched her hand. Leaning forward, he strained to understand the words. Suddenly, he heard a man's voice coming from Brigit's bent head. Lucas gasped and pulled back.

"What is it?" Alina whispered. He held a finger to his lips and, pushing the curtain aside, leaned in the open window. There, across the table from Brigit, was Nikolas. Lucas retreated but not before Nik caught his eye and raised one startled eyebrow. "What do you see?" Alina whispered again. Lucas shook his head. He led her away from the window. "What is it?" she giggled. He grabbed the tools that they'd leaned against the tree and dragged her away from the cottage.

She pulled away and stopped. "Tell me! What did you see, Lucas?"

"Brigit and Nikolas having supper, that's all," he grinned. The cottage door opened. "Lift your skirts and run," he cried as they lurched away.

Once they were back in the shimmering city square, Lucas stopped. And Alina, panting, brushed her hair out of her eyes. "What was that all about? Is this how you've spent your years lighting lanterns? Peeping in windows?"

"Sometimes, yes." Lucas grabbed her hand and spun her in a circle. "But not with such blatancy. I like to glance from a distance and observe for a moment someone else's world."

Alina laughed as she spun with him in the amber light. "I see that I don't have to encourage you to be childish after all."

He grabbed her and kissed her until she pushed him away. "Lucas we are outside in the center of the square!"

"I don't care who sees us. It's Brigit. I cannot understand that she is my mother's sister. She is not like us."

"To me, Lucas, you and Brigit are very much alike. Wild and whimsical."

He took her hand, and they headed toward the boarding house. "Do you really think so?"

"I do."

"I just wonder what she's brewing in that lively head of hers. She has so many unusual tendencies."

"As do you, my love."

Lucas stopped and kissed her again. "Tis true, I suppose. And I think I know who can explain myself to me."

"Your father, Seppo."

"Yes, him, Seppo. But I doubt he can explain Brigit."

"Or her exotic green porry mash. It smelled like mud!"

"Ugh, it did. And tasted worse." Lucas remembered Brigit stomping through the canal with her dripping satchel. He wanted to tell Alina, but he and Brigit had promised to keep each other's secret. He hesitated considering to whom he should show more loyalty, but then he didn't want Alina to ask where he had been going that morning, so he said, "She can brew tea, but I think her talents end with that." Lucas stopped in front of the door and turned to observe the city. "Here we are Alina. Did you enjoy lighting the lanterns this evening?"

"Yes! More than you realize." She reached up to caress his neck and plant a soft kiss on his lips. "I love the world in which you dwell. I am no longer afraid of it."

They stood for a long while enjoying the silent luminance. When Lucas noticed the gray cat slink toward the garden wall he wondered if their feline friend had followed them throughout the evening. "Let's see what Irene has left in the pot for us and take our supper in the courtyard garden."

Beaming, she said, "Yes. I will light the candles."

Lucas shoved open the door. "And I will bring the bowls and wine."

That sat together on the stone bench holding their bowls of stew in their laps. Alina slurped a large gulp and gravy dribbled on her dress. Lucas dabbed it with his finger. She laughed, "How peaceful and easy life will be from now on." They clinked the pewter goblets in a toast and sipped their wine. After finishing their meal, they cleaned up the kitchen and took the wine to sit in front of the fire. Lucas startled when he saw the gray cat stretched out on the floor, basking in the warm fire light. "She's so bold!" he exclaimed.

Alina bent down to pet the cat. "I'm very fond of her. I've been setting out bowls of goat milk."

"Milk?"

"Yes, she likes it."

"Good, Alina. A cat helps keep vermin away."

"I'm glad you don't mind. Let's give her a name then!"

"Sure," Lucas said scratching the back of his neck. He twirled his goblet between his fingers. "What would you like to call her?"

Alina bit her lip. "I don't know. But I'll think of something. I'd like to meet your father, Lucas."

"You will, my darling." He leaned his head back and closed his eyes.

"When?"

"I don't know. Soon."

"After the wedding?"

Lucas half smiled, "Yes, after."

"We can ask him lots of questions, Lucas. You won't have to wonder about yourself or your mother anymore." She stroked the palm of his hand.

"I would like that," he murmured sleepily.

"I know you love your mother still." Her shoulders slumped. "I wish I could have met her! She brought you into this world. Do you think she would have liked me?"

"Of course. Everyone does."

"No, they don't," Alina blushed. "What is it now, after so many years that you still yearn for?"

Lucas opened his eyes and peered into the low licking flames. "When my mother and I walked and gathered flowers together, I could feel her heart. I could feel the life humming in the swaying grass and fragrant flowers alongside us. It felt as if that beautiful land could hold the two of us together throughout the ages."

Alina leaned back and closed her eyes. Knowing she was trying to imagine what he described, Lucas took her hand. They sat silently for several moments before he said, 'I'm sorry, Alina. You didn't know your mother."

"No. My father and I were remarkably close, but I will never know the feeling of what you described. With a mother, it is different. I have felt that pull of my heart to you."

He sat up. "And I to you, right from the instant I saw you." Lucas brushed an amber curl away from her cheek and kissed her tenderly.

She stroked his arm. "I know a little about what you describe. I feel a cloak of safety when we are together."

Lucas frowned. "Even though I have not always protected you?"

Alina smiled. "I believe it has always been your intention to do so." She rubbed her cheek. "At first, I didn't want you to. I felt that place was for my father. But for you, the drumming in my heart is extraordinary."

Lucas wrapped his arm around her shoulders and pulled her legs into his lap. "I understand. When I first saw you that morning in the street, I felt your heart reach out to mine. I felt dazzled by your beauty, your face, your hair, your boundless eyes. But more than that, I recognized you even though I knew that you were not a young lady who would find me a proper suitor. When my hand brushed your skin, I knew the depths of your kindness and fervor, young and innocent as you were, and I felt that you matched me."

Alina giggled and fluttered her eyelids at Lucas. "As much as your effort to snatch my ruby startled me, I somehow knew you would not harm me."

"Never! My foolishness annoyed you. I'm relieved I didn't scare you away."

"I am strong like my father, and you are kind like your mother. Inside us, we hold our loved ones who are gone. And soon the wedding ceremony will affirm that."

Lucas laced his fingers in hers. "We don't need a ceremony to confirm us. Your father knew our hearts were the same. He knew I would recognize it." He tilted his cup and finished the last of his wine.

Alina did the same. "When we speak with Seppo, I'll ask the questions that you don't think of. But now," she said, taking the goblet from his hand and pulling him to his feet, "I will leave you at your bedchamber door so you can get a night's rest on your own."

* * *

Early the next morning, Brigit made her way to the boarding house. She knew it unlikely that she would find Lucas alone long enough to confront him for peeping in her window. Nikolas had found the incident amusing, though confusing, and told her, in a gesture of reassurance that she didn't need, that he would speak to Lucas. Nikolas, of course wondered if there was something in the cottage that Lucas wanted to steal. But what he said to Brigit was that he thought Lucas was reverting to his old tricks. Brigit knew better. She knew Lucas had intended to spy on her.

She found Irene in the kitchen discussing the wedding menu with Carissa and Perina. Irene explained that Ikarus had returned from Arcana with wonder and excitement about the lodgings at the Grande Inn. Bernard and Wentworth were thrilled for the invitation to the wedding ceremony and would arrive in a few days. Brigit engaged in the planning with enthusiasm although she had deep doubts about the constancy of Lucas' mind after seeing him scurrying around the canals like a rat while carrying Irene's market bag, which now hung in its usual place. Brigit sauntered over and peered inside the bag even though it was obviously empty now. It bulged the other day.

"I have tried to get Lucas to help me select garland to decorate the staircase for Alina's grand entrance, but he is ambivalent. He knows much about flowers. He should participate in this," Irene said with knitted brows to Brigit.

"No bother, Irene. I will take care of the decoration for the staircase," Brigit said offering a reassuring smile. *And in case he is as elusive as his mother, I will lock Lucas in his room the night before the hand-fasting ceremony,* she thought to herself. *Of course, if he wants to escape, he will simply climb out the window onto the tree. Perhaps a special tea. . .*

but no, that won't do. We don't want him stumbling and intoxicated. Hmmm. Brigit looked up to see the women watching her. Had she muttered aloud? Nodding, she said, "The floral tiara. We will save the absolute best flowers for that."

Chapter 4

In the ensuing days, vexed by Brigit nagging him to 'do something' as she put it, Lucas tried to avoid her. He was doing plenty, and what he did was none of her concern. Irene, on the other hand, doted on him as if he were about to embark on a long journey with the potential to never return.

Brigit and Irene cornered him one afternoon as he attempted to slip out to the monastery. They dragged him into the courtyard garden where they forced him to sit while they discussed the cord for the handfasting ceremony. Brigit wanted the cords braided in green for fertility and growth, purple for spiritual growth, and gold for wisdom. Irene nodded, absently sipping her endless cup of tea. Lucas patiently explained that Alina had already chosen white for purity and blue for fidelity, and he had chosen red for passion. In the end, the three of them agreed it was sensible that there would be two separate braided cords of three in all the wished-for colors to make six.

When he finally made it to the monastery, there was only time for Seppo to reassure him that he had the situation in hand and was following the directions Lucas had given him for the wedding day. As he circumvented the usual route back to the boarding house, Lucas felt sure Brigit was lurking somewhere in the shadows. He made his way to the Blue Gate, and to his great satisfaction, found Nikolas seated just inside the open window and enjoying a pint.

Nik hailed the serving girl and kicked out a chair. "Sit before you crumple your own weary bones," he said. Lucas narrowed his eyes and gulped. Nik hailed another pint for each of them. "Once you feel that ale course through you, why don't you tell me why you've been avoiding everyone, except at night when you're poking your head in windows."

Lucas laughed so abruptly that he spewed ale into Nik's face. "Sorry, friend," Lucas said and offered a handkerchief, but Nik had already used his hand to swipe his face.

Nik drummed his fingers on the table. "I'll have to bathe again this evening. You've got Brigit in a mighty stir. What were you doing the other night? Was that Alina with you too?"

Lucas swallowed and glared at his empty tankard. "Uh, yeah. Look Nik, Brigit is strange. She is up to something. She wanders around in the canals digging up poisonous plants."

"I thought you two agreed to keep that encounter a secret," Nik said.

"Apparently we did not," Lucas replied stonily.

Nik laughed. "You'd be surprised what a woman says at certain times."

Lucas held up his hand. "Nik, she may be your mistress, but she's practically my mother. I mean she's my aunt, after all."

"She's just concerned about you."

"I'm concerned about her. That mumbling and chanting, the odd gatherings of things, and that horrible porry mash she tried to feed us!"

"I've talked her out of that particular concoction. Is there anything you want to tell me, Lucas? You're pale and distracted. Is it the wedding?"

"It is," Lucas said as he stood to leave. "But nothing for you to concern yourself with. Be careful what Brigit feeds you. Tell her I don't want any frightening food to show up at the boarding house." He reached in his pocket, but Nik waved him away. "I've got this. Don't keep your secret too long, Lucas. Some things do make you sick."

Lucas grimaced but nodded. He gave Nikolas a squeeze on the shoulder before walking out into the now dusky street. He took a deep breath and reassured himself that he was doing the right thing.

When he went inside the boarding house, no one was about. He found Irene in her chamber and asked her to take a walk with him before supper. She donned her shawl, although the night was warm enough, and followed Lucas down the stairs and out into the street. Without saying so, they turned toward the river. Lucas strode in grateful silence that Irene knew him well enough to let him speak when he was ready. All the questions and plans of the past weeks had charred his mind. Finally, he said, "I have a carriage coming just before the noon bells toll."

"The ceremony commences when the bells toll," she murmured.

"Yes, I know."

Irene peered up at him. "Is the carriage bringing someone in or taking someone away? Lucas, the ceremony is the day after tomorrow. Wentworth and Bernard arrive this very night. That is why supper is later. I told everyone that. I thought you were in the room when I said that."

"I was. I know."

"Who will this carriage carry? Where would anyone want to go on your wedding day."

"Lucas stopped walking and gazed in the direction of the river. "The carriage will carry me . . ."

A sob burst from Irene. She clutched her throat. "What? Where are you going? You will leave us, all of us . . . after all! Brigit was right? She has been nettling at my ear that you are not ready for this wedding ceremony."

Lucas grasped her flailing arms. "Irene, please trust me; this plan is for the best. I've been thinking about it and, I'm sure. But we must not let Brigit know. Not Carissa, Perina, Nik, nobody. Only you and me. Please, Irene, I need your help."

Irene stared solemnly. "Of course, Lucas. You know I will do anything for you. She crossed her arms over her chest. "Tell me your plan."

* * *

On the morning of the ceremony, Lucas who had bid Alina good night each evening at her chamber door, awoke early. He stood outside her door for several moments before deciding not to knock. In silence, he descended the staircase carrying over his arm a long valise of belongings. He stepped so softly outside into the early morning murmur that the front door didn't even click as he shut it. The tall steeple of Saint Sempre glimmered in the dawn light. Lucas released a long breath of relief and walked away from the boarding house.

* * *

Alina rolled over onto her back and stretched. She'd slept more soundly in the past few days than she had even back in Ingleena at her father's house. Her tranquil slumber came from the deep sense of safety she felt now that she and Lucas were to wed. And today was the day! She leapt from her cozy bed just as Carissa rapped on the door. "Alina miss, I have tea and bread for you." Carissa pushed open the door and stepped in. "Mrs. Kempel says we should stay up here until the ceremony, so Lucas doesn't stumble upon you in your dressing gown."

"She's right. I don't want to encounter Lucas until I descend the stairs and see him waiting below. Did Perina arrange the garland that Brigit made for the banister?"

"Yes, it's done. In a few minutes, she and Irene will bring up the flowers Brigit selected for the bridal crown. It's going to look so magnificent when Perina weaves it through the length of your hair. She is the absolute best at it, I promise!"

Alina smiled to herself and sat on the cushioned stool while Carissa combed her hair. She was able to take only a few nibbles of the delicious warm bread.

Irene burst in carrying a long parchment. She lay it carefully on the bed. Alina stood beside her with her hand over heart as Irene unwrapped the rose-colored wedding gown. the bodice with a square neckline trimmed with fawn lace. The V-shaped waistline dipped at the center with flowing pleats and ribbons trailing down the back. The sleeves, tight lace and trimmed with fawn ribbon and tiny deep pink roses stopped just below the elbows. Alina gasped in delight. "I fear I will never want to remove this glorious gown!"

Perina entered the room with the crown of eucalyptus vine and daisy that she explained Brigit had chosen for innocence, purity, and loyalty. She had a bouquet of tiny red roses for love, and willow for balance and harmony. Alina peered at herself in the mirror. Her eyes watered as her heart filled with so much joy that she forgot to inquire of the women if any of them had seen to Lucas to give him his morning bread.

* * *

Carrying her special flask, Brigit scurried from her cottage toward the monastery. She'd sent Nikolas home the afternoon before explaining that he couldn't spend every night in her cottage. She had women things to tend to. How she would force Seppo to drink the potion she didn't yet know. But he would drink it, of that she was sure. He would not interfere in the lives of Lucas and Alina as he did Linnea.

When she and Linnea parted ways many years ago, Brigit had no one to consort with. She sought answers from the earth and the sky and made choices based on fragmented words she had overheard round the fires late at night. She'd found her own way, but Seppo deserved to pay recompense for the sister he stole from her, for the fear and sadness he caused. Linny had promised to stay at the farm, but when Brigit went looking for her there, she'd already been gone for weeks. She thought her sister dead. Everyone she inquired of agreed it must be so.

Her throat felt dry as she hurried over the canals. She had forgotten to drink any water upon waking. If she didn't know better, she would take a sip from her flask. The thought made her laugh. As the monastery came into view, she crawled through the weeping mulberry and emerged in the secret cemetery. Stopping in front of her lost sister's grave, she swore an oath: "I promise, Linny, I will protect your boy from that creature who absconded with you!"

She tiptoed through the lonely gravestones and searched the ivy-covered walls of the monastery for the opening that Seppo used to appear and disappear. Her eyes could discern no cracks or gaps in the walls. She felt with her hands until her fingers began to scrape and bleed. She feared she would ruin the ceremony with blood dripping from her fingers. Disappointed, she finally turned away deciding not to leave the flask in hope Seppo should appear and drink it on his own. The dead were already dead, and it was not right to leave a poisonous potion as further insult to them.

Back at her cottage, she hid the flask, bathed, and dressed in a flowing dress of pale yellow. She tied a purple sash around the waistline and let her long black hair flow freely over her shoulders and back. Nikolas clattered up to the door atop a black horse and with one on a tether for her.

"Why are we riding?" she asked.

Nik tilted his head. "I don't know. I had a feeling. In case anyone needs a horse, we have these two." He stroked his mounts shimmering mane. "You look astonishing!"

She glanced back to the cottage. "Too much?"

"As always, Madame."

"I could change to some sack cloth. It's Alina's day."

"Then you best show up as yourself; otherwise, you'll alarm everyone. No porry mash, though. You are forbidden to bring food or drink." He leaned over and brushed her cheek with his lips. "You're naturally beautiful."

Brigit smirked. "That's the right thing to say, especially if you mean it."

"I mean it, Brigit. You have a fierce and unsettling beauty all your own."

Embarrassed by Nik's ardor, she glanced down at her fingers They weren't bleeding even though she'd forgotten to dip them in oil. They rode to the boarding house in the midmorning light under a calm blue sky.

In front of the boarding house a long cart with Igmus and Rathbone squished onto its driver's bench waited. Nikolas and Brigit dismounted. "What are you doing sitting out here?" Nikolas asked. He glanced over to the front door that was outlined with ivy and white flowers.

"Good. The flowers and greenery are as I wanted them," Brigit murmured handing the lead rope to Nikolas before going inside.

"Tie your mounts to the wagon, and we'll pull up out of the way," Igmus said. Nikolas pursed his lips, but did as Igmus suggested. He noticed the two men were dressed in what looked like new black trousers and clean beige shirts.

"See you inside," he said.

"We'll be here," Rathbone said.

Inside, Wentworth and Bernard stood holding their pewter goblets and taking small sips as if they weren't sure if they were supposed to drink before Alina descended the decorated staircase. Nikolas went upstairs where the women gathered inside and out of Alina's room making it impossible to pass through and knock upon Lucas' door. "Good day, everyone. I am here," he announced loud enough for Lucas to hear in case he was pacing inside his chamber. The ladies overlooked him, and Lucas' door remained firmly closed.

Back downstairs Brigit came out of the kitchen wearing an annoyed expression. "Something's wrong," she muttered to Nik.

"What?"

"I don't know, but something doesn't feel right."

"I agree. I expected Lucas to be crawling the staircase in anticipation, but he's nowhere to be found, unless he locked himself in his chamber." Nik dragged his hand through his hair. "I've never been to this kind of thing." He poured them both a glass of wine. With his eyes, he implored Bernard and Wentworth to offer an explanation. But Bernard shrugged and Wentworth murmured something about not remembering. Irene dashed down the stairs and brushed past them into the kitchen. She returned dragging by the wrist a young girl clutching a flute. "Now," she said. "Play now!"

"Wait! Where in blazes is Lucas?" Nik demanded. Brigit's hair shot up and spun so quickly it would have slapped him in the face had he not deftly ducked.

Irene gaped at him in surprise. She propped the front door wide open and dashed back upstairs. The young girl with long wavy brown hair began to play her silver flute in lilting notes.

Alina stood elegantly relaxed in her flowing rose-colored wedding gown. The silk ribbons matched the fawn ribbons that Carissa and Perina had braided into the sides of her hair to match the delicate crown. It blended into her loose amber hair and streamed down the open back of the gown. She barely heard the words the women had been saying to her.

Since she opened her eyes early that morning and heard the last notes of the lark, she had felt as if she drifted in a story from a book. Her eyes glistened with joy at everything she saw, from the water pitcher to the blue sky outside her window. Her skin tingled in anticipation of Lucas' arms and his betrothal kiss. Even though her father was not here to see her wed, she knew that he somehow was aware of her ecstatic joy. She silently thanked him for having found Lucas for her and in a way, for leaving her alone in the world to learn how to make her own path and allow Lucas to love her.

This feeling she had never experienced before, and in the depths of her heart, Alina knew this kind of love did not come more than once in a lifetime and for some unfortunate souls, it did not come at all. She offered a prayer for the lonely, as her heart swelled with relief and appreciation for the future that lay ahead for herself and Lucas. Before she made an oath and vow to Lucas, she made a vow to herself never to neglect the sad and forsaken.

Carissa and Perina led the way to the top of the stairs where they left Alina and descended to stand among the guests. Irene came down next. Brigit began to tremble, and the hourglass that Nikolas hadn't noticed earlier flipped up from the top of her bodice. It contained no sand at all.

Alina appeared resplendent at the top of the stairs. She glowed like a seraph. When she glanced down at everyone gathered there, Nikolas gasped. Lucas should not be missing this magnificent moment!

Nik clutched his stomach, and Brigit slid her damp hand from his. He shook his head and glanced toward the front door. Why did Igmus and Rathbone remain outside? Where was Mr. Pagett and the other guests? Would Lucas come down after Alina? He sucked on his goblet but gulped only air. It was only two long sideways strides to the sideboard, but Nikolas dared not move.

Alina took one step and then another. Brigit started to mumble, "Wait."

Irene nodded and dabbed her eyes with a handkerchief. Alina held the banister with one hand and a glorious bouquet in the other. Nik feared she would slip and fall when she realized Lucas was not waiting for her at the bottom of the stairs. Outside, a clatter of hooves and a shout.

Nikolas let go of Brigit's hand and rushed toward the door; he was certain that Lucas had managed to die on his wedding day. Alina gasped. Her foot slid from the step, but she remained upright. Nikolas turned from the door to the stairs and back again when from the corner of his eye, he saw a glittering carriage. The door was open, and Lucas leapt out, landing on both feet. His eyes were dark and wild, his hair blown away from his flushed cheeks. He wore his newly tailored midnight blue breeches, matching doublet, a white linen shirt, and cuffed black boots. He shot an impish grin at Nikolas as he brushed in the door. The cathedral bells sounded.

Stopping at the bottom of the stairs, Lucas gazed up at Alina. He placed his hand over his heart and bowed. Their eyes locked together as she came down to him. He took her hand and kissed it. "Darling Alina, I have a surprise for you. We will take this carriage to Saint Sempre and wed in the beauty of the old cathedral as I had promised." He cupped her cheek in his palm. She blinked and nodded.

All the women except Brigit had tears streaming down their cheeks. Nikolas took his swig of wine and then followed Bernard,

Wentworth, and the others outside. Brigit stood transfixed while Lucas, Alina, and Irene climbed into the carriage. The others found seats in the long cart, now draped with white linen cloths. The flute player, Lily continued to play as she sat in the back of the long cart. For a moment, as he settled into his seat inside the carriage, Lucas noticed Brigit. The hourglass was full, and by what seemed a trick of the light, it appeared as if the sand eked out over the top. "Afterward, we will return here for the celebration feast," he announced.

Brigit pouted. He'd tricked her into thinking the wedding was not going to take place. Surely, his father was behind the intrigue. She shivered in horror that Seppo already had such a hold over Linny's boy. Yet her heart expanded with pride that Lucas had found such a suitable bride and that they would live a normal life together. Certainly, Alina had no intention of allowing that sepulchral Seppo to worm too deeply into their lives.

As the carriage pulled away, Lucas flashed her a stunning smile that wholly resembled his mother. Brigit clutched her heart as she realized how very much she missed her sister. Nikolas waited atop his horse. Brigit mounted and they fell in place at the back of the procession. As they made their way through the City of Dreams, the throng grew larger.

Brigit grumbled as she rode alongside Nik. "How did you know?"

"I didn't," Nik said. "I had a feeling . . ."

"You had a feeling, and I didn't?"

Nik tapped his chest, "I had a feeling that someone would need a horse today. Maybe I have the gift and am a seer as well." Brigit rolled her eyes but allowed herself to laugh.

The carriage came to a halt in front of Saint Sempre. Wentworth waited at the bottom of the steps. Lucas and Alina hugged and kissed Irene who dabbed her eyes with a handkerchief. Wentworth took her arm and led her into the cathedral. The guests proceeded inside. "We wait here together," Lucas said.

"Lucas," she gushed, "How did you do this? I cannot believe it. I feel like I have fallen into a beautiful dream!"

Lucas kissed her fingers. "You have. We have. I'm relieved that you're pleased, Alina. We had said we would wed in the cathedral. I didn't want to disappoint you. I realize I hurried you into the ceremony."

She giggled. "I'm glad that you did. And this surprise . . . you make me beyond happy, my darling Lucas. Truly, it's better this way. I had little to concern myself with."

"As intended, my love. I will never suppress you from walking your own path. Just please don't run away again." Above them in the tower, the bells continued to chime in splendid unison.

With an impish tilt of her chin, Alina pronounced, "I intend to stay," A quick kiss, then Lucas stepped down, took Alina around the waist, and lifted her out of the carriage.

Inside the arched dome of Saint Sempre, the cathedral overflowed with flowers. Mr. Pagett, the widow Van Dessen, the flower vendor, and all the many citizens who had followed, sat waiting in the long rows. Irene had diverted the guests that morning at the last moment, as they'd made their way to the boarding house.

The delighted guests filled the wooden benches inside the arched cathedral below a green, yellow, and red roundel glass window depicting a clear-winged angel. The workmen and laborers had fully hidden evidence of their toil and mess with several carved wooden rood screens. The talented, young flutist now climbed the narrow stairs of the loft to the organ console, took her seat on the smooth bench under the tall dome of the nave, and waited for the priest. Off to his side, stood Seppo waving like a gentle white feather.

Brigit shook her shimmery head in disbelief. Nikolas clutched her hand so tightly that she had to whisper in reassurance, "Of course, I have no intention to disrupt the ceremony and ruin this wonderful day for the people and our family." Releasing her hand, Nikolas excused himself to shake hands with Lucas and take his place beside Alina to escort her down the long wide aisle of Saint Sempre. Lucas made his way to the front where he kissed each of Irene's cheeks before stepping onto the alter where he embraced Seppo, and then stood alongside the priest.

Lucas swallowed and blinked resisting the urge to weep in awe when Alina stepped forward with her delicate hand resting on his best friend's arm. Her flower-braided hair cascaded over her slender shoulders and down her back eliciting a huff of admiration from their guests. Lucas had allowed Perina to adroitly comb his normally tangled mane and give him a smooth shave with a straight blade.

Nikolas kissed Alina's fingers before placing her hands into Lucas' open palms. Nikolas nodded to the priest, and Seppo then turned to notice with relief that Brigit hadn't moved. Lucas couldn't resist planting a kiss on Alina's lips which elicited a titter from the congregation. He stood in proud reverence when the priest spoke in a language that no one understood. Yet, upon this day, everyone in the Cathedral Saint Sempre understood the sentiment of true love. Lucas shuddered, unable to hide his exhilaration as Alina promised herself to him.

Wentworth mused about his first wife. Bernard squirmed in his fine clothes as if they were a snare. Knowing she would never ask for such a spectacle, Nikolas glanced gratefully at Brigit. Carissa and Perina wished for such a handsome husband. Ikarus remembered a wide-eyed girl he'd met in a terraced village on his way to the City of Dreams, and Irene wiped tears from her cheeks with the handkerchief that Lucas had just given her. She held it tightly wadded in her clammy hand. She was finding it difficult to breathe. She hoped no one noticed her distress, mixed with joy, and misunderstand her emotion. If Irene had only glanced around, she would have noticed the reassuring presence of Mister Pagett who stood poised to catch her should she faint.

Lucas and Alina faced each other with clasped hands. The sun poured through the stained-glass window and framed the two of them in a sphere of tranquil color. When the priest nodded, Lucas took his mother's ring from his pocket and slipped it onto Alina's finger. They both glanced at Seppo who slightly smiled.

Then it was time for the handfasting ceremony. Nikolas had to nudge Brigit to remind her that she carried the cords. As she stepped up into the chancel, Seppo came forward. Nikolas held his breath hoping she would not strangle him. He couldn't understand why she detested the man. Apparently, he'd stolen her sister away, but Nikolas doubted the truth of that. Two are usually involved in these things. He watched her compose herself before gracefully presenting the cords to Seppo. A twinge in his chest caused Nikolas to wonder for an instant if a wedding was such a fearful thing after all, but the feeling quickly receded.

Seppo murmured in a voice as soft as a song as he wound the cords around their wrists. Once Lucas and Alina were joined as husband and wife, the priest handed them in turn a golden goblet from which they drank. Alina's eyes watered, "Oh, my goodness, the wine is as strong as whisky!" she exclaimed. The cathedral erupted in laughter, applause, and the vibrating tone of the organ. Leaving the green, purple, and gold braid on their wrists and the white, blue, and red draped over Lucas' shoulders, they made their way outside into the brilliant day.

As soon as they arrived back at the boarding house, Irene realized she had made a terrible mistake. The crowd of guests and well-wishing citizens had grown so large that they couldn't possibly fit inside the parlour and garden. But as the carriage clattered to a stop in front of the house, they saw that banquet tables had been set outside in the street and several market vendors were carrying baskets of bread, cheese, and fruit. Alina clapped her hands together in delight. "There are so many surprises today!"

Lucas and Irene glanced at each other in concern for neither had made such arrangements. Carissa jumped down from the long cart and hurried over to Irene to explain. Early that morning, the woman Drusilla, sister of Gacheru the locksmith, had come to the boarding house to offer her assistance. "And she has arranged for three additional roasts as well! There's plenty for the boarders also, and Perina and I can enjoy the feast because we need not work throughout the day!"

Having formed an unsavory opinion of Gacheru whom he noticed loitering near the front door, Lucas grumbled under his breath. He couldn't imagine Gacheru's sister would be a capable woman, although she had clearly taken charge of the food. Keeping his thoughts to himself, he realized he was smiling anyway. He nodded his approval. Nothing could upset the wedding day. Irene, her cheeks rosy, laughed and followed Carissa inside.

Lucas and Alina made their way through the two-sided receiving line. Once they finally reached the parlour, Nik handed each of them a crystal goblet and offered a toast to their long life and continued good fortune.

In the courtyard, the pretty flutist was now accompanied by a handsome lutist. Bernard surprised everyone by helping Drusilla as she lugged platters of food and pitchers of ale to the parlour, the courtyard, and out onto the street. Wentworth watched in contentment from a chair by the fire that was filled with twinkling candles. Ikarus protested but took turns dancing clumsily with

Carissa and Perina. Once Brigit realized that Seppo would not attend the celebration, she gleefully danced with Nikolas and managed not to frighten anyone. Irene, who couldn't seem to relax, finally drank three glasses of wine and allowed Mister Pagett to escort her through two vigorous dances. Lucas and Alina drank toasts, swirled among the dancers, and accepted kisses and acclaim from the entire city.

By the time the feasting ended, and the last guest went home, the midnight bell had long since tolled. Lucas had not forgotten it was his wedding night, but as they opened the door to his chamber he felt as if he had not yet had enough to drink. Alina flung herself on the bed and giggled. "It's your duty to get me out of this gown." Lucas was not inexperienced with women, yet he suddenly felt apprehensive. He and Alina had spent some innocent, intimate moments together, but his heart skipped several beats as he helped Alina slip the lovely rose-pink bridal dress from her silken shoulders. The candles and fire had been lit by one of the girls and there were bouquets of flowers decorating every table in the room. Somehow Alina had helped him undress as well.

As they lay down together, she kissed him with such passion his body lit with fire. Slowly, he explored and caressed her warm body. They gazed deeply into each other's wide eyes and smiled, each a little timid now. He brushed a single tear from her cheek. Together they discovered each other in the amber glow of the crackling fire. He felt her shiver with his touch. He kissed her hands, her arms, her shoulders, her throat, and her eyelids. She wrapped herself around him. With tender, gentle strokes of love and adoration, Lucas took Alina as his wife.

Chapter 5

When Lucas and Alina emerged from their chamber, afternoon shadows slanted into the courtyard garden. Cool water, fresh bread, and jam had been left for them. The house showed no remnants of the large gathering. They sat quietly side by side reveling in the blush of their passions.

Irene passed through the parlour twice before Lucas realized she awaited an invitation to join them in the garden. "What a grand celebration it was!" Alina exclaimed.

They agreed it was more than any of them had imagined or ever seen. There were amusing stories about the guests, many having simply invited themselves. "I'm surprised to see the house put back in order so quickly," Lucas remarked.

"Yes," Irene glanced around. "Drusilla, Gacheru and many of the spontaneous guests stayed until everything was put back in its place."

"Remarkable," Lucas said.

"Will you go to the Grande Inn this afternoon or wait until morning?"

"I'd like to go this afternoon," Lucas said.

"And I too," Alina agreed. "We could stop by the monastery and leave some flowers on the way."

Lucas grinned and kissed her cheek. "Excellent idea, Alina."

"Why didn't Seppo come to the feast?" she wondered aloud.

"I don't know," Lucas shrugged. "We can ask him, but I believe he prefers to remain mostly unseen. I'm just glad that he was willing to participate in the ceremony."

"Nikolas has left horses at the stable for you," Irene said. "I'll have Ikarus gather your satchels and tie them on."

Lucas hugged Irene and kissed the top of her head. "Take some time to rest while we're gone, Irene. You have done so much for us. I must find a way to thank you."

She winked. "Thank me by enjoying yourselves." Alina embraced Irene and kissed each cheek before rushing upstairs to change into her riding gown.

"Are you well, Irene?" Lucas asked.

"I am, Lucas child. More well than I dreamed I'd be in these old years."

"Maybe well enough to walk by the river with Mister Pagett."

She blushed and slapped Lucas. "Maybe."

Lucas and Alina rode away from the boarding house with a basket of flowers slung over the rump of each horse. Ikarus had done an admirable job of securing their belongings. Alina, of course, carried more than Lucas. A teary-eyed Irene waved from the door.

Having discovered a cart path alongside the far edge of the mulberry trees when preparing the cathedral for the ceremony, Lucas took them that way and pointed out to Alina how he had first discovered the cemetery by following the cat under the mulberry branches. They made their way to the secret cemetery each carrying a basket of bluebells, Queen Anne's lace, and ivy. Alina followed Lucas over the dewy grass to Linnea's stone. They placed the woven baskets on either side and bowed their heads. Lucas placed his hand upon the marker that bore his mother's name. "Dearest mum, at last, I return our flower baskets to you."

Alina brushed tears from her cheeks and slipped her hand into his. They stood silently for several moments. "Do you know who else is buried here?" Alina whispered as she glanced around. Hand in hand they approached the other gravestones. The names had been carved with mush less care than Linnea's. The letters appeared backward and possibly upside down. Alina bent down to examine the markings. "I only remember crawling out of the moat when Dugald dragged me here, and then I woke up inside."

Lucas hugged her to him. "I don't know who lies in these graves or what language this is. We best go, but I had hoped to see Seppo."

"Let's go inside and find him," Alina said. "It would be sad not to let him know we visited and left these glorious flowers. We have not yet been officially introduced. I want to thank him for contributing to our wedding. And I can show you the tunnel that leads to the road to Arcana."

Lucas frowned and glanced around. "I'd like to see it. But let's go quickly and greet Seppo."

"It's easy to find from the inside, and we can tell Seppo to meet us on the road on our way home in a few days. I also want to know him. He is your father and someday we will tell our children about him."

Lucas wrapped his arms tighter around her. "My darling, Alina, how I admire your thinking. Once you show me the tunnel, we must come back this way for our horses. We'll ride quickly and reach the Grande Inn just as the lanterns and garden candles are lit."

Keeping clear of the moat, they made their way along the walls to the small, paneled door. It had been painted green. "My goodness! It seems your father is expecting visitors."

"There are other monks living in here you said, right? Did you see them?"

Alina thought for a moment. "Um, I can't say I saw them, robed as they were. But I did feel an ancient presence. I know now that Seppo was the tall one. I remember him, but anyone else I'm just not sure."

"Really?" Lucas hesitated before shoving the door. "I still can't believe Dugald took you here. Are you certain you want to do this?"

"Of course. Dugald is gone. It turns out he was mostly a harmless wretch. I was safe here. After all, it is your father's house."

* * *

With Lucas and Alina off to the Grande Inn, Irene, hoping to ward off melancholy, decided to take a walk around the city to thank the citizens who joined in the festivities. Many had contributed food and wares from their market stalls and stayed late to help clean up.

After walking and chatting for over an hour, Irene craved a cup of tea. She couldn't think of a tea shop where she would enjoy sitting alone, so she strolled in the direction of the apothecary shop. There was surely no harm in allowing Mister Pagett to prepare a blend for her.

At the boarding house, Carissa, Perina, and Ikarus discussed the offer from Drusilla to come to work and help with extra cleaning and lifting. "She is certainly built sturdy enough for it. But I don't think Irene will agree," Carissa said with a worried glance toward the door.

"It would also mean extra expense for her," Ikarus agreed.

"The city pays your wage. Is that correct Ikarus?" Perina asked.

"Yes, and I get almost as much as Lucas did. I help around for my room and board since Irene doesn't charge me. I think the three of us are enough assistance for Irene. And Lucas helps with everything as well."

"Yes, but he and Alina will move on their own soon. And Drusilla has offered her services for next to nothing," Carissa said.

"Where did she come from?" Perina asked.

"She is Gacheru's sister."

"He's a bungling charlatan as Lucas says," Ik remarked.

They all laughed. "Did you see him idling around yesterday? He offered to help only after the platters were already set down," Ik added, enjoying the lady's laughter.

"He helped himself to the wine and ale often enough," Perina commented.

"It's up to you, Carissa, to speak with Irene about the situation. You've lived here the longest," Ikarus said.

Carissa sat silently for several long minutes. "I don't think I will say anything to Irene. She is tired these days, tis true. But we can all do more to help. There is something off with that Drusilla woman. She's overly friendly. She wanted me to call her Drusy, like we were old friends. And I noticed Madam Trousdale frown at her more than once yesterday."

"I myself feel sorry for her," Perina said. "She has to live with Gacheru!"

"Well, it seems we have settled nothing." Ikarus said.

Over in the cottage, Nikolas lounged in Brigit's overstuffed bed. She bustled about, murmuring as she separated herbs and plucked leaves from drying plants. "Whatever are you doing? Why don't you come over here and relax with me?"

"I have much to do," she said in an impatient tone.

"Let me help you then," Nik said getting up and pulling some leaves from one of her drying racks.

"Don't touch that!" she snapped.

Startled, Nik dropped the plant and then bent to quickly retrieve it. Hair swirling, she raced over and grabbed it from his hand. "I'll go then," he said.

"It's near dusk. Go get some bread and come back. We can supper together." She glided over to her divination table and slid the purple cloth from the crystal ball. "But first, a man and his wife are coming for a scrying."

Nik turned away from the gleaming crystal. "Maybe, I'll stay away. The Blue Gate beckons me."

Brigit reached her cool fingers up to his throat, pulled him toward her and planted an alluring kiss on his gaping mouth. "Bring wine and bread. Come back," she teased.

* * *

Once inside the walls of the monastery, Lucas remembered how very narrow the snaky hallways were. "No wonder Seppo is so thin and thread-like. He must be able to fit through these strangling passageways."

Alina nodded as she walked ahead, her skirts brushing against the walls. For a time, the small door they'd left open at the entrance lit their way. Lucas wondered if he and Nik had mistaken that daylight for the phantasmal illumination they experienced on their first entry. As they walked on, Lucas had a sense of heaviness inside his ears. Alina was steadying herself by running her hand along the wall. He did the same and sliced his palm on something. He sucked it, but the blood kept coming. *What's going on here*, he wondered.

Skirts swishing, Alina held her head high, but Lucas had to duck now. "I think we are descending," he said.

Giving a quick glance back at him, she replied, "It does seem so."

Lucas noticed her expression was calm, and she kept descending along the tapering wall. Suddenly, a damp darkness engulfed them. Lucas stopped. His blood ran as cold as the dank air. "Alina!"

She reached out, and they clutched each other. "That's enough. We turn back right now," Lucas said.

"I don't remember this. Where is he? Seppo," she called out.

Lucas gave her a yank. "Forget about him. We go now. Hurry, Alina before it's too late." As the walls squeezed around them, Lucas lurched forward into the inexplicable blackness, with one hand following the curve of the wall and the other clutching Alina's hand so tightly she winced and tried to pull away. But he would not lessen his grip on her, this girl, this woman, his wife now, the only reason for him to exist at all. She breathed heavy behind him. They should be halfway to Arcana by now. Why had he brought her in here?

His stomach churned, his head throbbed, and his eyes found nothing to see. He took deliberate but measured steps. His mother, buried in the secret cemetery, was long dead, and Seppo nearly so himself. Lucas and Alina belonged up and above, in the sunlight with their entire lives ahead of them. He didn't care about anything but that. He had found and lost her once already. How could it be that now they were slipping into a perilous chasm? There was something deeply wrong within this monastery. He'd known so for years from observing from outside its walls. With relief, he felt the cut on his hand scab over and slide off. But daggers of pain stabbed his heart as he realized he and Alina were being pulled by a force beyond their control, to a place they undoubtedly did not belong. His trepidation spread through his veins and into hers. He knew she understood now that they'd made a dreadful mistake.

Chapter 6

If Bernard and Wentworth hadn't accepted Irene's invitation to stay on at the boarding house for the next week, they would have known that Lucas and Alina never made it to the Grande Inn. The men busied themselves by cooking up a potful of farm stew, as they called it. Carissa and Perina had just finished tending the courtyard garden, and Ikarus had set the empty wine barrels outside to be picked up. Since there was nothing left to do, the five of them sat down with a bottle of wine to wait for the meal to simmer.

Irene strolled away from the apothecary shop after two cups of revitalizing tea. Mister Pagett had many interesting stories to share about their neighbors and fellow citizens. He was not as wearisome as she had imagined he was. In fact, she had promised to think about his offer to stroll along the river some afternoon. She wouldn't though. They were both far too old for that sort of conduct. But still, it pleased her that he suggested it, for she doubted whether she and Lucas would ever have a picnic by the river again.

Gacheru and Drusilla were just departing from the front steps of the boarding house after having been turned away by Carissa when Irene approached. They rushed to her, gushing about how well served the wedding feast had been and complimenting everything from the flowers to the food to the wine and the very house itself. *It seems that today the world was full of fun and flattery*, Irene thought as she entered the house after agreeing to take on Drusilla as extra help some evenings.

* * *

At the edge of the dark zone where Gacheru and Drusilla lived in the back of the blacksmith shop, the two of them set to work forging and filing skeleton keys. They each carried four because the locks in the City of Dreams were sophisticated devices. Gach and Drusy were not adept at their work, and their poorly smelted keys often broke.

Gacheru, having lived in the city all his life, knew which type of locks accepted which keys, but as the city grew, the locks and keys changed, and he struggled to keep up with the complicated details.

Drusilla had been sent off by their parents at the age of twelve to marry a tenant farmer in the low southland. She failed to bear children, and after twenty-two years, the farmer could tolerate no more of her shrill scolding and complaining. He lunged at her with a pitchfork that cut a gash on her left shoulder, marked now by a silvery scar, that she claimed still ached when the rain fell.

Upon her return one year ago, Gacheru laboriously explained that their mother had run off shortly after Drusilla was sent away. Their father had died while working in the blacksmith shop. His death involved an unfortunate incident with a hammer. Neither the blacksmith nor Gacheru could recall who had been wielding the hammer at the time. But the mishap had resulted in a mutual agreement that Gach could live in the cluttered quarters in back. As dismayed as Drusy was to find that she had to make herself a cot in the corner of the steamy shop, she was grateful that neither man asked what had become of her husband after the fork matter.

Having discovered on the long journey that she was with child after all, she had hoped Gacheru could provide for her and the babe. He did string a curtain around her cot, but only as he   complained that watching her belly grow frightened and disgusted him. Once the baby was born—a difficult birth that she had somehow managed alone—he forced her to go out and work as a nursemaid. Taking on the feeding of five additional babies drained her strength and her milk. It was the nursing, lack of nutritious food in her own pot, and the blacksmith shop, full of noise and smoke, that took the life of her infant girl. She knew then that her brother didn't care about her any more than her husband or their mother had.

Gacheru was the favored child. He didn't protect her as a brother would a sister. She knew her baby's death wasn't her fault. Knowing so offered small comfort, but she took it, not allowing herself to think about her dead husband and how things might have been different if the baby had come sooner. How could a woman with no husband and no thatch above her head care for a child? The citizens of the city seemed to agree with that sentiment and when her ability to perform her duties dried up, they dismissed her offer to work as a maid or a cook.

Drusy did not experience heartache over the loss of her baby as much as anger. She did not feel sorrow, just resentment that soon turned into a suppressed rage. Too many things had gone wrong. Someone should pay for her plight. Because she had suffered, others should suffer as well. Whoever they were did not matter to Drusilla. The possibility of revenge lulled her to sleep at night and roused her in the morning.

* * *

Nik didn't know how long it took for Brigit to peer into the minds of her patrons. Bored, he left the Blue Gate after only one whisky. Just outside, he noticed a rat scurry across his path. Fearing it bad luck, he decided it was not yet time to return to Brigit's cottage. *Bernard,* he thought. *I'll go see if Bernard would like to stroll about the city and visit the pubs and taverns.*

He entered the kitchen through the service door expecting to see Irene bustling about. But to his surprise, Bernard stirred the black iron pot. "Women's work, Bernard?"

The man Lucas once called "Giant" turned and shrugged. The apron stretched across his abdomen made him look even larger. Nik broke out in laughter, and Bernard joined him. "Wentworth and I have taken to cooking lately."

"It actually smells good," Nik said. "Perhaps I could send Brigit over for a lesson."

"We always make the same thing," Bernard explained. "Where is your whimsical woman?"

"Weaving spells." Nik plopped down at the table and poured from the jug of red wine. "Feels strange without Lucas here. The entire city seems empty."

Bernard stared for a moment and then nodded. Nikolas realized his big friend had barely spent any time enjoying the city. "I came to take you out, but I see you're busy."

"Tomorrow, Nikolas? In the meanwhile, stay for supper. We're all here lounging about." Pointing toward the parlour with the ladle, he splattered stew across the floor.

Nikolas followed Bernard into the parlour, where Irene entertained the girls, Wentworth, and Ikarus with the apothecary's stories. He wondered if he should ask Ik to stop by the cottage and tell Brigit where he was. He scratched his chin. He'd forgotten to buy the wine and bread. Frowning, he sat on the hearth in front of the fire to ponder. Ikarus went to the kitchen and retrieved his tools.

Would the lad mind taking a quick side trip from his rounds? Feeling somewhat bewildered, Nik stretched out his legs. A gust of wind blew through the garden door and fanned the flames. From the kitchen, Ikarus called, "Good night."

Most evenings Nik enjoyed the close comfort of Brigit's cottage, but this afternoon when she uncovered the crystal ball his stomach churned, and his ears rang. "Ik!" he shouted.

Ikarus poked his head through the doorway. "Would you mind . . ." Nik began. The boy startled when a shadow loomed behind him. "Ah, never mind," Nik said as he recognized Brigit. Ik nodded and angled around Brigit. She glided into the parlour waving a wine bottle at Nikolas. He got up and went over to her. "This is better, right?"

She flashed a knowing smile, "We all miss Lucas and Alina. They'll be back soon enough."

* * *

"We return the way we came. Stay close my darling."

Her knees bumped the back of his as they scrambled back up the narrow passageway. "I'm sorry, Lucas. I should not have suggested we come inside. We should have waited for Seppo to lead us. I thought I remembered this place. It feels like everything has changed."

"Did you see evidence that Seppo actually lives inside these walls?"

"There was a large room with many candles and the passage to the road to Arcana. I hope we find it soon. I want a bath now."

"Yes, we will bathe together and then enjoy the dining room, several glasses of wine, and the candles in the garden. We will still have daylight when we emerge from this close chamber. I can't wait to leap upon our horses and sprint toward the setting sun."

Moisture gathered under his shirt and his hair clung to his neck. Lucas could feel Alina perspiring also as she let go his hand intermittently to wipe her palm upon her skirt.

They ultimately reached a point that no longer felt as if they were climbing. The stone beneath their feet was level and smooth as if many others had walked there before. But the walls still brushed their sleeves and Lucas could not see any hint of light ahead. He heard Alina's stomach gurgle. The bread and ale were in the saddlebags. He tried to think of something to say to reassure her, but at this moment, he didn't trust his own voice. He had no concept of how long they had been trapped inside the monastery walls. His heart resounded in his ears like thundering drums or was it rushing water within the walls. He fell. Alina landed on top of him. "Ouch!" she exclaimed.

"Ugh! Swords in hell! Are you hurt at all?" He clutched at her in the dark, running his hands up and down her body and squeezing her limbs. Tears wet her cheeks. "I'm sorry."

"I'm not hurt. We're trapped," she cried out, "Look, Lucas! We fell into a sand pit. We're never getting out of this place!"

Chapter 7

The next afternoon Nikolas left Brigit's cottage with a satisfied grin. The discomforting crystal ball was once again hidden under its purple cloth. She had more than forgiven him for not returning to the cottage with bread and wine. "I knew where you were," she'd said. Nikolas frowned finding her comment unsettling. *I never go anywhere but the harbour, the Blue Gate, or the boarding house,* he thought, *but why did she know exactly where I was?* Glancing back at her curious cottage, he realized just how much he relished their enchanting nights together.

He showed Bernard all around the secret sections of the harbour and pointed out where Alina's trunks had been hidden. Bernard remembered the ship that had carried Dugald away from their shore. From there, they went to the river. "This is Lucas' favorite place," Nik explained.

"So, I've heard," Bernard said. "He loves the land as well as he loves his city."

"He does," Nik agreed. "I believe we will all spend time between Arcana and the City of Dreams more often now." They walked on toward the Grand Boulevard to check Alina's house. The ivy that

Brigit planted had grown more quickly than Nikolas thought possible. "They'll be able to move in here when they return."

As they walked through the square, Nik noticed Bernard ambling with the confidence of a bull, meaning no harm but nonetheless clearing a path. And he was adept with the bow. A great skill to possess. Although it was his arrow that had killed Linnea, Marion was to blame. Bernard was not just burly in body; his spirit was also strong. He had not shrunk away from the bow and arrow. He became more proficient. Of course, the dagger was still most useful in the city but out in the countryside, for protection at a distance, the bow and arrow would be helpful. After all, nobody knew when the life you knew and enjoyed could be threatened by the ruthless and avaricious.

"Bernard, may I join you at the farm sometime soon and learn to use the bow and arrow?"

Bernard stopped walking and peered at Nikolas for a long moment. "Is there something you want to tell me?"

Nik thought for a moment, "I want to learn. I feel I will be good at it."

"It would be an honor to teach you and Lucas as well and also the ladies, if they so desire."

"I'm sure at least one of them does," Nik laughed as he pushed open the door to the Blue Gate.

* * *

Gacheru and Drusilla, prowling about trying their keys, had happened to notice Nikolas and Bernard roaming the city. They followed them at a distance. Expectation grew as the men's path led along the tree-lined boulevard and halted at the steps of a three-story home with wide windows and a thick wood door. Unlike the other homes on this enviable street, the drapes were drawn. The men disappeared around the back but reappeared momentarily and walked on. Gacheru scratched his stubbly chin and spat, "Vacant me guess."

Eager to please her brother, even though he disgusted her, Drusilla said, "I'll do some poking this evening and find out whose house this is."

"Do that," Gach replied, slapping her on the back a bit too hard. "A place as fine as this should be occupied, me think."

* * *

Brigit sorted through her potion vessels making sure to keep the dangerous ones sealed with wax and separated from the curatives. She didn't want Nikolas accidently to ingest anything. She was glad he had gone off with Bernard. She felt detached from herself since awakening. Something in a dream told her to let Seppo be. As she thought about the old monk, she realized he could have interfered in Lucas' life years ago if he had intended to. But no, he had waited for Lucas to go to him, to find him on his own.

Now she wondered why he would do that. He clearly had deep love for his and Linnea's child. What prevented him from showing himself years before? It crossed her mind to go to the monastery and have a conversation with Seppo. He did seem kind after all. Perhaps, she had corrupted her own mind with contempt for him all because she thought he had taken Linnea away. But as she thought back to the woeful time when Linnea left the caravan—and weeks later when Linny chose to remain at that farm in Arcana, she knew what was to blame, not just the caravan that taught the girls how to peddle and pilfer. Those lessons aided them. Her parents tried to keep them safe, but they themselves were powerless over the horrible event. And much more harm would have come to them, Brigit knew. She shuddered. Her older sister, Linnea, was an untamable spirit; nobody could have absconded with her against her will. Brigit decided she would visit Seppo and root out the truth from him. But not today.

Wearing her drifter dress, tinted in tones of the sky at dawn and sunset as well, she set out toward the sea where the breeze would tousle her hair and untangle the bothersome memories.

* * *

Irene hummed to herself as she tended the courtyard garden. In the house, Carissa and Perina were preparing supper for the boarders. After the boarders left for their evenings toil, the woman, the locksmith's sister . . . her name difficult to recall, would come to do the evening chores. And when she left, the girls would serve the family their supper that Irene had made earlier. Now, she could finish her day by three o'clock and relax among the plants and herbs. It was possible, she mused, that there would be time some afternoon to walk along the river with Mister Pagett. She blushed. What would Lucas say? Well, she need not tell him right away.

Once he and Alina returned from the Grande Inn, they would be too busy beginning their new life together to bother with her idling. She sat on the bench and imagined the two of them strolling through the candle-lit garden this evening. To think, if she hadn't insisted Lucas go back to his home in Arcana, they would never have discovered the Grande Inn or met Bernard and Wentworth.

Oh, Wentworth! She remembered; he'd asked her to wake him from his nap. Well, in a little while. The sunlight was lovely now, and she felt no urgency to move. Bernard might not return for supper. If Nikolas had his way, they'd prowl the streets beyond the midnight bell. She sighed; all was well. There was nothing for this old woman to worry about. Her eyes closed, and her head nodded.

When Drusilla rapped loudly on the back door, Irene sat up. She heard Perina open the door and welcome the woman to the kitchen. Rubbing her eyes, Irene shivered, for the afternoon sun had slipped away. Wentworth was sitting in the parlour holding a glass of red wine. "I didn't want to disturb you, but I hope you'll join me now," he said lifting his glass.

"I forgot to wake you," Irene murmured as she plopped down onto the divan.

"That's fine, Irene. A long nap in the afternoon is as welcome as an old friend."

Irene smiled. "By now, Lucas and Alina will be settled in and dressing for their second dinner at the Grande Inn as husband and wife." Her eyes sparkled. "I feel such a sense of tranquility now that they are finally wed and safe together."

Wentworth nodded as Irene accepted a glass of wine from Perina. "I remember the concern on your face that first evening at the Grande Inn when Marion and I met you and Lucas. Now, we are all at peace."

"We are," Irene agreed. "Perina, have you shown Drusilla what is expected of her this evening, the washing and drying of the plates and serving dishes?"

"Yes, Mrs. Kempel. She's already halfway through the boarder's dishes. And after that there are linens to fold. Shall I serve you and Mr. Wentworth supper here beside the fire?"

Irene smiled. "Yes, Perina, thank you. That is a lovely way to finish up this lazy day."

* * *

In the dark, they had fallen asleep, and now they awoke in a circular cavern about as large as the parlour. Chilly air rushed in from somewhere and with it a dusty plummet of light. Looking up, Lucas determined they'd tumbled close to the height of his second story window. The sandy floor had saved them from injury.

He leapt up and searched for a way out. He ran at the stone wall several times in an attempt to launch himself up. Alina huddled on the floor and spilled the sand through her fingers. "Madam Trousdale would just love this." She giggled. Lucas sank down beside her and held her in his arms while she shivered and laughed and then wept. If he could, he would take his dagger and slice his own throat for allowing them to get lost.

Her stomach gurgled again, and his did as well. He wondered what they were serving in the elegant dining room at the Grande Inn this evening. It was the first night of their weeklong wedding retreat, or was it the second? He couldn't tell how much time had passed. He and Alina were supposed to share his luxurious bedchamber with the green and gold coverlet.

Lucas wanted to scream in fury, but he calmly continued to reassure his bride that their dire situation was not her fault. How could they have known that the ancient monastery held such impenetrable passages? He should have known better. He'd always avoided this place.

When Alina finally cried herself to sleep, Lucas took out her wedding gift, the pocket watch. As he feared, they had missed their first night and were about to miss another. He stretched out beside her and placed his arm and one leg protectively over her. He covered them with his cloak as the last strand of light dissipated from their stony prison.

In a paralyzing dream, Lucas lay at the bottom of the rushing river, unable to surface. When he roused from his torpor, he found Alina lying beside him, twitching and murmuring in troubled slumber. Lucas carefully untangled himself and got up. He didn't want her to wake up in here. He must find a way out now.

Crawling and feeling around the walls, he found the source of the cool air. He dug and clawed with his hands until he reached a small chasm formed by what must be a foundation of boulders. He took a deep breath and lowered himself into the hole. His feet hit solid ground. That was enough for him. He didn't stoop down and look around, lest he lose his nerve. Hoisting himself back up, he felt his shoulders burn with pain.

"What are you doing?" Alina was sitting up and staring at him. You just crawled out of the wall."

"There's an opening. We can fit through."

"I'm not crawling into a hole in the wall, Lucas! We must go up. The light is above us."

"Yes, but the air is below."

"Can't we go up?" She pointed to the ledge from which they fell. You could lift me up. I could stand on your shoulders." She bit her lower lip. "Maybe."

"It's too high Alina. That is not the way out." Lucas wrapped her in his arms. "I can hear water. We must go this way."

Alina stood and brushed sand from the folds of her skirt. "If we die, we die together. And nobody will ever know what happened to us." She covered her face with her hands.

His eyes turned black, he glared at her, and his voice came out deep and stern. "I will never let you die."

Lucas grabbed her hands; they were as cold as a silver goblet in winter. Peering into her wet eyes, he declared, "We will live. We will ride to the Grande Inn and feast on roasts and sumptuous wine."

Alina swallowed hard. "Who goes first?"

"Me," Lucas said offering his hand. "When I feel the ground under there, I will reach up and pull you in." And as he spoke, the hole in the corner began to glow with the light of what had to be dawn.

* * *

In the morning, Wentworth strolled through the city visiting the market stalls. Bernard had returned to the boarding house so late the previous night that he was still in his chamber recovering, having called out once pleading for water. After the isolation of the farm, the city excited Wentworth. He enjoyed watching the citizens mingling and gossiping, the delivery wagons clattering through the narrow lanes steered by alert, if not brash, steersmen slapping the reins and shouting to make way.

Once his basket was filled with goods for the house, he remembered one of the women whom Alina had introduced him to at the wedding, the widow Van Dessen. Perhaps she would enjoy some sweetmeats. He didn't know where her cottage was but had heard that she lived nearby the river so he headed off in that direction knowing he could ask for directions once he got closer.

With the day mild and sunny, he ambled along at a slow pace. Soon, the impressive tower of the old cathedral came into view. He heard the banging and droning of the laborers who worked on the restoration and wished he had enough to bring them all a pleasant indulgence. In the shadow of the cathedral walls, Wentworth noticed the monastery as the morning sun crawled up its limestone walls and bathed it in sunlight. It did not look as daunting and frightening as the stories he'd heard around the city. Perhaps, now that Seppo had emerged from his hiding place, the mystical structure could shake off its eerie history.

As he wandered closer, Wentworth observed horses grazing in the lush grass. Squinting, he went further along the path to discern if the horses bore saddles. It seemed that they did. Apparently, Seppo was not such a recluse after all. He stood watching the horses nibble the grass. They nudged each other like old friends. He thought of whistling to them to see if they would come to him but decided their keeper would not appreciate his interference. Wentworth felt a pang of longing for his farm and changed his mind about making any new friends here. He turned and headed back toward the boarding house.

* * *

Drusilla argued with Gacheru. She was tired from working so late at the boarding house. The ladies had taken full advantage of her she thought. She had not expected to work so hard. She had no time to even try one of their keys to enter any of the rooms. "What am I looking for anyway?"

"You may find valuable goods or coins in one of those rooms," Gach spat his words at her. She stepped back.

"We've been forging and filing keys to rob the boarders then?"

"What else is there? I tried many grand houses on the Boulevard. None of our keys work on that street They have complicated locks that I cannot duplicate."

"Huh, you stupid slob." She shoved herself out of the tight chair and went to stir the porridge. "I'm not going back to the boarding house. It's too hard for me." She didn't mention that she'd overheard Carissa and Perina discussing Alina and Lucas' house on the Boulevard. It was the very one, with the curtains drawn, that Gacheru admired. If he found that out, he would not hear it from her. She didn't know what his plans were from one day to another, but she was sure he would only make a repulsive mess of things as he always did.

Gach glared at his sister. "You think you can live here for free? You will go back. Make friends with the maids."

"No," she grunted as she sat down with a bowl in her lap. "They are polite and kind. They will never accept me."

Gacheru got up to dish out his own bowl of porridge. He kicked her shin as he passed her chair, and the bowl of slop spilled into Drusilla's lap.

* * *

Nikolas lolled in the bed at Brigit's cottage. The third cup of tea was beginning to ease his headache.

She stared at him while he sipped and moaned. "It doesn't help that your eyes bore holes through me," he said.

"Something's wrong," she replied.

"It certainly is. I'm about to die from whisky consumption." Moaning, he lay back and clutched his stomach. "My guts churn as well."

She dipped some bread in broth and served it to him in a pewter bowl. "I feel as if someone is in trouble."

Nik laughed. "Someone is. It's me. You don't need a crystal ball to see that!"

Brigit smiled but turned and lifted her gaze into the distance beyond the open door. When she glanced back at Nik, she said, "Please don't retch in here. I must walk and listen for answers." She bent to kiss his forehead, but her kiss sent shivers down his spine. Her lips were stone cold.

* * *

Lucas and Alina landed on their feet in an elongated antechamber. Light shone from a carved louver window high above their heads. "There is light!" Alina exclaimed.

Lucas stood silently still.

"What are you doing, Lucas?"

He blinked. "I'm thinking. We have to decide what to do next. There is another tunnel leading downward."

"No, I saw anger cross your face. I've never seen your eyes so dark, and your jaw is tight."

"Alina, my darling, you did not see my face while you were missing."

She wrung her hands. "I've aged you."

Lucas laughed. "Well, if it's possible I've aged myself."

"Are you fearful?"

"I only fear the inability to protect you, Alina."

"Lucas . . ." she hung her head.

He tried to smile as he encircled her in his arms, "We must not entrust fear as our guide. Come, I hear water below."

Alina stayed close to Lucas, but she wanted to turn around and run. She would have if there were anywhere to go. They had gotten trapped in this dreadful place by going down. Maybe they shouldn't have turned around . . ..

"It's too late now," Lucas said, as if he could read her mind, and she wondered if she had spoken aloud. He squeezed her hand. "I can feel what you're thinking. But it's not your fault, Alina, and if I hadn't demanded we turn around yesterday, we may very well have found that passage you mentioned or found Seppo, or something wonderful may have happened. But now we have only this perplexing juncture. We are here now, and we must keep on trying to get out of this place."

Alina nodded and took a step forward so that he would keep going and not notice that her eyes were again on the verge of spilling torrents of tears. She suddenly felt so childish and so soon after having just become a woman. She wanted to get out. She wanted to go to the Grande Inn and be welcomed as husband and wife.

Her stomach churned with dread. The life they'd imagined together may never be theirs. It wasn't possible to remain as children after all. She scratched at the damp hair that gripped her head like a heavy hat. She reminded herself of a mad woman who had roamed the crowded streets of Ingleena. Alina clasped her hands and silently prayed. *If we survive this, I will do something helpful for Seppo. We must take him out of this terrible tomb. No wonder he looks so ghostly.* The thought made her shiver and sweat streamed down her back. Somehow, she felt cold and hot at the same time. Her legs dragged as if they'd been weighted with iron chains. Why was she thinking about the future at all?

At least, the light from above accompanied them as they wound their way downward, although by now there was no way to discern from whence it came. A green door carved from heavy wood blocked the tunnel. Lucas' heart leapt in hope that it was the way out. After struggling with the latch, he slipped his hand into a gap above the door and felt around until he found a clasp that when lifted at the same time as the latch, the door swung open like a gate. Clasping Alina by her clammy hand they went through.

She wondered how Lucas knew how to open the door but didn't bother to ask. She had all she could do to keep her feet moving. They went down and wound around in the serpentine tunnels—some leading nowhere— and descending ever downward. They reached another cellar like the one where they'd spent the night. Lucas kept going, pausing only long enough to consider the potential for escape. Alina groaned and dragged her feet like a willful child. She felt distraught and wretched, and she could not stop blaming herself for their plight.

Lucas took a deep breath, "I know you're tired, but we can't stop here. We need to drink. I can still hear rushing water, but we haven't reached it yet."

"I hear no water," she said flatly.

"Not only can I hear it, but I can smell it." He pulled her by the wrist. "I would carry you, but the tunnel is too tight." She sighed so long and deep that he stopped and held her to his chest. "Take strength from me." Kissing the top of her head, he promised, "I will fix this."

* * *

Ikarus spotted Brigit skirting through a dark alley gesturing angrily and muttering strange words. He followed at a discreet pace. He thought to approach and inquire if she felt ill, but something told him to keep his distance. He remained several paces back, ducking into a doorway or behind a thick-trunked tree whenever she hesitated and turned her resplendent head in his direction. She went nowhere in particular but never retraced her steps. Ikarus pursued her same path until dusk drew near, and it was time to prepare for lantern lighting. When he turned back to the boarding house, she was headed in the direction of the monastery.

Irene sat with him while he ate his supper. He knew she missed Lucas and did his best to engage in conversation with her, but he avoided mentioning Madam Trousdale's odd behavior. Not even Lucas understood that woman, and he wouldn't want Irene to worry. Tonight, Ik would keep watch for her around the city. Because Lucas and Alina were reveling in the passions of their nuptials at the Grande Inn, Ikarus thought it helpful to sort out Madam Trousdale on his own. In the next few days, if necessary, he would find Nikolas and mention something to him.

As the sun fell below the edge of the sea, Brigit returned to her cottage. Nikolas was outside chopping wood. "Did you discover the problem?" he asked.

"No, I fear not. But whatever is wrong, it isn't getting any better." She went in and came out with two large cups of crimson wine. They stood shoulder to shoulder gazing into the distance.

Nik took a sip then peered at Brigit, "I intended to meet with the merchants tomorrow, but I can help you search instead."

"No." She forced a smile. "Thanks Nikolas," she ruffled his hair with her long fingers, "but I'm not certain what I'm searching for."

* * *

After passing through four more latched green doors, they reached a third cellar. Lucas knew they could walk no farther. The light was fading, and he feared Alina would collapse with exhaustion. He led her to a smooth recess in the rock where she could recline. She sighed as he wrapped her tenderly in his cloak and tucked his waistcloth under her head. Lucas caressed her smooth cheeks until her eyelids fluttered. Wishing to examine the room while they still had beams of phantom light, Lucas peered around at the speckled dark angles and corners. He still heard rushing water, or was it the rumblings of a melodic chant? It could be monks, he supposed, if there were monks at all.

He gazed upward, wishing for a long length of rope. The slants of light and shadow confused his vision and caused his stomach to ache. His head suddenly pounded. Alina was already groaning in a fitful sleep. But as he stood over her, she became peaceful. Was something else in the cellar with them? The far corner was engulfed in darkness. Expecting a spectre of red eyes to appear, he stared there. Then, he drew his dagger and waited.

His pocket watch ticked loudly in rhythm with the pounding in his head and the abysmal throbbing beyond the walls. Sinking to his knees, Lucas clutched his forehead with both hands. He wanted to shout in agony. The noise, the pain, the trap they were in, it must cease! He squeezed his eyes closed and covered his ears.

He must have slept there on the ground because something woke him like the brush of a feather across his back. He jolted upright and rushed to the nook in the wall. Alina still slept, he gazed down upon her until he could discern the rise and fall of her chest.

The room was somehow brighter now. A slender ray of sunlight had beveled its way into the chamber. Lucas fathomed a seraphic presence with them in this crypt. Unnerved, he painstakingly perused the carved walls as the light made its way in. Stepping toward the farthest corner, a strangled gasp caught in his throat. Once he heard it, he saw it. Glowing within a fingerlike ray of bluish light, a cascade of melodious water plummeted through the chiseled rocks into a polished cistern of glistening gold.

Stunned, Lucas stood transfixed. He blinked, rubbed his eyes, and blinked again. The vision did not change. Swallowing hard, he went forward. He reached out a trembling hand and touched the smooth edge of the carved pool. The stone was cool and damp, and a fine mist rose from the radiant water.

Lucas swallowed and glanced back to Alina. "Look at this," he murmured. She did not stir. He crept closer. The tumbling water mesmerized him, and his fear faded away. Lucas leaned forward and extended both hands. He let the water pour through his fingers. "This . . ." he whispered. "Alina, come here." Lucas dipped his hands into the water. It tickled his skin. It was as soft as Julian's silk. Chuckling with relief, he splashed his face. He bent to drink from the glistening gift and instantly felt refreshed and nourished.

"Alina. This is the sound of the water. The water is chanting and plunging at the same time. Alina. Alina, it is a marvel. Come see!"

Elated, he turned to Alina. She lay silent and motionless in the narrow niche. "Alina!" His heart thundering, he rushed to her.

Grasping her shoulders, he shook her firmly. "No." He placed a cold palm upon her brow. "My darling, wake up. We're saved!"

She moaned. Her eyelids fluttered.

"Come drink!" Lucas gently pulled her upright. "Please wake up."

Her eyes opened and then closed as she grumbled, "I'm not thirsty."

"You must drink. Come on, Alina, please get up my love." She stared at him vacuously and then flung an arm across her eyes. Lucas pulled her arm away, "We're spared, sweetheart." He felt her forehead and ran his hands along her body checking for injuries or excessive heat. Soon, he heard her take a deep breath. She relaxed under his touch. He ran to the pool and cupped his hands carrying water to her. He insisted she drink three times. Sitting up on her own now, Alina gaped in astonishment at the shimmering pool.

"What is this place?"

"I don't know. The light is fading already. It's a glorious pool of salvation."

"It's imbued in gold," she gasped.

In the dimming light, Lucas noticed color had returned to her cheeks. "The light will return, and we will find our way out. He slipped into the niche beside her and kissed her deeply.

Tears wet her cheeks, but she giggled and returned his kisses. "This is not the place," she murmured.

"It is the place. It's the perfect place. We are quite alone here. Tomorrow we will walk out into the light of day. Believe me, my darling, we will."

She nestled against him, her breath warm against his chest. Entwining their legs, Lucas and Alina breathed in rhythm as they hearts pattered together. Darkness fell like a delicate drape upon their heads.

Chapter 8

In the morning, Nikolas and Brigit had tea and sweet bread together. Nikolas didn't ask her to speak about whatever she felt was wrong. If she wanted to discuss it, she would say so, Nik reasoned. They drank their tea quietly, each gazing away into their own thoughts. Soon afterwards, Nikolas returned to his room at the harbour to prepare for a meeting with the textile merchants. Brigit hadn't suggested they meet up later. Perhaps dinner at the Blue Gate was in order. With a twinge of envy, he thought of Lucas.

Ikarus made his way along the familiar back paths until he found Brigit where she gathered plants along the reedy canal. After watching her for several moments, he mustered the nerve to approach. "Madam Trousdale," he said softly so as not to startle her, "May I be of assistance? You appear troubled these days."

Brigit spun around, sending hair twirling. Stepping back, Ikarus clasped his hands in deference. He received a marbled glare, but then she said, "You may walk with me. But I warn you, I'm looking for trouble."

"Of course, you are," Ikarus replied.

"And you? What are you looking for?" she narrowed her eyes at him.

"Me?" Ikarus placed his hand on his heart. "I'm not looking for anyone."

Brigit laughed. "I believe you are seeking someone. I asked what and you answered who. Is it I who needs assistance or you, Ikarus? Don't think I haven't noticed you skulking behind me these past few days."

Ikarus winced. She strode away but glanced back to smirk at him. He followed. Her skirts swished as she walked. Her claws and hourglass clanked together. He found these things a familiar comfort as they walked side by side. After a while, Ikarus was shocked to hear his own voice asking Madam Trousdale to glimpse into her crystal ball and see if she could find a special girl from a distant hillside village.

She raised one eyebrow and nodded as if this question was what she was waiting to hear. "I can find her of course. You must tell me more about this girl you are looking for."

Ikarus struggled to walk as quickly as Brigit. He explained how he, his sister, and brother stopped with their herd in a village where they spent three days. "A young girl named, Camille knew much about sheep, and we walked together in the high pasture. We enjoyed a few words together but mostly minded the sheep in quiet companionship, holding hands and gazing at each other. When it was time to leave, she asked me if I would return someday. Alas, Madam . . . er. . . Brigit . . . I did not understand until these past few weeks what she meant by her question. I think she was inviting me to come back." He frowned and gazed toward the hills. Brigit poked his shoulder. Startled, Ikarus stammered, "May I call you Brigit, Madam Trousdale?"

"One or the other. Make up your mind. Silly boy-man, of course, the girl, Camille invited you to return. Why have you never mentioned her before?"

"Well," Ikarus gazed again toward his mountains, "It was only at supper that evening when Irene and all of you, asked from where I came. Until now, I kept my own secret."

"Tsk," Brigit shook her thick mane. "You thought nobody cared?"

Ik frowned and shoved his hands into his pockets.

"Or is there another reason you kept this a secret?"

"No." Surprised, Ik shook his head. He pursed his lips and lowered his gaze.

"Timidity won't get you anywhere. Where is this village?"

Ikarus sighed and pointed toward the distant peaks. "Somewhere up there. My brother was the guide. I only followed."

"Ahh, then there is a journey in your future." Brigit walked off again, and Ikarus noticed they were almost at the monastery.

"You will help me?"

"Yes, but first we must discover what is wrong here. I thought it was Seppo, but I believe the problem goes deeper than that. Come, I will show you the secret cemetery."

Ikarus shuffled behind her, and as they ducked to go through the mulberry trees, he muttered, "I hope my brother did not go back that way."

Brigit turned to him with a finger to her lips. "Hush. I see horses."

* * *

Awakened by splendid sunlight, Lucas sat up and looked around. He rubbed his eyes with his fists and blinked. "Alina," he murmured. She stretched and smiled up at him. He brushed tendrils of hair from her face and kissed her softly on the mouth, "My darling, you are not going to believe this place!" He pushed the cloak aside and pulled her to her feet. The carved walls glittered with wide streaks of gold.

As Alina got up and walked over to examine the walls, Lucas noticed with relief that she looked well again. The two of them ran their hands along the gold veins in absolute wonder. Sunlight poured in from angled openings as high up as Lucas could see. They were in a grotto of gold. Barely speaking, only gasping in amazement, they handed pure gold rocks back and forth to each other. In time, Lucas sat beside the pool of flowing water and realized that it too shimmered with gold. He cupped his hands, drank, and then held his hands up for Alina to drink. "It's as if this water tastes like gold," she uttered.

"I know what you mean," Lucas agreed. "I've never known anything like it." They sat on the edge of the golden pool contentedly holding hands. He pointed to a far corner. "That, over there is the passage out. Through that green door."

She nodded, "I can see it now. It's blue after all. And I can hear the water echoing in the walls. You saved us, Lucas."

He grinned and kissed her. "I can't accept praise for any of this. There are powers beyond our understanding at work here." They glanced around and took it all in. "I suppose we should go." He squeezed her hand. "Are you ready?"

"Well, we must. But it is difficult to walk away from this." She set the rocks she had gathered on the edge of the pool, and Lucas did the same.

"We take nothing," he said.

"Do you think Seppo knows?"

"I suppose. Perhaps it's why he has never left. We will ask him. But not until after we go to the Grande Inn and celebrate our wedding."

Lucas went ahead and opened the door. They entered the passageway and began to walk upward. This time the walls didn't seem so close, and they could feel a flow of fresh air. After hours of weaving their way upward Lucas realized they were in the same tunnel where he and Nikolas had first met Seppo. He thought of calling out for his father, but he feared he would appear now, and they would be delayed even more, so he kept walking.

When they came to the green door that led out to the moat, another passageway led to the right of it. Feeling it would lead to the secret cemetery where they'd left the horses, he took it. He was worried now about the horses. Would they still be waiting? Did they find water? There was plenty of grass for them.

They arrived at yet another green door, and clutching Alina's hand, Lucas shoved hard against it. They burst out into the cemetery and fell upon each other in the green grass. The horses neighed a warning. Peering up Lucas had to shield his eyes from the glaring sun. Two silhouettes sat atop their horses.

"Hey!" Lucas shouted. "What are you doing!?" He jumped up, grabbing the halter just before his horse, with Brigit atop, reared up in panic.

"Lucas!" Ikarus shouted as he slid off Alina's horse and rushed to help her up.

"Why are you here?" Brigit demanded. "We were about to take these horses back to the stable and raise the alarm!"

"We stopped by to visit Seppo," Lucas explained.

Brigit glared at him. "You've been in there visiting Seppo all this time?"

"Yes, we had such a lovely time that we stayed a few days," Alina added.

Brigit stared incredulously at them. Alina's hair was dirty and matted. Her dress torn, and she had smudges on her face and hands. Lucas' trousers were ripped, and his white shirt stained with sweat. "It appears you did have a lovely time."

"Yes, it was quite pleasant," Lucas said as he reached up to help Brigit dismount. "If you don't mind, we will be on our way now. Please let Irene know we will stay a few extra days at the Grande Inn since we were delayed here."

Ikarus began to say something in protest, but a sharp glance from Brigit kept him quiet. He helped Alina mount her horse and then turned to Lucas. "All is well in the city and at the boarding house."

"Your horses are fine as well," Brigit stated.

"Thanks, I'm glad to hear that." Then nodding to Alina, he said, "Shall we, my darling?" They led the horses slowly through the gravestones and out the way they came in three days ago.

"That was very odd," Ikarus said to Brigit as they watched them go. He glanced around wishing Lucas and Alina hadn't departed so quickly. Her eyes dark, she curled her upper lip. He'd never seen Madam Trousdale's eyes so fathomless and black without any swirling colors. He peered deeper and then jumped back. A face inside her eyes glowered back at him.

Brigit sneered, "What are you gaping at?"

He shook his head. The face reflected in her eyes was his own. Ikarus clutched her forearm, "Is that what was wrong? Was that it? Lucas and Alina, you were looking for? They didn't even ask us why we were here."

Without answering Brigit turned and walked away. Ikarus groaned and followed, hoping she would not forget to look into her crystal ball for his lost Camille. Behind him, the gray cat scooted from behind Linnea's stone and fell into step.

* * *

It was midday. Lucas and Alina exchanged an ecstatic gaze before turning the horses toward Arcana. They galloped at full speed toward the Grande Inn. They did stop twice to water the horses that seemed as glad as they to run at last. In the exuberant joy of riding, Lucas barely wondered why Seppo never appeared. It did occur to him that in the past few weeks Seppo had always met him outside the monastery to discuss the bridal ceremony. Other than this time, he'd only been briefly inside the monastery with Nikolas and then to rescue Alina.

Upon arriving at the Inn, Oliver greeted them with an inquisitive expression but took their bags without comment. Mr. Hartwinn inquired several times if all was well. Lucas assured him that it was, but requested the bath be made ready. "The hot water is on its way and wine as well! I'm sure you want bread and wine."

"We certainly do," Alina agreed with a bright smile.

They bathed together while enjoying soft cheese, warm bread, and goblets full of red wine. They washed and combed each other's hair. Once clean, they pulled back the multi-colored coverlet and climbed into the fourposter bed. The white linen sheets were enough, for the day was warm and the window open. Lucas stroked Alina's arm and hoped the spotted brown bird would appear so he could show her. She snuggled against him. Although he had intended to let her rest, he could not contain himself as he slid on top of her.

They awoke as dusky orange light moved across the bed. Alina stretched and yawned. Lucas laughed. "Shall we dress or would you rather we order our supper brought to the chamber?"

"I am rested, and you will help me dress."

"I will, yes, and then I will help you undress again after we walk in the garden."

Alina giggled and kissed his cheek. "Lucas, I am so glad that we are out of that place."

"Also I. But I cannot help but wonder why Seppo didn't appear. How could he not know we were there? And what about those other two monks? Are you sure you saw two others or not?"

"I'm not sure anymore. When I was led out, I perceived that there were two others, and beforehand I thought that they brought me bread, water, and wine. Only Seppo though, being the tall one as I said I realize now, only he seemed tangible as I think back on it. I was upset, of course. And it seems like so long ago. Like a story someone told me. It's difficult to believe that happened to me. You should ask him, Lucas, but I am never stepping inside that place again. Gold or not!"

Lucas half smiled. "Yes, I'm sure you've had enough of that eerie place. It seems they have been hiding those golden walls for a long, long time."

Alina gazed lovingly at him and ran her fingers through his hair. "We both lied to Brigit. And did you see the look on Ikarus' face? What was he doing with her at the monastery?"

"I can't imagine what brought those two together. She, of course, would have been looking for us. She does know things. But she will not know the monastery is full of gold."

"We certainly can't tell anyone," Alina agreed.

"It's Seppo's secret, and we will help him keep it." Lucas said. "Come, my darling, let's prepare for dinner."

Chapter 9

When Nikolas finished his work at the harbour, he went to the boarding house out of habit. He found Irene, Wentworth, and Bernard finishing their supper. The girls were through for the evening, Irene explained and offered to serve him. Realizing that he often showed up at supper time, he declined awkwardly. Instead, he asked Bernard if he would like to visit the Blue Gate. Bernard nodded as he got up and cleared away his bowl.

As they walked, Bernard admitted that he grew weary of the city and yearned to return to Arcana. "I don't want to disrupt Wentworth. He's enjoying the company of these fine women here at the boarding house, and they don't expect anything from him."

"I'm sure he could stay on if he likes and when he's ready, I will escort him home."

"Would you?" Bernard asked with relief.

"Of course. But for now, you and I will enjoy the fine ale at the Blue Gate." Nikolas slapped Bernard on the back and then wondered if the giant man even felt his show of fellowship.

When they arrived at the tavern, they found Brigit and Ikarus slumped at a table with a cluster of tankards strewn out in front of them. "Well, this is a surprise," Nik said as he dragged over a chair.

Brigit nodded the slow nod of the fully inebriated. The eyes of Ikarus, usually bright blue, were hollow and bloodshot. "What about the lanterns, Ik? It's near dusk."

"Ohhh . . . I forgot." He tried to focus on Brigit's face. "What should I do?" he pleaded.

"I don't know, laaadd," she drawled.

Nikolas and Bernard exchanged a worried glance. "What happened. Why are you two drinking together? Ik, are your helpers nearby?"

"Go boarding house now." Ik muttered as he swigged his ale.

"Hold on," Nikolas put a hand up and then turned to Bernard. "Stay here with them. "I'll go find the other lads and let them know they must work alone tonight." Nik rushed out calling over his shoulder, "Get our pints but don't let those two have any more."

Nikolas hurried back to the boarding house to intercept the lamplighters. After he spoke with them, he notified Irene who sat reading beside the fire. "That's fine, Nikolas," she said. Wentworth dozed in a chair, and Nik wondered if the old fellow would ever return to Arcana. That might upset Mr. Pagett, he mused, but Irene didn't seem to mind if either of them accompanied her.

When he ambled back into the Blue Gate, he was more than ready for his ale, the finest in the City of Dreams. Bernard shook his head and rolled his eyes as he slid the mug to him. Brigit and Ikarus had managed to procure more ale, but now they chewed on chunks of bread dipped in a hearty stew. "I could eat," Nik told the serving girl.

As Brigit and Ikarus obliviously stuffed food in their mouths and alleviated their drunkenness, Bernard repeated what they'd managed to tell him about seeing Lucas and Alina at the monastery and that they were just today headed to Arcana intending to spend extra days. Nikolas could make no sense of what he was hearing. He prodded Brigit for more information. She shook her shiny mane, and her eyes splashed a collection of colors. "He's a sneaky one," she said. "Takes after his . . . uh . . ."

"His aunt," Nik finished her sentence.

"I meant his father." She waved a hand and hiccupped.

"I'll ride back to Arcana in the morning," Bernard said. "If there's anything wrong, I'll send word."

Nik thought for a moment and then nodded. He would have liked to go himself, but it was best for Bernard to do it since he wanted to go home anyway. Nik felt sure Lucas would confide in him once he and Alina returned. There must have been a good reason for them to delay their excursion to the Grande Inn. Outside the Blue Gate, the men shook hands. "Farewell, Bernard. Remember to tell Irene that Lucas and Alina are spending extra time in Arcana."

Bernard tossed Ikarus over his shoulder like a sack of flour. "I'll take him through the back door."

"My room at the harbour is closer than the cottages." Nik had a firm arm around Brigit's waist. She gripped his neck and pulled his hair. Nik glanced back at Bernard and waved as he and Brigit stumbled across the cobbles.

* * *

Drusilla was leaving the boarding house when Bernard skulked up to the back door. "What is that?" she screeched.

"It's me, Bernard, and this is Ikarus," he whispered. "He needs a bit of help getting to bed. Don't worry, Miss, I've got him."

"Everyone just turned in." Drusilla smiled, flattered that he'd called her miss.

"Much appreciated," Bernard said with a droll smile.

Drusilla walked away with a light heart. She'd had a pleasant evening drying pots and then folding linens while chattering with Carissa and Perina. They'd even pulled out a chair for her. "There's no need to stand while folding linens," Carissa had said. Then she and her sister Perina, included her in their gossip, and before she left for the evening, they served her tea and sweet buns. No one had ever given her anything before.

She had so enjoyed the banter and lighthearted conversation about the citizens of the City of Dreams that she had completely forgot to try any of the fake keys. As she neared the blacksmith shop, it occurred to her that she'd left Gacheru's keys in the pocket of her apron that now hung on her own special hook in the scullery. She tiptoed past his putrid shape in the rumpled cot.

"Did the keys fit?" he demanded.

"No," she grumbled, wishing he were dead.

"None of em?"

"Nope. None. All useless just like you." She retreated behind her makeshift curtain.

"What about that big house on the Boulevard? Did you ask about it?"

"Nobody knows whose it is," she lied flopping on the cot and pulling her tattered blanket over her head.

Chapter 10

In the morning, Lucas and Alina awoke tangled up with each other in the soft white linens. After enjoying an ample dinner of roasted meat, vegetables, and wine, they had strolled in the candlelit garden. They agreed to forget about their terrifying ordeal in the monastery until they returned home.

"Good morning, lovely wife," Lucas murmured as he stroked her back. "It seems we have slept through half the morning."

"With you lying beside me, I could spend the entire day in this bed," she said in a velvety whisper.

"Then, we will." Lucas met her moist lips with his own. When they finally emerged from the bed, the room was bathed in sunlight, and Lucas had to pull the curtains. Downstairs, the dining room was empty since they'd missed breakfast. Lucas and Alina sat at a table overlooking the garden. The serving girl brought tea and warm pastries murmuring that she'd saved some for them. Laughing at themselves, they ate voraciously. The door flew open, and Bernard burst in. Lucas dropped his spoon.

"There you are!" Bernard stated.

Lucas gawked. "Yes, we're here. What are *you* doing here, Bernard?"

Alina smirked. "You look as if you're being chased."

Bernard plopped into a chair and swiped a pastry from Lucas' plate. "I rode from the City of Dreams this morning."

"Is something wrong?" Lucas groaned.

"No, they're all fine. Well, they will be after today, I suppose." He spoke with his mouth full.

Lucas reached across the table and squeezed Alina's hand. He had no intention of rushing back to the city, no matter what had happened. "Once, you finish chewing my pastry, Bernard, will you please tell us what the matter is. Who will be all right after today?"

Bernard swallowed, the serving girl set a goblet of water in front of him, and he gulped loudly. "Brigit and Ikarus, once they recover from the bottle ache."

"Ah, well all right then. Is Irene having celebrations without us?"

Bernard laughed. "No, in fact she and Wentworth spend so much time sitting around staring at books and the fire that I had to leave."

Lucas grinned. "You got so bored that you rode off this morning and stopped at the No Horses on your way here."

"Yes, but no, I didn't stop at the tavern. Brigit and Ikarus went to the Blue Gate and got themselves stupid drunk."

Alina raised her eyebrows and looked askance at Lucas who examined his hands before he said, "I see."

"They told Nik and me that they saw you two yesterday. As drunk as they were, we believe them." Bernard narrowed his eyes and gazed at Lucas.

"We stopped by to visit Seppo," Lucas and Alina said at the same time.

Bernard frowned. "For three days? Listen, you can spend your days how you like, but I imagine that an hour of that strange man in that spooky place is more than enough."

"Yes," Lucas agreed. "We were quite bored. But he needed some help so, we stayed on." He stroked Alina's hand. "Certainly, longer than we would have liked to."

"Certainly," Alina agreed.

Bernard leaned back in his chair and signaled to the girl. "I'm really hungry, if you don't mind," he said to Alina.

"Of course, Bernard, please join us. We're happy to see you." She patted his huge shoulder.

When they finished their meal, Bernard rode with them as far as the flower fields, and then, he turned in the direction of the farm. Lucas and Alina dismounted and walked hand in hand among the fragrant flowers. As they walked through the woods toward the pond, Alina asked, "Bernard doesn't believe us, does he?"

"No, he doesn't believe us, and Nik won't either. But we don't have to think about that now." He glanced around and gestured outward. "This is the beauty I remember from childhood. Having you beside me, Alina, evokes the innocent joy I once felt here. Now, I can feel it again." She encircled her arms around his waist and tilted her head so that he could kiss her forehead, each of her eyelids, her flushed cheeks, and soft lips. Lucas led her to the edge of the water. "Would you like to swim? The water feels like silk." She nodded and he began to unlace her dress.

* * *

Two days after their drinking bout, on a muggy morning buzzing with irritating insects, Ikarus hovered outside Brigit's cottage. The dusty lane felt hot under his feet. Finally, he saw Nikolas leave. Ikarus didn't like answering questions and wanted to keep his yearnings secret. Nobody from the boarding house needed to know that he was seeking Camille, especially because it was their prying that was to blame for his sudden discontent. Believing that he'd return in the coming weeks, he'd left the high country with his brother, sister, and their sheep. Even when he found himself alone, he still intended to go back. But as time passed, like the yawning gap of an unbridgeable chasm, he'd become doubtful and wavered.

Now, here he was wondering what to do. The exhilarating ease he remembered sharing with Camille was a memory that often haunted him. The feelings had not slipped away from him, but occasionally her image blurred in his mind. Madam Trousdale understood these things. He hoped she could explain how the tranquility of Camille's presence had been replaced by queasy bafflement. When they inquired at supper of his earlier life, he'd hedged and nearly lost his appetite. That day outside the monastery, the ache in his heart spoke out to Brigit without his consent.

Lately, Ikarus realized his boyhood had slipped behind him. He had to take action; he was a man now. Doubt persisted whether or not Brigit would keep his secret, but he couldn't find the girl without her. Taking the sheep down the mountainside with his sister and brother took many weeks. In that time, they passed through several cliffside villages. In one of those warm and welcoming villages he had met Camille.

She had peered out at him from the window of her hut. In the dappled interior, he could make out only her pale face, cream colored hair, and sky-blue eyes. He smiled in her direction, and she ducked out of sight, but when her mother beckoned, she emerged carrying a basket of wild berries that she offered to him before anyone else.

Over the next few days, she showed him the best areas for good foraging and warned him of poisonous plants. They walked alongside each other on the slender trails. When he slipped his hand in hers, she didn't pull away. While his sister and brother slept, and it was his turn to keep watch over the herd, she sat with him until the sun rose behind the mountain peaks. They noticed the flicker of grass that indicated wind on the way, a still rabbit waiting to make its escape, and the brush-stroked clouds of a rainless day.

Neither spoke much, both at ease with long looks and shy smiles. It was in the cathedral during Lucas and Alina's wedding ceremony, when Ikarus realized what he had known with Camille. He could tell by the expressions of the captivated citizens whether they had experienced that rare emotion or not. It did not happen to everyone. In witnessing the rapture of Lucas and Alina's love, Ikarus understood what he had left behind in the mountains. And in the awareness of it, he felt more helpless than ever. He could think of no way to get back to Camille's village.

Seated at the table, Brigit asked Ikarus to describe the girl. His eyes glazed over as he stared into the flickering ball. He swallowed hard and felt his blood drain from his limbs. "Close your eyes," Brigit demanded.

"Well, she's um, her hair is the color of mine. She has small hands." He looked up, "And they are clean! Her fingernails are white. Her skin is pale. Her eyes are blue."

"Are you sure you weren't gazing at your own reflection?" Brigit quipped. "Except for your work-worn hands of course."

Feeling belittled, Ikarus stopped speaking.

"Go on, Ik." Brigit fingered her claw necklace. Since their encounter with Lucas and Alina, she kept the hourglass out of sight. Ikarus knew Lucas thought it was talking to him. Everyone thought that when they saw it. "I will help you. Tell me," she blurted out startling him.

He opened his eyes. Avoiding her gaze, he studied the cottage. "I've never been in here. It's as odd as Lucas described."

Brigit got up. "Would a cup of wine help?"

Ikarus laughed. "We best not, I think."

"True you are. Tea then. Lucas loves my tea."

"I'm worried of late that my brother went back that way and claimed her for himself. Her face is always in my mind." He stared at his hands. "I haven't known what to do. How to see her again, but I feel like she needs me."

Brigit set the teapot on the table. "Did he know you were fond of her?"

Ikarus shook his head. "I didn't say anything about us, but he had to notice we spent those three days in close company."

"Why did you stay here and not go back yourself?"

"I thought I would go right back. But when I didn't, I hoped she would come find me." Ik blushed.

"Ahh, that *is* embarrassing, my boy." Brigit's hair swirled outward and brushed his crimson cheeks. "You told me the other day that she invited you to return. How would a girl, who looks like a lamb herself, make her way down the mountain alone?"

Ikarus clutched his head in both hands. "Once we got here, my brother and I had a terrible disagreement over the price for our sheep. We fought. He knocked me out. When I awoke, I was alone in the holding pen. Except for the sheep of course. My sister and brother were gone. They had left me behind."

"And you didn't know the way back."

He nodded his head.

Brigit pressed her lips together. She removed the teacups from the table, sat down, and bent over the crystal ball. She began to hum, and her eyeballs rolled under her lids. Ikarus gripped the edge of the table so tightly that his fingers ached. As her humming grew louder, Ik gasped. He saw figures appear and disappear in the ball. He saw the snow-covered mountains. He saw the sheep that Camille milked in the morning. He saw her! He saw his sister and his brother. He leaned closer as the image of his brother faded. Brigit's hair fell around the ball, covering it. He waited until she finally tossed the purple cloth over the ball and looked up.

"Your sister and brother did not go back through that village. But Camille is alive. And she is still there."

Ik's heart pounded with apprehension and excitement. "She's there still."

"Yes, I saw her on a mountain trail."

"Did my sister and brother make it back to our village?"

"I don't know. It's hazy. I can't answer everything at once," she snapped. "Is it Camille you want to know about or your kin?"

"Camille."

The door swung open, and Nikolas stepped in. His hand, poised halfway to brush hair from his eyes, dropped to his side. Looking from Brigit to Ikarus and back to Brigit he said, "Are you two drinking companions now?"

"It's a reading," Brigit smirked. "And we've had only tea so far."

"A reading. Well, what is it that you want to know, young Ikarus?"

"Nothing," Ik murmured. But Brigit proceeded to tell Nikolas everything that Ikarus had told her and that they needed to go to the mountain village right away.

"It's an urgent matter, I understand," Nik said pouring himself a cup of wine. "But who will light the lanterns? Your helpers can't do it on their own. They missed many streets the other night."

"I know," Ik groaned. "I hope you won't tell Lucas. I do want to light the lanterns. I like it now. But first, I must go to the mountains."

Nikolas handed Brigit a cup of wine. "Well, if you must, then you must." A nervous smile crept across Ikarus' face.

Nik flopped into a chair. "If you go with him, Brigit, I'm going with you. Ikarus is still a colt. And you, Brigit, you're as wild as a lunatic's leer. The two of you out there together, you just might spin right off the edge of the world."

"Good, the three of us." She grinned. "How do we get there?"

Nikolas scratched the back of his head. "It's a long walk, isn't it, Ikarus? We can't just jump up and go. Julian, the silk merchant, arrived with bolts of cloth and crates of wine today. He can work with Lucas once he returns, and we will go then. There's a lot to think about. We'll try before Lucas and Alina get back to find someone to light the lanterns. It's an important job."

"It is," Brigit agreed. "It can't be just anyone who takes over while we're gone."

Nik gazed at the floor, "No it can't. He who lights the lanterns is privy to the activities of the citizens." He frowned. "You're going to have to wait, Ik. We can't leave before Lucas and Alina return and we have a replacement for you."

Ikarus sighed and hung his head.

Nikolas raised one eyebrow, "Why is this suddenly so urgent, Ik? You've been here for . . . how long?"

"It will be two years come November."

Brigit leaned back in her chair and peeked at the hourglass pendant under her blouse. The sand rushed through.

"May I have one cup of wine?" Ikarus asked.

"No!" Nikolas and Brigit said at once.

"She's old enough now," Ikarus said. "I must get back before someone else claims her."

"He's right," Brigit mumbled and turned to Nik.

"Arrangements must be made," Nik said. "A couple of weeks. For now, lad, keep the lanterns lit."

After Ikarus left, Brigit and Nik took their wine outside to the bench under the linden tree. Brigit focused her gaze on the distant peaks. "I want to get to those mountain terraces and collect plants there."

"I'm in favor also," Nik said. "I've never left the City of Dreams. I suppose I'm going to have to explain all of this to Lucas as soon as they come home. And he should tell me why they stopped off at the monastery. I hope nothing is amiss there."

"The two of them came out all dirty and disheveled," Brigit reminded him.

Nikolas groaned. "First, I'll tell Irene that we're going. If she's not concerned, then Lucas will hopefully agree as well. After all, it's up to him who lights the lanterns. We should have asked Ik how long the journey down the mountain took. It will take longer going up. I hope this girl is willing to come back with him."

"She will be," Brigit assured him, hoping to convince herself. She didn't bother to mention that Ikarus didn't know the way to Camille's village or that she had her own doubts about making this journey to her former home.

* * *

The next evening after spending the day with Julian distributing goods and wares, Nikolas stopped by the boarding house. He was surprised to see Irene sitting alone in the garden. "Where are your suitors?" he teased.

"They'll be along soon enough. I sent Wentworth out for a walk with Mr. Pagett."

Nikolas laughed aloud. "You sent them?"

She chuckled. "Yes, the two of them keep pestering me to go out for a stroll. I just want to sit here and enjoy my herbs and plants."

"They're lonely men," Nik suggested.

"It seems so," Irene said. "But I'm not lonely, so they can keep each other company for a while. Anyway, they'll be back soon enough. The girls are cooking, and Drusy is upstairs folding. Join us for supper, Nikolas?"

"Ah, no thanks, Irene. I'm meeting Brigit at the Blue Gate. Although, I will take the time to tell you a story if you don't mind."

"Please, do tell me a story."

After Nikolas described the situation with Ikarus and the girl, Camille, he explained to Irene that he would have to help Lucas find someone to fill in with the lanterns while they were gone. Drusilla stepped in from the parlour to declare she was finished for the evening. Irene got up to fetch her weekly wage. "We'll work it out, Nikolas. We all appreciate a love story."

* * *

Drusilla took the long way to the blacksmith shop to enjoy the summer evening and allow Gacheru time to pass out. To her dismay, he was waiting up for her. She skirted past him to her curtained off cot. He came up behind her and grabbed a fistful of her hair. "Where's me keys?"

"I don't have them," she shrieked and pulled away.

"Go back and get em then!"

"I can't. They're gone."

She pulled the curtain and perched on the edge of her cot. "Leave me be. I want to put on my night dress."

She heard her brother step away. "Where's the keys, Drusilla? You'd better tell me."

She heard him pouring from the whisky jug. "I dropped them," she said. "I fell and they slipped into the canal." It was almost true. She'd thrown them in.

"You're gonna make new ones then, you clumsy boor," he slurred. "Now, fix me supper."

Tears stung the corners of Drusilla's eyes as she slipped her nightgown over her head. If only she could stay at the boarding house with the other girls. His stupid keys were useless, and she would not help him make more. Gacheru needed something to do in the evenings. Then, she might be able to wriggle away from him.

They hadn't invited her to stay at the boarding house yet, but she knew one of the masons had left after injuring his hand. There was a small room open. From an abandoned corner of her desperate heart a flicker of hope rose. Nikolas had said they needed a temporary lantern lighter. Gach could do it. He knew the city as well as anybody. People had once trusted him as the locksmith. She didn't know exactly when he had resorted to drunkenness and robbery. His fake keys didn't work anyway. Once Irene and Lucas saw that she was willing to help with anything they needed, she could request the little room. "There's a job you could do, Gach. Would you like to hear about it?" She pulled aside the curtain and scooted over to stir the cauldron.

When she finished explaining about the lantern lighter job, Gacheru narrowed his eyes and glared at her. He stood up and came toward her. Drusy cowered, but Gacheru's sneer turned into something resembling a grin. "You wouldn't try and trick me would you, Drusy?"

"How could I trick you? It's a job that pays money. It's what people do."

"I guess you know all about that now, don't you?" He scratched his chin.

Encouraged, she poured more porridge into his bowl. "It's a good wage, and the citizens will see that Lucas trusts you. If you bathe once a week and stay sober, they will come to you again. For their big fancy keys and locks," she added.

"I could buy my own fancy house," Gacheru snickered.

Drusilla felt a warmth creep over her. Her plan was beginning to work.

Chapter 11

Lucas and Alina cherished their time in Arcana exploring the flower fields, swimming in Lucas' pond, and strolling through the garden after dinner when the candles twinkled and created reflections on the tree trunks. They had kept to themselves and didn't spend any time in the parlour with the other guests. Their sumptuous bedchamber was their sanctuary.

As their visit ended, and they prepared to depart, Lucas' thoughts turned to finding Seppo without having to enter the monastery again. He may have to enlist Brigit's help with that. Alina began thinking about moving into the house on the Boulevard. To begin with, just for part of the time. They could still stay and help at the boarding house if they were needed. She loved the courtyard garden and wondered if it was possible to create such a place at the Boulevard house.

Her father had given her the house for herself and Lucas, as she now knew. But a part of her was still a little bit fearful of the initial memories she'd made there. The boarding house felt like home. She wondered what she and Lucas would do in that big house all alone. They would need a maid. But her heart didn't feel ready to trust a lady's maid again. She wouldn't take Carissa or Perina from Irene.

The more she thought about it, the less she could understand how to live in there. Perhaps they should just wait until someday in the far future when they did have children. She knew Lucas was thinking about Seppo, so she didn't tell him about her own qualms. She would discuss the matter with Irene.

Alina mounted her horse with a sense of sadness. They would come again to the Grande Inn, many times she was sure, but it would never be again as it was this remarkable time.

Lucas reined in outside the No Horses Tavern. Knowing he was as reluctant for their interlude to end as she, Alina grinned. They swung off their horses and walked inside hand in hand. As Lucas had hoped, Bernard was there leaning his thick forearms on the bar. They laughed and conversed with Bernard for over an hour before finally getting Bernard to promise to return to the City of Dreams soon. At dusk, they rode over the bridge turning to notice the flickering orange lamps dotting Saint Sempre and the voices of workers within.

As soon as they came through the door, Irene cheerfully embraced them and set the girls into action preparing a welcome home celebration. Ikarus offered to go out and find Nikolas and Brigit so they could join them for supper.

Before they all gathered around the table, Nikolas and Ikarus cornered Lucas alone in the courtyard to explain the situation with their proposed journey and the lanterns. Lucas gawked at them and shook his head. "That isn't even amusing, my friends. I've only just returned. I have Alina to put first. This is too much to think about at this point. I certainly don't have time to do it. I must meet with Julian. We have ledgers to write and everything else. You know that, Nikolas. We are just beginning here." Abashed, the two men peered mournfully at Lucas. "You're like a couple of lost kittens. Whose ridiculous plan is this?"

Ik glanced at Nik who gestured for Ikarus to speak up. "I . . . the thing is, you and Alina have us all thinking about love and romance these days. There is a girl I need to find."

"And you realize the timing is terrible, Ikarus?" Ik nodded as did Nikolas. "But you both are determined to go anyway."

Nikolas smiled and nodded. Ikarus turned crimson but mumbled, "We'll hurry right back."

Lucas laughed gently. "Well, even though I want to, I can't stop you. Ok then, if you must go, I'll try to oversee the lanterns as much as possible, and deal with Julian on my own. But my evenings belong to Alina now."

Ikarus embraced Lucas and rushed out of the garden before he could change his mind. "What were you doing at the monastery?" Nikolas asked bluntly.

Lucas turned white but answered calmly. "We got lost inside. It's as simple as that. I would like to lure Seppo out of there and talk to him. But there is no hurry. That place is nothing but tunnels that lead to nowhere." Nik narrowed his eyes and was about to ask more questions, but Lucas turned and went through to the parlour. Irene and Wentworth sat beside the fire. Ikarus was whispering with Brigit. Alina came in from the kitchen laughing. Carissa and Perina followed carrying wine.

Lucas and Alina mentioned little about their time in Arcana, and nobody was wont to pry. They did mention Bernard, and at his name, Wentworth announced he had enjoyed his visit so much that he'd overstayed. He would like to go home and check on Bernard and the farm. Nikolas offered to escort him home the next day.

As they finished supper, Drusilla arrived accompanied by Gacheru. The two loitered awkwardly in the back of the kitchen, visibly surprised to see the group of them gathered. Gacheru nudged Drusilla, and she nudged him back. Finally, he cleared his throat and spoke. "I've come to find out that you here are fixin to fill the lantern lighter position for a spell.

"Not a spell, a few weeks," Brigit stated.

"Yah, weeks, all right. I can do it." Everyone seated at the table gaped blankly at him. He lowered his eyes.

Drusilla mumbled, "I'll start my folding," and scurried out.

Ikarus stood up realizing it was time for him to go to work. He also didn't want to be around when the decision was made. If they said no, he couldn't bear it. Now that he'd decided he needed to go up the mountain for Camille, all he wanted to do was get going. Lucas watched him as he unlocked the cabinet and removed the tools. Ik felt himself blushing and hurrying so they could talk about him once he left.

He couldn't believe he'd found the courage to tell Lucas that it was he and Alina who had inspired him to return to the mountain village for his lamb-like girl. He hoped Lucas didn't think he was blaming him or using him and Alina as an excuse. What he'd said was true. Stepping outside into the pink dusk, he knew he would never stop thinking about her.

It wasn't until the past few weeks that he'd mentioned to his companions that he considered going back to find her. The lads who helped him light hand lanterns teased him; that she had already turned fat and shrill. Once they wed, he'd be trapped like a rabid dog by her complaining and demands. He'd never make enough money to satisfy her.

But those lads had not met her or anyone like her. They didn't know how he felt, how she and he felt together. Tonight, as he walked ahead of his helpers, he set his thoughts to remembering the trail to her village. Many shepherds followed this route. Hopefully it would not be hard to find. Ikarus gazed up at the stars; he would enjoy sleeping beneath them in the mountain air once again.

Irene pushed away from the table, "Tea anyone?" Lucas raised his goblet even though it was still half full of wine. Alina peered at Lucas. He'd told Gacheru to wait outside while they finished their supper. Once he was out of sight, Nikolas had passed the wine jug and the celebration resumed.

When Irene took her tea to the courtyard garden followed by Brigit, and the girls got up to clear the plates and platters, Alina spoke to Lucas. She reminded him he'd have to make a quick decision. He stroked her cheek and murmured, "You're right, my darling, but I like to see him fidget out there. He cannot think this choice is made lightly. You know I will have to oversee him. What are your thoughts about this?"

"I will walk with you most evenings. We can stop for wine along the way. I enjoy seeing the lanterns gradually light up the city." She pulled him to her and kissed his cheek. "We can behave like children while we keep an eye on him." Lucas laughed and nuzzled her neck. He distrusted Gacheru, but Irene and the girls approved of Drusilla and her work. He squeezed her hand under the table. He glanced at Nikolas still seated at the far end of the table.

"Should we give him a try?" Nikolas asked.

Lucas stood up and strode over to open the back door. He gestured for Gacheru to come in and sit at the laborers table. Lucas sat across from him and drummed his fingers on the table. "I don't like you," he said. "Once you were a man of reputation, but you have fallen from favor with the citizens of this city. The last time you were here, you could barely hold onto your tools. How will you raise a lighting stick and not smash all the lamps around the city?"

In the scullery, Drusilla hid behind the hooks of aprons. She basked in her brother's discomfiture, but at the same time, she hoped that they would take him on and thus set her free.

"Lucas, tis true. I'm old but not yet done for. If I leave off from the bottle for these weeks my foot and hand will be steady. I promise, sir."

"How eloquent you've suddenly become, Gach. I will give you a chance. But, and remember this, if you put one clumsy foot out of line, you will pay for your mistakes." Lucas lifted his pewter goblet and drained it.

"Do you understand, Gacheru?" Nik asked over Lucas' shoulder. "Lucas has offered you a splendid opportunity. Don't let us down."

Gacheru twisted his lips and nodded. In the back of the scullery, Drusy expelled her breath. As irritated as Lucas was that he would have to spend most evenings following Gacheru for a minimum of a couple of hours, he couldn't blame Ikarus. The lad only wanted what Lucas had wanted, and he knew nothing could stop him from pursuing his girl. And Alina was right, they may as well stroll the city in the pleasant summer evenings with wine in hand.

Upon returning later that evening and hearing the good news, Ikarus joyfully professed his undying loyalty to the lanterns and the city once he returned with Camille.

The next morning, Nikolas clattered up to the boarding house with a short cart to escort Wentworth back to his farm. Nik looked forward to spending time with Bernard and learning how to shoot the bow and arrow, a valuable skill to possess. It would be useful for hunting as well as protection on their journey.

While Nikolas was away, Brigit spent her days gazing into the depths of her crystal ball seeking answers for herself. The forthcoming journey seemed predestined since her arrival in the city. Now, that it was upon her, trepidation grew. When the ball offered no answers, she set to drawing maps on large sheets of parchment but made little progress. Her recollections collided like thunder clouds in the vast landscape of her perception.

As a child, daylight hours were full of wandering. Birdsong filled the sun-washed treetops. She remembered Linnea wistfully dancing along beside her, often stopping to pick the most fragrant flowers. But there were many bleak and troublesome days as she grew older. The mountain trails were often rocky and steep or muddy and narrow.

All of the Romany, regardless of age, banded together to push the heavy caravan wagons up and down in spring and fall. Everyone bickered on those days. Shadows lingered in the woods. Then, and now in the corners of her mind there was a memory of evil that she could not bear to face. There was much she had tried to forget about that time. But still she was compelled to go.

Each time she closed her eyes to recall the different directions of the worn paths dotted with leaves and dung, a fear gripped her, and her hand darted across the parchment blotting out the trail. Brigit thought she knew which way was best for them to go, so swearing an oath, she began again, this time drawing a route that felt passable. It would have to do. She carefully folded her makeshift maps and tossed the purple cloth over the ball. That was enough to remember today. She got up to prepare a brew. For now, in the comfort of her snug cottage she would pretend nothing had, or would, go wrong.

Chapter 12

Their day of departure quickly approached. Nikolas returned from Arcana and showed Brigit what he had learned about the bow and arrow. Bernard had given him three mules, one brown and two gray, to carry them up the mountain.

Brigit wished she hadn't promised to help Lucas lure Seppo from the monastery before she embarked on the journey. As far as she knew—all Lucas would admit to—was that he and Alina had gotten lost inside there. She doubted they were truthful when they said they spent a few days with Seppo. She knew Lucas better than that. Besides, nobody had seen Seppo since the bridal ceremony. When she observed him in the cathedral looking utterly frail and harmless, she realized her strong potion wouldn't be necessary. Now though, it occurred to her that it was possible in the thinking and making of the lethal potion she had heedlessly killed him. He might be decaying inside the leering old monastery. She didn't want Lucas to witness such a sight.

Lucas strolled up to her cottage bathed in early morning sun. His loose white shirt ruffled in the warm breeze. He had an easy smile on his handsome face. "You look so much like your mother," she said. "More and more every day."

Nodding, he offered his arm. "I was wondering," he said.

"Wondering what?" she frowned.

"Why is it that you want to know all my secrets but refuse to tell me your own?"

"No reason." She twirled around and walked on.

"That was not my question," he said. "I was wondering if your last name, Trousdale, is mine also?"

"Oh, that," she frowned again. "Why do you ask?"

"Why wouldn't I ask? I want to know. My mother never mentioned a surname that belonged to us. My father, it seems, is only called Seppo. And Alina would like to know as well."

"Ah yes, I see. Well, you can use Trousdale since you like it so much."

"How thoughtful of you, Madam Trousdale," Lucas said shielding his eyes as he looked toward the belfry tower. "But is there a surname for us?"

She shook her head, and the black sheen quickly turned a deep purple and then back again. "No surname. Why not go by Sutcliffe? That's a fine name."

"Huh? That's Alina's name, her father's name."

"Right, so use that."

Lucas yanked her arm as he turned to cross one of the narrow-arched bridges. "Where do you . . . where do we . . . come from?"

"I came from a lengthy line of thieves. You know that already, don't you, Lucas?"

"On that side of things, I suppose. I can't imagine my mother. She wasn't like you, a gypsy, a fortuneteller . . . a liar . . .."

Her eyes turned black then silver, and her hair swirled up and slapped him across the face. It stung like nettles. "Ouch! What in blazes? You haven't been lying to me, have you?"

"I'm your aunt. Mind your tongue. If I'd found you as a boy, you would understand respect. "

"I understand it simply fine. It was beat into me as a child when I roamed Arcana and here in the city before Irene found me. Irene taught mutual respect goes both ways."

Brigit smoothed her hair. "Yes, well, of course she did."

"Of course." Lucas nodded.

Brigit glared at him, "Don't try to trick me by agreeing with me."

"Same, aunty." Lucas shook his head. "Why do you and I always argue?"

"I don't know. Maybe that's what kinfolk do." She clutched his forearm and then pointed toward the monastery. "Steady yourself. Seppo awaits."

In the center of the secret cemetery and clad in a flimsy, tan cassock, Seppo moved among the gravestones like a hesitant butterfly. His dark eyes, all of him, looked faded against the brilliant sky and verdant grass. Lucas glanced at Brigit, "Ah, so there he is as if he was expecting us. I thought I needed you to help me tempt him out."

She chuckled, her relief apparent. "He looks ghostly for an old apparition. At first, I wished he were. Go on then. I'll wait here."

Lucas shook his head. "No, go on back if you like. This conversation could take some time."

"I'll wait with Linny," she said as she moved to the stones.

As Lucas approached Seppo, he wondered where he should begin. He had so many questions now. "You're here for answers," Seppo said as Lucas came closer. Lucas nodded, noticing that the baskets he and Alina had left weeks ago were refilled with fresh flowers. Seppo touched his arm and led him slowly around the side of the building to carved double doors that Lucas had somehow not seen before. He had walked around the entire perimeter of the monastery; he would not have missed this large entrance. Knowing Lucas' thoughts, Seppo explained, "These doors were covered with vines."

"I'm not going in there." Lucas planted his feet wide and crossed his arms.

"Hidden on purpose," murmured Seppo, opening both doors wide enough for Lucas to peer in. The scent of sandalwood drifted outward. Leaning inside, Lucas observed a long, rectangular shaped chamber. The soaring walls were adorned with dark crown molding, wainscoting in the same mahogany wood, and five rows of pews. A carved spiral of thirteen steps led to a crescent pulpit protruding above the benches.

At the other end of the elongated chamber and arranged around a sunken firepit was a scattering of overstuffed damask divans where someone had tossed embroidered pillows in a gesture of welcome. Stone sconces caked in wax held thick candles that cast warm light around the silent setting. The room, in contrast to the damp tunnels below, breathed an open-armed embrace that assured warmth, safety, and tranquility. Lucas stepped over the threshold as if he'd just returned home from a long journey.

Seppo blew across the room like a gentle undulating frond. He gestured to a divan. Lucas glanced back toward the cemetery, but he couldn't see if Brigit remained there.

"Come in, Lucas."

Curious, Lucas asked, "What goes on in here?"

"This is a place of prayer and contemplation. Here, I enjoy recalling moments sewn gratefully into memory and faint reminiscences that tarry in the dark fringes. After all that came to pass, I now abide in peace here."

Lucas scowled and remained rooted mere steps from the open doors. "I don't understand what you're talking about."

Seppo exhaled softly. "I have wine."

"I'm able to go places without wine," Lucas remarked as he moved to stand beside the offered seat. With hands firmly on his hips, he observed every facet of the secluded sanctuary.

After Seppo poured two golden goblets full of deep ruby wine, he gestured for Lucas to sit. Lucas gave in and sank down into the comfortable cushions and stretched out his legs. Admiring the golden goblet in his hand, he noticed a close resemblance to the gold-jewelled box from Brigit's cottage that had somehow ended up in Seppo's possession and then in his own hands. He decided not to mention he knew where the gold came from. Did Seppo even know that he and Alina had nearly died in the depths of the twisted tunnels?

"Shall I begin when I met Linnea?"

"That will be fine," Lucas said and took a long gulp. Then holding up his hand, he asked, "Where are the other two monks?"

"I'm here. To begin with, we were thirty-three. We once had eleven left, then seven, then three. That's it, more or less."

Noticing his goblet was near empty already, he asked suspiciously, "When I first came looking for Alina, you said, "We are three here."

Seppo took Lucas' goblet and refilled it from the tear-shaped jug on the floor. "We were three at that moment: me, you, and your friend Nikolas. The three of us stood together, did we not?"

Lucas flopped back against the pillow. "I know you are skilled at evasion, Seppo. Are there more monks here or not?"

"The pillows make a difference don't they," Seppo said gesturing with his goblet. "They were a gift from your mother."

Lucas picked up one of the pillows and ran his finger along the fine stitching, "It's marvelous. I don't recall seeing her sew. She made all of these?" Lucas glanced around the chamber, silently counting the pillows.

Seppo smiled distantly, "Yes, before you were born."

"May I have one?"

"They are yours already."

Lucas furrowed his brow but settled in among the pillows, and tucked one under his elbow. "When you said, 'We are three here' to Nik and me, Alina was in the monastery too. She would have made four if you were referring to ourselves."

"Yes, but she was not in the hallway at that time."

Lucas shook his head and smiled. If Seppo didn't want to tell him about other monks, he clearly couldn't persuade him. "Does this stately chamber lead to the maze of passageways?"

Seppo shook his head. "Not today."

Lucas rubbed his palms on his thighs. "What does that mean? Will you at least tell me what this place is about, such as why the monastery contains a jumble of disrupted passages?"

"Lucas, I want you to understand that this sanctuary was built over many decades by afterthoughts of fearful secluded men."

Lucas leaned forward and placed his goblet on the floor. He rested his elbows on his knees. He could hear Seppo quietly breathing and wondered what his unusual father thought about him. Did he mind that he asked so many questions? Lucas realized he asked all these things as if he had a right to, but Seppo need not explain anything if he didn't feel like it or had reason not to. Maybe he should excuse himself and leave. Then, he noticed the inscription etched into a white marble rectangle in the floor. Lucas bent over and read the artfully carved words:

Now, I shut out the day before it turns to creeping darkness.

This night, life outside my window with its teeming waves of weary shall pass me by.

I will remain inside, haloed in candlelight, safely shrouded in shuttered contentment.

"Extraordinary," he murmured peering up with bewilderment at Seppo. "Who wrote this?"

Seppo gazed quizzically at Lucas. "You know I find it unnerving to meet you as well. I wrote those words. I don't carve. One of the others created the tablet."

"Are you the abbot?"

Seppo almost smiled. "No. I would be though if this were truly an abbey."

Lucas tilted his head. "What order of monks are you?"

Seppo gazed so long at the goblet on the floor that Lucas wondered if he'd fallen asleep. When the old man looked up, his eyes were veiled with sorrow, "We were not monks. Not ever. Never," he exhaled wiping a white hand across his weary face. "But after a time, some of us were holy men."

"Some?" Lucas repeated.

"Yes, some of us, some of the time. We were holy in our intentions and deeds by then."

Lucas gazed long and deep into his father's familiar eyes. "And you, Seppo, were you a holy man?"

Seppo twisted his white eyebrows, leaned back on the divan, and drifted into thought. Lucas sipped his wine and waited. Glancing around the room, he wondered which of the occasional holy men stood in the pulpit and spoke. He thought he could hear water running. Was it the golden pool below them? He got up and refilled both their goblets. The gold would not be discussed today. Lucas squeezed his father's shoulder. "Go on then. Just tell me how you met my mother."

Seppo's face lit with the hint of a smile. He handed Lucas a wedge of hard cheese from a platter placed behind the jug. Slowly, painstakingly, he explained how the thirty-three men disguised themselves as monks and left the crowded city where they had taken advantage of the people there. He told Lucas some of the men had committed unspeakable offenses on others. And others endured similar offenses turned upon themselves. He explained how the struggle with the land taught them to become more like the monks they had pretended to be. He described the building of the monastery and how the arduous work freed their souls from their guilt and taught them how to work together. He patted tears from the corners of his eyes when he spoke of the death of men who had become like brothers and protectors to each other. Lucas forgot about his wine and listened with rapt attention without interrupting while Seppo explained how they dug the tunnels and then out of desperation lied to the newcomers to get them to help build their roof.

All while keeping their secret in the crypt, Lucas thought. As if reading his son's thoughts, Seppo admitted, "We had much at risk and kept our precious secrets." Lucas sat up in anticipation of Seppo revealing the truth about the golden crypt. Another long silence ensued.

When Seppo spoke again, he seemed to gaze through Lucas like he was a sheer curtain. "But the seven monks, as we came to believe ourselves to be, although we were not reverent men, as I said, we had surpassed the limitations of discord."

"You found peace," Lucas suggested.

"Yes," Seppo smiled candidly, revealing a frank resemblance to Lucas in his suddenly youthful face. Finally, he explained to Lucas his desire to wander alone. He had grown restless and began to roam a little farther from the monastery every day. "In Arcana, in a field of flowers, I came upon Linnea. You know how it feels to encounter a woman like that. I don't need to describe our instant fervor to you."

Lucas stared unblinking, picturing his mother, and a somewhat younger version of Seppo, walking toward each other in the flower fields. "Were you not so very much older than she?"

Seppo hesitated and then went on. "We felt each other's hearts. We held hands and ran through the fields together. She taught me about flowers." He sipped his wine and stared vacantly at Lucas who returned his gaze while trying to picture this curious man dallying with the vibrant mother he carried in his mind's eye.

"She came with me. We travelled to Ingleena by ship. We stayed as guests in grand houses. I bought her exquisite gowns. I felt like an authentic person, part of civilization, how the world is for others. And she did too. We were remarkably content. We planned for our future. As you now know it never came. I suppose it had no foundation."

Wide-eyed, Lucas asked, "What happened? How did the two of you became a part of upper society? And then what ended it all?"

"You," Seppo said. "Linnea was with child. The gold I had pillaged from, well you know where, ran out."

Lucas gasped.

"I told her the truth about who I was, invited her to live here so that we could gather more gold, but she chose to take you back to the farm. Even after all we'd experienced together, in the end, I frightened her." Seppo hung his head and covered his face with his capacious sleeve.

Lucas moved to sit beside him. His own hands trembled, but he enclosed his father in his arms. It felt as if the ancient man's bones might crumble under his touch. "Did you ever see her again?" Lucas whispered.

"Ah, yes. I went to the fields in my hooded cloak. I watched the two of you. It was agonizing for both of us. She let me hold you sometimes when I let her see me. I had never meant to frighten her. I hoped Linnea may accept one day all that I'd done. She seemed to be calmer as you grew. Then one horrible day I came upon the two of you dead in the field. I waited in disbelief willing her to rise from that dreadful sleep. I had a little bit of water with me, I tried to force you both to drink. As I considered how to bring your lifeless bodies back here, along came a young boy. I hid in the brush. He also tried to wake you and your mother. Finally, he gave up and snatched the arrow tip. Fearing he would alert others, I collected the willow baskets and fled."

Lucas, seated next to his father, turned his gaze to the timbered ceiling. Bright colored scenes of trees and hills were painted between the beams. He took several deep breaths before asking, "The boy who took the arrow tip saw you hiding in the brush?"

"I think he must have. He screamed. My cloak and my eyes were all he would have been able to see."

"It was Bernard," Lucas said more to himself than his father. "You did not see me get up?"

"I did not." Seppo said. "When I returned the field was empty."

A flight of twittering swallows dipped below the arched door. When they swooped upward and out of sight, Lucas heard Brigit calling his name. "Enough for today," Seppo murmured. Lucas stood, glad to leave but reluctant as well. He had forgotten Brigit was waiting. His father had easily mentioned the gold, so he must have known that he and Alina were inside.

"Remind Brigit that Linnea made the correct choice by going to the farm. The farm was the best place for your mother, under the circumstances. And I did not abscond with her. We chose each other."

"I think you should tell her," Lucas said. "You know Alina and I were trapped down below."

Seppo nodded.

"Why didn't you help?"

"I did help," Seppo said. "I left you to discover something for yourself."

Lucas levelled his gaze, "I thought Alina was going to die!"

Seppo sighed, "I am wholly aware of that."

Lucas knitted his brow. "Is there anything more you'd like to tell me?"

Seppo shook his head, "Not now, son. Hurry along. Brigit is waiting."

Walking slowly over the foot bridges, past Brigit's marshy gathering ground, Lucas asked her, "Why would my mother, being with child, run from a man with an unsavory past when she herself came from gypsy blood?"

Brigit glowered then glanced around. "Linny lived in harmony with dirt, the earth, flowers, herbs, all of it. She knew more than me, if you can believe that," Brigit chortled. "When we were children, the adults, they slept in drunken heaps, and scoundrels came in from the woods. Your mother, she was like you, or you like her. Not even I could foresee what she might do. The farm offered refuge. She wanted to plant herself in a beautiful place. And then it seems that peculiar monk came along. I can only assume that once you were born, she had all she ever wanted."

They went the rest of the way in silence. Lucas felt that Brigit was holding back, but he thought it best to let it go. She was entitled to her secrets. He felt content enough now that he knew who his mother and father were. A gypsy and a thief. God knows what else Seppo had been. He didn't want to know everything just yet; it was unnerving enough just sitting there with the man. Lucas could understand why he'd frightened his mother back to the farm. And what was it about her family that had sent her there to begin with, he wondered.

Glancing at Brigit, he sighed aloud. She gave him a sidelong glance but kept walking. Well, he had his own secrets, he reasoned. The thoughts and words of others should only occupy a small place in a man's mind. As the roof of the boarding house came into view, he looked forward to telling the entire story to Irene, except about the gold of course. Seppo, without saying, trusted him and Alina to keep his secret in the depths, but there was more that the ghostly man was not yet telling.

He turned his thoughts to his own life. It was past time to speak with Irene and give her the acknowledgement that she deserved for how far he'd come since that first trip back to Arcana. It was all because of her insisting that they had gone there in the first place. He looked forward to spending time alone with her — perhaps a picnic by the river — and letting her know that she was correct about everything, including Alina. The day she caught Alina's veil for him was the same day he met Madam Trousdale. Such remarkable events! Alina seemed content here in the City of Dreams and Arcana too, of course. But if the day ever came, he might attempt to board a ship to Ingleena again. If Seppo and Linnea could go, why not he? With Alina at his side, things might turn out differently.

Brigit drifted ahead of Lucas on the road. Amused, he wondered if she forgot he was there. Then she turned and said, "We leave for the mountains the day after tomorrow. I'd like to tell you everything I can remember about Linny but there isn't time. For now, you will enjoy knowing that the chandelier at the No Horses once belonged to our parents. Linny and I traded it for buckets of ale." Lucas and Brigit left each other laughing.

Chapter 13

In a solemn procession, Lucas, Nikolas and Ikarus followed several paces behind Gacheru on his first evening of lighting lanterns. The three spoke in hushed voices so as not to disturb the grumpy Gacheru. He knew they followed and made a meticulous show of his efforts. An uneasiness as oppressive as the viscous fog curling in from the sea clung to the three friends. Lucas recognized that Nikolas had misgivings about leaving the City of Dreams, but the pull of adventure was stronger than his apprehension. Ikarus of course thought mostly about Camille even though a noticeable sense of duty beset him.

None of them were pleased with Gach roving the city with purpose and permission. It seemed the decline of Gacheru had occurred suddenly as if he'd had just one whisky swig too many. As for himself, Lucas preferred that his friends remained close, but it wasn't for him to decide. They were going. All he could do was wish them a successful journey. The evening crawled by as they straggled in Gacheru's irksome wake. Every movement he made was overdone. "He's purposely dragging his heels. Let's stop for an ale. Perhaps he'll move quicker when he loses his audience," Lucas suggested as they turned toward the Blue Gate Tavern. Lingering over their draughts and hoping Gach would finish up soon, they discussed the path ahead.

"Brigit has drawn maps from memory." Nikolas remarked. "As a child, the troupes travelled the hills a fair bit. And we have Ikarus here. Of course, you remember the path you took, right, lad?"

"Sure," Ikarus mumbled and gestured for another ale.

Lucas gazed at him overlong. "Just don't let Brigit lead you off in some murky woods."

"Brigit and I have good sense," Nikolas said. "We can always turn around and return in our own footsteps. She wants to gather plants. I look forward to escaping the harbour odors. We will return with unusual gifts and exciting stories, I'm sure. And our first day home we will meet right here at the Blue Gate for this magnificent ale."

Lucas raised his tankard. "I look forward to that very day, my friends." They all drank and grinned hopefully at each other.

"And Camille will be with us," Ikarus added.

"I'm sure," Lucas agreed as he concealed a growing unease.

Back on the slippery, cobbled street they spied Gacheru heading toward the cottages. "He had no trouble following the route," Lucas mused. "But if I can find someone else, I will replace him."

"I'm sorry, Lucas," Ik said. "I promise I'll hurry right back. As fast as Camille can travel," he added with a nervous grin.

They made their way to the harbour where Nikolas retrieved his possessions that he'd bundled for the journey. From a distance, they watched Gacheru light the last of the lanterns and head back toward the boarding house to return the tools. Lucas would not allow him to take them to the blacksmith shop. After that there was nothing left to do but for the men to part.

Walking the familiar road to Brigit's cottage, Lucas wondered how it would feel without her presence here. The three of them lingered in the silent street outside the small stone cottage, each immersed in his own thoughts. Candles flickered merrily behind the vaporous windows suggesting a warmth that Lucas knew was about to end. The sky above overflowed with stars and the distant mountains were mere hulking shapes in the distance.

As if they all came to the same conclusion at once, they turned to each other, shook hands and clasped their forearms as well. Ikarus swallowed, then lunged at Lucas and hugged him tightly. Patting Ikarus' back, Lucas mumbled wishes for safe travels. Ik stifled a sob and wiped tears from his cheeks with the back of his hand before shuffling over to wait in a rectangle of light beside Brigit's window.

Nikolas and Lucas regarded each other, their eyes speaking the unnecessary words of abiding friendship. When a wispy cloud drifted away, the moonlight bathed them in inky light. Lucas pressed his lips firmly together, for words eluded him at this melancholy moment. Nikolas shrugged and said, "I'll be right back." He laughed, forcing a thin smile from Lucas.

Lucas gripped Nik's shoulder. "Until the tavern then. Farewell, Nikolas." He had taken several steps backward before finally turning away when the cottage door opened, and Nikolas and Ikarus disappeared inside.

Lucas followed the lantern lights home. He wished he'd lit them was on his way to the Blue Gate to meet Nikolas now. When the gray cat appeared, Lucas whistled in delight. It was then he realized he hadn't formally bid farewell to Brigit. Gazing down at the cat, which returned his lonesome stare, he thought it best to leave the last words between himself and Brigit with her story about the chandelier at the No Horses Tavern. She and his mother had traded it for buckets of ale. He smiled down at the cat. He had forgotten to tell Brigit that upon first entering the No Horses, he had hit his head on that chandelier.

He remembered a time that seemed long ago when he first came to Brigit's cottage late at night. She was Madam Trousdale then, and she had nearly clobbered him with a fire poker. He laughed aloud when he remembered his desire to steal the gold-jewelled box that ultimately was simply handed to him. The gray cat trotted companionably alongside him, glancing up only when Lucas laughed. He wondered if Alina had given the cat a name yet. That would be something enjoyable for Irene to get involved with.

Very soon, he must find the time for the stroll and picnic he imagined for himself and Irene. A twinge of guilt pecked at him, he hadn't told Irene about his and Alina's time lost inside the monastery. Now, it felt too late to bring up their ordeal at all, especially since he couldn't mention the gold. Irene would probably know he held something back. As his footsteps slowed, he felt a familiar glimmer of the mysterious atmosphere of the City of Dreams. The thick stone walls, marked by ever changing images dancing in the lantern light, drew him into their secret philosophy. It might not be so bad to follow Gacheru and savor the spirit of nightfall. "Will you accompany me and Alina on the evening rounds?" he asked the gray cat. "You are good company."

As the peaked roof of the boarding house came into view, he hoped Alina would be waiting for him beside the fire, and there she was. The cat scooted ahead of him and leapt onto Alina's lap. "Both of you home together." Alina smiled as she stroked the cat's soft fur that moved beneath her slender fingers like waves. "I was about to get up and pour the wine, but I'm afraid you'll have to do it. This girl has caught my attention first."

Lucas poured the wine and then dropped down onto the divan beside her. "I hoped to find you here just like this, my darling. Now, tell me how you spent your evening."

Alina stroked the cat from head to tail. "You just missed Irene. She and I had a lovely evening together. We found ourselves having supper on our own and were planning to read here beside the fire, but our own chatter distracted us."

Lucas laughed. "Good I'm happy to hear that. My two favorite ladies dining together and getting to know each other better. I was thinking today that I want to spend more time with Irene. I'm glad she had you for companionship tonight. Why don't you and Irene choose a name for our cat here?" He stroked the soft fur behind the cat's ears. "She's part of the family now; since everyone feeds her."

"Yes, we all feed her, but it's you she reveres. I'm certain she'd come around even if we didn't set out goat milk and scraps for her if she knew you were here."

The cat arched and leapt to the floor. She brushed between Lucas' legs before trotting off to the kitchen. "We do often seem of the same mind," he mused. "Similar characteristics and an unusual fondness. At one time, I thought she was a bewitchment sent by Madam Trousdale." Alina laughed and leaned over to kiss his cheek. Lucas caressed the nape of her neck. "Tell me more about your evening with Irene."

"Well," Alina said curling her legs up underneath her and nestling closer to Lucas. "Irene told me all about her married life and how you came along at just the right time to assuage her loneliness after her husband passed on. We are sent the people we need when we need them, don't you think? Like you and your cat."

Lucas twirled her hair between his fingers. "Like you and me."

She grinned and blushed. "Most certainly!" She wrapped her arms around his neck, and Lucas pulled her onto his lap.

"What else did you and Irene discuss?"

"She is a remarkably determined and accomplished woman. So, I suppose that's why she doesn't want to come live with us in the

Boulevard house." Alina frowned. "But she has promised to visit and spend the night as a guest on occasion. Won't that be wonderful, Lucas? We can host celebrations over there!"

"It will be absolutely wonderful, Alina. I'm delighted that you and Irene enjoyed your time together." Lucas held her hand and kissed her palm while she spoke.

"And also, we have new boarders. A young couple newly betrothed. She's young, not him, however. She's so lovely, although a bit pallid. They sail tomorrow for Ingleena, or did she say the day after?" She pursed her lips. "We're all intrigued by them, but you probably won't get to meet them."

"I don't mind. The only young woman I'm interested in is you. Shall we sweetheart?" Lucas stood and offered his hand to pull her to her feet.

"Oh, Lucas, you look tired or maybe a little sad? Our friends go tomorrow, and I didn't even ask how your taking their leaving went."

Lucas gazed at the flames before answering. "It was . . . I don't know. . . there comes too soon the moment when one must turn and walk away. But we all hesitated in that empty space." He looked away in search of the distant trail his friends would soon take. Turning to Alina and smoothing her hair back, he forced a smile. "We were hoping to hold onto the moment, I suppose. For me, looking at the three of us from aside, perhaps from the eyes of our cat companion, I wanted to grab hold of the three of us, Nikolas, Ikarus and me standing there in the glow of Brigit's cottage and somehow shove that moment into a burlap sack and carry it away with me."

Alina encircled her arms around his waist and rested her head against his strong chest. She heard his steady heartbeat and slow intake of breath as he spoke. "It was sad for me, yet I'm thrilled for all of them. I can't even imagine the adventures they will have. But you, dearest Alina, you revive me. Let's take our wine upstairs, and you can divert my thoughts to more comforting things."

She nodded. "I believe I know how to comfort you."

"I'm grateful that we're married at last."

"Also, I, Lucas. I wondered up until the last minute if you would be willing to give up roaming the streets with your lanterns and deep brooding."

Lucas tilted his head in amusement and then pushed open the door. Four candles atop the mantle flickered but didn't go out. Alina giggled. "Irene says she is pleased too. She was concerned about your solitary nature."

"More selective than solitary, I'd say. Ah, you lit the fire for me."

"Yes, and now it's ready for you to place another log. I like to watch the light reflect in your eyes as the blaze comes to life."

"And I like to watch you slip out of your dress in the warmth of this light."

The logs crackled and sparked, and the blue-flamed candles made dancing images against the wall.

Chapter 14

Nikolas, Brigit, and Ikarus departed from the cottages under a sapphire sky before dawn. Their mules were laden with sheepskins for the impending cold and bundles of dried meats, hard bread, herbs, and plump skins of ale and wine. As they quietly led the beasts out of the city, the vast sky opened up like a canopy of diamonds. Nikolas wondered if they would find any highland whisky to bring down from the mountains to share with Lucas upon their return.

Brigit went first and then Ikarus, for she and Nikolas in a protective instinct had decided to keep him within their sight. None of them looked back as the path led up and away from the City of Dreams.

Nikolas thought the softly glowing lanterns of home would tempt him to turn around. The excitement he'd held for the past few weeks dissolved into determination. His jaw set and his shoulders straight, he kept a watchful eye out for threats. Of what nature he had no idea. He carried the bow and quiver full of arrows that Bernard had given him slung across his back.

Brigit hummed to herself and soon Ikarus imitated her. Nikolas found it difficult to create the sound and quietly amused himself with sailor songs. In the slow moments just before dawn, Nik was struck with a sudden stab of worry that the trip would turn into nothing but a tedious travail. Then, he suddenly remembered he'd forgotten to mention to Lucas, as they walked the Boulevard last night, that he'd noticed the ivy was broken at Alina's house. He'd fallen behind when he stopped to tighten the laces on his boots and when he caught up Lucas was discussing with Ikarus the art of discretion in approaching Camille. Lucas told the lad, "Do not go dashing up to her right off. Hold back with patience so she may grow fond of you again." The advice Lucas gave Ikarus amused Nikolas because Lucas had done the very opposite in approaching Alina, as everyone knew by snatching at her throat on the street. The three laughed about that moment and Ik promised that if Camille wore any jewelry, he would not attempt to grab it. Thus, the ivy was forgotten.

Now, Nik wished there were a way to send a warning. If only he could stand atop one of the large boulders they were passing and shout across the widening gap to Lucas. The ivy that had grown strong so quickly was broken in several places moving from the ground upward. It appeared that someone had climbed up to the second story window. Damn! How had he failed to say anything? If something were amiss, he could never forgive himself for failing his friend. Feeling too warm now in his night cloak, he unfastened it and tried to shove it in his saddlebag, but it fell, and the mule stepped on it. Swearing, Nikolas swung himself to the ground to retrieve the garment.

Twisting in her saddle, Brigit raised and dropped an arm in objection. "What are you doing? We're barely underway."

"It's been over two hours already. I just dropped it," Nik grumbled. "Give me a moment." He looked back toward the City of Dreams just as the city—looking dwarfed in the vast landscape around it—became awash in the yellow, pink, and pale blue radiance of dawn. The three of them stopped and gazed in wonder. Even the mules stood motionless.

"We are quite far already," Ikarus declared. As long rays of sunlight shot across the land, they could see the steeple of Saint Sempre and the bell tower at the monastery shimmering golden beside the silver river, and the road to Arcana looked like a ribbon of pink marble. The foothills changed from brown to ripe green when splashed by the sweeping slant of sun that shot up the hill and spilled down upon them.

When Nikolas glanced at Brigit, her head was titled back, her eyes closed, her black tresses specked with gold in the glory of dawn. After several minutes, she opened her eyes and smiled radiantly. Remembering her youth, Nik mused. They beheld their home one more time and then drove their mounts up the hill.

It was near midday when they stopped beside a sparkling pond where Nikolas shared his concern with them about the broken ivy. "Oh no," Ikarus groaned sprawled on the grass tossing pebbles into the pond. "There's nothing we can do, is there?"

"We can't go back," Nik complained and reassured at the same time. Brigit's expression lost the serenity the dawn had brought and clouded with apprehension. She laid a hand to her chest and then pulled the hourglass from inside her blouse. Her eyes went from blue to black, and her hair spun into purple wrath. Nikolas held his breath as Brigit flung her shawl over her head. Ikarus let the pebbles slip from his hand.

The two men gazed silently at each other. There were only six years separating them, but as they waited, Ikarus could have easily passed for Nikolas' son. His youthful detachment contrasted with Nik's apprehension.

"It's moving," Brigit finally said, tossing aside the cloak that tangled with her hair as if not willing to give up. "Lucas will notice the ivy."

"That's a relief. Let's go," Ik said. Dusting his trousers with his hands, he leapt onto his mule.

Nikolas and Brigit let him lead the way up the migratory trail. "It's beautiful out here," Nik said, "I can't believe either of you left it behind."

"I left the caravans and thieves behind," Brigit answered moodily. Since the sun had risen, she'd been struck by the familiar scent of the high meadow grass and the memories it stirred. As a child running wildly over the hills, she had never imagined leaving the magic of this ancient land. When the evil came, it was Linnea who first suggested they run away. Neither of them would have left if they hadn't been forced to go.

The trips they made down to the hamlet of dreams—that's all it was at the time—delighted her, and she profited from them. Their entire tribe did. But Brigit was always the first one to lead the caravan back up the hill, which was why she thought she might remember her way around out here. However, she noticed the trails had grown over and new paths trampled the old ones.

"I hope Camille is willing to come with me," Ik worried. "Is it right to request she leave her village for me?"

"You are going to try," Nik said. "I daresay I wonder why she would leave beauty and peace for the tumult of the city. You must have considered that, lad, before we embarked. No?"

Ik shook his head. "Didn't even think of it until now."

Nikolas made a funny face and slapped Ik on the back. "I would have come anyway. We will find a way to convince her. How could she turn down such a handsome troupe as ours?"

"Some grow restless out here and run off, among other things," Brigit stated. "There's no talking yourself out of this, Ikarus. You've already made your choice, and the consequences await." She urged her mule forward. They came to a lush meadow with swaying grass as tall as the mule's shoulders. "Which way from here?" she asked Ikarus.

He glanced around and stopped. All of a sudden, as if some unknown force had stamped down the grasses, he saw five different trails. One led over the curve of the meadow seemingly away from the mountainside, perhaps back downhill. Another led toward a copse of trees. Ik remembered travelling through trees on the descent with his sister and brother because they'd lost two sheep to a predator.

He swallowed hard and glanced sideways at his companions. They appeared relaxed and confident in his ability to direct them. Hadn't Brigit drawn some maps? He wondered what happened to those. His stomach grumbled. It was wearisome to feel hunger so often. It would be weeks before he enjoyed one of Irene's bountiful stews. He pushed the thought of it, along with warm bread, out of his mind and took a deep breath. Pointing a dubious finger toward the trees, he said, "That way." His voice came out in a high squeak but neither of them laughed at him.

"You two go first," Brigit said.

"Why?" Ik asked.

Sitting indifferently in the saddle, she combed her hair with the two claws. "Because you know the way, and I'm busy." She narrowed her eyes and scanned the tree line.

Nik scowled. Brigit had fallen into one of her stubborn moods. Clicking his tongue, he kneed his mule forward. Ikarus wasn't sure if Nikolas was encouraging the animal or himself. As he hesitantly fell in line behind Nikolas, he remembered Lucas' departing gift to him.

He slid his hand into his satchel, retrieved the pistol and tucked it into his waist band under his cloak.

When he glanced back at Brigit, he caught sight of her sliding her long dagger from its sheath. She grinned and waved it at him. As he turned forward with consternation, he noticed a movement in the thick wood. His heart thumped, and his breath stopped short. Up ahead, Nikolas plodded onward. Brigit trotted forward, and the claw necklace and miniature hourglass swayed and tangled together. She narrowed her eyes and scanned the trees.

Unable to form words, Ikarus peered into the woods, his clammy hand wrapped tightly around the pistol grip. A cluster of green-leafed saplings wavered in a small patch of sunlight that had penetrated the broad crowned trees. But just behind them and forming a curtain of gray, a thicker clump of trees huddled together like conspiratorial soldiers. *Just shadows* he told himself. He glanced at Brigit who motioned him forward. Nik didn't seem to notice the eerie presence in the forest, but he was certain Brigit did. She didn't speak, so neither did he. Once they passed through this woodland, he'd take a long swallow of ale.

As the shadows grew longer, they came upon a bubbling stream. Nikolas stopped and dismounted. "The mules would like to rest here."

"The sun goes down early with these peaks around us," Ikarus announced. Slipping from his mule, he immediately groped for the ale skin. When he finished gulping, he noticed Brigit staring intently at him. Ignoring her, he untied his bedroll and placed it in a patch of soft grass surrounded by boulders for protection. Nikolas tied the mules on a line beside the stream where they could drink and munch sweet grass. He tossed his belongings onto the ground and went off with his bow and arrow in search of game. Brigit's eyes burned holes in the back of Ik's head.

"What are you so scared of?" she derided.

"Nothing!" Ikarus glowered. "What's to eat?"

"Pudding pie," she quipped. "It's bread and dried meat until we catch something." Ik nodded and helped her make a circle of stones for the fire. "You changed your mind about your girl, or you're frightened. Which is it?"

Ik twisted his mouth and glanced in the direction where Nikolas had gone. "I don't know if we are on the right path. There are many more sheep paths than when I came down," he muttered.

"Then we're both lost," Brigit whispered.

"What about your maps?"

She shook her head, "They don't make sense. Well, now that we're out here. I don't know . . . maybe something will become familiar."

Ik slapped his forehead and sank to the ground. Glancing again over his shoulder, he asked, "What do we do?"

"Keep going of course. Eventually, we will probably come upon a traveller who can direct us." Brigit drew some lines in the dirt with a smooth stick. "This is how far we've come in one day. The tops of the mountains are only three more lines of this length. You see?"

"Sure, seems right. We'll find a village if we keep going up. I hope so, anyway." Ikarus said and laughed uneasily. "It's not like the city where one can simply ask a passerby for directions."

"Nikolas is enjoying the adventure, so we need not worry him." Brigit spread a cloth on the ground and laid out the bread and dried meat.

"All right," Ik agreed. "How many paths can there be after all? So, when we do return home, I'm thinking that Lucas and Alina will move to the Boulevard house, right? Camille and I can live in their rooms." He smiled with the buoyancy of a child dreaming about an easily attainable future. "You know, until we're married. And then we'll both stay in Lucas' room."

"That's a fine plan, Ik. That way Lucas won't have to worry about leaving Irene at the boarding house. Good enough, I'd say." She tapped the ground three times with the stick. "I think Camille will happily welcome your return, even after so long away."

Blushing, Ik said, "I think so too." He leapt up. "I'll go find Nikolas. Maybe we can get a hare for the pot."

It was dark by the time Nikolas and Ikarus returned with the hare, but Brigit had started a fire and the black pot was full of boiling water and herbs. After they ate and discarded the scraps away from their encampment, they relaxed in the glow of the crackling fire and passed the ale skin back and forth. "That's it for ale, just wine from now on," Nik said and leaned back on his elbows. "Tell me what to expect in this village we're headed to?" he asked. "What are the people there like?"

Ikarus' eyes shone in the firelight. "They are friendly and beautiful," he said. "I've also brought a sack of coins to present to Camille's father. And some jewelry that Lucas gave to me. He gave me silk, too, for her mother. It's customary to offer sheep, but all of this is better. And if we don't have any wine left by the time we get there, they make their own. It's dandelion wine."

"Wine without grapes?" Nik asked.

"Yes, it tastes nothing like grape wine. I bet she knows how to make it, don't you, Brigit?"

"I do. But we will buy it from your new family."

"Thanks, Brigit. And Nik too. The family will think well of me showing up with the two of you."

Nik laughed, "You can stand up for yourself, Ikarus. You're a fine young man, no longer a quivering lad."

Ikarus and Brigit exchanged a glance. She got up and went over to check the mules. Ikarus saw her pull her maps from her satchel. Was she planning to throw them into the fire, or did she think they would magically make sense? He lay back on his blankets and gazed up at the stars. *It's wonderful to be out here again,* he thought. *Nothing can go wrong now.*

Nikolas and Brigit sat murmuring beside the fire long after Ikarus fell asleep. Brigit explained her plan to gather herbs along the way, and that choosing the yellow, gold, or white blooms may add an extra day or so to the trip. Nikolas didn't think Ikarus would mind. The more gifts they could take to Camille's village the better their welcome. He admired that Ikarus had thought to bring gifts. Well, Lucas had taken care of it.

As he and Brigit mounded the fire and nestled in their blankets, he wondered how old Gacheru was doing with the lanterns. The City of Dreams seemed so far away it was difficult to imagine that its inhabitants were real. Up here in the cool mountain air, under the sky overflowing with stars, Nikolas felt powerful and free. He wondered what creatures roamed beyond the fire's glow. Part of him hoped to return to the city with stories of mythical beasts and brave achievements, but also, he hoped they met only stalwart people who lived easily among the elements.

He looked forward to the vast scenic views ahead of them and to Ik's excitement when meeting Camille again. He mumbled goodnight to Brigit who didn't answer. He was glad she slept and had no inkling that as she lay quietly beside him, she couldn't stop thinking about the footprints she'd seen in the sand beside the stream. Flat, wide, bare feet. She knew of only one soul who walked that way.

Chapter 15

Irene settled back into her routine of walking to the apothecary shop for her special tea blend. Lucas usually accompanied her halfway before visiting the merchants that Nikolas had procured. The dealings with Julian were settled for now, and the merchant had already left the city.

In the early evening, Lucas, Alina, and the gray cat, named Shadow by Irene, followed Gacheru along the meandering streets, some in dappled afternoon light and others split down the middle with the final angles of afternoon sun. The shopkeepers pulled their wares inside and latched the shutters. "This is my favorite time of day," Lucas said. "I don't know why, but I enjoy watching them wrap up their wares and go inside to their supper. By the time the lanterns are all lit, the streets are mostly empty. The light glints off the cobbles. It is quiet."

"And then you are alone," Alina finished.

"Yes, as a boy I felt safe, and the city became mine."

"And there were no threats but darkness."

"I've never feared it. Do you, Alina?"

She shook her head. "I should, but I don't. Even that night, when I was looking for you in the rain and couldn't find my way back to

Uncle Vasil's house, it wasn't the darkness that frightened me but those who lurked in it."

"That kind of thing will never happen to you again, Alina. We walk together now."

"Yes, we certainly do. And what of Seppo, Lucas? Have you told Irene about his secrets?"

"No, I haven't even told Seppo that I know. He knows I know, but we didn't actually discuss the situation. For now, I suppose we put it away from our minds. I have more answers than I ever thought I would."

Gach glanced back at them with a wry smile as he turned down a narrow, twisting street.

"It's difficult to remain inconspicuous in this section," Alina said.

"He knows we follow, so there is no chance he will miss a lamp or steal a lantern. Let's go to Le Cameé for wine and bread," Lucas said.

"I don't mind walking around, but I understand why you don't want to do it anymore, Lucas." Alina said taking his hand as they turned away from Gacheru.

"It's a younger man's work."

"And for you, it was a lonely man's work," Alina remarked. She reached up to brush his hair away from his cheek so she could place a kiss there.

Lucas stopped and clasped both her hands. They gazed steadily into each other's eyes. "This extraordinary gift of love we share grows stronger when we spend time alone together." He kissed the top of her head. "The evenings are pleasant for walking sometimes, but not always. And my days are busy without Nikolas here, but I'd rather sit with you beside the fire and wait for Irene's supper."

Alina laughed as she stepped through the iron gate into the courtyard dining house. "I enjoy the evenings together in the boarding house also, and the courtyard garden is as lovely as the Grande Inn."

They took their seats at a secluded, candlelit table. "Tiny in comparison, but charming. There is good soil at your Boulevard home garden, Alina. Unkempt as it is now, we will tend it together."

"Yes, it needs nurturing, Lucas." Alina picked up her wineglass and then set it down abruptly.

"What is it, lovely?"

"I . . . it's . . . well . . ." She blushed. "I just realized that I don't know how to cook. How will we manage on our own in that big house?"

Her eyes were wide and confused. Lucas realized she had quite startled herself with this revelation. "Well, I hadn't thought of those details."

"Neither had I!"

"Someone will be able to show you, won't they? Irene or one of the girls, Carissa. We will start cooking lessons right away, and I will learn also. It can't be difficult. I've seen Brigit prepare food or some semblance of it. Wentworth and Bernard even." Lucas gazed into the distance imagining them enjoying their simple farm life.

Alina beamed her girlish smile bringing Lucas back from Arcana. "It seems we don't even have to try to behave like children. Well, speaking for myself, I don't." She reached for his hand across the table. "Are you disappointed?"

Lucas laughed. "That you don't cook? I must confess, Alina, that first day I met you in the street my thoughts were only about how well you might cook!" Now, they both laughed, and Lucas refilled their glasses. "After this, we will go home and enjoy one of Irene's wonderful stews and save our concerns for cooking until another day."

On the way back to the boarding house they strolled past Alina's house. Right away, Lucas realized the ivy was broken. Someone had clearly climbed to the second-floor window. Not wanting to alarm Alina, he suggested, "Let's walk around the back and peruse the garden." By the light of a single hand lantern, they discussed what to plant and where to place a bench and the candles. By the time they left, Lucas felt certain the house was empty. He would have to wait until tomorrow to find out if whoever had made the climb had gotten inside.

Before Alina awoke in the morning, Lucas slipped from their warm bed. He found Irene in the kitchen serving tea and bread to the boarders. Lucas enjoyed his breakfast standing near the great fireplace so he and Irene could murmur to each other away from their guests. He explained his concerns about the broken ivy. Irene suggested he take Mr. Pagett with him because he didn't have Brigit to tell him how to restore the ivy.

"What do you think about those two?" Irene whispered and pointed toward a young lady and her male escort.

"I don't know. What do you think about them?" Lucas asked. "I can only see their backs from here. A girl and her father."

"Hmm, not likely, the way he looks at her, like a hungry wolf. A father or brother wouldn't behave so lasciviously. I don't know if he's her husband," Irene clucked her tongue, but they took only the one room."

"Maybe he's not her father, brother, or her husband," Lucas teased.

"It's scandalous!" Irene blurted out, fanning herself. "I suppose I sound like an old fish wife, don't I?"

"You said it, not me," Lucas squeezed her shoulder. "How long are they staying?"

"They're not even sure," Irene hissed. "Seems they laid about too long and missed their ship."

"A scandal indeed! What are their names and from where do they come?"

"Mr. Plimpton." Irene said.

"Nothing more. No name for the girl?"

Irene pulled Lucas closer so she could whisper in his ear. "Mr. Plimpton, from far and away. That's what he wrote in the register."

Lucas observed the couple. "I thought we were going to be more careful who we let stay after Dugald."

"I was careful. Mr. Plimpton has a letter stating that he is an emissary for Lord Brimley of Ingleena."

"Oh, Lord Brimley. Well of course," Lucas said giving a little bow.

"I don't know who he is either," Irene admitted.

"Ask Alina. I'm sure she can entertain you and the ladies of this boarding house with tales of Lord Brimley and his protégé, Mr. Plimpton or whoever he calls himself. I must go. If Alina awakes before I return, please distract her with your gossip. I don't want her to concern herself about the Boulevard house. Her father intended it to be a place of repose for her. And so far, it has not fulfilled that assignment. I'd wager that by the time I return, the mystery of this clandestine rendezvous will be resolved."

"We shall do just that," Irene said with a wink.

The apothecary took along with Lucas and him a young boy who helped in his shop. He climbed easily up the timbers and stones and pushed the broken ends of ivy into the mortar. Mr. Pagett assured him the ivy would refurbish itself quickly and that it was possible the wind had broken the ivy. But Lucas decided they would delay moving in, as he was certain Brigit would advise.

Afterward, Lucas unlocked the door and the three of them went through the house to be sure all was in order. He noticed nothing missing but nailed all the windows shut anyway. Lucas explained to his companions that Alina was hesitant to live here since she'd used it as a hideaway, and it was full of sadness and confusion. "Remove the gloomy drapery," Mr. Pagett suggested.

"Excellent suggestion. This house should not sit empty much longer." Lucas said. "I need time to help Alina make preparations to move in."

"I have a small cart and donkey," Mr. Pagett said. "I can follow Gacheru along the lantern route."

"I'd like to come along," the boy piped in.

"Maybe sometimes," Mr. Pagett said, "but I thought I would invite, Irene, er, Mrs. Kempel to accompany me. What do you think, Lucas? A young handsome man as yourself should be at home with your new wife in the evenings."

Lucas hesitated to respond. He wondered if he should agree since the offer seemed based upon Irene consenting to the plan. "Well, I would like very much to take you up on that, but only if Irene agrees of her own will."

"Of course, Lucas. Irene enjoys my company more than she lets on. I think she will appreciate getting away from the kitchen and the endless cooking."

"I hadn't thought of that. Never mind though, we have Carissa and Perina, they cook. You must keep a keen eye on this house." Lucas regarded Mr. Pagett with sympathy. He would probably never get what he actually wanted from Irene. She enjoyed her independence and would never marry again. He couldn't imagine her riding in a donkey cart either.

"I will guard this house," Mr. Pagett promised, and the two men shook hands. As if he'd read Lucas' mind, he added, "The cart is fancy with cushioned seats and backrest."

"I can guard this house too," the boy offered.

"All right but only in the daylight hours. And if you notice anything amiss run for help. Most of all remember, I know your mother and father and you will be home safe in your cottage by dusk," Lucas said. "Your time will come to roam the streets, lad. For now, stay close to your mother at night."

The boy rolled his eyes. Lucas guessed he was not more than ten years old. "The safety of a warm hearth should never be taken for granted." He took some coins from his pocket. "I appreciate your assistance today. When Alina and I begin work on the garden, you can help us again. For now, take these coins and go home."

Lucas and Mr. Pagett strolled to the boarding house together, each immersed in his own thoughts. Lucas guessed that Mr. Pagett was planning his invitation for Irene to ride out in his fancy cart. His own thoughts were about the Boulevard house. He felt it desired occupancy. Three weeks should be enough time to wait for the ivy to reestablish itself, and they could move in. By then, Nikolas, Brigit and Ikarus would be back. Ikarus could take a few days to show Camille around the City of Dreams and then resume his duties. Brigit would make sure the new garden was planted with harmonious flowers and herbs.

He left Mr. Pagett in the parlour to seek out Irene and then bounded up the stairs to tell Alina they would be spending the evening in. One of their private bedchamber picnics was in order.

* * *

Drusy had grown so comfortable at the boarding house that she had completely forgotten that her frowsy brother existed. So, when she overheard Mr. Pagett telling Irene that he was doing a sufficient job and that she and he would be his guardians for a while she was overjoyed. Later that afternoon, as the sun made its escape from an exceptionally sweltering day, she slipped in the back door of the smithy and stuffed the remains of her belongings in a gunny sack. There was no reason to remain any longer behind the shabby curtain. Irene had given her a permanent room! From remnants in the crusty pot, it appeared that Gach had managed to fix himself some gruel, but the layers of grime revealed that he hadn't bothered to clean it between meals. Soon the sludge would run over the top. He'd need to forge himself a chisel if he wanted to eat again.

The thought made her laugh so hard that tears ran down her plum-colored cheeks. She picked through the rest of his belongings with one hand while the other pinched her nose closed. She hurried, lest the stench from his discarded clothes permeate her freshly washed hair. How had she ever lived in such a repugnant place? Squatting down to take a quick peek under his sagging cot, she pulled out an oil-stained sack. New skeleton keys? she wondered. But to her surprise the sack contained a silver hairbrush and mirror, and along with those women's implements, a silver tea set with a tray that was so heavy she could barely lift it.

Her good mood now ruined, she shoved the sack back under the cot. The items came from the Boulevard house she was certain. She would report him immediately to Lucas. But as she made her way back to the boarding house with her small satchel of old clothes, she changed her mind. They needed Gach to light the lanterns, or her new life as a respectable house maid would fall apart. Maybe Alina wouldn't even notice those things were missing, at least not until she and Lucas moved in.

Drusy would monitor him herself. He couldn't be so ignorant to rob anymore, not from that house. And if he did, she would find a way to make him stop. She didn't have time to follow him in the evenings. The others were doing that, although not very well it appeared. She'd have to make regular trips to the blacksmith shop to snoop. He repulsed her even more now, but following her worthless brother was worth it to protect this new life she'd stumbled into: her own little room with a spacious bed and crisp linen sheets, in a warm house with meat and vegetables to eat at every supper. And although she was older than Carissa and Perina, they accepted her. Carissa had promised that the next time they took an evening to themselves to go out in the city she could join them. Her eyes misted at the thought.

The girls shared secrets with her. None of them especially important, women issues mostly and secret hopes that certain young men had noticed them. Drusy didn't have any secrets that she could or would share. The girls were polite and didn't ply her with questions. They assumed she had the same hopes and dreams they did. Maybe now with her new life upon her the day would come when she had an admirer of her own.

She found plenty to chat about. Even though it wasn't possible for her to tell them things about herself, she could gossip about who she saw at market and those kinds of things. Having friends was new to her, but she very much enjoyed the feeling of inclusion. Even Irene was nothing but kind to her. Drusilla believed she would absolutely die if they ever found out about the misdeeds of her brother and herself too. But there was a difference. Gach gained satisfaction from his own evil nature. He ate up meanness like food. She, though, was actually good inside. It wasn't her fault evil had sought her out in the past.

Chapter 16

Just after dawn, Brigit slipped from the warmth of the blankets and crept around the campsite in search of tracks. Nikolas, Ikarus and she were in a lush little valley resplendent with tall grass, abundant wildflowers, and the echoed tones of a gurgling stream. She lifted a single layer of skirt and began to fill it with specimens of the flowers and herbs. Many she remembered from her childhood, but not all.

Absorbed in the glorious morning and unexpected, pleasant memories, she forgot about the footprints until returning to their encampment. But now, the prints she'd noticed last night were stamped out by the mules' hoof prints. Quietly, before Nik and Ik awoke, she sorted her plant treasures into separate twill pouches and then placed them carefully side by side in the morning sun.

She searched each side of the muddy stream bank. The mules twitched their ears and followed her movements with their large brown eyes but didn't seem eager to begin climbing again. As far as she could tell, there were no more footprints. None that she could find before the men awoke anyway. Sitting up, Ikarus looked confused.

Brigit laughed as he rolled from his tangled blankets. "You forgot where you were," she teased.

"I did! To wake up and see sky instead of walls, I'd forgotten how that feels." He stumbled to the stream and plunged his entire head in. When he emerged, he shook like a dog and howled, "That's cold!"

Nikolas, standing with his hands on his hips, exclaimed, "I never slept so well. This grass is spongey, softer than feathers."

In spite of her wariness, Brigit had to agree. Once she had finally fallen asleep, she had descended into the welcoming folds of restful oblivion that only children enjoy. They shared a breakfast of porridge boiled in spring water and then made ready to go.

Brigit thoughtfully packed the flowers and herbs in layers inside her basket. This slender valley provided everything that they needed for their brief time here. It was comforting now to remember the times with her tribe in places exactly like this.

But the footprints alarmed her. It was him who'd forced her to leave and go live among people in the city. That horrible man, a demon, or whatever he was. If not for that creature, she would still be roaming these foothills. Of course, she would never have encountered Nikolas or Irene or even met Lucas, her own nephew, but she was not like them and never could be. She had tried over the years to be somewhat normal. Still, she stood out, and she knew it and had found a way to make her unusual talents help her survive.

At first, she used her powers to trick others into believing she could help them with their dreary and tiring lives. And that was all it took. Even when some came who were beyond help, she promised them all was well, that their afflictions were temporary. As the days passed, and people continued to come, she made promises and predictions. Her words flowed easily. Soon, even she began to believe what she said, especially when her predictions began to come true. "Life is magical," she pronounced. And often it was. Sometimes, she did help others, a lot, and she delighted in their relief.

She began to make potions for her patrons based on things they told her. A soothing tea for one and an invigorating brew for another. Her memories and dreams guided her. She began to care very much about improving situations for individuals. Of course, there were circumstances when she couldn't help at all. She felt incapable in those cases and wanted to know why.

She began trading potions with peddlers and travellers and one wizened wanderer presented her with the crystal ball. There were answers for everything, but the answers differed for every person. Brigit still didn't fully understand from where her gifts flowed, but the more she used them the stronger they became. All she did know for certain was that the world of nature constantly called to her.

Even in the City of Dreams, the back alleys and mossy arched bridges lured her to the outer edges of the civilized world. The voices she heard in the wilds calmed her, taught her, and even reassured her she was in the right place to do her work. Often times, she sought out citizens, without asking for pay, to warn them of impending danger. She'd never intended to leave the wildland, but that vile wizard had driven her away. He forced her into exile where she carried her gift to those who needed her. In the City of Dreams, she felt safe.

But they were in his territory now. She would never forget he had attacked her mother, viciously and violently, and she and Linny had seen the whole thing. That's why Linny left first. Lucas didn't need to know that. He had not asked about any other members of the family, and hopefully he never would. She wouldn't tell him. He didn't need to hear about everything that transpired before his birth. A bright blue butterfly landed on the back of her hand and broke her reverie.

The men waited rather impatiently astride their mules. "Are you ready now?" she japed.

"Just about," Nikolas said with a grin. Ikarus took the lead, and Nikolas, giving Brigit a calming nod, fell in behind him. It was a lovely place, but they would probably not stop here on the way back. It seemed that somehow Ikarus had led them into her own forbidden ground. Of course, she couldn't be sure. She had drawn the maps in part hoping to avoid sites from the past.

Glancing around one last time, she noticed a spectral shape emerge from the tree line and rush up the hill to cover her two companions in shade. There were no clouds in the sky. The silhouette was in the shape of a thick man in baggy trousers, and square-shaped hat. The tree wizard man, she and Linny had called him. Nobody knew his real name, and everyone feared him. Wherever they went, he lurked in the trees in the dale.

She held her breath until the apparition dissipated. Dappled sunlight burned its way through the gloom without the men noticing anything at all. Did she conjure him up, she wondered, or had his pervasive malevolence permeated these enchanting hills.

By evening, they had travelled far enough for Brigit to believe she had been there many times before as a young girl and also not ever at all ever. Exhausted from the good and bad memories that besieged her all day, Brigit brought her plodding mule to a halt. Nik and Ik jabbered about the infinite views they had experienced. Sharp craggy rocks rose in the sky above them. Brigit pulled her wineskin from the saddlebag and went over to a patch of grass that had been tamped down by sheep. She lay down flat on her back. Nikolas came and squatted beside her. "You will tell me if anything is troubling you."

"Of course," she said cupping his cheek in her hand. "All is well now. Today was a day of reminiscence, but tomorrow, all will be new to me."

"Ik and I will lay the fire and cook the broth. Enjoy your wine and the earth." Nikolas leaned over and kissed her cool forehead.

She clasped his hand. "I'm surprised at how much you understand me," she said. "Especially in this land that is so foreign to you."

He nodded slowly and swept one arm outward, "In this vast land, I see how it must have been for you as a young girl." Nikolas took a moment to smooth her hair down along her shoulders. When he went over to help Ikarus, who was blowing the fire into orange spires, she closed her eyes. By the time Nikolas sat next to her offering a bowl of broth and dried meat with stale bread for dipping, it was nighttime. The stars were so close she reached out a hand and let it drop to Nik's shoulder.

In the morning, they set out anew, crossing over two pastures before coming upon a large flock tended by two boys many years younger than Ikarus. One of the lad's had blonde hair like Ikarus' while the other had hair as black as Brigit's. Their skin was tanned as well. They were shy and wary but answered the many questions the three had for them. Where was the closest village, did they know the family of Camille or Ikarus, and had they any cheese to sell? The lads didn't know the families, but they drew lines in the dirt and pointed to the cliffside villages, one more day's walk. They were proud to sell some of their delicious, soft cheese.

The excitement grew for Brigit, Nikolas, and Ikarus now that they had encountered at least two of the very people they sought. Ikarus and Brigit were both secretly relieved to have those who knew the paths point the way for them. They stopped often and collected wild onions, sorrel, cattail, purslane, and mallow. On occasion, the trails were so steep and narrow they dismounted and led their mules over the rocky terrain. Brigit felt better as they climbed above the tree line.

"If you spot a hare, Nik, take it. I can make a stew with all that we've gathered," Brigit said cheerfully.

"I've noticed many. Let's choose a spot and stop early. The mules can use the rest after these precipitous paths."

Ikarus agreed. "We should relax and eat well tonight. There are many creeks and streams around. I will wash myself in case we find Camille tomorrow."

Brigit laughed and asked Ikarus, "Does this land look familiar?"

"Yes, it all does. I expect to see my irascible father lumbering along the trail any minute."

"He'll be glad to see you," Nik said, and Ikarus shrugged.

Brigit motioned to a wide flat outcropping alongside a tinkling creek. "This spot looks alluring. We have all we need. We can view the trail above and the valley below." Ikarus gathered sticks for the fire, and Nik promised to return quickly with a hare. Kneeling by the creek, Brigit filled the pot and thought about which roots she could add to the porry that wouldn't be too stringy. For many years, she vowed never to return to this land, but right now she was delighted that she did. In this moment, her concerns and misgivings gave way to the tranquil beauty of the landscape.

Sitting on stones around the fire, the men ate their meal as if they enjoyed it and they all finished the last of their wine in anticipation of reaching a village the following afternoon.

"Tell us more about your family, Ik," Nikolas implored.

Ikarus shook his head, chewed, swallowed, gazed away as if perplexed. Finally, he began to speak in a soft voice. "My mother is kind. She works hard but sings as she does. I have one sister, and she is similar to my brother. They look alike, their hair and skin are as dark as our father. I'm the only pale-haired one, except my mother had golden hair I'm told. As long as I've known her, it's been gray. She's tired but doesn't complain, not like my father who can't speak without complaining and swearing. He favors my older brother over me. They are both proud of themselves. For what, I do not know."

Abashed, Brigit said, "Oh, that's why you didn't go back."

Ikarus tossed a handful of sticks into the fire. "That's another reason why. I go now only for Camille. When we reach this first village, we must ask everyone if they know her. Maybe we don't have to go to my village." He pulled on his empty wineskin and tossed it aside.

Nikolas and Brigit exchanged disconcerted glances. "Don't you want to see your mother after coming this far?" Nik asked.

"Well, I'd like to make her come with us. But she won't, so . . . I don't know. I would like Camille to meet her, yes." A smile flashed across his face, and then he squinted and gazed up the mountain. "Should we go there and try to convince my mother after we find Camille?"

"Of course, we should." Brigit handed him her wineskin. "There's a wee draught in there, lad."

"Thanks." He sucked on the wineskin. "I suppose you're both right. We've come all this way and I don't want to go back without hugging my mother again." He smiled to himself, "Maybe she'll come with us when she sees that I will have a wife. I can take care of them both. And Camille will enjoy the company of one of her own."

Brigit nodded. "All right then." She hoped her words were not misleading. Nikolas looked as if he would say something encouraging but knitted his brow and crossed his arms instead.

In the morning, they resumed the climb, Brigit riding ahead on the brown mule that was taller and more acclimated than the two grays. Peering ahead toward the bend in the switch backing trail, she thought for an instant that she saw a caravan up ahead. Her hair spun outward alerting the others. "What is it?" Nik shouted from behind Ikarus.

She kneed the mule, and braying in protest, it darted forward. It was a gypsy caravan of three horses pulling plank carts and four mules hauling two brightly painted, intricately carved vardos.

Excitement and dismay simultaneously roiled in her stomach. Turning to them, she ordered, "We wait here until they approach us."

The eldest man held up a hand, whether it was in greeting or warning, Brigit couldn't be sure, as she courteously dismounted. She counted six men, seven women and eleven children of varying ages. The men and boys were dressed in hand-cut, ashy colored woolen trousers and tunics. The women and girls wore long frocks with bright red and green sashes tied around their waists. The necklines and hems were embroidered with tiny edelweiss. Both groups stood and stared for what felt to Brigit like endless minutes.

Ikarus murmured, "It doesn't appear they have wine." Slapping her hand over her mouth, Brigit muffled a chortle. Finally, a small girl broke from her mother's firm grip on her shoulder and ran toward them. Brigit smiled grandly as she instinctively opened her arms to the child. One of the men nodded.

Holding the girl's hand, Brigit walked toward the girl's mother. Nikolas and Ikarus followed her. Brigit stroked the girl's silken hair and beamed at her mother. The other children ran their hands along her skirts, and examined her shoes, clothes, and bracelets. The heaviness in the air eased.

When the chieftain approached, the women stood back murmuring among themselves. After the men greeted each other with clasped forearms, Brigit explained that she and Ikarus hailed from the region and that they were travelling to a certain village to locate his future wife. Everyone nodded in appreciation and the mood eased even more.

A few of the women sneaked shy smiles toward Ikarus. With much gesturing and pointing, the man explained to Brigit which of several paths that they were soon to encounter in the woods ahead led to a village of fair-haired people. It was one of many, the chieftain told Ikarus and advised that if they didn't locate the correct village, then

Ikarus should find a wife where he landed. The gypsy men found this comment overtly amusing, so Ikarus laughed along with them. Brigit and Nikolas tugged the mules off the trail and let the caravan pass.

"That was interesting," Nik said. "I didn't really believe those people lived out here."

Brigit and Ik snickered at him. "Where did you think our Madam Trousdale comes from?" Ik prodded. "She is not just the stuff of whimsy."

"She's certainly not," Nik blushed. "I know it, but it's a bit unnerving to see for myself though. I never expected to. Was it like that, Brigit, in your caravan?"

"I could have been one of those young girls," she said. "My sister Linnea too."

"People are such mysterious creatures," Nik declared. "In those few minutes, I learned very much more about you, Brigit."

"Does it help explain her uncanny habits to meet people of her kind?" Ik teased.

"People of our kind," Brigit corrected. "It's your turn to cook tonight, Ik," Brigit ordered.

"That would be something we all regret," he said with a groan. They trudged upward leading the mules so the animals and themselves could stretch their stiff legs.

The trail led away from the steep ledges through a verdant pasture, where they stopped to gather plants, and then into a dense forest with thorny dead underbrush. Almost immediately they were lost. Brigit had stopped to investigate the darting figures she'd seen on both sides of the trail. Nik and Ik, thinking she wanted them to lead, plodded on until Nikolas reined in. He threw up his hands. "There's six different trails now."

They waited for Brigit to catch up. "What do we do?" Ik asked. "Which trail did the gypsy say?" Brigit's hair turned red and swirled straight up, and her eyes went from blue to black and back again. When her hair settled back into black silk, Nikolas suddenly remembered that he'd once walked past her in the street when something must have angered her, and her hair went red. He hadn't recognized her at all.

"Oh no," Ik said. "Damn all. I really wanted wine tonight."

Brigit stroked her chin with her long-fingered hand. She cleared her throat, "Listen, he said to take the middle path."

"All right," Nikolas said guiding his mule forward.

"But I don't think we should."

Nik turned and raised his eyebrows at her.

"I think I recognized one of those young men back there." She pulled out her claw necklace, combed her hair and sneaked a peek at the hourglass.

"You did? How?" Nik exclaimed. Ikarus glanced at Nikolas and rolled his eyes before clutching his forehead with both hands.

"The barefoot one," she said softly.

Nik shrugged. "I didn't notice their feet."

"Come closer," she murmured. When the two of them flanked her, she explained. "When I was a child up here, there was an old man, a wizard, a Mumblecrust really. He followed the caravans from the woods to the dale. Some offered him bribes to go away, which he accepted, but he always came back. A greedy hateful creature, he was. He had bought himself a wife with stolen goods they say. That poor sad woman." She shook her head, and a noticeable shiver ran through her. "His family dwelt in a forest much like this one. That man took from others in despicable ways. Evil eked from him. He deserved his punishment. I remember his leathery peeling skin. My sister, Linny," she glanced at the two of them for emphasis, "said he looked like a dying yew tree. But he refused to die on his own, aged as he was."

She envisioned, as she often had, the night he attacked her mother. Her fists clenched, and her hair struck outward. Brigit waited for the moment to pass and turned away from their stricken faces without relaying to them the details of that unspeakable incident.

Wishing to avoid hearing whatever she said next, Ikarus moved away. Nikolas sighed uneasily. "So, you did something?"

She frowned and then sneered. "I poisoned his grandson. That one back there."

"The one you just recognized?" Ikarus gasped.

"Yes, him. I see it didn't work."

In truth, she hadn't intended to kill the lad, only subdue him in order to retrieve the hourglass. Her mother had removed it only once in the hours after the attack. Brigit and Linnea helped her mother scrub herself with sand until her skin was red. In those few moments when they cleaned and comforted their mother, they had all been taken advantage of again. Brigit gazed beyond the tree trunks into the past. She spoke coolly, "That boy stole the treasured hourglass while we cleaned and comforted our mother! He had the audacity to wear it. It was made for my mother by a seer as a talisman for guidance and protection.

"There were twin brothers," she said with a deep breath. "One was a good and pure man. He was my tribe's chieftain. The other, the wicked one, had been banished before I was born. Our chieftain wouldn't kill his despicable brother, although many entreated him to. The evil one burned with jealously and resentment. He coveted all women, but mostly my mother we found out. The tribe protected its women and children, but he was cunning, and sometimes he slipped into our camp undetected."

A shudder went through her. She went on to explain in a hushed voice about the stolen hourglass and her effort to retrieve it. She described how her mother had been attacked by the foul one, but in the telling she left out the extreme violence of it all. And the others never knew. Brigit and Linnea had sworn to keep their mother's gruesome secret.

As she spoke, the sting of her own words made her stutter, and she abruptly attempted to conclude the story. "Those were dark days that should be left in the past lest we invoke the bad spirits of these woods." However, the blank faces of Ikarus and Nikolas compelled her to go on.

"Linny said we had to flee after our mother's attack. I followed her later as you know, but for several weeks I stayed. One day, I got my chance. I spent weeks all by myself hiding in the thick trees. When my chance finally came for the only revenge I could manage, I dosed the boy and snatched my mother's hourglass back. I hoped the wizard tree man would spend his days in torment knowing that his grandson no longer possessed the gift of insight and protection." The two men stared. She'd said too much. They didn't understand the ways of her people, or the innate fears of women. "One must take their own revenge. This is our belief. That's all."

"All right, well, I don't think he recognized you." Nikolas said. "Why did you wait so many hours to tell us this stuff? Let's just get out of these dark woods. Come on. Ikarus is thirsty for wine. And after that story, I am too."

"Someone was dead. I saw the body wrapped and rolled." Realizing she'd spoken out loud, she threw her hand over her mouth. This time in a barely audible whisper, she muttered, "The lad drank the potion. He lay on the ground completely still. He was dead. I didn't wait to think too much about it. I did what I intended to do and easily recovered my mother's hourglass. But in my haste, I left my chalice behind."

"What?" Nik shook his head. "We don't know what you're talking about, Brigit."

"You're not listening to what I'm trying to tell you. If the grandson died, then why is he roaming the hillsides? I didn't expect to see him! I have always feared the grandfather, the horrible tree wizard man. He is the one who would want to come after me for revenge. I wanted him to suffer for what he did. He harmed my mother, destroyed her body and soul. In return I destroyed one of his own. My chalice that held the potion was sitting upright on the hard ground. He might have recognized it as mine. The concern was never that he would come down the mountain. He never followed the caravan when we travelled down there. But I have walked into his territory now. Someone is following us. The lad should be dead. You two saw him, I know you did."

She covered her face with her palms. "Now that we're here, I recall too many things, bad memories from this land." She glanced at Nikolas. "It's beautiful, yes. But for some of us, it's forbidding as well."

"He doesn't know who you are," Nik insisted. "Body rolled where? I don't want to hear these phantastic tales."

"Nik's right," Ikarus said. "If that man is the grandson, and he knew it was you, wouldn't he have just clobbered you over the head just now and been done with it?"

"We roll our dead into a crevice, or off one of these cliffs. A stone tomb." Her voice trembled with a fear that quickly infected her companions.

Nikolas reached for her mule's bit and pulled. "Let's get out of this forest. We don't even know which lad you are referring to anyway. There were several young men standing around. They greeted us amiably. If he, the grandson, or the wizard comes for you, we will all deny everything. Right, Ik? Pretend you're someone else. We'll call you Mairy. How does that sound?"

Brigit smoothed her hair down with both hands. "Very well, if that's what you want to do. Let's go. But someone does follow us. I saw a dark figure just now lurking among the trees."

They rode on in silence. Ikarus was dejected now. He had looked forward to the village that may have word about Camille, fresh bread, and wine. Who knew where they would end up? He realized that wherever they stopped for the night there wouldn't be any wine.

Chapter 17

Just before dusk, Mr. Pagett pulled up in front of the boarding house in his stylish cart. It was painted black and tan to match the amiable donkey, and the seat was indeed padded with overstuffed red cushions. Irene, who had foregone her afternoon tea for a goblet of red wine, plopped into the seat next to the nervous apothecary like she'd been waiting for this very occasion. As they clomped away, Lucas slipped his arm around Alina's shoulders. "Perhaps he will allow us to borrow it some evening."

Alina grinned. "I would go. I'm sure it's about to become the newest fashion for moving about the city."

Carissa and Perina served the boarders supper while Drusy folded linens in the scullery. Seated at the table sipping wine with Alina, Lucas noticed Drusilla hummed while she worked. He was glad for the poor woman. She wasn't old yet, maybe a few over thirty years, but he could tell she had seen her share of grief. Unlike her brother, she was very tidy and thorough.

Lucas wondered how things went with Ikarus and the others up in the mountains. It had been three nights since their departure, and it seemed possible that they could have reached Camille's village by now. There was no way of knowing, of course. He could only hope that they would return soon. Alina watched the two new boarders who sat at the far end of the guest table, keeping a distance from the masons and laborers. The girl nodded absently as the man spoke. "She's bored to death," he whispered to Alina who covered her mouth and giggled.

Lucas got up, carried the wine jug over to them, and poured for the girl but not the man. Her face lit briefly, before settling back into a pervading woe. She seemed to have nothing to say herself, or maybe she just didn't have a chance to speak. The man only stopped jabbering long enough to shove food into his mouth. The girl picked at her food but finished her wine and refilled her glass.

Carissa handed Lucas the basket for their chamber picnic. As he and Alina climbed the stairs, he asked her if she knew of Lord Brimley.

"I know of him. He's a pompous heir to some ill-gotten fortune."

Lucas snickered, "So there actually is someone with that name. His so-called emissary sitting there seems to take after him."

"I agree. She must be his daughter, the girl. Don't you think so? I can't imagine anything else," Alina said. She held the bedchamber door open for Lucas. He stepped through and set the basket on the table by the window.

Taking her into his arms, Lucas said, "We can forget about everyone else for a while."

Irene and Mr. Pagett trotted around the city doing their best to follow Gacheru. Some of the passages were too narrow for the donkey cart, but they managed to work their way around and greet him at the other end. Even grumpy Gach managed a chuckle at their antics.

He finished his work without pilfering anything. After he handed over the tools to Carissa at the back door and received a few coins, he headed to the Duck Tavern. A few pints might help him come up with a plan to shake off his guards. This opportunity would last only a little while before Ikarus returned. He needed to stash as many goods and merchandise as he could. "Get it while the getting's good," he always said to himself. And after all his demanding work, Drusilla had better come home and make herself useful again.

In the morning, Lucas left Alina in the kitchen with Irene who described the evening following Gacheru around the city in the donkey cart as a grand adventure. She was eager to go again. It pleased Lucas that she was enjoying herself and it was helpful as well, given the situation.

In the afternoon, Lucas, Alina and Perina would meet at the Boulevard house to begin preparations for their move. There was cleaning to do and furniture to rearrange or give to the disadvantaged. Now, though, Lucas went to meet merchants for business.

The summer days were long and luxurious. Over his gossamer white shirt, he wore a black jerkin with a small pocket for the watch Alina had given him. He'd usually calculated time by the position of the sun. Now, every time he checked the gold watch he thought of Alina, and his heart warmed. He no longer carried the black lace veil for fear of losing it. It hung now from the mirror in their bedchamber.

After concluding his business, he left the square and headed toward the monastery. He carried fresh flowers for his mother's grave. When he arrived, he noticed that the secret cemetery was carefully tended. Seppo was not allowing even one decaying flower to remain there. The double doors to his sanctuary were open. Lucas called out and then strolled in. Seppo paced with his hands clasped behind his back. Noticing Lucas, he gestured for him to sit. "Thanks for coming."

Surprised, Lucas asked, "Were you expecting me?"

"Yes," Seppo blinked. "Shouldn't I be?" Confused Lucas accepted a golden goblet of water from his father. "You have more questions," Seppo stated.

"Yes, many. I was just now wondering where you get your supplies, food, and such?"

"I care for the small vegetable garden myself. We had a larger garden before and gathered fish in those days. Once the city built itself up around us, we went to market hidden in cloaks. Some days, I still do. Nobody notices me. I enjoyed going on my own late in the afternoon when you started your rounds, but since your nuptials, some of the devout and curious citizens bring baskets of food and leave it at the cathedral for me. More than I need. I don't eat much."

"I see that," Lucas said. "Did you say you noticed me on my rounds lighting lanterns?"

"No, I was saying that I followed you. Often, not always."

"You followed me?" Lucas looked surprised.

Seppo smiled and nodded. Lucas slowly shook his head. "I had no idea."

"Of course, you didn't."

"Normally I would notice something like that. Someone following me." Lucas narrowed his eyes. "It's hard to believe that I never saw you."

Seppo gave a slight nod. "Most people see what they want to see, or not."

"Hmm, now I'm going to try and mentally retrace my steps over the past few years. I should have felt someone following me." Lucas gazed curiously at his father. "Would you like to come live in the city? The boarding house, or, as Alina has mentioned, we have many rooms in her inherited home. We think you must feel quite lonely out here by yourself."

"Ah, well thank you, and Alina as well. I am simply fine here. I don't want to live among others. Even If I wanted to, I cannot. I keep vigil in the monastery."

"Oh," Lucas scratched at his chin. "We don't want . . . well, I don't know what the vigil is, or perhaps I do. What do you mean exactly?"

Seppo got up and walked to a wide window ledge. He crumbled some breadcrumbs there. "The birds would miss me. I have much to do here. I am where I belong. I have seen the world, Lucas, and it is not for me."

"I think I understand," Lucas said, "but you are welcome among us." He held up his hands and let them drop. "We thought we'd ask, Alina, Irene and me. So, then I wonder if you would tell me what you and the other monks did so long ago that forced you to leave your home and travel here?"

"We and those who came with us, suffered poverty, starvation, and ultimately blame for our former deeds. Damnation to be clear. Eternal damnation. We were forced to fight for our lives. People died."

"Did you kill someone?" Lucas asked calmly.

"I think we all did," Seppo said gazing through Lucas into the past. "We were just beggars, that's it. Beggars from birth. We lived without purpose." He gestured with an invisible arm inside his wide sleeve. "Here we found our purpose."

Lucas waited, their matching dark eyes regarding each other. Finally, Seppo stood and murmured, "It's finished."

Lucas had questions about the crypt hidden beneath the monastery. But understanding that his father would not speak about it, he pressed his lips together and got up. He reached out a hand. Seppo's cold fingers gripped Lucas' wrist so hard Lucas winced. "That's it then. You won't tell me anything more, and you don't want to come live with us."

"No and no again." Seppo shook his head. Noticing the helpless expression on Lucas' face, he added, "Think about it, my son. Nobody actually wants me hovering around. Not only that, but this is also my home. I have no desire to leave this peaceful sanctuary. Why do you think I waited all these years for you to find me? The time had to come on its own. And more times will come for us, here and there." He stood up and placed his hands on Lucas' shoulders. "Thank your people for me. I enjoy your visits. Go out there and live now."

Unable to think of anything else to say, Lucas simply hugged his father, turned, and stepped through the double doors into the brilliant summer day. The music of nature filled the warm air with a symphony of buzzing bees and singing birds. The sky appeared brighter and bluer than he'd ever seen it. The lush green grass carpeting the cemetery nearly devoured the old stones.

He knelt beside his mother's grave and whispered to her. "Something unspoken has kept this man alive all these years. He must have been old when you met him. Did he not seem so? What secrets did you not have time to tell me? I miss you still," he murmured as he placed his hands on the spongey grass and pushed himself up.

Lucas chose to take the long way home on the path through the mulberry trees, over the fallen log, and alongside the gloomy moat. He was in no hurry and had much to think about.

Irene and Alina awaited Lucas in the courtyard garden. The three of them strolled over to the Boulevard house where Mr. Pagett would meet them with two lads and a long cart to carry away to the needy extra items from the overstocked house. Alina had set aside several household items, pots, and plates for Irene to use at the boarding house. She and Irene selected a few items to give to Brigit and extra coverlets for Nikolas and Ikarus. The men finally finished loading the cart just after dusk.

After watching the others ride away in the over laden cart, Lucas and Alina meandered through the house. Lucas was relieved to see everything in order and the ivy out front looking vigorous again. "The house will be ready when our friends return from the high country," Alina said. "We will have a grand celebration!"

"Nikolas promised to bring highland whisky," Lucas said. "I must say it feels strange with the three of them gone."

"I think so too." Alina agreed. "I look forward to their return. I wonder what they're all doing right now. Whatever is, it must be wonderfully exciting for them!"

"I'm sure it is a most wonderful adventure," Lucas said as he locked the door. Glancing back at the house, he imagined the candles lit, a fire blazing, and their friends walking through the front door.

* * *

Gacheru, just picking up the lighting tools, noticed that they had all forgotten about him. This time he was glad they had. Each night he attempted to chat with Irene or the girls in the kitchen, but they rudely hurried him on his way.

And somehow Drusilla, that ungrateful woman, always managed to be out of sight. She could invite him into the kitchen for a cup of tea at the end of the evening, but she remained hidden. It had been several days since he'd seen her. Did it not occur to her to offer her dutiful brother a respite? Somehow, she'd managed to trick them into letting her stay at the boarding house. He wondered what kind of accommodations they'd given her. Probably a mat in the scullery. Or if she had Ikarus's chamber, she would surely lose it upon his return, and then she'd come skulking back to her cozy cot in the smithery.

He lit the lanterns leading away from the boarding house and then, changing the route, he headed directly to the house on the Boulevard. Weeks ago, he'd found it easy enough to follow Carissa there one afternoon. He wasn't as ignorant as they took him to be. If nobody were willing to help him, like they did Drusilla, he would just have to help himself.

Circling the house, he tried the doors and windows, but none opened for him. The ivy was already growing back, and he didn't want to risk the climb before full dark. Last time, his arms and legs ached for days afterward. Huddled at the back door, he decided to take one last chance. They might snap in pieces, but he reached into his deep pocket for his two remaining fake keys. He cursed Drusy for losing so many as he jammed two at once into the lock. He twisted slowly left, then right, and back again. Nothing happened. Pulling the iron handle toward him, he tried again. This time, to his amazement the lock gave way; the door hadn't been firmly closed. The rich feel safe everywhere, he grumbled to himself.

He quickly slipped inside and closed the door behind him. This would probably be the last time he could get in, so; he'd best make the most of it. They had already removed some large pieces of furniture, but the study was untouched. The girl, Alina would not remove her father's personal belongings he reasoned. The man must have used the house to store his excess belongings. How could anyone acquire so many things all in one place?

He knew all of the furniture was fine and valuable, but all of it was too large to haul out and sell. As he skulked through the house, Gacheru realized that Alina's father dealt in many goods. He bought and sold things. Just like himself. The only difference was the wealthy man conducted his business within the confines of the law.

An uneasiness settled over him, and he searched around for a bottle of whisky. After ignoring the glasses and swigging from the bottle, he took his time looking around. The lamp lads would keep lighting until he caught up with them. He didn't think they would notice his absence for a while since they mostly did their share of the work and avoided him. When he did encounter them in the amber glowing streets, they poorly hid their laughter and disdain. He crawled under the large mahogany desk, tapping, poking, and prodding. What wealthy man doesn't hide valuable items in his desk?

Drusilla was upstairs when they came in, but she recognized their voices. Nobody was following Gacheru! She hurried down the back stairs with an armful of linens. Lucas and Alina were happily slopping stew into bowls while Irene and Mr. Pagett sat at the table. Carissa and Perina had already finished for the day and gone out for their evening stroll. "Have you had supper, Drusilla?" Lucas asked. It took a moment before she understood that Lucas offered a place at the table. Her mouth fell open from surprise, not hunger.

She stammered, and finally managed to say, "Well, I had a little something earlier, but that smells delicious."

"We're learning how to cook," Alina giggled.

"Just set those clean linens in the cupboard and join us," Irene said as Mr. Pagett took another goblet off the shelf. Drusilla could barely breathe. She was invited to supper with the family. She couldn't possibly warn them about Gach now. Maybe somebody else followed him tonight she reasoned.

Sitting gingerly on the bench she accepted a bowl from Lucas as Alina filled her goblet. Irene passed a platter of warm bread. The red wine filled her veins with joy, and the stew calmed her nervous stomach. She chewed carefully so as not to slop any food on herself. She even accepted a small bowl of seconds and tried not to guzzle the wine. Her villainous brother could burn in hell for all she cared right now. She prayed he would not return the tools while they were seated at the table.

Irene poured a little more wine in Drusilla's glass. "If you would like to begin your shifts a little earlier, we could use your help with a few of the rooms. We all take care of our own chores, but Lucas and Alina are making preparations in their new home. Would you like to help with the firewood and water hauling for their bedchamber until they go?"

Another surprise for Drusy who nodded and glanced at Alina who gave her a friendly smile. "Of course," she murmured and stood to clear the bowls.

Squeezing her arm, Irene said, "Tomorrow then. We forgot about your brother this evening, but I suppose he managed on his own."

A regretful look crossed Lucas' face. "Don't worry," Mr. Pagett said. "I'll take a stroll about the city on my way home. If anything is amiss, I'll come right back and let you know."

"We appreciate your help with this and everything," Lucas said.

Irene bid Mr. Pagett good night at the front door, mumbled something about her nightdress awaiting her return, and went up the stairs to her bedchamber. Alina and Lucas took wine goblets outside to the courtyard garden where Lucas lit the candles. As soon as they sat down together on the bench, Shadow leapt from her hiding place among the greenery and curled up at their ankles.

Drusilla dreaded the thought and had no idea where exactly to start but wondered if she had better go out and check on Gacheru herself. She swept the ashes and banked the parlour fire. What could she do even if she found him drunk at the Duck and the lanterns only half lit?

The back door opened, and Drusy scooted behind the corner column. She heard him dropping off the tools and held her breath until he left. Even if he'd glanced into the parlour, the dim lighting offered cover. It seemed Lucas didn't hear Gach come or go. He was busy whispering what must be scintillating words to Alina, guessing by the look on her face.

After making sure the front and back doors were bolted, she waved goodnight to the two of them and retreated to the comfort and safety of her own small bedchamber. She pulled a light night gown over her head and splashed water onto her face. Gazing at her reflection in the oval mirror she couldn't help but notice that her brown hair shone from more frequent washings, and some of the weariness had left her face. She was not homely and useless as Gacheru claimed. Once Ikarus and the others returned, she would explain to Lucas that her brother couldn't be trusted. He would be sent away, and she would never have to feel ashamed of him or herself again. The wine and soft bed helped her drift swiftly to sleep.

Gacheru carried one small hand lantern to make his way over to the dark zone. He hoped his old mate was still huddled down over there and could help get this new treasure sold and out of the city. He avoided the huts still lit with candlelight or with doors hanging open. He kept to the shadows but couldn't bring himself to extinguish the lantern from fear of who might lurk in the dark pockets of these suspicious lanes. If anyone knew what he carried they'd cheerfully stab him for it, he was sure.

The smoke was so thick on this windless night he couldn't help but cough and spit. Soon, shrouded faces appeared in windows and a gravelly voice shouted, "Shut up!" A dog barked, and another growled and then yelped. He pressed on, walking sideways to watch his back as he went forward.

It wasn't long before he realized he was lost. Now, more huts seemed crouched together here. It had been a long time since he'd ventured this way, and he had never come at night before. He didn't dare stop walking. Three dogs trailed him. What good was his plunder if he couldn't sell it? He trod on, wishing he'd had patience enough to wait until daylight. Every little cottage looked the same. The only way to know which one housed his mate was to approach and call out or poke his head in a window. *I'd like to keep my head though*, he thought.

Frightened and confused, he decided that his quest was hopeless. He would have to return in the daylight when shadows didn't change the shape of things. Planning to walk straight back the way he'd come, he turned around. But up ahead, in front of a hut with dim light emanating from the only window, a stout figure stood watching him.

Gacheru darted sideways between two dark huts. When he came out on the next lane, the same figure was there blocking his way. He took a step forward. The burly man put his hands on his hips and made a growling sound. Fear bubbled up in Gach's throat. He turned and ran deeper into the dark zone, stumbling over discarded rubbish and slipping on slime. He kept going until he left the angry cottages behind and reached the canals. With his breath croaking out in intermittent rasps, he bent forward with his hands on his thighs and wheezed.

He stumbled over to an abandoned well and perched on its rim. The air was cool and smokeless. Crickets chirped. Glancing up, he noticed the stars peering down at him. For a fleeting moment, he felt a sense of wonder. It seemed he was the only one foolish enough to wander this far so late. It would be a long trudge back along the edge of the river and over the barely discernable canal bridges.

Gacheru swore at the world and everyone it. The crickets halted their serenade. Even though he was all alone, he kept his hat pulled low over his face as he picked his way back toward his cot in the back of the blacksmith shop. Why did the city let people live out there in those cottages? It wasn't right to put a bunch of thieves and murderers all in one place. When he made his fortune and became a respected citizen again, he'd have something to say about it.

Finally, he emerged unnoticed on the main road. Feeling the reassurance of the cobbles underfoot, he made his way back toward the square. Three dogs still followed him. Had they been there all along? He shivered and shouted and waved his arms. One bold mongrel darted in and nipped at his ankle. A swift kick sent it and the other two yipping into the night. They had a lot of nerve ushering him out of the dark zone. They could have that menacing place.

When Gacheru finally saw the lanterns up ahead, he broke into a lurching run. The lads had done their job without his assistance tonight. He slipped his hand into his pocket and cradled the gem-studded bracelet. Tonight, he would sleep with it safely hidden right there in his pocket.

The next morning, Drusilla made the tea and helped Perina knead dough. It wasn't part of her duties, but she enjoyed working in the large, clean kitchen. The boarding house felt like home. Once the boarders left for the day, she had nothing to do until the afternoon when she would help in Lucas and Alina's room. As much as she dreaded seeing her brother, she knew she needed to check on him.

As she meandered toward the blacksmith shop, she unpinned her hair and ruffled it a bit. She had dressed in her shabbiest work gown. She entered through the front door of the shop since she didn't live in the back room anymore and wanted to make a point of that. Two men swinging hammers sent sparks flying in all directions. She couldn't tell if they noticed her.

She made her way over the sagging boards and around the back of the blazing forge. Gacheru lay wheezing on his cot. His body was twisted sideways with one stocking foot atop a soiled blanket and one barefoot grazing the grimy floor. One arm was flung over his eyes, and a sparkling gold, ruby-studded bracelet dangled from his pocket. Drusy's breath caught in her throat and before she let it out, she was out the back door and clutching the bracelet in her clammy hand. What had he done?

The farther she got from the blacksmith shop the more she regretted taking the bracelet. She stopped, glanced around, and carefully slipped it into her cloth purse. She knew it had to belong to

Alina because it perfectly matched the ruby pendant. Since Drusilla had never seen Alina wear it, she had to assume she kept it in the Boulevard house. It didn't make sense though, unless her generous, deceased father had left it among his things for her to discover.

She hurried to the Boulevard house in hopes that she could get inside and stash the bracelet there. The doors were locked, the windows out of reach. Just as she decided she had no choice but to either return to the smithy and hopefully stuff the bracelet back in Gach's pocket before he awoke or report him to the constable, she saw Lucas and Alina coming down the tree-lined street. If they found out what Gacheru had done, her life at the boarding house would end. She darted to the side of the house and waited for them to enter. There she waited for a quarter of an hour before strolling up to the front door and knocking. The two of them opened it together and showed only mild surprise to see her there. "I was talking a walk in this lovely neighborhood and thought I might offer my assistance," she explained.

"How thoughtful of you, Drusilla," Alina said, stepping back so Lucas could open the door wide. Once inside Drusilla made an effort to hide her amazement at the elegantly appointed home. She had to think like Gacheru now and determine from where he had taken the necklace.

"I was about to go talk to Mr. Pagett about some plants for the garden. Would you mind keeping Alina company while she goes through her father's study?" Lucas flashed his charming smile. "You're timing is excellent."

"I'd love to," Drusy said thanking the heavens for her good fortunes of late. Lucas embraced and kissed Alina, winked at Drusilla, and went out the front door.

"I should have thought to ask you last night," Alina said. "I haven't gone through my father's personal belongings yet. When I stayed here for that time, I was too upset to look through the personal items he kept in this study."

Two walls were lined with bookshelves from floor to ceiling, the other a row of windows, and one with colorful paintings of nature. There were four plush upholstered chairs arranged around a small table for reading and then the huge desk. Instinctively, Drusy knew this is where Gacheru would search for valuables. And to her trained eye, there was one drawer that had been pried open then closed crookedly. Alina went to the bookshelves. Drusy plopped herself in the tall wood and leather chair.

"I need to sit a spell if you don't mind, Alina."

Alina glanced at her and laughed. "Of course, rest a moment. It's a long walk from the boarding house and since you've been walking all morning . . ." her voice trailed off as she removed a heavy book from a shelf.

With shaking hands and her eyes fixed on the amber tresses streaming down Alina's back, Drusilla silently slid open the drawer and carefully slipped the bracelet inside. She pushed herself out of the chair and closed the drawer at the same time. Alina had seated herself in one of the upholstered chairs with the beautiful red, leather-bound book in her lap. Drusilla sat across from her.

"Would you read a little to me? I don't know how."

Alina only hesitated for a moment before smiling and taking a breath. "This book is titled: *Before the Winter Nigh*, by Carlo Trieste." She cleared her throat and began to read from the first chapter: *It befell the young lady to accept a visit from a most unsavory suitor.*

When Lucas came in from the back door he could hear Alina's pleasant voice coming from the study. For several hours, Drusilla had listened rapt to the enchantment that could emerge from a book. She'd forgotten all about the bracelet. Alina set the book down and stood to greet Lucas. "My darling," she said, "Drusilla and I are reading. Well, today I am reading to her, but once we have settled in here, I would like to invite her and other women to come and learn to read also."

Lucas took Alina's hand before kissing her full on the lips. "I like that plan, Alina. I believe your father would be pleased to see this splendid study put to such beneficial use."

Turning to Drusilla, Alina said, "You will be my first student. And please if any of your friends would like to learn how to read, they are welcome as well."

Drusilla rose to leave, her eyes moist. "I'm afraid I wasn't much help today after all."

"You were more helpful than you know," Alina assured her.

Drusilla walked along the Boulevard with her head held high. Soon, she would be able to read. And she had done a remarkably good thing today. Alina would find the bracelet. Even if she hadn't returned it to exactly the right place, it didn't matter. It wasn't possible that Gach could ever figure out that she was the one who took it. He would wake from his drunken stupor and believe he'd lost it.

This theft would not be the end of it though, she knew that. He would continue to pilfer from her new family. If he tried to enter the Boulevard house again, someone could be harmed. Probably not Lucas, but what if Gach got in when Alina was home alone, absorbed in a book or bathing even. No, that could not occur. Lucas and his bride deserved to live in peace and safety. Who was he to intrude on that? He was nobody. Nothing but a filthy and immoral man. Maybe he wasn't really her brother. She hoped not. After all, who really knows the truth about these things. Her mother wasn't a kind or careful woman. Her stomach churned as she got closer to the boarding house. She was hungry that was true, but something else ate at her.

Then, she saw him, Gacheru making his way to the back door to pick up the tools. She didn't have time to follow him this evening. She hoped somebody would. Before she could dash through the front door, he spotted her. "Drusilla!" he shouted in his boozy, bugger voice. She could barely fix her gaze upon him. He approached, so she waited lest he make a scene in front of the house. "Where've you been you old wench? Do you think you can just prance off and live with these people? Think again. You are not their kind."

He peered at her waiting for a defensive retort, but she was thinking about the extra man she'd noticed in the blacksmith shop earlier. He had a ring of keys hooked to his belt. Gacheru had already been replaced. Did he even notice someone had taken his job right under his dribbling nose? She clapped a hand over her mouth to conceal a smile.

Gach spat near her shoes and continued his barrage of insults. "Sure, they may feel sorry for you now, but once they discover who you really are, this sham will end. You best clear out of here while I'm still willing to take you back at the smithy."

Drusilla grimaced. Gach knew nothing about her. She'd rather drown herself in the river than go back to the grimy blacksmith shop. She crossed her arms across her chest, "Never."

His bloodshot eyes bulged. He grabbed her arm. "Come on, Drusy. I took you and the babe in, don't forget. It's a shame the wee one was a weakling." He scratched his stubbly chin. "You're a good cook by the way. I know I haven't mentioned it, but you are. I miss you. I do. And I need your help. I lost something important. I need you to help me find it. Will you come back? We're kin after all."

She turned, shoved the front door open, and then slammed it behind her. Fortunately, the parlour was empty. Closing her eyes, she took three deep breaths. She would never go near him or the blacksmith shop again. Drusilla pressed a firm palm against her throbbing chest. He was right about one thing though. If her new boarding house family knew about the rubbish that she and Gacheru had descended from and how she'd gotten free of her abusive husband, they would kick her swiftly to the gutter. But not even Gacheru knew how her husband died. He couldn't.

Irene was in the kitchen placing bread and a flask of wine in her market sack. "Mr. Pagett will be here in a moment," she said. Someone knocked, and Carissa opened the back door to let Gacheru in. He shuffled to the tool cabinet, sneaking only a sideways glance at Drusilla. "We can't leave him on his own too often," Irene whispered with a finger to her lips. "You girls have the house to yourselves for a bit this evening." As Gacheru went out, Mr. Pagett pulled up in his cart.

Drusy rewarded herself with a slice of warm bread and butter before going up the stairs to Lucas and Alina's chambers. Alina now only used her small room to change her dresses, but they kept a clean linen on the bed for her to lay them out. She hung two gowns in the wardrobe and lifted the edge of the crisp linen to smooth it. She heard footsteps and turned to see Alina and Lucas returning for the evening. "Oh, I'm just getting started up here," Drusilla said.

"It's no matter," Lucas said. I'll remove the linens from our bed for you. Alina wants to change her clothes, and you can help her."

Drusilla cheerfully helped Alina unbutton her pale-yellow gown and step out of it. "What is this belt? Oh gosh, it's a dagger!"

Alina laughed, "Ah yes, don't worry. I wear it for protection."

"Indeed? I never noticed."

"That's the point," Alina said softly. "I've used it too. You should have a way to defend yourself, Drusilla. All women should."

Drusy chewed her bottom lip as she placed a soft shift in Alina's arms. "I wish I did," she mused wondering where people bought that sort of thing. Her meals and room were included in her wages, so there probably wasn't much money in the stocking stuffed under her mattress.

Reading her thoughts, Alina unbuckled the strap and handed the dagger and sheath to Drusilla. "Take mine. I will get another one."

"Oh no, I couldn't." she said, blinking and gingerly reaching for the dagger. "But you need it, Alina."

"I can get another one. In fact, I have one that belonged to my father. You take this one, Drusilla. It will offer protection, especially if you find yourself out after dark, walking alone. Of course, the hope is you never need it. But if you ever find yourself in serious danger . . ." Alina demonstrated an upward jab into the air, "use it."

Chapter 18

The three rode until dusk when they reached a grassy meadow in a high valley with a slender but sparkling creek. Nikolas had wanted to stop earlier, but they hadn't seen any water, and Brigit insisted on putting as much distance as they could from the threatening tree shadows. They hurried to gather wood and start the fire, and just as they settled themselves around the blaze, a lone figure approached on foot. He followed their same trail. Brigit leaped to her feet, upsetting the pot she'd been tossing root plants into. "Who is it?" Ikarus whispered standing behind Brigit and peering over her shoulder.

"One of them," Brigit muttered.

Nikolas grabbed his bow. He set an arrow in place. The wind direction changed and engulfed him in smoke. He coughed, "Bloody hell, I can't see! Is he still coming?"

"Halt!" Brigit shouted.

"Get away!" Ikarus warned.

Nikolas choked and coughed. His arm wavered. "Where . . . what do you see?"

"He's still coming," Brigit shouted. "It's him. The dead boy." Nik coughed and let an arrow fly.

It hit the man with a dull thud, and he fell backward.

"What happened?" Nik gagged and spit.

"He's down. Damn you hit him!" Brigit ran with Ikarus on her heels. Nik stumbled to the creek to splash water on his face.

"It is him. Oh no, it's the grandson just as I thought," Brigit declared. She squatted beside him and said, "You won't die."

He groaned and clutched his shoulder. He was lean with taut muscles. His dark hair fell across his face. He brushed it away. His piercing eyes were pools of black. Raising up on one elbow he grabbed ahold of the arrow.

"What in blazes . . . have you all gone mad? Why would you do that?"

For a moment, Nik watched from the creek and then approached cautiously. Brigit turned and frowned. "I can't believe you actually shot him."

"I . . . didn't mean to," Nik stammered, "Not exactly. I couldn't see. Isn't this the one you fear, Brigit? You just said so. We were all startled, weren't we?"

Ikarus shrugged in agreement. "I was scared, yeah."

"Don't pull it." Brigit said to the moaning man. "Wait. I'll help you. Why do you track us?"

"Beltree . . ." he murmured.

She leaned over him. "You remember me?"

"Aye, but you forgot me. I don't believe it. I'm Mabon."

"I didn't mean to hurt you," Nikolas stammered. "I couldn't see. And everyone was panicking. Brigit thinks you're . . ."

She swirled and glared at Nik, and he stopped midsentence. Turning back to Mabon, she said, "I had forgotten your name, but I remembered you too. Why are you here? What do you want?"

Nikolas reached under the lad's shoulders and lifted him to his feet. "We have a fire and food. Brigit will tend you."

She nodded. "I will. But first he needs to explain."

Nik and Ik helped him across the meadow to the fireside where he slumped down on the blanket Brigit spread out for him. She sat down beside him. "Why did you not speak earlier if you remembered me?"

He stared at her. "You look the same. At first, I wasn't sure. Then, it all came back to me. Why did your husband shoot me?"

"I'm sorry," Nik said. "We aren't from around here."

"I know that," Mabon snapped.

Brigit refilled the pot and set it in the fire. "We'll remove the arrow when the water is hot."

"This is not the first time you tried to kill me, Beltree." Mabon rummaged with one hand in his rucksack. "I'll have a quaff to ease the pain."

"He has wine!" Ikarus gleamed.

"Good thing you didn't pierce the wineskin," Mabon said to Nikolas who still looked aghast.

Brigit rummaged in her satchels mumbling to herself. When the water boiled, she took a cloth, dabbed around the arrow, and asked, "Will you share your wine?" When Mabon opened his mouth to respond, she yanked the arrow out and then quickly squelched a trickle of blood from the wound.

"Ahhh . . ." Mabon dropped the wineskin and lay back.

She took a gulp and handed it back to him. "You will stay the night with us. In the morning, when I'm sure you are well, you can go back to your tribe." She made a bandage out of cloth torn from a layer in her skirt. "Luckily, Nikolas is new with the bow and arrow. The wound isn't deep. Now, tell me why you came."

"I wanted to talk to you. We are kin in a way. All of us from the Treesdale tribe. Why does your husband call you Brigit? I know that you are Beltree."

"He's not my husband," she gestured toward Nik. "This is Nikolas, and the lad is Ikarus. We are looking for a girl from a mountainside village."

"The girl is Brigit? Your husband keeps saying Brigit." Mabon said.

"No. That's me. I am Brigit now," she murmured. "The man, Nikolas there, who is not my husband, calls me Brigit."

"And the girl is Camille," Ikarus said gazing woefully at the wineskin.

Mabon nodded his head and offered the wineskin to Ikarus. "Ah, Beltree, I am not surprised. You return an unmarried woman traveling with two men."

Ik eagerly accepted the wineskin and turning to Brigit asked, "Your true name is Beltree? I like it better. It makes more sense."

Nik chimed in. "It does. And Treesdale! Is that Trousdale? Brigit? Is that where your name comes from?" Nik exclaimed.

Brigit smiled at last. "It does. But that's not who I really am."

"She's Beltree," Mabon said. "You gave yourself a city name. But you will always be the wild Beltree."

"It's grand!" Ikarus said wiping a dribble of wine from his chin.

"We make good wine," Mabon said reaching for the skin. Ikarus sat close to Mabon and described Camille, her village, and his own home village, including his brother and sister, but Mabon didn't recognize any of the names. He did know how to reach the nearest village of sheep herders, where many people had light colored hair, and he offered to take them there. "We already told you how to get there," Mabon reminded. "Your fear confused you it seems." Ikarus nodded with excited anticipation.

Brigit tossed more of the fresh vegetables and herbs they'd gathered into the pot. "No meat tonight, but there's some old bread for dipping." They ate and moved closer to the fire. Mabon pulled another wineskin from his rucksack.

"You didn't come for revenge," Brigit said.

"Nah, of course not. You freed us when you brought that potion to me. I should not have been wearing your mother's hourglass. My father forced all of us, especially me, to do many things that were wrong." Mabon said reaching for the strings around Brigit's neck.

She pushed his hand away and withdrew the hourglass from under her shawl. "I still have it."

"And it's full," he said, as he turned it in the palm of his hand with his thumb.

Brigit's expression softened. She reached out and tenderly stroked Mabon's hair. "I'm glad I . . . we. . . didn't kill you. Now or before."

"You were always the tameless one, Beltree."

A wistful smile flashed across her tanned face, and Nikolas caught a glimpse of the girl she once was. She returned his gaze for several seconds and then focused on Mabon. "It was your grandfather who died then?"

"Aye, it was him. I didn't drink that potion. I feigned sleep. I knew what you wanted. When grandfather came to my side, I gave it to him saying it was wine. I dispatched him with your help, Beltree." For a moment, Nikolas expected Mabon to shrug like Lucas often did. But Lucas had picked up that gesture from Bernard. Mabon waved one arm in the air simulating a bird in flight and then he stretched out on the ground with a sigh. His eyelids fluttered, and his head lolled to the side. He was instantly asleep. Brigit tucked his knapsack under his neck and Nikolas brought a blanket.

The three of them sat silently around the fire watching the flames flicker. Nikolas liked Brigit's real name, Beltree. He needn't ask why she had changed it. She thought she killed someone, that was reason enough. Gazing at the peacefully sleeping Mabon, he considered tossing the bow and arrow into the flames, but then he remembered it was useful for hunting. "Is he your cousin then?"

"No. Our fathers were brothers, that's all."

"Well, that means . . ." Ik started, but Nikolas shook his head, and Ikarus took a gulp of wine instead. "We best save some for him since he brought it," Ikarus said, setting the skin aside before slipping into his bedroll. Brigit smoothed her hair with the claws and then curled up and went to sleep with the hourglass clutched in her hand. Nikolas stretched out on his back beside her. Gazing up at the stars, he realized he actually knew nothing about this woman. What would Lucas say when he told him about Mabon and the tree wizard man?

Nikolas imagined him and Lucas meeting at the Blue Gate and Lucas sitting across from him ordering two tall ales and demanding to hear about every step of their journey. He hoped he would remember everything he wanted to share with his friend by then. He rolled over and thought about the taste of that distinctive brew found only at the Blue Gate Tavern.

When Nikolas awoke, Ikarus had packed up the entire camp except for Nik himself. The mules, laden with their satchels, waited eagerly. Brigit and Mabon were sitting alongside the stream with their dark heads together. "All set," Ik said brushing dust off his hands and squatting down next to Nikolas.

"What are they talking about?" Nik asked.

"Dunno. The past I suppose."

"They are kin," Nik said.

"Yeah, before they went over there to the stream to whisper, Mabon explained some to me. His grandfather, the poisoned one, was his mother's father, of course, and he was the brother of Brigit's chieftain. Her chieftain was the good man and Mabon's grandfather was the wicked one who crept around in the trees. Beltree says she doesn't share the wicked side of the bloodline. Mabon told her that the entire clan disowned that connecting thread once the evil brother died. So, her poison helped set them free, and Mabon made sure to finish the job."

"Strange," Nik murmured.

"It happens," Ik said. "They had to stop that part of the bloodline. The brother should have killed the brother. It shouldn't have been left to Mabon, the grandson."

Nik scratched the back of his head. "I'm damn glad I didn't kill anybody. Mabon looks like Lucas. A little older and more rugged I'd say, but remarkably similar."

Ikarus nodded. "Too bad he won't come back with us," Ikarus said.

"Have you already asked?" Nikolas looked confused. He was trying to discern what all he'd slept through.

"Yes, Bel, I mean Brig . . . she asked. What do you think we should call her from now on? Beltree or Brigit? I can't tell which she prefers yet. I might just go back to Madam Trousdale. I wasn't even used to addressing her as Brigit yet."

Nik laughed. "We'll call her what she tells us to call her."

"Ok, let's go, Nik," Ik said yanking on Nik's blanket. "Mabon will lead us to the forked trail and point the way to Camille's village. This journey has already taken too long. I must see Camille today. We're only hours away." He pulled the blanket right out from under Nikolas and handed him a chunk of hard bread. Brigit and Mabon each tossed a pebble into the stream and, then rose simultaneously. Mabon set out in front on foot and soon proved to be more sure-footed on the craggy trail than the mules.

* * *

Lucas awoke with a start. He was shivering and sweating at the same time. The sheet was twisted around his legs. Alongside him,

Alina lay peaceful, but uncovered. He kicked the twisted linen to the floor and got up to grab a fresh one for Alina. After carefully draping it across her, he crept over to the fire that had gone out. He didn't stoke it since the days were warm enough. Only evenings did they need a small fire. Leaning on the mantle, he rested his forehead on his hands. It had been many weeks since his last nightmare, but this latest one wasn't about him. It involved Ikarus. With his eyes squeezed shut, Lucas tried to remember the meaningful fragments of the dream before his thoughts twisted the images.

The dream had begun with himself plunging into the pond in Arcana. At first, it was pleasant enough, but then he was stuck in the narrow passages of the monastery that were filling with water. He couldn't breathe. What frightened him the most was his face scrunched into thick gagging mud. As he struggled there, he saw Ikarus. A sudden darkness had enveloped the boy. Lucas could feel how it gripped his young friend's heart just before he appeared to fall a long distance into complete darkness. Lucas felt the lad's distress with such intensity that he ran to the window and thrust his head out searching the far-off jagged horizon beyond the buildings for his pale-haired comrade. The tranquil peaks were dotted with puffy white clouds.

Stealing a glance at Alina, Lucas considered waking her, but he didn't want to remind her about the panic of the suffocating halls inside the monastery. He slumped into the chair beside the fire to stare into the cold ashes. For several long minutes, he waited but no more images came to mind. Ikarus had disappeared from the dream. Sighing, Lucas got up, pulled on his trousers and a soft shirt, and crept from the room. To his relief, he found Perina alone in the kitchen.

"Oh! Good morning, Lucas. So early . . . my goodness you look like a ghoul!" She exclaimed. "Here sit." Getting up from the empty table, she hurried over to the kettle. "Irene isn't even down yet."

"All right," he accepted the teacup and stood in the doorway.

Perina peered up at him. "She'll be disappointed that she missed the departure of our intriguing gentleman guest and his lady."

"Where did they go?" Lucas muttered.

"Off to the harbour at first light. They sail today."

Lucas nodded and tried to focus on Perina's prattle, but he didn't care that the pompous man and his young companion were gone. Perina gestured to the bench, and Lucas sat. She scooted next to him and whispered, "I did get some gossip for Irene though. The young lady is his wife. They are actually married!"

Lucas laughed in spite of himself. "Well, I daresay that Irene will be disappointed to hear that. She suspected something much more scandalous with those two."

"Would you like to tell her the story, Lucas?"

"No," Lucas said, understanding Perina hoped to cheer him. But gossip didn't have the same curative effect on him as it did the women. "It's your story to tell, Perina. Irene will appreciate it more coming from you. I think I'll go for a walk."

Once he stepped out into the street, Lucas felt renewed. After spending so many years working at night, he rarely found himself out this early. There was a fresh anticipation to the morning time. The river smelled crisp as it coursed toward the sea. The familiar scenes helped assuage the disturbing images of the nightmare. The mountain peaks, in their splendor against the vibrant blue sky, suggested only exquisite beauty. In the square, the vendors chatted as they stocked their stalls. The aroma of bread and pastries was so fresh that his stomach urged him to stop. He bought two baguettes along with a sack of apple tarts and cheese blintzes, one of which he consumed on his way back to the boarding house. He heard his name and looked up to see Alina, still wearing her nightdress, standing at the window. She was smiling and waving at him.

* * *

Ikarus followed closely behind Brigit who kept her mule apace with Mabon. He tried to overhear their conversation, but either the words or their tone of voice made it impossible for him to understand. At one point, they both turned and looked directly at him and quickly glanced away. "They must be talking about me," he told Nikolas who looked like he was half asleep. The morning stretched into afternoon, and just when Ikarus had started to prepare himself for another night on the trail, Mabon stopped. Brigit dismounted, and Nik and Ik did as well.

"Here my friends, I leave you," Mabon said. Nikolas noticed the hourglass glinting against the young man's chest. Brigit, or Beltree rather as it suited her in this moment, clutched his hand. Her eyes were misty black and swirling blue.

"Will we see you on our way back down?" Ik asked hopeful. "It will only be a couple of days before we return with Camille."

"No," Mabon said rubbing the hourglass. "You won't see me. That way," he pointed to one of two trails. "The village you seek lies at the end of that trail."

"Thank you," Nikolas said. "I hope I still have your forgiveness for the accidental arrow. I will repay you in any way you wish."

"Take care of our Beltree. That's all I ask." He shook Nikolas' hand. To Ikarus he said, "Fare-well. Remember, every path leads to a new turning point." He turned to Beltree, and they embraced like two people who didn't expect to ever see each other again. The three of them watched in silence as Mabon sauntered off swinging his arms. He did not turn around as he reached the bend in the trail but raised one hand above his head. Then he was gone.

"Beltree?" Ikarus whispered.

Brigit shook her head. "Beltree and Mabon are gone."

Ikarus looked at Nikolas and made a face. "Along with the hourglass," Nik said.

She smiled and nodded. "Mabon will take care of it now. And if they ever meet, that is how Lucas will recognize . . ." her voice trailed off.

Nikolas and Ikarus exchanged a glance and waited. She peered down the trail where Mabon just went as if they'd agreed he'd go a short distance, turn around, and come back. The scent of sage surrounded them, and bent-legged insects leaped on and off their shins.

Nik squinted up at the sun and finally asked, "Lucas will recognize what?"

"Something. I don't understand," Brigit said pulling her glance away from the empty path.

"I don't either," Nik said.

"Huh?" Ik shook his head as he climbed up on his mule. "Well, let's get along this path and find Camille."

Before the end of an hour, the village came into view. Ikarus kneed his mule that brayed in protest and came to a stubborn stop. Ik leaped off and ran forward, then turned back, grabbed his water skin, and splashed water on his head and face, smoothing his hair back with both hands. He straightened his shirt, and pulled up his trousers, and swiped dust from the cuffs. Nikolas and Brigit grinned at him. "Shut up," he said.

Laughing, Nikolas waved him forward. "Lead the way, Ikarus."

Ikarus blushed, swallowed, and went toward the village. Nik and Brigit dismounted and followed a few paces behind.

The village was comprised of dozens of ochre walled and slate-roofed huts winding up and around the terraced slopes of long, tawny waves of grass. Sheep bells clanged a chorus of welcome as the villagers stopped what they were doing and funneled toward the newcomers. People and sheep surrounded the three, pulling them away from their mules, laughing and grabbing at their clothes and Brigit's swirling black hair. Standing among the bleating, the bells and the varied strange sounding voices, Brigit, Nikolas, and Ikarus could only gape at each other. They had not anticipated such a rousing welcome.

They were led to a circular center of piled stones. Dirt-smudged hands offered them loaves of round bread and bowls of warm milk. Ikarus grinned with relief and joy. This was Camille's village at last.

They were besieged with questions from the adults while the children frolicked nearby, sometimes stopping to listen in on the conversation. Having met many of them before, Ikarus, of course, was the center of attention. He noticed that one familiar girl, just two years older now, held a babe in arms.

Soon the bowls of milk were replaced by cups of watered wine and soft cheese. It wasn't until the sun slipped behind the craggy peaks, and the clouds dotting the powder blue sky turned pastel pink that Ikarus felt a jab of fear. Camille did not come down from the hillside path. Ikarus wished he'd had the forethought to skirt around to the high pasture and find Camille resting there alone in the soft grass humming to the sheep.

A few of the shepherds emerged from their family hut wearing fresh trousers and shirts, or soft sinuous dresses. In the instant he panicked, her mother caught his eye. Ikarus stood. Surely this sharp woman knew why he was here. She broke away from the gathering, and Ikarus followed. The stiff beat of his heart eased a little as he followed Camille's mother to the large family cottage. He prayed Camille was not sick, but if she were, Brigit would heal her. Nikolas and Brigit, seeing him go, slipped away and followed as well.

There, inside the tidy but empty cottage, Camille's mother, who wore her gray hair in a loose bun, took both of Ikarus' hands in her own deeply calloused ones. Ikarus held his breath and waited, terrified that the woman was about to tell him that Camille had somehow fallen from the hillside and died before he could return. In the end, Ikarus thought for a small second that an accident would have been better news than to hear that, *great luck* as her mother called it, had befallen her. A gentleman from across the sea, seeking solace after the loss of his first wife, had stumbled upon their village, showered them with gifts and bank notes, and taken Camille away as his new wife. Ikarus stood chilled and dumbstruck until Brigit's hair slowly, but fully rose above her head and swirled like a thunderstorm.

"Damn all to hell!" Nikolas exclaimed before clapping a hand over his mouth. As he watched Ikarus, he knew he would never forget the expression on the lad's face; startled at first, then, crumbled, and suddenly turned whiter than the lambs. His eyes reflected a brief moment of doubt and hope in the same instant the realization that the unbearable blur of words were true. His body went rigid, and Ikarus crumpled like a cast-off sack of hollow bones.

"Oh dear!" Camille's mother pressed her palms together and leaned over Ikarus. "Have I said too much?"

Brigit pushed her out of the way as she dashed to Ikarus' side. She leaned in close to feel his shallow breath on her cheek. She brushed the damp hair from his cold forehead and murmured to him. Frowning and helpless, Nikolas waited.

Camille's mother wrung her hands and moaned. She paced, then went to the door, and peered out as if she were deciding to flee or summon help. After a few moments, she brought a cup of plain water and attempted to hand it to Ikarus. "You and your companions are welcome to stay, Ikarus. Camile has young sisters as you know."

Brigit glared at Camille's mother with disgust. "The boy has fainted."

Nikolas took the cup of water, knelt beside Ikarus, and cradled his head in his arms. "Go on then," Brigit said and waved the mother away. "Take your unwanted news from us. We will not be staying here." And to Nikolas she said, "We will take him to his own village."

"He has been gone too long," Camille's mother whined. "His sister and brother came through here just before winter. Their mother had died. They asked us to deliver the news if Ikarus ever returned here. Please stay. All of you are welcome. We can help you revive Ikarus. We accept him as one of us."

Brigit vehemently shook her head. Nikolas scooped Ikarus up into his arms and carried him outside to the impatient mules. "What in blazes do we do now?' he asked Brigit.

"I don't know yet. Here, give me some of the dowry coins. We will compensate the villagers for their kindness. And a bracelet for the mother. I should not have spoken so rudely." They wrapped a blanket around Ikarus and laid him over the back of the mule.

Nikolas handed her a pouch. "Take these extra coins and ask if they have any highland whisky to sell. Stay calm, Brigit. They could not have known that Ikarus would return after all this time."

Brigit nodded. "It's his own fault that he's too late. I wish he told us sooner." She hurried back to the stone center. Nikolas kept Ikarus under the shade of a short tree and tried to rouse him with slaps and water. Brigit finally returned carrying three wineskins and a folded parchment. "They have no whisky. But the youngest sister gave me this just now. It's from Camille to Ikarus," she said. Nikolas carefully unfolded it. It was a drawing of a young girl and a boy standing on the hillside among the sheep. They were smiling and holding hands.

"Well, this isn't much help," Nik grumbled as he stuffed the drawing into his saddlebag. They traipsed back as fast as the mules were willing to go, away from the village before any of the well-meaning people could stop them. Brigit said it was just as well that Ikarus didn't awaken right away.

Chapter 19

Mr. Pagett showed up with his cart, and Irene had their picnic ready, but Gacheru did not appear for his rounds at the appointed hour, or even three quarters past it. Drusilla, who had started her chores early this afternoon, was vigorously scrubbing the stone garden benches. "Have you seen your brother?" Irene inquired from the threshold.

Startled, Drusilla dropped her scrub brush and began to cough. "No." Shaking her head and leaving the brush where it lay, she began to replace the plants to their proper places.

Irene tsked. "Well, I suppose we're going to have to alert Lucas." Drusilla nodded, her expression wooden. She had seen Gacheru this morning through the filmy window of the Duck Tavern. It was not noon yet. The sight of him sitting there like a fool and snickering with three other idlers repulsed her.

Lucas and Alina had just sat down at the table with Carissa and Perina who had finished serving the boarders their supper. The men, weary from their long work shifts, had shuffled to their rooms at the first sign of dusk. Lucas served Alina her stew, teasing her by dropping tiny spoonful's into her bowl just to watch her giggle and motion for more. In return, she grabbed his wine goblet and downed the contents. "Ah lass," he exclaimed, "you are victorious in the supper skirmish."

They'd had a lovely day arranging furniture and linens in the Boulevard house and taking flowers to the widows and to Linnea's grave. Seppo had given them a sack of sandalwood candles for the courtyard garden. He, as always, declined their invitation to supper. In the course of this easy day, Lucas had forgotten about his nightmare.

Irene clomped into the kitchen with Mr. Pagett following a few steps behind. "That Gacheru isn't worth a tinker's damn," she blurted.

"Oh no, what now." Lucas turned to her with his hand poised in the air as he poured wine into his goblet.

She lifted her hands and dropped them. "Didn't show up and it's getting darker every minute."

Mr. Pagett frowned, holding his hat in front of him as if the absent Gacheru were somehow his fault. "I have the cart loaded, and we were ready to follow him," he said. Frowning, Lucas turned somberly to Alina. She stopped chewing and wiped her hands on a cloth as Lucas got up and went to the supply cabinet to retrieve the tools.

"What's in your picnic basket?" Alina asked Irene.

"Pretty much the same as what you have here."

"All right then," she nodded to Lucas. "You go on ahead and get started. We will follow shortly in the cart. We can finish supper along the way until Gacheru appears.

"You don't have to," Lucas said, but he smiled his approval of the plan. He didn't feel like roaming the streets to light lanterns, but with the three of them following him, the chore would be more like a festive occasion than a nuisance. He couldn't wait for Ikarus to return.

Then, he remembered the terrible dream. The sooner the better, he thought, for all of our sakes. He offered a silent prayer for the safe return of Ikarus, Nikolas, and Brigit, along with Camille whom they all looked forward to meeting. He kissed Alina's cheeks and hurried out the door.

"Gacheru sure is a bumbling bloody biscuit," Irene griped as they climbed into the cart.

* * *

"There is nothing to be done but wait the anguish out," Nikolas said as he led Brigit, Ikarus, and himself back down the trail that they'd just come up that morning with Mabon. Just then, Ikarus began to stir. They stopped and pulled him off the back of his mule. Not only did they have to remind Ikarus what Camille's mother had said that caused him to faint, but Nikolas and Brigit also had to deliver the awful news about his own mother having passed away.

The two of them took turns reciting encouraging words to Ikarus who sat on the ground so close to his mule's hind end that Nik feared the lad would get kicked, along with everything else that had gone wrong for him this day. They spoke for nearly an hour to the mute Ikarus.

In the aftermath, only the birdsong remained. Nik leaned over to Brigit who put a finger to her lips and whispered, "Never stop listening until the birdsong has ended the day."

Nikolas let his eyes close and listened. The sun had long since finished its daily errand when silence ensued. "Now, I know why Lucas enjoys the evenings. The chorus of birds, although there aren't as many in the City of Dreams."

"It takes only one," Brigit agreed.

Ikarus groaned, lay down, and curled into himself under the mule's swishing tail. Nikolas gave the animals' rump a shove. "I'll make a fire." He unpacked the bundles and carried them several long paces away from the trail. There was no stream, but they had full water bags. A cluster of broad-leafed trees stood in a warm cushion of sandy soil. Once the camp was ready, Nik gathered up Ikarus and led him to the fireside. Brigit managed to make a bready broth that went well with the wine. She was pleased that Ikarus ate, and he didn't inquire where she got the wine.

When they finished, the three sat silently staring into the flames. Ikarus took a stick and stirred the orange embers of the fire. Brigit placed a cool comforting hand upon his wrist. "What would you like to do now, lad?"

The tone of her voice and the gesture reminded Ikarus of his mother. He had dreamed of taking both Camille and his mother back with them to the City of Dreams. Now, he would never see either one of them again. His throat closed upon itself, and sharp hot tears pierced his eyes. He heard his heart fiercely thumping in his ears. Then, it slowed and, as far as he could tell, stopped. It may as well. Ikarus knew—as if he saw his future appearing in Brigit's crystal ball—that before him lay a life as empty as the vast wound that opened inside him and created a hollow ache that would carry through his lifetime.

Not a day would pass that he did not think about Camille, wonder what she was doing and with whom. Did she ever think of him, wish he had come sooner, or was she glad he never returned? Would there ever be a single day that his thoughts were not full of her, that his eyes did not yearn desperately to see her. A day that his soul could forget the incomprehensible sense of peace that he experienced with her.

And what of his mother? Was her heart broken that her youngest son had never returned to her? Would she have told him he was a fool for leaving Camille behind? His skin hurt, his blood ran cold, his feet could not feel the ground. To have been so close and walked away, believing in his young naïve self that they would easily find each other again. How could he have thought in this vast treacherous world that two souls would have the chance to fall together in the perfect time, in the perfect place ever again. His life, mere hours ago a promise of joy, would forever pass in the gloom of longing and loneliness. The relentless sadness, a sickening cloak of suffering in which to bury himself. "I am the stupidest man ever born."

Ikarus realized Brigit was rubbing his back and that Nik had spread out his bedroll. He crawled over to it. Brigit helped him adjust the blanket, making sure his feet were covered even though the night was not too chilly. She spoke softly, "We can go wherever you like tomorrow. Do you want to continue up the mountain to your village?"

"No."

"All right. It's fine. Someplace else then . . ." Brigit cast a helpless glance at Nik who frowned and pulled his hand through his hair. "Ikarus," she said, "do you remember your sister and brother are not far from here? They are your blood kin."

"They will mock my plight. I cannot go there," he moaned.

"Shall we return to The City of Dreams, then?"

"Yes, I want to go home," he murmured. "Please take me home."

Nikolas, who had placed the drawing from Camille into his pocket to show Ikarus once he had eaten and had some wine, shoved it back inside the saddlebag, stuffing it all the way to the bottom. He and Brigit lay on the other side of the fire close enough to reach Ikarus if needed. They stared up at the stars, some of which seemed to loosen from their perch and shoot across the inky sky. Brigit whispered in Nik's ear, "Her sister said that Camille cried and cried when Ikarus left. She could not be consoled."

"Nonetheless, someone showed up and managed to console her, it seems," Nik grumbled. Brigit sighed but said no more. She seemed burdened with sadness over Ikarus or maybe Mabon. He couldn't be sure. After the jubilant arrival at the village, the news of Camille dismayed him. The entire journey was founded on a thrilling and romantic reunion for Ikarus and his beloved. The disappointment and embarrassment would follow Ikarus all the way home to the City of Dreams where he would have to tell his sad story over and over.

Gazing upward, Nikolas wondered if the twinkling stars had answers hidden behind their inexplicable illumination. He should be glad to end the journey that had turned out to be difficult, and now melancholy, but Nikolas wondered how he could ever leave the vast, unpredictable mountains, the purple, pink, and incredibly blue sky, the plentiful birds and creatures, the streams, the rich mud, and the rippling waves of green and ecru grass. He appreciated even the rocks that tweaked his neck as he slept.

As he listened to Ikarus and Brigit breathing in ragged slumber, he wondered how a man recovers from the complete absolution of nature in its fullest form. As the night grew longer, Nikolas realized that no man ever could, or should, forget how it feels to lie vulnerable and awed under the limitless sky.

Chapter 20

The evening lantern lighting rounds were completed without anyone spotting Gacheru. They'd made light of it by taking turns driving the little donkey cart and pouring cups of wine for the scattered citizens who leaned out their windows or stepped into the street to greet the pleasant band of lantern lighters. Lucas denied that he was taking up the task again but assured them that Ikarus would return soon. Nobody cared where Gacheru had got off to, and most hoped he wouldn't come back.

At first sight, the boarding house looked so bright and cheerful that Lucas half expected to find Nikolas, Brigit, and Ikarus waiting for them inside. But the parlour and garden were empty with nothing but a hushed breeze riffling the trailing plants in butterfly silence.

As Irene straightened the kitchen, Lucas and Alina went to the courtyard to enjoy the scent of jasmine from the delicate plant's buds. The widow Van Dessen had given them the shrub as a wedding gift, and Drusilla had managed to find the best place to plant it in the small garden. She'd dug for over an hour with a large kitchen spoon. "I wish Gacheru could learn something from his sister," Lucas said. "She is a diligent worker and a pleasant woman as well."

"I think so too, Lucas. It seems that she has had a troublesome life so far. Carissa says she was very shy at first, but now she laughs with them and even offers some gossip of her own. I'm glad Irene had a room for her. A woman should not live in a blacksmith shop."

"Certainly not. If her brother weren't so lazy and unreliable, he could have been more of a support for her. I wonder if he will ever show up again." Lucas rubbed his forehead. "I have a feeling he won't, and it's probably for the best. It's just as much a nuisance to follow him as it is to do it myself."

"And it's quite clear that none of the residents like him. It's nice that Irene and Mr. Pagett have managed to make some fun of it. Besides, Ikarus should be back any day now with Camille. He will be so excited! Oh, my goodness, I must discuss with Irene which room to give them. Is the ivy grown enough?" Alina jumped up. "We best move to the Boulevard house and make our room ready for Ikarus and Camille. We don't want him to be embarrassed!" she dashed off to the kitchen in search of Irene.

Lucas laughed and followed. "I'm glad you thought of that, Alina. Ikarus barely fits himself in the tiny room he sleeps in. And he can't take his betrothed into the boarders' lodgings."

Alina spun around. "But wait, they need separate rooms until they are wed. . . Camille can have my room."

"Of course," Lucas agreed, "and Ikarus will have to wait it out on his closet cot." He wondered what sort of ceremony they would have and where. "Although, I just thought, perhaps they have already wed in Camille's village."

"Why yes, of course, that makes the most sense! I'm sure her family wouldn't let her leave without a bridal ceremony. Then, absolutely there must be a room ready for them right away." Wringing her hands, She peered at Lucas.

"Don't fret, my darling. Your cozy room is the most romantic solution."

"What are you two scheming now?" Irene asked with a bemused grin as she hung her apron on the pantry hook.

"Irene, we think Ikarus, and Camille will arrive quite soon, and we're sorting out where they will stay. We think we should put them in my room. I can move the remainder of my things to the Boulevard house or into Lucas' room."

"Brigit will want to inspect the ivy first, I suppose," Irene said hesitating. "You're not ready to go so soon. There is much to do yet, isn't there?"

"We can wait a few more days," Alina suggested. "It's easier with the lanterns, right, Lucas?"

Blank and distracted, Lucas stood staring into nothingness. He'd suddenly remembered pieces of the disjointed dream. In this latest nightmare, Ikarus had fallen into complete darkness. Lucas looked at the ladies and his stomach lurched. Usually, he told Irene his nightmares, but he certainly didn't want to bring this last one up now. It would fade. It had to. Alina, so happy and hopeful about every little thing, should not have to worry about his foreboding nightmares.

He felt like Ikarus had fallen off a cliff. Was that possible? How steep were the trails up there? He didn't know. There was no way of knowing exactly where his friends had gone or if they had even reached their destination. They might return any minute or never. He closed his eyes for a moment and then squeezed Alina's hand. "Yes, we would like to keep our room here after we move to the Boulevard." He answered a question no one had asked.

Irene gazed long and hard at him before nodding. "Fine, that's the best choice. I'll be off to bed then."

"Go on up," he told Alina. "I'll blow out the candles."
* * *

"Let's take our time going back," Nikolas murmured to Brigit as they watched Ikarus who was kneeling beside the stream and splashing water onto his face. "This land up here it's a remedy, isn't it?"

"It is," Brigit said with a soft smile. "We will remind him who he is, and where he comes from, and after some time in the cloister of the forest and sleeping in the high grasses, and drinking the clear water with just a little bit of wine by the evening fire, he can decide what he wants to do."

"Yes, I think so too. He said he wants to go home, but he doesn't understand his heart must heal. This is the place to allow that."

Bemused, Brigit briefly embraced Nik. "The land appeals to you I can see."

Ikarus, blank-faced, walked toward them.

Nik nodded. "Everything up here charms me. I never knew the earth and the sky could be so alluring. It's a wonderment out here. At first, I felt uneasy, but now the vastness, the roar of the wind, the melody of the streams and the birdsong . . ."

"Has turned you into a poet," Brigit finished.

Nikolas blushed. "What do you say, Ik? Shall we take the long way home?"

Ikarus shrugged. "Why not."

Brigit and Nikolas exchanged satisfied glances. They'd noticed a slight smile on the lad's forlorn face. It's a start Nikolas thought, and for himself, he was glad to have more time in the wild land he knew he may never visit again. As for Brigit, now they could travel through the hillsides of her former home without fear. There was hope, he thought, now that they were staying, that they may see Mabon again and meet others from Beltree's tribe. Nik decided he would still call her by her original given name. That is, until she insisted he do otherwise.

The morning was crisp with dewy sunlight glistening down upon emerald, green leaves as wide as Nik's hand. "I belong here," he said holding up his hands. "I'm a tree too, Beltree." He tilted his head back and took a deep breath. Ikarus waited quietly, but Nik noticed him reach out and stroke one of the soft leaves.

They stood there waiting for nothing until the mules began to complain and tug on their leads. Reluctantly leaving the dappled patches of green and gold, Nikolas thought that it had been the perfect place to camp after all. If there had been a stream, he would have suggested they spend another day. The mules were nimble as they followed each other in single file into the green forest. "Which plant is this, Beltree?" Nikolas asked after nearly an hour walking silently.

Brigit reined in her mule and peered down at the tall, yellow-flowered plant. "It's fiddleneck. Do you remember, Ikarus?" Ikarus laughed to the surprise of Brigit and Nik. He asked her to name another cluster of wildflowers in fiery red, and deep purple. Her referred to her as Beltree also, and Nik and Brigit smiled at each other. They had made the right choice. His land would heal him, with or without Camille.

"Where is the edelweiss?" he asked. "I remember how Camille looked in those few days that we knew each other. Her hair was nearly the same color as mine." He gazed wistfully away. "She had soft hands, clean white fingernails, and her voice when she spoke to me, so calm. Did I tell you she had a face like an angel? It was so pretty and perfect like the delicate edelweiss I thought then." He sighed and shook his head. "I can't actually describe her. But I remember what it felt like to take her hand. Before I left her village, she hugged me, and I felt it in my bones and my blood." He glanced at Nikolas and Beltree who sat atop their mules and listened captivated by his words. "To the ends of my hair. I can feel her still. I will feel her if we ever pass in the street, even if it is completely pitch black."

"It had better not be," Nikolas said. Brigit frowned wondering if she had enough herbs to make a potion to calm Ikarus down. It did no good for her him to sentimentalize about Camille now.

"I wonder how Gacheru is doing," Ik said. "He will have to relinquish my job when I return. I know we will meet again, Camille and me. Someday, somewhere, I know it."

Brigit made a mental list of the herbs she had in her satchel. There must be something to induce forgetfulness. But Nikolas was glad to hear Ikarus talking, even if he rambled and mostly about Camille. He had yet to mention his mother, and Nikolas wondered if he'd somehow forgotten or if the shock made him cling to a delusional strand of hope about his young love, Camille. He thought it unlikely the two would ever meet again, but there was nothing wrong with imagining it while he adjusted to the truth. Now though, Nik wondered how things went in the City of Dreams. If only there were a way, he could reach Lucas and speak to him, just for a moment to let him know they were delayed.

* * *

Gacheru did not show up the next night, or the three after that, and then it turned into seven nights. Feeling annoyed and out of sorts, Lucas took up his old routine. Alina did her best to cheer him with plans for their friends return. She took over the readying of her old room for Ikarus and Camille. She had Perina change the linens in Ikarus' tiny room in case they had not wed in the mountains. She borrowed Mr. Pagett's cart and hauled many of her possessions into the Boulevard house with the help of Drusilla and Carissa.

Everyone offered to accompany Lucas on his rounds, but he declined. He had once relished the days when he walked alone, but that was before he had so many other important responsibilities. As he roamed the familiar streets, he felt like an observer in his own life.

So much had changed that he could not recapture the feelings he once enjoyed while lighting the lanterns. Some days, he worked to carry on the merchant trade that he and Nikolas had begun and even there, Lucas felt adrift. He didn't have the comradery with the harbour lads as Nikolas did, and several times they forgot to let him know when a shipment had arrived. When that occurred, he had to locate the shipment in one of the warehouses and arrange for the delivery to the respective merchants.

Some days, he was able to forget the nagging traces of his nightmare, but the ongoing absence of Nikolas, Brigit, and Ikarus gnawed at the edge of his mind like an infectious tick. Every time he heard even the slightest sound outside the boarding house, he thought it was them returning home. It never was though, and his frustration began to make him angry. He held it inside but felt like he was about to burst with impatience.

Every other day, he stopped by to visit Seppo who always greeted him with wine, water, and delicious bread—like none he'd ever tasted—and evasive answers. Mostly to distract himself, Lucas asked discreet questions about the gold in the tunnels and Seppo simply said, "It remains a secret, doesn't it?" And it did, so of course, Lucas agreed and let the matter drop until next time. In truth there was not much for he and Seppo to discuss, for his father would speak only to a point and then fall into meditation or sleep.

Lucas wondered what he was holding back, but also wondered if there was nothing more to know. He reasoned that Seppo's silence was not yet a problem that he must address. He wondered how the old monk and the others had kept the secret for so long, even now, with so many new residents arriving in the city. One afternoon, Seppo asked, "And what of you?"

Lucas didn't want to reveal his concerns about the delayed return of his friends. He thought for some time before mentioning, "There's a suspicious man who has gone missing. He could be dangerous," he warned Seppo as he described Gacheru.

"I will keep an eye out for him," Seppo assured, "but I doubt a man like that will come near this hallowed place."

"He's probably too lazy to walk this far, but he might come begging for food." Lucas cocked his head. "I don't know much about him except he has a sister he should be looking out for. Irene has taken her in though. So, it doesn't even matter unless you happen to come across him. Then, I'd want to know."

Seppo blinked, "I never liked waiting either. Now that's all I do and it's not so bad after all."

Lucas got up to leave. Seppo in his own way was trying to reassure him. He left his father resting comfortably on one of his pillowed divans. He stepped out into the twilight. It was still his favorite time. He pulled the tall double doors closed behind him.

Lucas walked past Brigit's cottage every night. When he went in, he found everything as she'd left it. He knew her clan awaited her return as impatiently as he did, but they had no insight to share with him. If they had an inkling of when she would return, certainly they would tell him. Shadow often kept him company in the curious but distracted manner of a creature that had better things to do. It seemed that she felt sorry for him plodding through his old routine.

At the end of each evening, he entered the Boulevard house. Once he found Alina there and hoped to spend some time alone together before going back to the boarding house, but Drusilla was dusting and folding, even at that late hour. Lucas paid her wages since she worked more for he and Alina than for Irene. The three of them locked up the house together and walked back to the boarding house. Although the ivy looked ready, Lucas didn't want to move into their new home while he was still lighting lanterns. He wouldn't bring the tools in, and the location of the house would disrupt the timing of his long-held route.

Noticing the dour expression on Lucas' face, Alina brought up Gacheru. "Where do you think your brother has got off to, Drusilla? The blacksmith has not seen him. Nobody has. When did you, yourself, see him last?"

Drusilla stopped and glanced around fearfully. "Why? Why, Miss Alina, do you ask me?"

"Well, he is your brother," Lucas snapped. "You must know something about his habits!" Drusilla cowered. "Damn, I'm sorry, Drusilla. I know it's not your fault." He patted her shoulder.

"We wonder if you can think of someplace to look for him," Alina said.

Drusilla chewed her bottom lip. "I guess. . . well, I don't know."

"Where did you see him last?" Lucas asked repeating Alina's question.

"I . . ." Drusilla thought about how she'd spied him through the misty window that dreadful morning and how her breakfast had roiled up into her mouth. "The Duck," she muttered pointing in the direction of the tavern.

"Ohh," Alina sighed as she recalled her own terrible experience with the place.

Lucas scratched his cheek. "All right, ladies. Let me take you back to the boarding house, and then I will go check there." They walked on in silence, but when they reached home, Lucas went in with them. "I've changed my mind," he said. "If Gach can't crawl out of the Duck Tavern, he's useless to us now."

"He is," Drusilla agreed, and nodded briskly.

"I can manage," Lucas said. "I have the two lamp boys and the route goes faster with their help. I will give Brigit, Nikolas, and Ikarus a few more days before deciding what to do next."

"They're probably caught up in Ikarus and Camille's wedding ceremony," Alina said. "Brigit was very keen on helping us with ours."

"That's true," Lucas said, cheered by the thought of a wedding.

"Irene says we will have a big celebration when they come home," Drusy said.

"I'm sure we will," Lucas said with a smile "I look forward to it. Good night, Drusilla. Thank you for all your help."

Upstairs, he and Alina were pleased to find a cool bath awaiting them. They undressed and slipped in together and crossed their legs around each other. Lucas splashed water over his head and shoulders. They sipped from the same cup of wine.

"It does make sense that they are delayed by the wedding ceremony. None of us thought to even ask Ikarus what his exact plans were once he found Camille. But it would be up to her father and mother."

"Yes, perhaps Ikarus had to take a few days to prove he is worthy before obtaining permission. I wouldn't let my daughter go too easily," Alina said.

Lucas grinned. "What are you saying, Alina?"

"Oh nothing, no. We are not having a daughter any time soon. Or a son. No, Lucas stop it. The day will come, but it's not here yet. In a few days, they will be home, and everything will go back to the way it was. The house is ready for us, but I think we should wait so Irene doesn't feel lonely."

"Yes, let's wait. I'm not quite ready either."

"What's wrong, Lucas?"

"Nothing that I know of. I just wish I could speak to Brigit and ask her what to do, in case there is something wrong. It's just a feeling. Maybe it's here in the city. I don't know what it is, but I can feel it."

"I know," Alina said. "I can see how worried you are. I miss them too. It seems like a long time for them to be gone, wedding or not. I've been trying to distract myself and you, but it sounds like it's time we did something. What shall we do, Lucas?"

He leaned back and closed his eyes. Alina poured a pitcher of water over her head and washed her hair, rubbing her scalp with her fingers. When Lucas was ready, she would do the same for him. "I've got it," Lucas sat up suddenly. "I'll let the lamp boys take the route tomorrow with Irene and Mr. Pagett. You and I will ride to Arcana and get Bernard." He picked up the pitcher and helped Alina rinse her wavy tresses.

"Bernard?" Alina asked as she rose from the tub with water cascading from her hair and shoulders onto Lucas. She took the water pitcher from him and, stepping from the tub, fetched the second pitcher from the wash basin. Dripping onto the rug, she stood behind Lucas and washed his hair. He groaned in appreciation and remained silent until she finished. Then he rose, wrapped them both in a large linen, and led her to the bed.

"Will Bernard light lanterns?" she murmured.

"I'm not sure yet. I just know we need him. Someone may have to go up the mountain. Come here, Alina. Let's relax now."

In the morning, Lucas found Irene in the kitchen and told her their plan. "That's a brilliant idea," she said. Lucas couldn't tell whether she was more pleased that Bernard would visit or that she and Mr. Pagett would follow the lantern lighters again. He strolled over to the stables and found the stableman who cheerfully saddled Lucas' usual mount and even remembered which horse Alina preferred. Lucas promised to pay the man upon their return, but the stableman waved him off saying, "Take your time, you and your lady. And don't fret, Lucas. Nikolas will show up with his flock before you know it!"

Lucas walked the horses slowly through the cobbled streets wondering if the entire city could read the concern on his face. Perina stood outside the boarding house and offered to hold the horses while he gathered their baggage. Alina had packed a picnic basket for them, and his bread, jam and tea waited on the table. Soon, they were galloping across the bridge and out of the city with the summer wind blowing through their flowing hair. Lucas glanced over at Alina. They smiled at each other. He'd made the right decision.

It was early still when they reached the No Horses Tavern, so they weren't surprised not to find Bernard there. They continued on, stopped at the Grande Inn to drop off their things, and gratefully sign the ledger for Lucas' regular room. Lucas' mood already improved by the invigorating ride that also restored his confidence.

By the time they reached Bernard and Wentworth's farm, he felt certain that when they returned with Bernard to the City of Dreams that Nikolas, Brigit, and Ikarus would already be there, and the arrival of Bernard would turn out to be just another cause for celebration. Wentworth stepped out the front door as they rode up, and Bernard came from around the back of the house. Both Lucas and Alina were surprised to see a young lad following him.

Once they were settled in chairs under a weeping willow tree, Bernard explained the lad helped with the farm work, and as young as he seemed, he was already married. His wife did some of the cooking, but Wentworth still enjoyed preparing most of the meals. Bernard said he no longer spent as much time at the Grande Inn. They spent the afternoon walking around the farm and relaxing in the shade of the long swaying branches of the willow trees.

Lucas found a moment to follow Bernard into the house to fetch wine. Although by then, his concern for Nikolas and the others had dissolved somewhat. Still, he said, "I came here hoping to enlist you to accompany me up the mountain, Bernard. I don't know where they went exactly, but I believe one of Brigit's cottage clan members may accompany us as well for guidance. I had a dream that Ikarus is perhaps injured or worse." He hesitated, "What are your thoughts? I don't want to burden Alina with this journey, but I don't want to leave her behind either. Now though, since I'm here in Arcana, the urgency to do something has dissipated a little bit."

Bernard scratched his burly chest. "I was glad to see you and Alina ride up, but I thought there had to be a reason other than lounging about with Wentworth and me. I think you should stay here with us for a few days. We can talk it through. I don't mind going up the mountain with you, but if we go up one way and they come down another, then what?"

Lucas grimaced. "I guess, you're right. If that happens then we will all just spend weeks roaming the mountainside looking for each other."

"Have you dreamed about Nikolas or Brigit or just Ikarus?"

"Only Ikarus." Distracted by the buzzing of insects, Lucas glanced around. "I miss it here sometimes."

Bernard gestured around the farm. "It's not the old farm from our childhood, but I want you to feel that this is your home as much as mine. Never forget that." He slapped Lucas so hard on the back that he had to take a step. The men laughed and exchanged more back slaps.

"Will you and Wentworth join Alina and me in the dining room at the Grande Inn this evening?"

"Of course, we will. Wentworth will love it."

"All right then, Alina and I will meet you there. We'll go now and have our walk in the garden. We are planning our own garden and it will provide ideas for us. And like you say, well what I think you mean to say, even if Ikarus has been injured, Brigit and Nikolas will take care of him."

"They will. I'm certain of it, Lucas. And when Ikarus returns with his lady the two of them can wed right here under these trees if they like."

"If they haven't wed already," Lucas said. "But even if they have, we will try to bring Irene next time. I think she would enjoy a visit with you and Wentworth here."

Lucas and Alina rode back to the Grande Inn slowly so Lucas could tell her what Bernard had said. She took a deep breath. "You look relieved, Lucas, so I believe that must mean that Bernard is correct. We cannot speak to Brigit or Nikolas from so far away, but I think Brigit would send an intuition to you somehow, if they needed our help."

"Now, that we are here, it does feel that way." He still hadn't told her about his nightmare, but it didn't matter now. Bernard was probably right. "Which dress did you bring for this evening? The green one, I hope."

Alina's eyes sparkled, "You see Lucas your instincts are very keen. I have brought the green dress."

They walked in the candlelit garden and took notice of the flowering plants and lush greenery. Some trees and shrubs were better suited to hold the candles than others, and they paid attention to that and to which plants produced the most flowers. Seated on the bench, Alina wrote detailed notes. When Bernard and Wentworth arrived in the dining room, Lucas felt renewed and sure that all was well for himself and his friends. Alina glowed, radiant in her green dress that matched her eyes and highlighted her amber hair.

They dined on juicy roast, abundant green and red vegetables, and potatoes that had been stirred until they were soft and fluffy. A berry tart concluded the meal. Wentworth spoke fondly of his days staying at the Grande Inn but never mentioned his errant wife, Marion. Bernard agreed to accompany them back to the City of Dreams if they would agree to spend the next day with them again at the farm and also add another night to their stay at the Inn.

"We will do that, Bernard. Every time I come to Arcana, I find it difficult to leave. Irene will understand that and take care of things at home. Perhaps my concerns were nothing more than restlessness."

In the morning at early light, after another walk in the garden and a breakfast of delicious and unique pastries and teas, Lucas and Alina rode out to the pond. They removed their clothes and plunged into the abyssal blue. The cool silken water cooled them. Afterward, they stretched out in the grass and made love like they did on their wedding night.

Instead of riding over to the farm, they led the horses and walked hand in hand along the damp shady road that was puddled from a passing rain shower. "This is how I always hoped I would feel when I took a husband," Alina said. "But I never thought it would be here, in this place that I didn't know existed. This land is blessed by fairies," she whispered.

Lucas stopped and turned to her with a pleasured twinkle in his eyes. "I didn't know that you believe in fairies, my love."

"I didn't know that I did until just now. The land is so welcoming and full of magic as if the earth is telling us that everything is all right. Don't you think so, Lucas?"

Lucas laughed. "Well, when you say it like that, I have to agree. You help me to see things in a new way. Tis true. This visit to Arcana is the best one yet. I have never felt as at home here as I do now, not since I was a child and my mother and I ran free among the flower fields. You remind me not to let myself forget.

"When Irene and I first came here I experienced more confusion and sadness than anything else. I have always appreciated the elements of nature, but now at this time, it is as if this natural world welcomes and embraces us. You know, Alina, it's quite possible that

Brigit, Nikolas, and Ikarus are enjoying such a marvelous time that they just want to stay a bit longer. Just like us here."

"That certainly could explain their long absence. Ikarus has family and friends he must want to spend time with and Brigit probably as well. Who knows, maybe they will bring more than Camille back with them. That must be why they're delayed." Alina squeezed his hand. "It seems we have discovered why we needed to come to Arcana. We cannot go up the mountain, like Bernard says, without a better plan, and maybe our answer was here waiting for us."

"I hope our friends are at home waiting for us." Lucas wrapped an arm around Alina, pulled her close to him, and kissed her passionately. The horses nickered and chewed quietly with their noses in the grass. Lucas took her chin in his palm and gazed into her shining eyes. "Maybe we don't have to go back tomorrow either." Alina grinned in playful agreement.

Nestled in the valley, the red farmhouse was framed by a cloudless blue sky. They saw Bernard and Wentworth sitting in the shade under a sprawling curtain of swaying weeping willow branches.

"They're waiting for us," Lucas said.

Wentworth waved, and Bernard stood up. "Come join us. We have chairs for you here in the shade. I made them myself. I'm a furniture maker nowadays," he added laughing.

"Ah, Lucas, I see why everyone loves Arcana," Alina said as she led her horse forward. "I don't know how you stayed away for so many years. Irene told me she had to talk you into returning. Were you too sad to come back?"

"I don't know. I just avoided it. Looking back now, I believe I was more frightened than sad to return. My idyllic childhood turned into a nightmare in one single afternoon. Irene knew best though. I'm forever grateful to her for that. We will come more often," Lucas promised, "once our friends are home safe, of course."

They released their horses to clomp over to the water trough. Lucas and Alina took seats beside their friends under the tree.

Chapter 21

Brigit had enough information about flowers and herbs to keep them busy throughout the long, alpine summer day. They got off and on their mules so often to collect herbs and roots that Ikarus was glad when he noticed the sun curve toward its final arc and leave them in the purple and blue hue of twilight. He'd learned more about the land today than in his entire childhood here. They had travelled to a high plateau through and above the tree line. A massive formation of boulders created a lean-to with remnants of a previous campfire. "I didn't think the herdsmen would come up this high," Ik mused.

"I wonder who was here before us," Nik said as he pulled three sticks from a neatly stacked pile and began to lay the fire.

"Not all who wander are herders," Brigit said.

Ikarus laughed. "Yeah, we're here." He pulled the saddle off his mule and stood absently scratching its back and behind its long ears. They could hear the sound of rushing water but couldn't find the source until Brigit discovered a blast of frothy white gushing from a small rock cluster below them. "It's coming from an underground spring!" They all rushed over to drink from the chilly water and refill their waterskins. Brigit filled her pot and promised the best root stew they'd ever had.

"What's the difference between stew and porry?" Ikarus asked.

Brigit glared at him for a moment and then gave him a friendly shove. "You are about to find out, lad."

Nikolas stretched himself out on a warm flat rock and watched Ikarus and Brigit prepare the supper. The birds sang their evening songs, and he wished he never had to leave. After the most delicious root stew anyone had ever eaten, they nestled beside the fire and passed the wineskin around. Nikolas decided the firelight was the perfect setting for Ikarus to view the drawing from Camille.

He dug it out of his saddlebag and explained that Camille's sister had given it to Brigit when she went back for the wine. Ikarus took it with trembling hands and stared at it for so long that Nik and Brigit looked at each other, bewilderment flashing in their eyes. Eventually, Ikarus reached for the wineskin but instead of drinking from it, he poured some onto the drawing. Brigit grabbed the drawing, shook it and held it above the flames trying to dry it. The boy and girl were doused in red. Ikarus took a long drink. Brigit handed the drawing to Nikolas who set it on the warm rock.

"Why did you do that?" Brigit demanded.

"There's something wrong with him," Nik muttered.

"It doesn't matter anymore. Besides, it looks better with some color on it. Do you think I'll forget who she was someday?"

"Maybe," Brigit said.

"Do you want to?" Nik asked.

"Not yet. I can't. But I think it would be good if something could make me forget about her." He shook his head and let out a long sigh. "Not my mother. I should have returned to her. I wish so much that I did. My dear gentle mother will always be with me." Without looking at Nikolas or Brigit, Ikarus mumbled, "Good night." He got up and left them to sit on their own alongside the crackling fire.

"That is a confusing young man," Nikolas exclaimed.

"Yeah, but in some ways he's recovering," Brigit murmured. "I think we can go home soon." As Brigit spoke, the drawing from Camille was lifted by the wind and carried away. Nik thought to chase it and started to stand but sat back down and let the boy and girl from the past spiral upward and float away. He glanced over toward Ikarus who watched and closed his eyes.

"Yes, today he seems well. But still, it's best not to rush him. Who knows what he will say or do tomorrow." Nikolas said. "It could be the land that revives him."

"Are you not concerned about what our friends in the City of Dreams are thinking after all this time?" Brigit leaned forward and gazed intently at Nikolas. Her hair reflected blue and amber sparks. He returned her gaze with a slender smile. Her eyes flashed an array of colors. "You don't want to return?"

Nikolas leaned back on his elbows and stretched out his legs. "I do . . . just not yet. I don't miss the harbour or the smell of fish and sweaty men or their voices shouting and arguing all day long. Here, the blue sky greets me every morning. The wind whispers through the tall grass and swaying branches. You and Ikarus and me, we three are of similar disposition, don't you agree? There is nothing to do but walk on and enjoy what awaits us down the trail."

Brigit listened quietly. She understood his sentiments. It was similar to what she had experienced so long ago when she left these high hills and travelled to the City of Dreams. It was a new world to her, and everything was extraordinary and exciting. She didn't miss the things she had grown up with and ultimately taken for granted. Although, after listening to him describe her former home as he did, she wondered briefly why she left it. Did she want to stay, she asked herself, but even in her sudden doubt, she knew that she loved the City of Dreams as much now as the first day she arrived. And she had Lucas there. Her true kin.

She had changed her name to Brigit on her first day there. It was fitting they called her Beltree here and now, but that part of her had grown and gone away. Even though she had made peace with Mabon, she knew she did not belong up here anymore. The sense of wonderment would fade once the ordinary set in again. For now, though, since Nikolas enjoyed the land and the adventure so much, they could take their time. She got up and held out her hand to Nikolas. "Come on. Let's lie down and enjoy the stars together."

In the morning, Nikolas awoke at first light. He stole away quietly from the camp and followed the rushing stream downhill. He wandered on a zigzagging trail until he came to a copse of trees and sat down alongside a gurgling tributary. Gazing into the swirling depths, he noticed a large fish, then another and another. He reached in and after a few misses, he grabbed one. "Ha!" he shouted flipping it onto the ground beside him. *If only the harbour lads could see me now,* he thought.

Brigit was sitting on her blankets combing her hair with her claw necklace. "Breakfast," he grinned holding up the trout.

"Well done!" Ik said. "I'm famished."

They cooked the fish directly on the embers. Nikolas offered the largest pieces to Ikarus who appeared so content that Brigit worried he might want to stay now too. If he decided to remain, she may never get Nikolas to go back. Of course, he would have to, if for nothing more than to explain to Lucas that he no longer wanted the lantern lighter job. A long simple day awaited them, and although she wanted to get back home, she looked forward to the wandering easiness. She, herself, could almost be persuaded to stay in the high country. But soon enough, in just a few more weeks the chilly nights of fall would come and then the frigid snowy winter. For the next few days though, she would enjoy the land as if, like Nikolas, it were her first time here.

Nikolas showed them where he had caught the fish. The tributary led to a wide stream. They followed it as it traversed the green and gold mountainside, winding in and out of the trees and sometimes plunging them into deep shade and then abruptly back into the full warm sun. Occasionally, in the distance, they could hear the clanging of bells. They waited, hoping to encounter more sheep or goat herders, but the sounds echoed around the hills. To their disappointment, they didn't encounter anyone on this trail that was narrow, sloping, and deeply rutted.

As they went, the vigorous stream widened. At one point, Ikarus, having leapt from one side to the other to pick some wild onion for Brigit, found himself on the wrong side, and had to take a running leap to get over to a flat boulder jutting from the rushing water and then to the bank where Nik and Brigit with arms linked pulled him back. Later, Brigit managed to wander across a sandy rock bed and had to traverse a narrow log to rejoin them; her hair stood out parallel to her shoulders aiding her balance. "Let's all try to stay together on one side," Nikolas said.

They were still traversing the mountainside, but by afternoon, they were going downhill on steep rocky terrain. They had to dismount and allow the mules to make their own way. Then again, they came to a plateau, and the stream was more of a wide creek that was full of fish. Nikolas waded in and made a game of grabbing a fish and tossing it to Ikarus. "We will have a hearty supper tonight."

Nikolas waded and floated while Ikarus ran along the bank laughing and catching the fish that he then tossed to Brigit. The banks were mostly muddy, but also slick with green grass. Ikarus slipped in a couple of times and dropped their prize. Nikolas had to catch the fish again. They argued between their laughter whether it was indeed the same one or not. Brigit warned that the basket was filling up fast and they should throw some back. "We're hungry!" Ik shouted. "And the water is refreshing." They frolicked in the surging current as they tossed fish to Brigit.

Brigit caught one after another and arranged them in her collecting basket so as not to disturb the roots in the satchel that was slung over her shoulders. Focused on arranging the fish in the cumbersome basket, she didn't see what was coming. When she looked up, the water was thundering toward the edge of the world. For a second, Nik from where he stood in the center of the rushing water, turned around and stared at her. His face was impassive, almost curious. His sand-colored hair, dark and wet now, clung to his neck.

Then, suddenly he was spinning. He whirled away from her and went under. Her hair shot outward, reaching for Nikolas. One of his arms was flailing high above the raging water. Then, his head popped up. The swirling tumult spun him around. His eyes filled his entire face that was white with shock. He went under again. Brigit saw a knee. She saw the bottom of one foot. And then he was gone.

The water plunged, tumbling and slamming over the edge. Ikarus stood on the bank clutching his head with both hands. He screamed and kept screaming until his screams and the pounding of the water all sounded the same.

Brigit, frozen in place with the soggy satchel cementing her to the spot, suddenly lurched forward, her hair flying up like a sheet of black. She tripped and fell flat on her face. "Oof!" she said as she clawed to untangle her feet from the satchel. The flopping fish with their bulging eyes glared at her in horror. She heard her own voice screaming, along with Ikarus, as she scrambled to the edge of the cliff. Crawling on her hands and knees with Ikarus shouting behind her she peeked over the edge of the deafening white waterfall.

The water moved so fast that her eyes could not adjust to what she was seeing. Tumbling white water. Nothing more. Frantically searching the landscape around them, she saw the mules following each other along a dusty, switch backing trail through the green meadow off to her left. The indifferent mules had noticed nothing as they lazily plodded along. Safe passage, so close, she thought.

Ikarus grabbed her arm and shouted something that she couldn't understand. He raced to the edge, and for an instant she thought he intended to jump in, but he stopped and tore off his tunic. His back and shoulders were rippled with tawny muscles. He turned around and began to climb backward down the slippery rocks. She looked from him to the mild mules and wondered what to do next. She ended up doing nothing but standing there, gripping a boulder with one hand, her other arm outstretched as if Ikarus, who had managed to climb far below her, would need to reach for her. She held her breath as she watched his bare feet struggle to find the next ledge. His hair splayed back from his face that was as gray as the raging water. His trembling lips were purple, and his blue eyes filled with fear. But Ikarus climbed swiftly and skillfully like the mountain goats he'd grown up with. Still Brigit could not move. If she abandoned the spot from where she last saw Nikolas she might never see him again. She hugged the boulder and watched as Ikarus reached the bottom of the sheer waterfall and ran along the precipice of the raging whirlpool. He was shouting and waving his arms around like a madman. He glanced up at her from time to time shaking his head. When he stared up at her for a long moment and then crouched by the edge to slip into the water, she screamed, "No!" Her hair flew up. He hesitated. Brigit released her grip on the boulder and ran down the path the mules had taken.

By the time she got to the swirling pool at the bottom of the waterfall, Ikarus was pulling his long, shivering body from the churning current. He looked twenty years older than he did just a few minutes ago. The stream, which was now a river, sped through a stone-walled canyon, around a sharp bend and out of sight. They clutched each other and fell to the ground sobbing. Over Ik's shuddering shoulders, she saw the mules munching on the sweet grass, their saddlebags securely in place. Nothing had changed for them. Brigit wanted to die. Her crystal ball reading that Camille was still in her village was absurdly wrong. She couldn't remember if she had any poisonous plants in those saddlebags.

———————

The sun moved across the sky and left them in shadow before Brigit and Ikarus finally clambered over to the mules and pulled them into a group of cottonwood trees. From there, they could still hear the terrible waterfall. But they could not see it. They built a fire in silence. They each pulled off their soggy clothes and wrapped themselves in blankets. Lying on opposite sides of the fire, they fed it with sticks throughout the night so that a lost traveller might see its welcoming glow and find his way home.

The next day, as Brigit watched the sun move across the sky, she kept telling herself that this time yesterday Nikolas was here, tossing fish, laughing. She repeated this thought until the hour hit that he had slipped over. Then she forced herself to stop reliving the moment by eating a handful of herbs.

The two of them spent three nights beside the fire. During the day, they stacked wood and sticks for the fire. They drank water but neither felt like eating. They didn't speak. Their shock and grief had created an immediate bond of understanding. On the third morning, they walked back to the top of the waterfall. They marked the place with rock cairns and one of Nikolas' warm shirts. Brigit made a figure out of sticks and placed it inside the shirt. Ikarus turned away to give her the moment.

They followed the mules down the trail that ran adjacent to the river. This river, Brigit knew, would ultimately lead them back to the City of Dreams. She walked as slowly as she could.

Some days, they didn't bother to start walking until the late afternoon and then only until the sun set. Brigit prepared broth, herbs, and roots. They ate from the pot and dipped the last of the hard bread they'd brought from Camille's village into it. Afterward they took small sips of wine. They remained quiet throughout the day as well as the evenings by the fire, each listening for a familiar voice to come out of the landscape.

One morning as they kicked their fire into ashes, Ikarus said, "I find it strange that we have not encountered one person at all. No herders, gypsies, nobody."

Brigit nodded solemnly. "I think so too. I hoped to encounter people in villages or the herders most of all and tell them to search for Nikolas. At night, I think I hear sheep bells. I can still see the look of triumph on Nik's face when we reached Camille's village. I've heard footfalls as well. I sit up and wait, but nobody comes." She shook her head and glanced around. "Maybe we are the ones who are lost."

Ikarus stared in the direction of Brigit's gaze, "It seems that way. What if Nikolas is already home sitting at the table in the boarding house drinking Irene's special tea?"

Brigit began to smile, but her face cracked into tears. "We can't go back, Ikarus. At least, I can't." Her hair turned white for a brief instant.

"I know," Ikarus moaned. "What will we say? We have let Nikolas get swept away! We are the ones who come from this land. How do we tell everyone how utterly stupid we are."

"You can go back, Ikarus. You can tell them it was my fault." She sniffed and plopped down on a smooth log as if she'd just found the home for which she'd been searching.

"What will you do, Brigit?" Ikarus raked his fingers through his hair, a move that reminded her of Nikolas.

"I'll just stay out here." She looked up at the sky and then back at Ikarus, "Take a potion or something," she whispered.

"A potion for . . ." Ikarus tilted his head, quizzical." Wait . . . no! No, you won't!" Ikarus grabbed her wrist and pulled her to her feet. "Listen, now we have both suffered a great loss. But this . . . this is so much worse than a girl choosing another. It happened to both of us. Well, to all of us. Now though, you and me, we have only one choice; we have to go back and explain to our friends. We will do the right thing for Nikolas. And, if after that, we can't bear to live anymore, we can go to the monastery. That's where people like us end up."

Brigit groaned but didn't bother to answer. She stared intently at the mules as they munched on the long grass. Each evening, they took the satchels and bundles off Nikolas' mule and in the morning put the same ones back on again. They hadn't added any bundles or taken any away. They'd been taking turns leading his mule behind their own and making sure it had plenty of sweet grass, water, and encouraging words. Their own mules, although they ate and drank the same as Nik's, drooped and stumbled under the weight of their forlorn riders. Now, even after a night of rest, they chewed with passive weariness. Yesterday, Nik's mule had tried to pass them on the trail. It trotted forward with vibrant determination. "We do have to go back!" she blurted.

Ik gaped at her.

"Ikarus," she said gripping him by the shoulders. "What have we been doing out here? We must go back and get Lucas. He can find Nikolas. Lucas healed himself! He can find Nikolas." She grabbed an armful of bundles and began to load up the mules. "Let's go. Don't just stand there. Bring Nik's mule. Hurry!"

They pushed the mules to the limit of their compliance. It was the final fringe of twilight when Ikarus finally reined in. "We have to eat now. All of us." He unloaded the mules while Brigit slopped something out of the pot where it had fermented all day. Ik hesitated but his stomach growled. He glanced begrudgingly at the grazing mules wishing he could eat grass as well. Brigit glared at him then poured some wine in his bowl and stirred it up. Whatever it was he couldn't tell and didn't dare ask. There was still plenty of wine left so they finished off all but one of the wineskins.

Afterward, Brigit who had been sullen through supper began to talk and describe the look on Nikolas' face when they showed up with Lucas. Nik would be camped at the edge of the river, trapped, but warm beside a fire eating fresh fish. They would pick up the laughter right where they'd left it at the top of the waterfall, where they'd goosed around grabbing fish. It will be as if nothing bad had happened at all. "Nothing at all," she told Ikarus.

Lying on his back looking up at the stars, Ikarus was relieved that they were going home at last. He liked better his own story that Nikolas was snug in the boarding house. Brigit had her own illusion. Neither of them was possible. He doubted there was anything Lucas could do at this point. In fact, he expected Lucas to fly into a rage at both of them. Well, he, himself, deserved it. Besides, nobody liked to confront Brigit. She would be the one to speak since she intended to compel Lucas to come out here and fix their wretched lives by finding Nikolas.

He memorized the route although all they needed to do was stay alongside the river. Wouldn't they look even more the imbeciles when they simply followed the river into the city?

Ikarus realized he didn't care about Camille anymore. His heart was completely empty when he thought about her. He tried to continue to pine for her, since that is why they came on this journey to begin with, but he didn't care. He might never care about anything again. Yet, as he closed his eyes, he allowed himself to nurture a small flame of hope that they would indeed come back out here with Lucas, and he would make Nikolas appear, just as he inexplicably made his own wounds disappear.

In the morning, Brigit cooked yet another unusual thing she pulled from the ground. She passed the wineskin to help wash it down. "We will reach the outskirts of the city by the end of this day," she said.

"How do you know that?"

"I can tell. So, today, we will take the time to restore ourselves. We must regain what we have lost of our spirit so that Lucas will be able to feel Nikolas through us."

Ikarus glared at the ground. She truly was a crazy wild witch. Did she actually believe that Nikolas hadn't died falling off that waterfall? No living creature could survive that plunge. Lucas had unique abilities, certainly. But Ikarus, and nobody else for that matter, ever thought that Lucas was capable of saving anyone's life or restoring the dead. She was killing his last hope of forgiveness with her bizarre scheming. Ikarus reached for the wineskin. Perhaps she'd risen earlier and begun drinking. He would try to find that level of delusion to get through the day. He forced a smile and nodded. "All right, Brigit, tell me what to think about as we take our last steps home with our dreaded news."

"Fine. Good. We will stop outside the city, close enough to bask in its glowing lanterns. We will invoke Nikolas' spirit. In the morning, his essence will accompany us to the boarding house where Lucas will know what to do. The rest is up to him."

Ikarus stopped himself from saying, *brilliant plan if there were any chance that it might work.* Instead, he nodded several times to hide that he was actually shaking. He would have to answer to Lucas once Lucas realized, and it would only take a few minutes, that Brigit had fully lost her mind. Perhaps, she'd been a lunatic all along and Ikarus hadn't noticed. Wouldn't Lucas have known though? Probably not, or surely he wouldn't have let them all go off together.

Nothing at all had gone right on their journey. The best part of it, in truth, were the minutes just before Nikolas disappeared. Ikarus couldn't stop himself from reliving those moments: the keen look on Nik's face, his tanned arms plunging into the water grabbing the darting fish, the utter joy as he tossed wriggling fish to Ikarus, and then his glance at Brigit to make sure she appreciated it too. And she had laughed and encouraged them as well. They all had been enjoying the most wondrous time.

Until it ended.

Chapter 22

In the murky hours just before dawn, off the coast of Ingleena, the ship *Le Peresi* dropped anchor outside the harbour. A bundled dead body was handed off to a waiting skiff. It was customary, if too close for burial at sea, to remove deceased passengers before arriving at port. The young perpetrator was also removed to an additional skiff, chained, and then loaded onto a ship that would return her to her original port of sail.

* * *

The tenant farmers on Bernard and Wentworth's farm grew onions, parsnips, garlic, and parsley. Alina and Bernard gathered sacks to take back to Irene. Before they returned to the willow tree where Lucas and Wentworth shared a few memories from Lucas' childhood, Alina spoke quietly to Bernard. "I understand your concerns, Bernard, about yourself and Lucas travelling into the high country alone to search for our friends, but I wonder if you could rally several of your companions to assist in the search as well. They are familiar with the natural world, and I imagine as strong and resilient as are you. I do not expect to find Brigit and the men at home when we arrive tomorrow."

Bernard smiled down softly at her. "Yes, Alina, I can tell that Lucas shares your concerns. Something must be done, and I believe you have come up with a good plan. Have you mentioned this to Lucas yet?'

"Not yet. I hoped to have your agreement first."

"I will help of course. I do know several men who would enjoy a mission like this."

"Thank you, Bernard!" Alina threw her arms around his thick waist. "Let's go tell Lucas! We will enjoy a few more hours here on your peaceful land, and then in the morning we can all head out to the City of Dreams and onward."

"Lucas will not allow you to come with us, Alina."

"Oh, I know that," she said with a sly smile. "But what he doesn't know is that I believe he must go along with you. I know you will look out for him, Bernard."

Bernard placed his burly hand upon his heart. "As my brother, I will protect Lucas with my life."

The Grande Inn served Lucas and Alina dinner in the candlelit garden among the abundant, aromatic flowering trees and plants. They sipped their wine from crystal glasses and held hands while they slowly enjoyed their meal.

In the morning they would return to the boarding house with Bernard and his men. At that time, unless a miracle had delivered Nik, Ik, and Brigit safely home, they would gather provisions for the search party, recruit from Brigit's clan as Lucas had suggested, and immediately launch the search. For now, though, in the tranquil twilight, they kept their focus on the serene garden, the special meal, and each other.

Just after dawn, Bernard rode up to the Inn with five robust men on solid horses all laden with supply satchels. The eight of them, including Lucas and Alina, made one stop at the No Horses Tavern to share a toast to good fortune. Lucas rode proudly behind Alina admiring her fearless horsemanship. She could ride as well as any of the men. Before midday, the bunch pounded over the stone bridge into the City of Dreams. Lucas noticed a startled woman on the riverbank turn in alarm at the racket. He turned quickly to Alina who, by her expression, also recognized Drusilla combing about in the thickets.

Bernard and his band rode directly to the cottages to question those who might have knowledge of Brigit's path, and from there they would stop by the harbour to rouse Igmus and Rathbone.

Inside the boarding house, Lucas embraced Irene and left it to Alina to tell her the plan while he changed into travelling clothes.

Irene wrung her hands and shook her head as Alina explained that the time had come to find out what had happened to Brigit, Nikolas, and Ikarus. They could no longer convince themselves that all was well. Carissa brewed a strong tea. By the time Lucas came into the kitchen, the women had stuffed a sack full of provisions. He kept his arm around Alina's shoulders as they walked toward the front door to say their goodbyes.

A loud knock made everyone jump, and Irene swore loudly. Yanking the door open, Lucas intended to reprimand the intruder, but he was greeted by his old friend, the constable.

"There's been a murder!" the constable exclaimed before noticing the women. "Excuse me, ladies. But well, you're going to find out soon enough. Mr. Plimpton has been stabbed to death in his berth."

Lucas glanced around at Alina, Irene, and Carissa who all appeared as confused as him. None of them recognized the name. "That is a shame, I'm sure," Lucas said, "but I must go. We have an important mission." He pushed past the constable, Alina's hand firmly in his as he wanted a few private moments with her.

"Wait, Lucas. He and his young bride stayed here not long ago. They awaited a ship to Ingleena. Somebody must remember them."

"What? That little blonde girl?" Irene squeaked.

"I didn't notice what color her hair is, but she is at the harbour now and has admitted that the two of them stayed here."

"Maybe it's them," Irene said turning to Carissa. "The young girl with that arrogant old man."

"We don't know much about them," Carissa said. "Why do you come here with this news?"

"We have to follow through on where she came from. Mr. Plimpton was a prominent citizen of Ingleena, an emissary for Lord Brimley." He peered at Alina. "Have you never heard of him, he travelled with his young bride, Ca . . .?"

"I've heard of Lord Brimley," Alina interrupted. "But I don't know any details or anything about him, other than his name. We have a pressing matter of our own right now."

"Did Mr. Plimpton stay here or not, Mrs. Kempel?" the constable asked Irene. "The young woman says he is her husband, or was, before she stabbed him to death." He looked at Carissa now. "His wife, did you meet her? She's about your age. Camille is her name."

A moment ticked in stunned silence. Then a hand flew to Irene's throat. "By the heavens in bloody hell," she cried. "Her name was Camille?!"

"Could she be the same one . . . damn it," Lucas pounded a fist on the door jamb. "What are you telling us, sir? What is going on with this Plimpton person? And, you say a young woman named Camille who stayed in this boarding house . . ." He looked at Alina, "Is that a common name? Someone stabbed Plimpton? It's not an often-heard name, is it?"

"I never heard of anyone with it," Irene said flatly. "Not that I remember now."

"She killed that man?" Alina said doubtfully.

"She stabbed him," the constable said making an upward gouging gesture.

Carissa bit her lip as if she were trying not to laugh, and Lucas caught her eye. "All right, you've informed us. We don't know anything about her, that supposed lord, or his emissary or whoever."

Still blocking the doorway, the constable crossed his arms and said, "Mrs. Kempel, I'm asking you, did the girl stay here?"

"They did stay here," Carissa admitted. "And we all felt sorry for that young girl. I can't imagine her stabbing a piece of meat let alone a stuffy old man."

"Quite unlikely," Alina added. "She never spoke to any of us. Lucas has to go now. And so do you." She gave him a small shove.

The constable glowered but took a backward step. Lucas followed him outside and explained their situation, "Nikolas, Brigit, and Ikarus are overdue. That is far more important to us right now. But bring the girl here. We can hold onto her. A young woman like that shouldn't be in the cells."

Lucas turned to Irene where she stood on the threshold. "She's coming here. Alina's chamber is ready. Lock her in there. Find out if she is Ikarus' girl. If so, then this is worse than I imagined."

He ran a hand through his hair. "I have to go Irene. Be careful and make sure the lads keep the lanterns lit. Extra if possible so the light can be seen from far, far away." Irene nodded somberly and then took his face between her hands and kissed each cheek. Carissa moved to stand next to her.

Lucas and Alina walked away a few paces to bid each other farewell. They wrapped their arms around each other and stood silently together for several long minutes. "Do not disappear," Alina murmured. She slipped the black lace veil inside his shirt and pressed her palm against his heart. Lucas kissed her wet eyelids, and still holding her hand as he turned to go replied. "I did not come here to fail."

* * *

Drusilla had just changed out of her muddy clothes and put on her apron in the scullery when the constable appeared at the front door. Usually, everyone was gathered in the kitchen at this time of night. She turned and scurried back into her room and waited there, her ear pressed to the door. Bad timing for the return of Alina and Lucas. They may have seen her by the river, but they wouldn't know why she was there, and hopefully they would forget to ask now. Ever since disposing of Gacheru, she'd walked the route from the canal to the sea to make sure her beastly brother hadn't left anything behind. And he had! Tonight, she found his boot. It was gone now, burned at the same beggars fire that took her blood-stained dress. She hoped that was the very last of him. Checking for remnants of the worthless lout was a tiring chore even though nothing else had shown up in all these weeks.

Drusilla could barely breathe when she heard what they said about Camille. How foolish of the girl to stab the man aboard ship! And now she was coming back to the boarding house. Drusilla plopped down onto her feather bed with a gasp. How short her run of good fortune had been. Camille was shrewder than anyone knew. But even this murder was Gacheru's fault. Nobody would be dead if not for him.

That morning when she saw him laughing at the Duck, she could bear it no more. He'd had that same delight on his face as he did that day so many years ago when he had assured their mother that she was doing the right thing by sending Drusilla away. "After all," he had said, "she's one more mouth to feed, and she eats too much!"

She had waited in the alley close next to the Duck Tavern. As she huddled there, she pieced together her plan without fully admitting she'd planned it. She hated him. He would never stop hurting her. He enjoyed it. He thought it was his right to control her and take everything away from her. Nobody could help her. She had to find courage to help herself. This time, she would keep what mattered to her. She couldn't bear to go back into his dark and filthy way of life.

When Gacheru finally emerged from the tavern, she was stiff and achy from standing in one place so long, but she waved and walked up to him. "Hey, there you are. I've been looking for you. I came across a house with a window open."

He looked sideways at her, his mouth slack from whisky and perhaps doubt. "It's on the Boulevard. Come on," she urged. "We got to get there before someone comes back. I saw a gold watch and earrings and rings and pewter cups and silver plates . . ." He perked up and followed her. Hoping not to be seen by anyone, she darted behind the square toward the canals. "Hurry, Gach. It's a shortcut."

Groaning, and complaining, he staggered behind her. "This better be good, Drusilla! I'll rip your hair out if not," he threatened.

"It's what we've both been waiting for!" she promised with a forced grin.

On a narrow path at the farthest edge of the dark zone, where the canals were constantly flooded by sea surge, Drusilla stopped. She had at least an hour before high tide. It would take a few minutes for Gach to catch up, sweating and panting as he was. As she stood waiting and shifting from one foot to the other, she glanced down at her reflection in the water. She almost didn't recognize the contented woman she saw there. Her brother shuffled up to her, the usual indignation on his face. "What are you doing, Drusilla? This isn't nowhere near the Boulevard!"

She turned and grinned at him with hooded dark eyes. "I know that," she hissed. He took a step forward, a hand raised to slap her, his twisted mouth open to spew one last insult that she would never hear. With both hands, she thrust the knife into his chest where his heart would be if he had one. He made the most disgusting gurgling sound she'd ever heard. Red goop shot out of his mouth and onto her frock. One of his crooked black teeth clung to the crimson mess. Her stomach flipped, and she dry heaved. He slumped backward, his knees twisting into an ungainly angle. "Why . . ." he croaked.

"At last," she whispered bending over him to shove the knife deeper, "I am free of you."

His bloodshot eyes showed one last look of confusion before they went blank. She waited until he stopped twitching. There was a gurgle, *like his last snore*, she thought smiling to herself. After a few moments waiting to make sure he didn't move, she went to the canal and rinsed the knife. Glancing back, she could barely see his bloody body in the twilight. She grabbed him by the feet and dragged him over to the canal. Exhausted now, she sprawled on the bank and waited until the sea tide made its way up the canal raising the water level. Then she rolled him in headfirst. The current caught Gacheru and carried him out of her life forever. She quickly walked away.

Weeks passed. She felt released, but the images of what she had done lived on in her mind.

When Drusilla finally crept out of her room, Alina was sitting alone and staring into the fire. She wished she could have bid Lucas safe travels and comforted Alina, who glanced at her and smiled thinly. Drusilla knew she'd forgotten about seeing her along the river. Her heart ached for all of them missing their friends. It seemed bad luck could happen to anybody. "Would a little cup of wine help at all, Alina?"

Alina shook her head and Drusilla turned toward the kitchen. "Wait, Drusy. Come sit for a bit, will you? Let's have wine and chat."

"Of course, Alina. I'll fetch it." Herbs grow along the riverbank, Drusy thought, in case Alina did ask what she was doing out there.

She sat across from her waiting for Alina to say something and hoping that she didn't have to lie about anything. "Would you like some bread and cheese? Carissa said you hadn't eaten. I'll just bring it in."

They sipped wine and nibbled on the cheese by the slim light of the low burning fire. "Do you wonder if you will ever see Gacheru again?" Alina asked.

"Uh, well no." Drusy took a long gulp of wine and swallowed hard. "I worry more for Brigit, Nikolas, and Ikarus. But Lucas and Bernard will bring them back soon."

Alina's face lit up. "Do you really think so?"

"Of course. I'm sure of it. They will return safe and sound, and we will have a big celebration." She stopped, wondering why she'd so boldly included herself, but Alina didn't seem to mind.

"Yes, Drusy, we will! You're right." Alina nodded cheerfully.

"Soon," Drusilla murmured.

"I agree. Thank you for your comforting words." She clasped her hands together and placed them in her lap. "And you, are you not too sad about your brother? Do you think he may have drowned in the river, or fell off the harbour into the sea? Perhaps he's taken ill somewhere and needs help."

"It's certainly possible," Drusilla said, a tear of relief sliding down her cheek.

Alina embraced Drusilla who, having never been comforted by anyone before, broke into sobs. Irene darted into the parlour and, — seeing the two women sobbing— wrapped her arms around them. All three women wept for their missing friends, and the joyful life they'd lost, and the possibility of everything getting worse.

Chapter 23

In the morning, Alina went to the monastery to speak with Seppo. She stopped first in the secret cemetery and placed a colorful bunch of flowers at Linnea's gravestone and a few at all the others as well. It was such a beautiful, warm day that she sat in the lush green grass and spoke to the long-gone occupants. When Seppo didn't appear, she went around to the carved double doors. Finding them open she strolled through.

The solemn wood walls and sandalwood candles created an ancient contrast to the living cemetery. Seppo was not there in the large room, so Alina sat down to wait and soon drifted off to sleep. Upon awakening, it took her several long moments to understand where she was. She couldn't remember ever having slept so well. Looking around she found water in a pitcher and drank half of it.

It was midafternoon. Where could Seppo be she wondered. She climbed up into one of the pulpits and looked over the room. It would be lovely if Seppo agreed to allowing Irene and some of the others to come in. *This is a sanctuary,* she thought. There was a narrow door behind the pulpit. Surprised to find it unlocked, she went through. It led to a dimly lit hallway. "Seppo," she called out, "it is I, Alina. Hello

. . . Seppo? Are you there?" She walked forward running her hand along the wall and calling his name.

When she came to a green door, she faltered in fear. A flash of heat rose up in her. Where was she? Had she turned any corners? Her heart thudded like a rock against her ribs. She spun around and hurried back the way she hoped she had come. Finding a small door up ahead she ran and burst through it onto the pulpit. But it was not the same one. She had emerged on the opposite end of the room. She was sure of it, or was she?

Alina ran outside through the cemetery and through the mulberry branches. Just on the other side of the cloudy moat, she saw a cloaked figure walking slowly and carrying a cumbersome bundle. How could rags be so heavy she thought as she realized it was Seppo. She stepped forward. A bare foot slipped from the layers of rags. She squinted trying to understand what she was seeing. A man's foot, it was twisted at an odd angle. Catching her breath in her throat, she backed up, tripped, landed hard on her rump, scrambled up, and ran.

* * *

Brigit and Ikarus had sat above the river looking down on the City of Dreams for two nights. Ikarus didn't care what came next, and since Brigit was busy with her incantations he simply lay in the dirt and waited. Now, she compulsively tapped her hair claws against a rock. "Are you trying to break that?" he finally asked her, "Because I can do it for you. You should have kept the hourglass. You know that now, don't you?" She refused to speak but he knew she could hear him as her hair responded by swirling up. She handed him a cup. Ikarus drank what she gave him and dozed.

* * *

Within hours of embarking on the rescue mission in the darkest hour of deep night, Lucas, Bernard, Igmus, Rathbone, and the five countrymen stumbled upon Brigit and Ikarus. The two had made no fire, but Lucas and his men all carried lanterns. Ikarus awoke with a shout seeing a circle of monstrous fireflies surrounding him. Brigit began to laugh in eerie satisfaction. Lucas gaped in shock and joy. Going to Brigit, he grabbed her and pulled her up. Her laughter stopped abruptly. Ikarus ran to Lucas and hugged him from behind. "Ik, what's wrong with her?" Lucas passed Brigit to Bernard who steadied her.

"Lucas, I'm so glad you came," Ikarus blurted out. The other men held their lanterns high. "I'm sorry," Ikarus exclaimed. "Forgive me."

They stared at each other in the circle of light. Ikarus stood forlorn, waiting as the terrible truth struck Lucas. Even in the orange light, Ikarus could see Lucas go pale. Nikolas was missing.

"Where?" Lucas finally asked.

"Waterfall," Ik whispered.

"What?" Lucas put his hand on Ik's shoulder and squeezed tightly. "What did you say?"

"Waterfall," Ik whispered again. He glanced at Brigit wavering at the edge of the circle of light. Bernard kept a firm hold on her, his burly arm gripping her around the waist. Her black eyes were marbled with red spider legs, her hair suddenly a silvery white. Ikarus slumped to the ground. Lucas' hand on his neck was clammy and cold.

"Sit down." Lucas demanded even though Ikarus was already on the ground. Lucas went to Brigit, reached inside her smock, and pulled out the claw necklace. "Where is it?"

"It's gone. Hopeless," Ik muttered.

"You lost the hourglass?"

"She gave it away," Ikarus said. "To Mabon."

"Who is that?"

"Her cousin."

"Why?" Lucas let the claw necklace fall against her chest. Brigit's eyes went back to blue and her hair black. Lucas slumped to the ground next to Ikarus. "Somebody light a fire. Ikarus, tell us everything that happened."

When Ikarus finished speaking, the sorrowful men and Brigit sat staring absently into the fire. Just before dawn, Lucas left them there.

* * *

Camille was already locked in Alina's old room when she got back to the boarding house. Irene paced in the courtyard garden complaining to Mr. Pagett. "We can't just leave her in that tiny room. I wish Brigit were here. She would know what to do. Oh, Alina, there you are! What did Lucas mean for us to do with this poor wretched girl? Where have you been all day. Is there any news?"

Alina sighed and chewed her bottom lip. She couldn't tell anyone what she just saw. "There's no news about anything right now. Has anyone questioned Camille yet? Let's bring her down. She won't run away. There is no place for her to go. I want to know what happened."

Wiping her hands on her apron, Drusilla entered the garden from the parlour. "I'm not so sure, Alina. We could all get into trouble. Don't you think you should do what the constable said and keep her locked up?"

Alina pouted and glanced at Irene who looked weary. "I suppose you're right, Drusy. We have to keep the promise that Lucas made. I wish he were here. I need to talk to him. My heart hurts." She took Irene's hand and squeezed it. "It's your house Irene. What shall we do about Camille?"

Irene frowned and rolled her eyes. "Well, for now, I suppose we keep her locked in. She refuses to speak at all. Nonetheless, we will serve her the same as ourselves: wine, fresh cheese, warm bread, just like any other guest. She will talk in her own time."

"Shall I fix her a tray then, Mrs. Kempel?" Drusy asked.

"No, Drusilla. You have enough to do. I, myself, will take care of this girl."

* * *

Bernard found Lucas pacing along the edge of the river. "My men and I will go up," Bernard told him. "I think you want to get these two back down to the city."

"I do," Lucas said. "But if there's any chance that Nikolas is still alive, I am going to find him."

"I'll go back up," Ikarus said. "I know where he went over."

Lucas turned pale; he squeezed his eyes shut and clutched his brow. Shaking his head, he turned to Igmus and Rathbone. "Take Brigit to the boarding house. Go slowly. Allow her to take her time. Enter through the outskirts of the city. If she wants to stop at her cottage, it's fine. But don't let her out of your sight. Make sure you take her to the boarding house. Once there, speak gently to the women. Tell them that we are all right, except that Nikolas . . . uh . . . that Nikolas, he quite possibly is not. Nikolas is not all right. Stay with them. Have Carissa bunk you with the laborers. He peered in earnest at the two of them. "Can you do that for me?"

"We can," Igmus grunted.

"We will," Rathbone nodded and shook Lucas' hand. "Fare thee well,   friend."

Lucas wrapped his arms around Brigit. "I will find Nikolas. One way or another, I will bring him back." Pulling away, she grumbled and sniffed. He couldn't make her meet his eyes. Lucas smoothed her hair. "I don't believe this is your fault."

Brigit closed her eyes, and Ikarus embraced her. She sobbed into his chest, then wiped her face with the back of her hands, and turned to follow Igmus and Rathbone. Lucas and the men took the three mules with them to help carry their supplies and for Nikolas as he may need to be carried. Ikarus broke away and ran back to Brigit.

"Lucas is right, Beltree. Don't blame yourself. I have a grain of hope. Your invocations may prove true." He squeezed her hand, and she tried to smile.

On the way back up the mountain, Lucas asked that Ikarus tell him the rest of the story. Ikarus reluctantly explained all the events that had unfolded on the ill-fated journey. Beginning with their dazzling view of the city that first night atop the hills, to the wonderment and beauty they discovered together in the terrain. He described the feeling of foreboding that came upon Brigit in the strange clustering of trees.

Ikarus recounted her tale of the tree wizard man and then meeting Mabon. He told Lucas who Brigit really was and that her given name was Beltree. With begrudging words that erased the last traces of expectation that lingered at the frayed edges of his heart, Ikarus described how Mabon helped them find Camille's village. Lucas stopped and held his breath when Ikarus lowered his voice to a whisper and struggled to admit that she was not there waiting for him. When Ikarus finished speaking, his arms hung helplessly at his side, his face void of youthful exuberance, his young face a mask of dejection.

Lucas was intrigued that Brigit had cousins in these mountains and secretly hoped that someday he could meet them. But now was not the time for that kind of hope. He could only count on his own determination to find Nikolas or somehow change what had happened or even make it not true.

When Ikarus got to the part where Nikolas slipped over the waterfall, they both stopped walking. They waited until the others trudged ahead. Ikarus spoke in a hollow voice, his moist blue eyes remained fixed on the trunks of swaying saplings in the woods. His hair was the color of corn silk, wispy strands ruffled by the fragrant breeze stuck to his dry lips. He didn't seem to notice.

Slowly but ultimately, he told Lucas every single detail about those glorious last moments with Nikolas. The tinkling rhythm of the water, the slap of the fish when Nik tossed it to him. Nik's shout of joy; *got it!* when he grabbed the fish with both his hands and held it high above his head. "We were laughing right up until the very end." When Ik's words faded away leaving tears on his tanned cheeks, Lucas gripped him in a fierce embrace. Ikarus mumbled into Lucas' shoulder, "Brigit said you can fix this. Can you?"

"I don't know," Lucas groaned between clenched teeth. He released Ikarus and walked forward. "Come on, it will be dark soon. If we find Nikolas . . ." he began. Sighing, he ran his hands over his face and through his hair. "We must find him. That's all I know." He realized as they continued upward that he felt as possessed as Brigit.

Lucas was relieved though that Ikarus hadn't asked how things were going in the City of Dreams. Lucas didn't have to tell Ikarus that Camille, in all likelihood, the girl he'd gone searching for, had slept for several days in their own boarding house, and with a man, apparently her husband, whom she was now accused of murdering. He did not say that even a slight variance in Ikarus' schedule may have changed her fate and their destiny. If only he'd come upon her in the kitchen. Nobody would ever know how closely their paths had nearly crossed. Lucas did not say that the journey to find Camille was futile before it even began.

Chapter 24

Alina couldn't sleep. The bedchamber echoed an eerie emptiness without Lucas there. She got up and pressed her ear to the wall to listen for Camille. The endless hour between three and four tormented her. Lucas had not taken his pocket watch with him. The more she stared at it, the less the minute hand moved. Lying down again, she began to drift off when fear shook her upright. Seppo.

She should have called out to him. What prevented her from doing so? He looked more like Lucas at that moment than a willowy monk. His jaw was set in fierce determination, and his frail frame had suddenly become sinewy strong. He carried a man shrouded in cloth. Although she only saw the dangling foot, the man appeared to be sleeping. But he could have been dead. Maybe an ancient monk who helped to guard the gold? Seppo was walking toward the secret cemetery.

She still wondered who had helped care for her when she was taken there by Dugald. Lucas wanted to know who was inside the monastery, but she couldn't discern exactly what she had seen. It was a frightening and confusing experience. She had felt the presence of someone at the time. Was it only Seppo? He certainly seemed to be alone now. But was there another, one who had fallen ill perhaps? Seppo spoke about others to Lucas, didn't he? She'd been escorted through the tunnels to the road to Arcana. Seppo was the tall slender one and maybe someone else was there. She had thought so afterwards, but she was distraught and scared.

Now, as she tried to remember, a part of her didn't want to know if there were other monks after all. If the monks were ill or dying, Seppo must be taking care of them. Lucas said he saw Seppo only when he was alone. She felt sorry for him. He was kind, Lucas' father, a man who had lost his life's love, Linnea. But he was keeping a powerful secret in the cellar.

Her own maid, Daria, had kept secrets for years. No one turns out to be who they seem on the surface. At least, that's how she felt in the nagging darkness with Camille's quiet presence looming behind the wall. The shadowy fire flickered leaping ghostly images on the walls. She wished she had the nerve to light a candle and go down the hall to Irene's room. She wouldn't mind at all, Alina knew. But she remained rooted in the bed. Her thoughts too heavy to move. By the time the first birdsong began in the pale gray dawn, Alina had decided to go back to the monastery and check on Seppo. Lucas would certainly want her to make sure his father was all right.

She knocked on Camille's door, waited, and then knocked again. She pressed her ear to the door until she thought she detected the sound of breathing, but she couldn't be sure that it wasn't the morning breeze coming in through the tiny window. Alina had felt such joy in the small room. She hoped it was some comfort to Camille as well. But how could it be? After knocking a third time and calling Camille's name, she hurried down to the kitchen where she thought she heard the boarders talking with Irene. Nothing could prepare her for what she saw upon entering the kitchen.

Brigit was perched rigid and dazed on the corner of the long table. Her hands waved in the air while she muttered curious words. Irene was seated beside her, rubbing her back. Igmus and Rathbone stood awkwardly off to the side, eyeing the morning loaves cooling on the sideboard. "Where's Lucas?" Alina gasped.

Irene squeezed her eyes shut, but several tears spilled out anyway. She held out a hand, and Alina grabbed it. Shrieking, she asked, "Where is he, Irene?"

"Lucas is fine. Why don't you serve Igmus and Rathbone." Irene gestured to Igmus who came forward and led Alina away from Brigit.

Alina sliced bread for the two men and the three of them went to sit at the far end of the kitchen at the laborers' table. The two gruff men gently conveyed the terrible news about Nikolas. When Alina began to tremble, Rathbone covered her small hand with his dirty, calloused one, and Igmus gracefully poured her a cup of tea. Her mind raced; how was poor Ikarus faring in this terrible turn of events. Did he blame himself? She felt certain that he must, as much as Brigit clearly did. When Mr. Pagett came through the door with a satchel of herbs, Brigit stopped mumbling. She followed him to the cauldron and the two of them set to work. On what Alina could only wonder. "How long did Lucas say he would be?"

"He didn't say, Miss," Rathbone said.

"They're looking for Nikolas," Igmus added. "One way or another, they will bring him home."

"Shut yer yap," Rathbone snapped.

"Tis true. Well . . . sorry, missy. We should go back up and help, Rath."

"Lucas said to stay here with the ladies. You could go Igmus. I can protect this house."

"No," Alina said. "You should both go back out there. Lucas might need you. Maybe something will happen that you can, might have to help out with. I can take care of things here. We have Mr. Pagett and the constable if we need him."

"Lucas told us to stay right here," Rathbone said.

Alina sighed. She twisted her fingers around the fringe at her cuff. "I'm sure he did. But go catch up with them. Tell Lucas we're all right and that I sent you back to watch over him."

"Yes, go. Eat first and take extra these loaves," Irene said placing warm, cloth wrapped loaves on the table in front of Igmus and Rathbone.

"Irene, what about Camille?" Alina asked.

Irene wrapped an apron around her waist, "I'm fixing her a tray now. She opens the door for me, but I haven't gotten her to talk yet."

"If she's going to talk to anyone, it will be you, Irene. Your kindness may put her mind at ease. Maybe she will confide in you why she murdered her husband. In fact, I thought Drusilla had spoken to her a few times when they boarded here. Where is Drusilla? Isn't she up yet?"

Irene shook her head. "I thought I'd let her sleep. Unwelcome news can wait. That poor woman looks like she has had enough problems of her own."

* * *

Lucas thumped heavily on the trail, walking so close to Ikarus that he caught his boot on the lad's heel more than once. Ikarus quickened his pace, but Lucas could see how tired he was. There was nothing left for them to talk about. Bernard and his men called out Nikolas' name. Lucas was grateful that they did, and he didn't have to speak his friend's name right now. He remembered the time when Dugald had slashed his leg, and Nik took him to Brigit's cottage for tending. Nikolas had asked how he healed himself from gaping wounds and how to patch himself up. What had he told him? Lucas tried to remember. *A force of will*, he'd said. *Make the choice to live.* A portentous thing to say. But he had no other advice to offer. He had no idea why he healed. Seppo had not spontaneously offered an answer either. No matter how this turns out, Lucas thought, I will sit with Seppo until he explains this mystery to me, and every curious thing about himself and that place.

* * *

Alina helped Irene carry the tray up to Camille. Irene knocked, "Camille, it's Irene. I have food for you."

Camille opened the door but shut it quickly when she saw Alina. "Camille, please talk to us. We want to help you," Alina said softly through the door. The women waited. In a few minutes, Alina spoke through the door again. "I'll go now. Irene will hand you the tray. Maybe you can talk to her. We all confide in Irene."

Downstairs, Drusilla paced in the parlour. She rushed over to Alina. "How is the poor girl? Has she said anything yet?"

Alina shook her head. "No, but I'm hopeful that she will speak to Irene soon. Brigit is in the kitchen."

They went through and found only Mr. Pagett sitting at the table in the steamy kitchen. The cauldron hissed and burbled. "Where's Brigit?"

"Gone. She poured some of that concoction in a bottle and swirled out the back door. I couldn't stop her. You know how she is." He shook his head in bafflement.

"Oh no!" Alina rushed out the door and peered up and down the narrow lane.

"She's long gone." Mr. Pagett frowned into his teacup.

"None of us ever knows what Brigit might do, Mr. Pagett. But, did she say where she was going?" He merely sighed. Drusy was curiously stirring the big black pot. "Don't drink any of that," Alina muttered, "What a mess our lives have become."

* * *

Lucas and the others stopped only briefly to eat. Even after sunset when it began to drizzle, they kept going. They took turns walking along the edge of the river and peering over into it, so that one of them may always be a look out for the other. Bernard served as the anchor man with a thick rope tied around his waist, a loop went around the man who walked the edge. The arrangement was tedious and unwieldy as the rope got tangled in bushes and around trees. Everyone knew they were looking for a body crushed on the rocks below. No one said it, of course, but the relief showed in each man's face when his turn ended.

It was a damp and chilly march up a craggy trail. Here, summer had already given way to the cool nights of fall. The lanterns guided them until the moon suddenly burst from behind silver black clouds. They walked through the night, one man peering over, another laboriously dangling a lantern down into the deep river canyon. Some places along the edge were full of thorny brush, thus impassable, so they marked them with white ribbon to check on the way back. A syrupy black brew that Bernard's men had brought along kept them awake. Numb but awake. Lucas hated the feeling of it burning his throat— not at all like whisky— but he didn't want to take the chance of turning it down and becoming lost in a globe of his own tortured thoughts. The brew made the men say pointless things that were also amusing, although none of them actually laughed.

Bernard refused to take a turn away from the rope position. If he did, they would have to stop for the night, for he was the only man suited for the job, tree-like as he was. Several times, Lucas had to squint through the eerie, moonlit, lantern glow to see if Bernard was still there. Sometimes, it was indeed a tree, and Bernard and the men had moved on. At first, he had taken more turns than the others hoping his eyes could summon Nikolas to appear below, perched on a ledge and grinning awkwardly at his mishap. Lucas practiced what he would say to Nikolas; Let's go to the Blue Gate became a tempo that kept him going. Apparently he'd staggered because Bernard's men abruptly claimed the edge for themselves. Ikarus remained in the lead since he was the only one who knew the way.

Ultimately, the long night passed and allowed the yellow line of dawn to creep over the peaks to reveal a glistening white dust of snow on the far summit. The astounding beauty of the sunrise mocked them by lasting for more than an hour, an orange ball suspended lazily in a golden sky framed with pale baby blue.

"We are almost to the bottom of the waterfall. The place where Nikolas would have come down, er landed," Ikarus said softly. Somber faced the men plodded on. The finality of his words took their breath away.

* * *

Alina and Drusilla carefully transferred Brigit's potion into jugs and set them on a high shelf. Alina showed Drusy how to make a sign of thick parchment and label it: *Madam Brigit Trousdale Only*. By the time they finished, Irene came down with Camille's tray. She appeared haggard. Alina worried for her. Mr. Pagett had already left, but before he left, he asked Alina to convince Irene to join him in his apothecary shop. Irene declined, but when she also refused to rest in her chambers for a while, Alina suggested she accompany Irene to the shop.

"I will guard Camille's door," Drusy promised.

"I've talked to her through the door," Irene said. "I didn't mention we think we know who she is. I only assured her that we wanted to help her. That's all she knows so far. She doesn't need to know about Ikarus going up the mountain to find her, not yet. And now Nikolas missing. She didn't know him. I don't want her to feel worse than she already does. Tsk, what will come of her. The poor girl must feel so alone."

"Did she tell you anything at all?" Drusy asked.

"No, but she rustled around in there. She'd unlocked the door so I could slide the tray inside. She ate well. That's good, I suppose."

"I suppose so," Drusy agreed as she looped an apron over her head.

Alina grabbed a shawl for Irene and one for herself. The sky was bright blue, but as they both gazed towards the crests, they saw clouds swarming there. "It will rain on them tonight," Irene said.

Alina felt as if everyone they passed in the busy streets stared at them. *They all know we are doomed,* she thought. In the market square they didn't stop, only waved at the vendors who called their names. She pulled her shawl over her head near the flower vendor stall. She feared she may burst into tears if she saw the woman's friendly face. There was no reason to celebrate with flowers now.

At the apothecary shop, Mr. Pagett set three chairs out front around a small table in the sun. A water pitcher filled with fresh flowers made Alina smile in spite of the sickening worry stuck in her stomach. Irene went to the table and sat down. "I do enjoy this little shop," she said.

Alina sat beside her and accepted a cup of tea from Mr. Pagett. They sat and watched people pass by. From time to time, Mr. Pagett had to jump up to go inside and assist a customer. Alina waited him for to settle so she could make a move. "I'll be right back," she said.

"Where are you going off by yourself?" Irene scowled.

Alina could think of no excuse. "I just want to look around," she assured. "We can buy fresh bread on the way home so you don't have to make it tonight. How does that sound?"

Irene looked worried, but Mr. Pagett patted her hand. "Alina is young and needs to move about. She isn't content to sit still like us."

Once away, Alina hastened over to the monastery. She scrambled through the mulberry trees and skirted over the log bridge.

She found Seppo in the secret cemetery shoveling dirt around one of the gravestones.

She went straight up to him and blurted. "Did you bury someone there?"

Startled, Seppo nearly toppled over. Alina grabbed his arm to steady him. "Oh, I'm so sorry Seppo." He leaned on her for a moment. Alina thought he was as light as a child. "Are you all right. What are you doing out here?"

He peered at her with his piercing Lucas eyes. "What are *you* doing here, Alina?"

She glanced around. "Have you seen Brigit?"

"No, I'm seeing only you."

"I mean before, earlier today," she said before abruptly asking, "What were you doing yesterday?"

Seppo patted the dirt with the back of the shovel and gestured for her to follow him through the carved doors to the sanctuary room. She hesitated. Did he know she'd just been here, uninvited. He poured a goblet of water for each of them. "Forgive me, I have no bread at the moment."

"I should have brought some. Are you hungry, Seppo? I hope you would feel comfortable speaking to me if you had a problem or needed anything." She gestured helplessly around the room.

"What is it that you want to ask me, Alina?"

"Nothing. Well, honestly, I was wondering, I saw you the other day, yesterday. You were carrying something . . . something heavy."

"Yes."

"Who was it? A man, I think. Is he dead? Did someone die here? Maybe one of your monks that nobody has ever seen?" Taking a gulp of the water, she spilled some of it down the front of her dress. Seppo's steady gaze unnerved her. She swiped at the water with her hand.

Seppo stood. "Don't worry, Alina. None of the monks suffer. Occasionally someone does get injured. Is that not true in the City of Dreams? I hope you *will* bring bread the next time you visit."

Alina handed Seppo the empty goblet. "So, the injured monk is all right. Shall I run for some bread and come back? I don't mind at all."

"No, no. Don't worry about bread right now, dear child."

His sincerity emboldened her. "May I meet the other monks? Perhaps tend the injured one?"

Seppo waved a bony finger, "Those who dwell here are beyond old. Souls tire as time passes for as long as it does." He smiled as he led her toward the exquisitely carved doors. She had so many more questions. The monastery and all its secrets fascinated her. Lucas had told her some things, but to hear it from one of them. Had Lucas ever mentioned that his father smiled? She couldn't remember. "There is nobody here for your to be concerned with, Alina. Nobody that needs tending. Bring Lucas next time." Seppo patted her cheek, closed the heavy doors, and left her alone in the glaring sunlight.

She dashed back to the apothecary shop hoping Irene wasn't upset with her. But when she got there, the table out front was empty. No one was inside either. She called for Mr. Pagett and paced before she heard sounds coming from down an unlit corridor in the house. Alarmed, she went toward the voice, calling Irene's name.

The slender hallway led to a large kitchen with huge open windows overlooking a garden layered in shades of green and partially covered with a muslin canopy. Plants climbed over other plants, many hung from invisible threads in bulging baskets, colorful dainty flowers trailed up and down the stone walls, and a delicate fountain gurgled in the far corner. Irene and Mr. Pagett sat side by side on one of four benches. He waved his arms in the air as Irene sat enthralled by whatever yarn he was spinning with his gestures and words. Alina began to back up but they both turned and noticed her at the same time.

"Alina, join us. Come and see this beautiful garden. Did you know that Mr. Pagett grows and tends all the herbs for the apothecary shop right here?" Irene exclaimed. Alina was astounded by the bountiful scents and tender plants growing up from fertile soil. Above their heads, rows of taut ropes were cramped with plants in various stages of drying. It never occurred to her to wonder where all the herbs came from. There was so much to see that she could barely look at all of it.

This unusual place suddenly exhausted her. Lucas should be here, she thought. She didn't want to experience such enchantment without him. Who knew what he was enduring at this very moment. "Oh, my goodness, this is too beautiful for me to take in right now. If you are quite well, Irene, I will make my way home and let Mr. Pagett walk you over later." He nodded agreeably.

"Alina dear, why don't you stay and have another cup of tea," Irene implored. "Even Brigit frequents this shop for what she can't harvest herself. It's a magical place."

Alina smiled but shook her head. "I'm terribly tired."

Mr. Pagett handed her a packet of herbs. "Here, take this before bedtime. It calms a restless heart."

Alina blinked. Her eyes stung with hot tears. Irene wrapped a soft arm around her waist and walked her to the shop door. "Our Lucas will return. They all will. Believe nothing else, dear girl."

Hurrying along the bustling streets, Alina felt, for the first time, in a very long time, wretched and lonely. For all she knew, Lucas might disappear just like Nikolas had. She slipped in the front door, hoping to escape to her room to weep for a bit, but she saw Drusilla perched on a stool outside Camille's door. It was open just a crack. The two women were speaking in hushed voices.

"Drusilla! What's going on?" Alina snapped. The door slammed from the inside.

"Oh, Alina . . ." Drusilla got up glancing over her shoulder. "I thought I would try to get her to speak."

"It looks like it worked. What does she say?" Alina brushed past Drusilla and pounded on the door while turning the knob. "She's locked it again. Tell me what she has told you."

"Uh, well . . ." Drusilla wrung her hands. "Perhaps we should go downstairs and speak."

Alina covered her face with her hands and sighed. She wanted to cry even more now. Regaining herself, she said, "Very well, let's go. I have a tea from Mr. Pagett." She started down the stairs when Camille opened her door. "I will tell you, Miss," Camille uttered meekly.

"Thank heavens. I can't bear much more hysteria. I'm fatigued, and it isn't even midday. It seems everyone has gone mad. Tell me what went wrong so I can help you, Camille. Wait, where are you going Drusilla? Come back up. She might be more comfortable with you here too."

Drusilla hesitated in the middle of the stairs. She looked up at Alina and then down at the front door. "I'll just make the tea."

"You can do it later. It's fine, Drusy. Irene is busy. You have time." Alina went into her old bed chamber. It looked different now that the young lady occupied it. There was only one chair, so Alina left it for Drusilla, and she sat herself on the end of the bed. Clutching a thick coverlet, Camille leaned back against the headboard.

"Go ahead, Camille. Tell me what happened on the ship."

Camille bit her lip and glanced at Drusilla. "You haven't told them anything at all?"

Drusilla shook her head.

"What do you know about this?" Alina asked Drusilla.

"I . . . well . . . I know that her husband . . . that man was too old for her. He was a bad man."

Camille nodded vigorously. "He was vile. We did not know it at first. In the hills, he lied and tricked my mother into letting me go. And me too. He promised the life of a queen. He hurt me as soon as we left."

Alina narrowed her eyes and pressed her lips together. "Hurt you how, Camille?"

"I can't say miss. Don't make me say. I was innocent. There was a boy. I was waiting for him. But he never came back."

Alina shook her head and murmured to Drusy, "You haven't told her about Ikarus?"

"No."

Startled, Camille asked, "Do you know Ikarus?" Her cheeks were dry, but tears had left salty streaks. Her eyes, which were such a pale blue they almost looked white, were red from crying.

Alina hesitated and then gradually explained how Ikarus had gone looking for her. "It was a horrible twist of fate," she murmured. "Somehow, I don't know how, you two just missed each other downstairs in the kitchen and parlour."

Camille's lips trembled, her face aghast. She pulled the coverlet up to her throat.

"I'm terribly sorry," Alina threw her hands up; there was nothing more to say. She didn't trust herself to talk about Nikolas and the search party. Drusilla chimed in and took over the story of the accident and the hastily formed search.

Alina, not wanting to hear it, let her mind drift to Lucas as it always did. She willed him to give up the search and return to her while he still could. Things had gone tragically wrong ever since Ikarus had set out searching for this girl, Camille. She feared the bad luck would continue as long as they kept traipsing up into those perilous mountains. What kind of life did Camille leave behind up there, and why would her family let her go? Money most likely played a part, of course.

Whether it was disdain for their child or not, it seemed simple ignorance had made the decision to give up their lovely daughter. Watching Camille, Alina noticed that this girl's willful naivete was possibly another cause for such a bad choice. Perhaps, her family felt blessed and fortunate at the prospect of a wealthy husband for her. Maybe, they imagined she would enjoy a life of ease and travel.

She could see why Ikarus hadn't forgotten Camille. She looked like a delicate seedling, a lily. What would he think now? Alina's thoughts had taken her so deep that she almost missed what Drusilla blurted out. "I gave her the knife."

Alina gaped. "Wh . . . what?"

Drusilla glanced at Camille, whose face had gone paler than it already was. "The knife that you gave me for protection, Alina. I gave it to Camille before she boarded the ship with Mr. Plimpton. I knew he was hurting her. I heard outside their door late one night."

"My knife," Alina repeated clawing at her throat as she felt suddenly flushed. "Camille, you stabbed your husband with my knife?"

Camille sniveled and peeked at Drusilla.

"I suggested she do so," Drusilla stated.

"Is that true?" Alina glanced from one to the other.

Camille nodded. "I was so scared. I didn't know anyone here. I wanted to say something, but I couldn't, and he never left me alone long enough. But when we boarded the ship and sailed away, I knew I was doomed. Once we reached Ingleena, I could never find my way back here or home."

"I see." Alina stared at the two women. Drusilla got up and fidgeted from one foot to the other as she edged toward the door.

Turning a stern face to Camille, Alina asked tersely, "Where is the knife now?"

"Oh! Gone! It's gone, Miss. I threw it overboard. It's at the bottom of the sea."

Alina released a long slow breath. She got up from the end of the bed and reached out to pat the top of Camille's head. Her soft hair tumbled down around her childlike face. "All right then."

Turning to Drusilla she said, "You must not interfere in the lives of others. This may turn out all right. We'll see. There are consequences. I know you both realize that what you did was wrong." She shook her head, "For the love of cabbage, we could all be imprisoned!"

Drusilla fanned herself with both hands and nodded. A part of her wanted to explain about Gacheru, but she swallowed hard and murmured, "Please don't tell Irene."

Alina peered out the tiny window. "I don't think Irene has to know just yet. For now, we will try this soothing tea from Mr. Pagett. Come downstairs to the garden, ladies. We all need fresh air."

Chapter 25

Brigit took her potion to the river and poured it in. She tramped along the banks—sometimes in mud up to her ankles—all the way to the harbour. The shipmates and wharf rats scurried out of the way when they saw her barreling toward them. Her eyes were black, their rims red. Her cheeks were white, and her lips a vehement vermillion. She ranted aloud in words only she understood. The men turned their heads and offered the sign of God as she passed. One young sailor ran for the harbour master, Mr. Merson. "All ships should be held offshore," the lad rambled. "A witch has cursed them."

Mr. Merson strode angrily past the crates and barrels. The spiraling hair had always amused him, but this time, when he saw Brigit, his stomach lurched. Her skin looked bluish gray, but her stricken face was white as ash. She fixed her lethal gaze upon him. He peered into her eyes for only a second and instantly felt as if he'd been run through by a sword. He spun and staggered behind a stack of cargo. Gesturing the lad away, he ordered, "Run along. Warn the others, make way. She'll go to the room of Nikolas."

"How can I warn them without passing in front of her?" the boy pleaded.

"Get . . . just go. She's not here for you. Off with ye now!"

The boy ran away, and Mr. Merson weaved his way back to his office, swearing as he went. "Damn the bad luck she's brought down upon us!"

Brigit saw nobody. She barged into Nikolas' harbour room that he rarely used in the days before their journey. But some of his things were still there. She soaked the bed and floor with the pungent potion.

* * *

At dusk, after long agonizing uphill trudging, the strained men reached the top of the vaporous waterfall. With each step, the sun retreated lower behind the canyon walls leaving them standing in a yellow and blue haze.

"The fog, it's like a gate," Bernard said in a hushed voice.

"The gate to hell," Ikarus answered softly.

As if in agreement, the men stood back waiting for Lucas to approach. When he arrived, Ikarus put a steadying hand on Lucas' shoulder, and together they inched forward into the blue mist. Silently, Lucas repeated his chant: *Let's go to the Blue Gate*. Then, he peered down.

The water thundered over the rocky cliff. It was almost as high as the cathedral tower. *Nobody survives this*, he thought. Unnerved, he stumbled backward, and Bernard caught him. The sun, gone now, left a swirling cloud of blue encircling him. It is a gate to hell, Lucas realized. He pushed away from Bernard and stood on shaky legs. Then, he saw the monument they'd left for Nikolas: his shirt and the little stick figure. Lucas slid to his knees, bent over, and vomited.

Ikarus stepped over to place a fiery hand on his shoulder. Suddenly remembering his nightmare, Lucas cried out, "Stand back, Ikarus!" In the nightmare, it was Ikarus who was falling into the darkness. "Get away. We must leave this horrible place!" Lucas staggered to his feet, shouting and waving his arms for all the men to move back. "It can't happen again. Let's go!"

Ikarus led them to the campsite where he and Brigit had waited for three days. One of Bernard's men made a fire. They lay down in the dirt in the circle of warmth since their clothes were damp from the mist. Someone passed a loaf of bread around. Lucas covered his head with his cloak to drown out the pummeling sound of water. He fell into a tormented sleep.

Somewhere in the depth of night, Lucas woke. He lay on his back listening to the men snoring. Their grunts and snorts almost blocked the sound of the waterfall. He was a fool to think they could come up here and find Nikolas alive. He tricked himself with thoughts of drinking ale in their favorite tavern when, in truth, Nikolas lay buried and broken beneath walls of water.

At first light, Lucas woke the men. "We go back now," he said. "How long will it take, Ik?"

"Three days if we don't follow the river. There's another way. The way Brigit and Nikolas and I came up. Summer is over," he added for no particular reason. "All of this water comes from the mountain springs. It will never let up."

"I know," Lucas said. "We go home without our friend. Bernard, I will pay your comrades."

Ikarus led the way. As they travelled, they passed through the thick forest where they'd all felt fearful of the huddled trees. If only he'd known then what the real threat was, and that Camille had not waited for him after all. He hadn't thought about her in several days. Perhaps he would forget her as easily as she had forgotten him. *But what if she had not forgotten him,* he thought. *She drew a picture of the two of them.* Ikarus gasped. Why did he spill wine on her gentle drawing and let Nikolas release it into the wind? He kicked the dirt, it didn't matter now. He would never know the answer to many questions.

As they ambled through the grassy valleys, Ikarus understood why Lucas had enjoyed walking the streets of the City of Dreams and lighting lanterns alone in the glow of his own light. Now, he looked forward to returning to it.

Lucas walking out ahead, and stopping only when the trail diverged, spoke to no one now. He was striding too fast for most of them, but the men didn't complain.

Lucas was the first to see the monastery and cathedral tower in the distance. He wanted to shout and run into the city, but he felt utterly bereft. He hoped Alina knew in her heart that he was on his way home to her. One more night of sleep out here.

All the way, he'd been wishing they would encounter Mabon. He wanted to bring him back for Brigit. Not as a replacement for Nikolas, but because Lucas didn't know what to do with her now. Maybe her ancient kin could help her regain herself. However, he knew there was no use hoping for anything.

He'd gotten himself up the mountain by dreaming about the Blue Gate Tavern and what had suddenly become the old days. He would most likely never go inside there again. Why was it called the Blue Gate? he wondered. And why was the waterfall shrouded in blue? Perhaps, that was the best Lucas could do with his ability. He couldn't bring Nikolas back through the Blue Gate Tavern; he could only frame the place where he perished, in blue.

They made their last camp and slept without eating. At dawn, Igmus and Rathbone appeared in the camp. At first, Lucas wondered why they hadn't remained in the city as he'd suggested, but then he realized Nikolas' mates, Ig and Rath, as Nik had fondly called them, had come back to safeguard himself now. He handed Rathbone the reins to Nikolas' mule and slung his cloak over his shoulders. He followed the men home. When they reached the first bridge, Lucas pulled the hood over his head.

He marched through the early September streets filled with the bustling energy of upcoming harvest season. His shoulders were squared, his back straight, but inside he trembled in his bones and shivered from the ice in his blood. For in the souls of his kindred, their last shreds of innocence were lost.

* * *

On her way home from the apothecary shop, Irene spied Brigit staggering through a narrow close. Irene caught up with her and grabbed a clump of her hair. Brigit stared, confused for a moment. Irene took her hands and peered into her wild colorful eyes. "Come now, Brigit. There is nothing left to be done. I will take you back to your cottage. We will stay together until the men return, and if Nikolas is not with them then, well . . .then, I will save you. Not the hourglass, not the potions, just me your old friend."

Chapter 26

Up ahead, Lucas saw the indigo windows of the Blue Gate Tavern. He focused on the cobbles. The muddy boots he followed stopped, and Lucas slammed into the back of Bernard. His giant brethren grabbed Lucas by his forearm, "They want to go in."

"Who does?" Lucas snarled.

"My men and your men."

Lucas looked up. Even Ikarus was skulking at the door.

"It's been a hell of a few days, Lucas," Bernard said.

"I'll never go in there again."

Rathbone spoke up, "Lucas, it's fitting. We will toast our fallen comrade."

Lucas groaned and tilted his head back to peer up at the annoyingly blue sky. Why was everything blue now? A hawk wheeled and dipped. Lucas looked away. The men didn't know about the agreement he'd made with himself in his mind. They only knew that the Blue Gate was Nikolas' haunt. It was the right place to toast Nikolas.

Lucas gazed at the familiar structure. Inside, on the ledge of the window, the gray cat lounged. She turned her yellow eyes toward him and blinked just once. He followed the others inside. Those patrons who leaned along the bar made way for Lucas and the men. No need to speak the news, their faces spoke for them.

They started with two whiskies apiece. Then ale. The door opened and closed so often that someone finally propped it open. Everyone from the harbour drifted in to hold a glass for Nikolas. Lucas remained numb. He couldn't drink enough to release the grip on his strangled throat. It seemed as if every working man in the City of Dreams came through the door. Lucas squinted into the bright sunlight unable to recognize a man until he'd stepped into the dim tavern. His head pounded. He gulped the ale as if it was water. A serving girl with brown hair decorated with several braids and green ribbons, stood nearby holding a pitcher and filled his tankard as quickly as he drained it. "You've always enjoyed the Blue Gate ale. You and your friend," she said.

Lucas narrowed his eyes; he'd never seen her before. "It's delicious. Better than water. Have I seen you before?"

"Of course, it is," she leaned her elbows on the bar next to his. "We're the only tavern with our very own well. Legend says it passes through the monastery before it comes here," she gloated and pushed her chest out. Lucas noticed his hand trembled, but he held it out for more anyway.

Bernard stood behind him. "Easy brother. Can I walk you to the boarding house now? My men are anxious to get back to Arcana before nightfall. We must ride while we still can." Lucas glanced around the room. Igmus and Rathbone were sitting in chairs along the wall on either side of Ikarus, each with a hand on his shoulder to hold him upright in his chair.

"I'll stay for now." Lucas stood and let Bernard embrace him like a ragdoll. "First, I will pay your men." He reached into his trouser pocket for his coin purse.

Bernard shook his head. "We are all kin in this. Come to the country when you're able."

Lucas watched Bernard's back disappear through the door. A shape lingered there. Lucas held his breath. But nobody else came in. He motioned for the girl. "Would you mind bringing bowls of your steadying stew for those three men and me." Lucas made his way over to Ikarus, Rathbone and Igmus. "We will eat before going to the boarding house to speak to the women."

They each consumed two servings of stew and tore chunks from a loaf of warm bread.

"The bread too," the girl said as she picked up the empty bowls. "All made from our well water." She seemed to know him, but Lucas didn't remember her. He supposed she didn't know he had a wife. "Would you like to see it?" she murmured leaning in close to him.

"No," he grumbled. "What are you talking about. I come in here all the time. I know this place."

"Not if you haven't seen the well."

"I've seen it. And all the wells throughout the city. Yours is not so special."

"Ours is inside, back there," she gestured. "Our well water passes from the monastery. The other wells around the city draw straight from the river."

"All right, show me whatever it is," Lucas said angrily. Who did she think she was talking to. The barkeep should teach her to serve the public and be quiet. He followed her to the back room thinking how he and Nik would laugh when Lucas told him the story. A stab in his side brought him back to awareness. He would never get to ask Nik if he'd been shown the special well in the Blue Gate Tavern.

But there it was, a circular stone well in the center of a small square room made entirely of stone. Lucas peered into its obscure depths. He hadn't seen this well since he was a lad and new to the city. He'd slept behind it on a few occasions. He didn't remember how ancient the stones were. Or more likely, as a boy, he didn't notice anything more than that it was a safe place to hide for the night.

"This is sacred water."

Lucas laughed at her and turned to leave.

She stomped a foot and folded her arms to block his way. "You don't know what I know. When I was little, my great grandfather took me to this place. Regular people can't get into the old monastery, but they can come here. The water is blessed by the monks. There's hundreds of them still living in there. They bless the water every day. This well comes directly from there."

"I heard you. Why do you keep saying that? Can't you leave a man alone to drink in peace." Lucas gaped at her. He was drunk and she was babbling nonsense. Until lately, not even he knew who actually lived in the monastery, if anyone. But now he knew what went on in there, although not everything. "Where do you come from?"

"The low country east."

"A dry land," Lucas remarked. "Why did you insist on showing me this?"

"I thought the ale would work better if you knew where it came from. And you can hear the strength of the water. We can't live without water, can we?"

"No, we can't. Bring me a lantern, then." he said. Bracing a hand on the rim of the well he held the lantern down inside as far as he could. The girl leaned in too. "I hear it, a river below," he said gently. Cool air rushed up the shaft of the well. Lucas felt his head clear, and the dizziness that confronted him since visiting the waterfall subsided. "It was kind of you to show me it. I have seen this well before, but not in many years and not from the inside. Mind yourself, miss. Don't slip over this edge." He handed her the lantern back. "Did you know Nikolas?" he asked her.

"The man you all grieve?" She chewed her bottom lip. "What do you mean by know him?"

"Never mind." Lucas left the girl sitting on the edge of the well. All he wanted to do now was go home. Shadow was no longer in the windowsill. Surprisingly, the cunning cat hadn't followed them up the mountainside. She led him places only to vanish and then appear again later. Irene had aptly named her.

The tavern was still full, Igmus and Rathbone stood just outside the door. Ikarus leaned on the bar wielding yet another full tankard of ale. Lucas regretted bringing Ik in here. But, all the men wanted to stop, and the cat and hawk appeared to want that as well.

Turning back to the serving girl, he tossed her a sack of coins. Her idea about the monastery and the deep well inside the Blue Gate being connected was thoughtful and observant. In a way though, the river connected everything. Or disconnected as in the case of Nikolas. He touched, Ik's arm and pointed to the door. "I'm staying," Ik slurred.

Lucas waited beside him for a moment, but Ikarus turned away and gestured to the barkeep for more. Igmus and Rathbone waited outside for Lucas. Clearly, they intended to walk him home. He wouldn't be able to talk them out of it. Crestfallen, Lucas left Ikarus there. He walked out of his and Nikolas' favorite drinking establishment for the very last time.

* * *

Alina used both hands to push open the large wooden door to the office of her solicitor. She'd been inside for over an hour and wasn't prepared for the glaring sun. A reeling man slammed into her, knocking her down to the hard cobbles. He scrambled to his feet and kept running. "Watch out!" she shouted. He was thin and dirty with pale hair. A young drover down from the high pastures with a herd, she mused. If only she could have asked him if he'd encountered the search party. Dusting herself off, she turned to the apothecary shop. Alina didn't want to intrude on Irene, but she hadn't come home last night. It was so unlike Irene that Alina felt she must check on her. Too many things had already gone awry.

Mr. Pagett startled when Alina walked into the shop. "Alina, what a pleasant surprise. Is Irene with you?"

"No. I thought she was with you."

He set down a green glass jar and removed his glasses. "She hasn't come by today. Was she planning to?"

"I haven't seen her all night." Alina's eyes brimmed with tears. "Mr. Pagett, I last saw her right here."

Mr. Pagett frowned. "That's not right. She went home not long after you," he stated. "I wanted to walk with her, but she insisted on going alone. She said she didn't need to be looked over like a child." The two stared dubiously at each other. Alina wrung her hands. If something had happened to Irene while Lucas was away, she would never forgive herself.

"What do we do? She didn't come back to the boarding house! Oh, dear lord, I'm going to lose my mind." Alina groaned.

Ashen, Mr. Pagett yanked his cloak from the wall peg. "Let's take the cart. It will be faster than walking all over the city."

"Yes, all right. We better search along the river first." As they trotted the path along the river Alina noticed her elbow was bleeding from when the drunken man had knocked her down. She hid her arm under her shawl. Slapping the reins, Mr. Pagett urged the poor, plodding donkey who seemed confused that they weren't following their usual lantern lighting route. Alina sighed thinking it would be faster to walk.

At least one thing had gone well today. The solicitor had assured her that he would speak out on behalf of Camille. He'd agreed that a young girl swindled into marriage couldn't be held responsible for her reaction to the dreadful arrangement. And he assured Alina that the constable would agree. So, there was no need, Alina consoled herself, to tell anyone where Camille got the knife.

Chapter 27

Igmus and Rathbone said goodbye to Lucas outside the boarding house. Feeling dreadful and relieved at the same time, he opened the door. The parlour was empty. It was such a warm day that no one had laid the fire. He found Carissa and Perina seated at the long table in the kitchen shucking peas. "Where is everyone?"

"Oh!" Perina clutched her heart. "Lucas, you're here. I didn't see you. Where did you come from?"

Carissa pushed up from the table. "Are you all right?"

Lucas knew he was filthy and haggard as well as droopy from whisky and ale. He shook his head. "Where's Irene? Where is Alina?"

"Alina has gone out. I'm not sure where. And I don't know exactly where Irene is at the moment," Carissa said, scratching the side of her cheek revealing her own confusion. "We're awfully glad you're back. Are you hungry?"

"No." He turned away. "I'll have a bath."

The two house maids watched Lucas as he filled buckets and climbed the stairs over and over. They didn't offer to help and did not mention Nikolas' name. He obviously had not been found.

* * *

Alina and Mr. Pagett discovered Irene in Brigit's cottage. For some reason, it was the last place they thought to look. Irene explained that she would wait with Brigit until the men returned. "I will send your things over, Irene," Alina told her. "You can try to be comfortable while you're sitting here."

Alina glanced around the cottage with curiosity. She'd never been inside before and didn't envy Irene for staying there. But someone had to remain with Brigit and keep her from wandering around putting curses on people. Mr. Merson had spread the word about the city, which is why it finally occurred to Alina to come here.

The tedious plodding of the donkey had made it impossible not to overhear the conversations of passersby. Apparently, even Brigit's own clan of neighbors found her actions unnerving. She held her breath when Mr. Pagett and Irene stepped outside to speak with each other for a moment.

Alina had previously found Brigit's company enjoyable, but now she found it difficult to meet the woman's eyes. Frankly, she was a bit unnerved, not only Brigit, but also by all of the tragic events lately. No wonder her inclination had been to remain as children. Of course, people couldn't stop the passage of time any more than they could stop their hair from growing.

Now she understood why father had tried so hard to protect her. She sighed and forced herself to offer Brigit a melancholy smile. Brigit nodded as she absently stroked the purple cloth covering the crystal ball, a low hum sounding from deep within her throat. Had she peered into the dreaded ball today, Alina wondered as she stepped away from the table hoping to distract Brigit from pulling the cloth away and revealing something that neither of them wanted to see.

Finally, Irene came back in and said, "Mr. Pagett will take you home now, Alina." Alina chewed her bottom lip. She didn't dare say that she thought it best for Irene to come with them. Rathbone could watch Brigit, she thought. But Irene assured Alina that she was fine in Brigit's mystical cottage. Her polite description of the intimidating cottage calmed Alina who couldn't wait to get back to the boarding house. She was tired of everything and simply wanted to soak in the bath, climb into bed, and wait until Lucas came home. She obligingly allowed Mr. Pagett and his donkey to take her home although she could have walked in half the time.

Mr. Pagett promised Alina that he would check in on Irene and let her know that he was following the lads who were lighting the lanterns. "They're doing a splendid job, slow, but it gets done."

Alina thanked him. She hoped he hadn't noticed how impatient the donkey cart had made her today. She quietly opened the front door and scooted up the stairs before the girls could notice her return. They were talking with someone in the kitchen, probably one of the lamp lads.

She was surprised to find the bedchamber door unlocked, but she'd been distracted all day. She pushed it open and stepped inside. Lucas, shirtless, leaned against the bed pulling off his trousers. "Oh!" she nearly shouted. For a long moment she stood dazed, just staring at him.

He laughed. "Don't be frightened. It's me, your husband." He reached for her, and she ran to him. Lucas enfolded Alina in his arms and covered her in kisses warm and deep. They pulled apart and gazed in wonder at each other. She clung to him, kissed his neck, and wept.

Soon their tears mingled together. She need not ask why. There would be no joyful celebration. Nikolas was not found. He helped her remove her dress, and they slipped into the bath. They washed each other, crying and smiling at the same time. Lucas cleaned the blood from Alina's elbow. She'd forgotten about it and couldn't tell him what had happened, blinded by the sun as she had been. Someone knocked her down was all she knew, but this time wasn't for speaking about herself. It wasn't the time for her to tell him about Drusilla and Camille either.

After Camille's confession, the two had kept to themselves. Drusilla took over taking trays of food to Camille who preferred to remain hidden in her room. The constable would not be coming for her. She understood when Alina had told her this good news but didn't have the courage to come out.

Somehow the girl had to be sent back to her mountain home. That would mean another trip up into those imposing peaks, but for whom? Certainly not Lucas. Still, the girl couldn't walk all the way back home alone. Maybe Igmus and Rathbone would be up for the task. Someone would accept payment to escort Camille, Alina felt sure.

In the meanwhile, Drusilla had proven herself to be a reliable and thoughtful woman. Even giving Camille the knife was well intended. Alina sighed and pushed those thoughts from her mind. Lucas was nearly asleep in the bath, and the water had cooled. She reached for the linen towels, and he stirred. They dried each other and wrapped themselves in thin blankets. Lucas opened the window and made a fire. They sat silently staring into the flames his arm flung around her shoulders. There was a knock at the door. Lucas groaned.

"It is I, Carissa. I've brought supper."

Pleased now, Lucas opened the door. "Come in, Carissa. Thank you for thinking of it. We had forgotten to feed ourselves."

She set the tray on the credenza. "Ikarus has returned. He was quite drunk. Perina and I put him to bed. He said to tell you, Alina, that he's sorry for bumping into you on the street."

Alina's hand fluttered to her elbow. "Oh goodness, it was Ikarus. I'm relieved you know, that he was drunk." Alina said. "Well, actually, that it wasn't some rude stranger. If I'd recognized him, I would have come right home, Lucas." She wrung her hands. "I'm overwhelmed. It's as if an entire shelf of dishes is crashing down around us. Don't you think so?"

Lucas took her hand. "Be calm, Alina. We will eat something and sleep. In the days to come, we start again, slowly."

Alina nodded. "Tell Ikarus not to worry, please, Carissa. I'm only glad he is home safely. And when Mr. Pagett comes by will you tell him to let Irene know that Lucas is home safely? Hopefully, she can get someone over there to help in containing Brigit for a while, or however long it takes for her to accept . . ." She wrung her hands and glanced at Lucas who grimaced and shook his head. "All right then. Thank you for bringing the tray."

Lucas opened the wine. They sat in front of the fire and nibbled their meal. He told Alina about stopping at the Blue Gate Tavern. "I didn't want to go in there at all. I had it in my mind all the while up on the mountain that Nikolas was telling me he'd meet me there, at the Blue Gate. But I tell you, Alina, you wouldn't have wanted to see where he went over." He shook his head, still stunned by disbelief. Alina stroked his arm while he spoke. "It was like the thundering forces of hell. I've never seen water as powerful as that."

He went on to tell her about the new bar maid. She was intriguing and annoying at the same time. "I've never seen her before. I don't know if she ever even met Nikolas."

Alina combed her hair with her fingers. "What do you think she really wanted? Why would she tell you all that?"

"I don't know. Everything is wrong. She wanted me to peer into the well, and it did sober me up. But after the journey, I only wanted to come home. I shouldn't have been drinking so much whisky. And ale on top of that. It was grim, not cheerful. No reunion. Then the irritating girl. I gave her some coins. So probably she got what she was after." He started to shrug but stopped himself. It was Bernard's movement, but he and Nikolas had adopted it in friendly jest. "Let's go to bed now. I think we should sleep for the next several days." Lucas pulled the coverlet back, and they both slipped underneath. They wrapped their arms and legs around each other to be as close as they could possibly get in an effort to block out the clamoring world.

Sometime, in the lull of deep night, Lucas awoke with an old enemy shrieking in his head. The nightmare of his nightmares had returned. The throbbing pain made him break into a sweat. He slid from the edge of the bed, dragging the sheet from Alina with his tangled foot. Half blinded by the agony, he crawled toward the fire.

He had seen a face in this dream. A face in the well at the Blue Gate Tavern. It was Nikolas. He reached for his friend and fell in on top of him. The raging water engulfed them. It was like the nightmare he'd had about Ikarus, but this time he was in it, and he was trying to reach Nikolas. Ikarus was safe downstairs in his bed, threatened only by the aftermath of besottedness.

Lucas considered making his way downstairs to ask Irene for a draught of laudanum. Then, he remembered she was with Brigit. The two of them surely had sufficient concoctions to fall asleep and remain that way. But it was too far for him to walk. He doubted he could get himself out of the bedchamber and down the stairs.

Alina sat up. "Lucas what are you doing over there on the floor?"

He put a hand up, tried to speak, and then let it fall. She came to him with the water pitcher. "Drink water. You need water."

He drank and let it spill down his chin. "Enough water. The water is a nightmare. I had another nightmare. There was one about Ikarus, but it was meant for Nikolas, it seems, and me too."

Alina sat on the floor next to him and stroked his sweaty hair away from his face and neck. "Go on, tell me."

Lucas told her about the two dreams as well as he could remember now. They ran together and blended with the girl at the Blue Gate. Alina listened until Lucas ran out of words. She helped him back into the bed and opened the window wider.

"As long as we are awake and talking about terrible things, I should tell you what I forgot. I saw Seppo carrying something. It was a person. I saw a foot. One of the monks I supposed, but he wouldn't explain. There must be others in there. Some as old as him who haven't died yet. Or maybe it was someone who just died. I think he buried someone. I tried to get him to speak to me, but he wouldn't tell me anything. He speaks in riddles." She pulled the sheet up around them. "I'm sorry, Lucas."

"You have nothing to be sorry for, my darling. I can't get him to speak much either." Lucas let his eyes close as she stroked his forehead.

"He did say I should bring you next time," Alina murmured.

"Ahh, well good. That's it then." He turned on his side and caressed her cheek. "Don't worry, my love. I have a feeling he is ready to speak to us. We will go together and make him answer our questions. It's time for him to explain the monastery, the wells, the gold, how he has lived for so long. All of it. We won't leave him alone until he tells us everything. And after Seppo is settled, we will find a way to honor Nikolas and fix Brigit. Let's sleep now, sweet girl, and whenever we wake up, we will go."

Chapter 28

They slept through the following day. Their slumber carried them beyond the sounds of the street, persistent bird chatter, night crickets, lonesome dogs, quarreling cats, aromas of life, and a few gentle knocks on their door. They slept through a day and into the untortured quietness of the next night. A rumbling in Lucas' stomach awakened Alina. She giggled as she watched him sprawled flat on his back with one arm dangling off the side of the bed. He was not awake, but his body called out for nourishment.

Thinking to creep from the room and bring some bread and tea for them, Alina slipped from the bed and pulled her day shift on. When the door latch clicked, Lucas called out, "Don't leave me, love."

"We are growing old in this bed."

"And hungry," he answered.

The world felt safe and beautiful in these early moments. Then, Lucas remembered, and his expression clouded and so did Alina's.

They splashed water on their faces and dressed for the walk to the monastery. "It smells like there's fresh bread waiting for us downstairs," Lucas said as he opened their chamber door.

Carissa and Perina were both in the kitchen, humming to themselves as they chopped and stirred. Again, Lucas and Alina felt safe as if nothing had happened, and for a moment they all looked at each other as if everything was the same as before Nikolas died. *The joy of seeing a familiar face, it has healing effects*, Lucas thought. *Somehow, eventually, Lucas knew the faces of those they had lost and could never again see would fade into the background. The anguish of the missing presence would ultimately subside and be replaced by an enduring sting of heartache.*

Lucas deliberately sat at the table in the seat where he last remembered seeing Nikolas sit. Nobody else was aware of his tiny tribute to his friend, but he would go through many days making these small gestures to console himself.

The girls sat at the table with them, to fill the empty places, Lucas thought. They talked about everyday things, such as Lucas and Alina having slept for two days. There was a new ingredient for the stew, an orange vegetable that tasted sweet. Mr. Pagett had brought it by and reported that Irene was fine, although restless in Brigit's cottage especially after hearing that Lucas was home. The days continued with and without the ones who were missing.

Drusilla came in through the back door. "Good day, everyone. I hope you've had a pleasant morning so far." Pleased to see Drusy, Alina nodded, but Drusy frowned and said, "I'm afraid there is more unwelcome news."

"Oh no," Perina exclaimed.

They sat, waited, and braced themselves for whatever might come next. "Drusy plopped down at the end of the table. She was perspiring. "It seems that Camille has run off."

"How did she get out?" Alina asked.

"Well, Ikarus wanted to speak to her. He stood outside her door. I'm surprised you didn't hear him." She gazed at Lucas and Alina. "Anyway, finally she let him in. I don't know what he said to her, but she fled through the open door."

"Bloody hell," Lucas swore. Alina realized she had forgotten to tell Lucas that she had spoken to the constable on Camille's behalf. She clasped her hands over her face. Would it never stop? she wondered.

"Where is Ikarus?" Lucas asked.

"He went after her," Drusy said. "The trouble is she has climbed to the top of the cathedral tower and is threatening to jump. Ikarus is at the bottom pleading with her."

Lucas laughed. He laughed for a long time, and Alina couldn't help but smile. It was all just too much. "It's like a fairy tale gone absurdly wrong," Lucas said.

"Most of them do," Drusilla said.

Slapping his hands on the table, Lucas said, "Well let's go get her."

"I tracked down Igmus and Rathbone. They're over there too," Drusilla said.

Lucas scratched his head. "What in ever for?"

"I thought that one of them might catch her if she jumped."

"Oh, well. Sure, that's a good plan, Drusy." He grabbed Alina's hand. "We'll talk her down, and then we can go speak to Seppo."

Ikarus met them in the street. He told them Camille wanted to speak with Alina and Drusilla only. "Would they be willing to climb the stairs up into the bell tower?"

"Go ahead, Alina," Lucas said. "I trust you can put an end to this nonsense. I will find Seppo. When you get Camille sorted out come to the monastery. Even though we have lost Nikolas, I want our lives to be as they once were." He placed a soft kiss on each of her velvety cheeks. "Take care but hurry, darling."

* * *

Lucas entered the sanctuary through the double doors. The candles had been lit long enough for clumps of wax to drop and sizzle on the stone floor. The air smelled of incense and the room seemed to hum with tranquility. However, it was empty. Ikarus whistled. Lucas cast an annoyed glance in his direction. Lucas had brought him along, so Camille didn't have to look at him. Apparently he was the reason she wanted to jump. Lucas hesitated. "Stay here, Ikarus. Sit down, and don't leave this room!"

Ikarus, sprawled atop a divan and called out, "Are you coming back? Where are you going?"

"I don't know," Lucas said as he grabbed a candle and went through the door at the far end of the sanctuary. When he and Alina were lost, he'd heard rushing water behind the walls. He might be able to follow that sound back to the golden grotto. He wanted to see it again. Without knowing where he was going, he ran his hand along the wall imagining the way he and Alina had taken. There were so many twists and turns. Soon enough, Lucas realized he'd made a mistake again. But he kept on, calling for Seppo as he went.

Suddenly, Seppo appeared. "You're here," they both said at once.

Seppo looked filmy and translucent as he always did, but his eyes were lively. Lucas stood still, and Seppo gestured for Lucas to follow him. "What's going on?" Lucas asked. "Were you expecting me?"

"Of course. I'll show you. This way. It's shorter this way. Follow me."

Lucas stayed close, but also far enough away if he decided he should flee. This greeting wasn't what he expected. Why was Seppo in the dark tunnel? He didn't carry a candle as Lucas did.

Lucas felt clammy under his cloak. "Where are we going?"

Stopping and turning around to place a skeletal hand on Lucas' shoulder, Seppo said, "Lucas, my son, I know why you have come. Do you?"

"No. Yes. Not really. I want answers. Alina and I have many questions for you. She will be along shortly we should go back so she can find us."

"What are your questions?"

Lucas heard the rushing water behind the walls. "Seppo, stop. What is that sound?"

"Where have you been, Lucas?" Seppo kept going deeper down the tight corridor.

"I was drinking ale, and a strange girl kept talking about water and the monastery. I had imagined I'd find Nikolas at the Blue Gate like always. He's dead, Seppo. My friend is dead. I can't believe it."

"I know." Seppo turned. His eyes glowed in the single candlelight. Lucas saw his own reflection and shivered. "Follow me, Lucas."

Although he was perspiring, Lucas pulled his cloak around him. Seppo walked quickly now, suddenly disappearing around corners then reappearing. Lucas caught up and held onto a piece of Seppo's tunic.

"You know that the river flows through here."

"I know," Lucas said."

"And lava once did. Creating underground tunnels."

"I never knew that."

"Ah, but you did. You just didn't know you knew. That's how it is with many people. They under value their keenness. You were born knowing what I know, but you forgot, dazzled by life as it was." Seppo waved his spectral hand in the air.

"The girl insisted that the well at the Blue Gate comes from your river."

"Our river. Amusing way to put it. The river belongs to itself. We diverted a portion of the water for the monastery. Water makes its own path. Well, that is the miracle of the earth. Who would have guessed a tavern would grow where we placed a well? But it's all for the best in the end."

"What are you talking about, Seppo?"

"The mountain springs flow endlessly." He gestured with both pale hands. "Down the river and where the lava once did, above ground or below, in your mouth, and out your ears . . ." Seppo broke out in laughter. *He's mad,* Lucas thought. *Everyone has gone mad, including me.* Seppo continued, "Water always finds its way. Occasionally, unusual things show up. But one never knows." Seppo pushed open a blue door. They emerged in the golden grotto. "And here, we have a surprise for you."

Lucas blinked and adjusted his eyes to the striations of gold veins throughout the crypt. He had doubted he would ever see it again. Some days, he and Alina thought they'd dreamed it. "Go forward," Seppo murmured.

Lucas took a deep breath and stepped into the gleaming light. He heard the cascading water and saw the reflected patterns dancing at the edges of the stone pool. Such pure beauty made him gasp. His heart raced. It was even more striking than he remembered. He glanced around recalling how ill Alina had been. He thought she was going to die in this glorious place as she lay prone on a stone ledge.

Turning toward the spot where she had lain, he saw something. "What is that?" He took a step forward. Something was there now. Someone. A man wrapped in a monk's robe. Startled, Lucas stepped back. He scanned the room for Seppo and couldn't find him. He narrowed his eyes and crept forward. Rippling, golden shadows shimmered on a face. His face, the face of his friend, Nikolas.

Lucas felt his stomach lurch into his throat, and he gagged. "Seppo, why would you do such a thing?"

Nikolas blinked. He raised a bandaged arm. Was that a grin on his face? Lucas went hesitantly forward. "Nik?"

His leg was splinted and propped atop a stack of pillows. A three-legged stool sat at the edge of the ledge. A pitcher and bowl of water beside it on the floor. Nik's sandy brown hair couldn't hide a glaring crimson gash on the right side of his head. Someone had laced it up with black thread.

"Flaming hell!" Lucas rushed over, grabbed Nikolas and pulled him up in a fierce hug. He didn't hear his friend squeal in pain.

"My God, you're alive! You muzzy mongrel, there's life and breath in you! Nikolas, aren't you dead? I thought you were dead!!" Lucas shouted. "We all did. Brigit has lost her mind. I saw where you fell. How can you be here?"

Seppo placed a restraining hand on Lucas' arm. "Your friend is healing. Careful." He helped Nikolas recline again, stacked an additional pillow under his head, filled a ladle with water, and held it up to Nikolas' lips.

Lucas gingerly touched the long gash on Nik's head. "How did you survive that waterfall? I cannot believe it!"

"I was dead. Or good as," Nik sipped and winced.

Lucas stepped away, stared at his friend, then came back, and sat on the stool that Seppo offered. "Nikolas." He took his hand. "It is really you."

Nik grinned. "Did you bring me an ale? Seppo only has wine here. And he's stingy with it. I never found any highland whisky up there."

"I knew you wouldn't die. I refused to let it be!" Lucas turned from Nik to Seppo and back again. "I would have brought a barrel of ale if I had known. What happened?"

Nik cleared his throat but still spoke in a gravelly voice. "I was catching fish. I saw them next to me. Their big eyes as I was falling and hitting boulders. Everything hurt. I couldn't reach anything. Just falling over and over. Water pounding in my mouth and ears. I thought my eyes blew out of my head."

"No one could survive that." Lucas exclaimed. "Not me. Not you . . ."

Nik started to laugh but winced again. "The water pulled me, and then it threw me. I saw the sky, and then I saw thundering bubbles. It tried to force me into another world. I felt like I wanted to go. I think

I saw what Brigit knows. And when I thought of her, I could see her shrieking at the top, her hair like fingers. I thought I'd better go back."

Lucas stared. He stood up, and sat down again, and grabbed Nik's hand. Lucas turned to Seppo who quietly held the earthenware jug.

"How long has he been here?"

"You best drink, Lucas," Seppo said. Lucas gladly accepted the water knowing it came from the golden pool. "How did you get here, Nikolas?"

"I've had him for several days," Seppo answered. "Not sure. It's best you didn't come sooner, all blue and bloated he was when he popped up in the moat."

"The moat? And you revived him?"

"Not I exactly."

"Then how?" Lucas raked his hands through his hair. He grabbed Nikolas' arm. "How do you feel? Am I dreaming?"

"I feel not too bad. This is a most comfortable place to recline. Where are Brigit and Ikarus?"

"They're home. Bernard, Ig, Rath, and some others, we found them on their way down."

Nikolas smiled.

Lucas patted Nik's hand. "They'll be all right now, won't they? Nikolas, you will remain alive now. Isn't that right Seppo?"

Seppo nodded. "Nikolas will survive. A little crooked perhaps."

"Tell me again what happened, Nik." Lucas insisted.

When Nik finished and answered all Lucas' questions, Seppo led Lucas away from the ledge. "Let your friend rest now."

"Of course. Listen, Seppo, I came here to ask you what is going on in here. Tell me now, in words please, not riddles."

Seppo raised his eyebrows. "I suppose the time has come to tell you everything since you and your friends keep penetrating the walls." Seppo sat on the edge of the pool. He ran his fingers through the water. "I will tell you. But not quite yet. You will have to wait only a little while more. For now, we will concentrate on the healing of Nikolas."

"Can you tell him what you told me, Seppo?" Nikolas sleepily whispered.

"Ah yes, I was getting to that. I will tell you, Lucas, that you were born of this place. Here in this very font."

Lucas jolted. "Here? How can that be true?"

"Tis true," Seppo said.

Lucas got up and paced. "My mother was here. Is that really so? You brought my mother here?"

Seppo nodded. "Yes, I brought my lovely Linnea here to have our child. That is, you. And when the time comes, you will bring Alina."

At the sound of Alina's name, Lucas settled down. He sat next to Seppo and ran his hands through the water. "I intended to bring Alina just now to speak with you. We wanted to ask you some things, many things actually."

"We will discuss them," Seppo said, nodding as if he'd planned that conversation himself.

Lucas gazed at Seppo and then at Nikolas calmly resting on the stone ledge. Strangely, it all began to make sense. Lucas wished Alina was here to see Nikolas recovering in the grotto, and for them to question Seppo together as they'd planned.

What a glorious surprise to find Nikolas! The encounter with the serving girl at the Blue Gate had compelled him to come here. When did Seppo intend to tell him? Peering at Seppo he wondered what secrets remained in the shell of this fragile man. A skip of his heart might erase those secrets at any moment. Seppo read his thoughts, "Don't worry Lucas, you will have your answers. Don't you want to go outside and tell everyone that Nikolas is alive?"

Lucas smiled at his father. "Thank you for saving Nikolas. Yes, I must go soon. There are a lot of curious things happening up on the surface. I best let Brigit know right away. When will Nikolas be able to come home?"

Nikolas tried to sit up. Seppo placed a hand on his shoulder. "Be patient, Nikolas. You have travelled a long way in a brief time." Seppo giggled to himself. "Send Brigit here, Lucas. Nikolas needs to remain for a while more."

Lucas nodded. He sat down next to Nik and took his hand again. Nik squeezed Lucas' hand and let his eyes close. "Come up when you're ready," Seppo said exiting the chamber. Lucas watched his friend breathe. He knew that later that night, secluded in their bedchamber at the boarding house, he would not be able to explain to Alina the incredible joy of finding Nikolas alive. He could still barely believe his own eyes. But he would tell her how it felt to see where he had been born. There was more to understand about who he was, and they would find out together.

He got up and stood silently listening to the water cascade into the pool. Time stood still. Finally, Lucas pulled himself away from the sight of the glistening pool. He embraced Nikolas. "I would never have stopped looking for you."

Nik's eyelids fluttered "I wanted you to know that we were delayed. There was no one to send as a messenger."

"In a way you did," Lucas said thinking about the strange serving girl. "But I certainly would have organized the search much earlier had I known."

"Next time bring ale," Nik quipped.

Lucas ruffled Nik's hair. "Next time remember you're not a fish."

Seppo waited at the threshold. "Go home now, Lucas. When Nikolas is ready, he will come back. For now, tell them that the monks are caring for him."

"Are there other monks here?" Lucas asked.
Seppo held the door wider and gestured for Lucas to go through it.

Chapter 29

When Lucas emerged from the tunnels into the sanctuary, Ikarus was gone. It was full dark outside, and the double doors had been partially closed. Of course, Ikarus would not have waited all that time when Camille was up in the bell tower. Lucas had forgotten about the plight of Camille and Ikarus.

He hurried over to the tower and found nobody but the evening masons. They assured him that the spectacle was over, and that the girl had come down at the insistence of Alina and another woman. They didn't know whether Ikarus was there or not.

Lucas ran the rest of the way home and burst through the door. The parlour was empty except for Shadow stretched out on the floor in front of the fire. In the kitchen, he found Alina seated at the long table with Carissa, Perina, Drusy, Ikarus and Camille. He was startled enough by seeing Camille and Ikarus holding hands that he didn't blurt out: *Nikolas is alive!* as he intended to do. Noticing his confused expression, Alina quickly explained. "We're discussing how Camille will get back up the mountain. Ikarus wants to take . . ."

Ikarus interrupted. "I can do it. I know the way better than anybody. It's all my fault what happened to her. She wants to go

313

home, and I should be the one to take her." He blushed and hung his head. Camille slowly shook her head no.

"Ahh," Lucas stroked his chin. He pulled out a chair at the end of the table, and Perina handed him a full goblet of ruby wine.

"I thought Igmus and Rathbone might be up for the trip," Alina said. "We can pay them well."

"Yes, maybe, but they have not been all the way up the trail," Lucas said. "Listen, there is something more important right now. I have remarkable news." Everyone turned their eyes toward him, their faces full of anticipation. "It is the most welcome news," Lucas said with a falter in his voice. He gazed at each of them before declaring, "Nikolas is alive!! He is alive, and he is well! Seppo has him." Lucas pounded the table with a fist and swiped at his moist eyes. "Our dear friend Nikolas survived the waterfall."

Ikarus broke into loud sobs. Dazed, Alina stood up, then flew into Lucas' lap and smothered his face against her chest. He was laughing and crying, and Alina was too. Carissa and Perina hugged each other, and Drusilla filled their cups and explained some details for Camille.

When they all calmed themselves, Lucas told Alina that they should make haste to Brigit's cottage. She could go right away to Nikolas, and Irene could finally give up her vigil and come home. "Ikarus and Camille, now is the time for the two of you to discuss your situation and be sure that the choices you make are the correct ones. But Ikarus, I think it best that you don't go back up that mountain unless you intend to leave us and stay there."

"I want to see Nikolas too," Ikarus said.

"Yes, Ikarus. Tomorrow, all right? We'll get Brigit over there first."
* * *

On the way to Brigit's cottage, with Shadow trotting alongside them in the warm evening air, Alina told Lucas how she had spoken to the constable on behalf of Camille. "She is free to stay or go."

"That's my girl, Alina. You always do the right thing." He pulled her closer and wrapped his arm around her shoulder.

"Not exactly," she said peering up at him. She stopped walking. "I made a rather large mistake."

Lucas chuckled and pulled her along. "And what could that be?"

"I gave my dagger to Drusilla for protection. You know she goes all around the city at odd hours and to the blacksmith shop searching for Gacheru."

"When did you do that? We must get you another one right away."

"Oh, I have one." She patted her leg. "It's, you see . . ." the cottage glowed in the distance. Alina walked slower. "Drusy gave my dagger to Camille and that is how she stabbed her husband, Mr. Plimpton."

"Ha!" Lucas stood still now. He took Alina's chin in his hand and kissed her gently. "So, you were very clever in speaking to the constable and making sure the issue is settled."

"Yes, I suppose so. You're not angry?"

He shook his head. "I didn't know the man. And the dagger is . . .?"

"Gone. She threw it off the ship."

Lucas nodded happily. "I do so admire the mind of a woman."

She laughed, and they walked cheerily toward the cottage. "I don't think the constable wanted to get involved in the matter anyway."

"Nor do I. Neither he nor the ship's captain had the stomach for condemning an innocent girl, I believe. I do hope Camille goes home. And I hope Ikarus stays." Lucas took a deep breath, squeezed Alina's hand, and then rapped on the cottage door.

After some rustling about, Irene opened it. She gasped and threw her arms around Lucas' waist. While they hugged and murmured to each other, Alina stepped into the cottage. She was surprised to see a young black-haired man sitting in a chair in front of Brigit who sat slumped on the edge of her cot. He was holding both her hands and speaking to her in a chanting sort of voice using words Alina didn't recognize. Brigit turned empty eyes toward Alina. "I know he's dead. Mabon has come to take me up to the pastures."

"He's not!" Lucas shouted from the door. "Nikolas is alive! It's true, Brigit. Come with us now. You can see for yourself. Seppo is caring for him." Brigit's hair flew up and engulfed her head for a moment. Rising, Mabon reached out a hand to greet Lucas. The hourglass hung around his neck and rested on his tanned chest. Lucas blinked watching it fill itself.

"We are kin," Mabon said. The two men shook hands and then clasped hands to elbows.

Alina helped Irene gather her things. Brigit stood alongside her scrying table, her face less pale, but her eyes still confused. She snatched the purple cloth away, leaned over, and surrounded the crystal ball with her hair. When she looked up, she was once again the illustrious Madam Trousdale to Lucas and the youthful Beltree to Mabon. Irene embraced her friend. "You need not leave us now, Brigit. All is well. We are restored."

They hastily made their way to the monastery, with Lucas leading the way and Mabon alongside him. They spoke like old friends. Alina and Irene kept Brigit between them for her hair couldn't settle for long, and they were afraid she would trip on the cobbles.

The double doors to the sanctuary were closed but unlocked. Irene marveled at the magnificent room. They didn't have to wait long for Seppo to appear. He greeted Irene and embraced Mabon, laying a hand on the hourglass momentarily. Brigit watched transfixed. Seppo and Mabon recognized something in each other. When Seppo turned to Brigit, he murmured, "Now, aren't you happy that you didn't poison me after all?"

She glared then giggled like a young girl. "You are not a monk at all! You come from gypsy blood."

Leaning close, he whispered in her ear, "Gypsy blood and gypsy ways. Your sister Linnea saw that right away." She let him take her by the hand and lead her through the narrow door. Brigit glanced back at Lucas, who grinned and threw up his hands.

Mabon and Lucas had many questions for each other and chattered all the way back to the boarding house. Irene exclaimed with delight when the house came into view. "In all my long days, I have never been so glad to come home!"

Drusy informed them that Ikarus and Camille had gone to their respective bedchambers. And exhausted by the long, sad days and sudden good news, Carissa and Perina had retired for the evening as well. When Mabon left them and went back to Brigit's cottage with a promise to return in the morning, Irene retreated to the comfort of her bedchamber.

Lucas and Alina slipped under the coverlet of their thick feather bed. Alina ran her fingers along his chest as he told her what it was like to see Nikolas alive after desperately clamoring up and down the hills in the pelting rain.

In a somber voice, he again described the terrifying waterfall. "We will never fully understand how he survived that." They agreed that only Seppo knew how it really all happened. When they did speak to him again he might explain, but it didn't seem understandable. All that mattered was that Nikolas lived. "I want to go to the Blue Gate and ask that serving girl a few questions too."

Lucas kissed Alina's eyelids and cheeks. Alina stroked his back as he told her how it felt when Seppo showed him where he had been born right there in the golden grotto. He'd been able to imagine his beloved mother in that very room. He felt sure that on the day she brought him into the world, she knew he would one day return there.

Alina promised that when the time came their own babies would enter the world the same way. They marveled at Seppo living for so many years waiting for just the right moment to emerge from the monastery and claim Lucas. "He will explain that," Lucas told her. "Above all we need to understand that."

* * *

When Seppo led Brigit into the golden grotto, she couldn't speak, her hair lay still, and her eyes did not change color. She went limp, and as Nikolas struggled to stand, Seppo guided her to the smooth stone ledge and left them alone. Nikolas handed her a cup of water. She drank and embraced him. "If I had known about this place, I would have followed you over the waterfall."

Nik stroked her sleek black hair. "I'm glad you didn't. Come, lie down and rest with me."

* * *

Two days later at dawn, Ikarus crossed the rickety log onto monastery land. He trudged along the narrow stretch of grass that paralleled the high walls. He found Seppo in the secret cemetery. Ikarus couldn't hide his unease. Seppo frightened him. But Seppo's dark eyes softened, and he reached out a thin hand and clutched Ikarus by the wrist. "Don't ask him for forgiveness. It's not necessary."

Nikolas and Brigit reclined in the sanctuary. Nikolas would continue to sleep in the grotto but in the daytime, he now rested among the candles and pillows with the doors flung wide open so that he could feel the fresh air.

Ikarus hugged Brigit and Nikolas together. They wept and laughed. "How many fish did we get?" Nikolas asked.

"I think they fell back in," Brigit admitted.

"Followed you over the waterfall," Ikarus said.

"Well, then we all survived," Nik said. "I think I will never eat fish again. If they are that offended by being caught it's best to leave them alone."

Seppo served them jugs of water, warm bread, and cheese. Ikarus stayed for most of the day. Nikolas told them how Seppo had sewn up the laceration on his head from threads off his own robe. And how he had yanked his bones back in place with his own spidery hands.

As he made ready to leave Nikolas and Brigit, Ikarus told them about Camille. "We were too late all along. I'm sorry I dragged you both up there."

"No, Ikarus. Have no regret. I enjoyed everything about it. I won't go again," he said and chuckled, "but I'm glad I've seen the beauty and marvel of the world outside our city. Arcana is far enough for me to travel, I believe."

"Will Camille stay?" Brigit seemed to know the answer already.

"No, and she doesn't want me to walk her home." Ikarus stared at a spot on the floor. "Mabon has offered to do it. He went to her village after he lost track of us. Did you know, he had intended to follow us back down the mountain? Her mother asked him to bring her home if he ever encountered her."

Brigit pouted. "I didn't know that. I thought he came to the City of Dreams to console me and take me home."

"I'm sure that was part of it," Nik said and smoothed her silken hair. "But you are home, Brigit."

Ikarus sighed. "I will never see Camille again. She will tend her sheep, and I will remain here and light lanterns. Our paths were meant to cross for only those few enchanted days."

"Many wonderful things await you, young man." Seppo spoke from an obscure corner, startling all of them. "The three of you belong here. Lucas will need your help. Please make yourselves at home."

* * *

The next morning, everyone gathered on the steps of the boarding house to send off Camille and Mabon. The girls had loaded them with satchels of food and Ikarus contributed several wineskins. Lucas made Mabon promise that he would return someday, and although these distant cousins claimed they would see each other again, neither believed it. Before he turned to go, Mabon took Lucas' hand and dropped something into his palm. "For Brigit," he murmured.

"They look like they belong together," Ikarus said watching the two highlanders walk away.

Once they were out of sight, Lucas opened his palm. It was the hourglass. He slipped it over his head for safekeeping. "Back to work tonight, Ikarus?"

"Yes, I'm excited for it." Ikarus grinned, and Lucas slapped him on the back.

"He'll be fine. Of course, never quite the same, but he will meet another girl soon enough," Alina said as she and Lucas made their way to the Blue Gate Tavern. When they got there and ordered two ales, Lucas looked around for the serving girl who had shown him the well. Finally, he asked the barkeep. "There was a girl here a few weeks ago. She took me in the back. She had brown hair, several braids and on that day, green ribbons.

"We did have a girl like that working here."

"Where is she?"

"Gone. She showed up that morning, insisted we let her serve, and then disappeared at the end of the day."

Lucas frowned, "Are you sure? You haven't seen her again?"

The barkeep shook his head and offered to pour another ale, but Lucas waved him away. Alina wandered toward the back room. "Can we go see it?"

"Go ahead," the barkeep pointed as if Lucas didn't know the way.

He and Alina peered over the edge of the well. The water wasn't visible, and they could barely hear it. Frustrated, Lucas said, "It was different that day. Let's go to the river. I want to see if I can tell where Nikolas floated in."

"I thought Seppo said he shot through a lava tunnel into the moat."

"He did say that." Lucas peered at her. "You and I have both been in that moat. Do you believe anything could pop up in there? It drags one down. I've never seen anything come to the surface there. The point is to drag intruders in."

Alina nodded slowly. "Yes, I remember Dugald nearly drowned while carrying me. It doesn't seem an injured man would just float to the top."

Lucas frowned. "There's the moat fed by the loch, fed by the river and the lava tunnels. And then the golden grotto. I wonder if Seppo will ever tell us everything he knows. It seems he wants us to discover his secret for ourselves."

"Perhaps, that's the lesson and legacy he intends to leave us," Alina suggested.

"Yes, he wants us to try to see, not only with our eyes but our spirit." He took her by the hand, and they stepped outside the tavern into the bright sunshine.

"Let's go get Irene and have a picnic by the river. We can bring Mr. Pagett too," Alina said.

Lucas took her hand. "I love you, Alina."

"Thank you," she blushed. "If we weren't already wed, I would ask you right now." They kissed right there in front of the tavern.

"We'll stop and brighten the flower vendors day with lots of coins and fill the boarding house with flowers."

"Yes, a wonderful idea. I want to get some for the Boulevard house too. Drusilla can take them over. She has the place all ready for us. And Lucas look!" She waggled her wrist. "Drusy was helping arrange things with me in my father's study and she found this marvelous bracelet that Father left for me!"

"Ahh, Alina my darling. Your father adored you, as do I." He kissed her and took her delicate wrist in hand to admire the bracelet. I agree it's a perfect time to let Irene know that we are finally going."

"Yes!" Alina beamed. "I'm ready at last."

"In a few days," Lucas said.

"Of course, not today or tomorrow. In a few days," she agreed.

At their picnic, Irene announced that she was giving over the kitchen and running of the boarding house to Carissa and Perina. Ikarus had brought them a lad who could help as well. She and Mr. Pagett would assist each other in tending their separate gardens. And they had a good start on the Boulevard house garden. Lucas wondered if Nikolas would want to resume the merchant trade business. It was a smooth and simple operation of talking and sealing agreements with handshakes.

"I'm going to the monastery with my donkey cart to gather Nikolas tomorrow," Mr. Pagett announced.

"Brigit came to the boarding house this morning to let me know that Nikolas is ready to emerge from his convalescence. He will stay with us in the room that Brigit and he have used before," Irene added.

Lucas grinned. He leaned back on his elbows and sighed with relief. He would again be surrounded by everyone he loved. The only thing left to do was speak to Seppo. He hoped his father was ready to divulge more of his secrets. How could he ever show his gratitude for saving the life of his remarkable friend?

"I'm glad we brought so many bouquets," Alina gushed. "We will have a grand celebration, won't we?"

"Yes," Irene said. "The girls are baking extra bread. We will have roasted lamb and fresh vegetables from Mr. Pagett."

"I'll tell the wine merchant to deliver a cask," Lucas said.

The following afternoon, Mr. Pagett clomped up to the boarding house in his little donkey cart with Seppo and Nikolas in the back.

Shadow rode in the cart nestled in Nikolas' lap. Brigit walked alongside. She had trimmed the ragged ends off her hair and sewn herself a new purple and red layered skirt.

Everyone gathered on the steps to greet Nikolas. The cathedral bells chimed to mark the joyous occasion. Nikolas was robust and handsome as ever. His hair had grown to cover most of the scar on his head. Lucas approached his friend. He took the hourglass from his neck and slipped it over Nik's head. It was full. "Welcome home, Nikolas."

Nikolas blushed when he saw everyone. Bernard and Wentworth had made the trip after Rathbone rode to Arcana to collect them. Ikarus, with tears crumpling his face, stepped up to help Nikolas step out of the cart. He walked with a slight limp, but the bones in his arms were straight and strong.

Igmus and Rathbone blinked and gently shook Nik's hand. Neighbors gathered on the street. The throng cheered as Nikolas walked up the front steps on his own. He turned with a sheepish grin, "That was one long journey. And I'm glad it's over."

Everyone was dressed in their finest clothes as if they were at the Grande Inn. Lucas poured ruby wine into the pewter goblets and made the toast to Nikolas. They all gathered at the table to enjoy the roast and an exquisite stew made with pure, golden grotto water.

* * *

In the weeks that followed, Nikolas and Brigit took long walks around the city and to the river. They went every day to visit Seppo who invited them to spend as much time at the monastery as they liked. He showed him his simple daily routine. Brigit admitted that she'd had ill intentions toward him at first, but now she enjoyed the mystical solitude of the ivy-covered monastery. "We will come every day, Seppo," she promised, and Nik agreed.

For now, they simply sat in the courtyard garden with Shadow taking turns napping on their laps. Some days, they went to Brigit's cottage but often returned for the evening meal and to sleep at the boarding house. There was room enough for them to stay at the boarding house, Irene reminded them, and Lucas and Alina offered rooms at the Boulevard house. But Brigit and Nikolas said they would remain at her cottage for now. They spent every sunset at the monastery.

Nikolas told Lucas that he would continue with their merchant dealings but leave most of it to him. And while Lucas was busy with that and adding to his lineage, Nikolas would help Seppo preserve the monastery for Lucas and his descendants.

He had given up his room at the harbour that was destroyed by whatever potions Brigit had doused the place with. Mr. Merson had that section of rotten structures burned to the ground. Many wondered if it was rats or Brigit he feared most.

One afternoon, as she wrung the linens, Lucas spoke quietly to Drusilla. "I believe, Drusy that there is no reason to wonder if Gacheru will ever return."

She turned crimson. "No sir, no there is not."

Chapter 30

One afternoon when the air was crisp and the leaves on the trees lining the streets turned scarlet and yellow, Lucas and Alina took the long way to the monastery through the mulberry trees and over the rickety bridge. They brought flower baskets to the secret cemetery and went through the double doors to the sanctuary. Seppo nimbly led them down to the grotto.

"What can you tell us, Seppo?" Lucas asked seated on the edge of the golden pool with Alina. "We don't understand how Nikolas could have popped up in the moat. Is that truly what happened?"

Seppo sat on the ledge where both Alina and Nikolas had healed. He smiled to himself. "That is true. The surface can be deceiving. Listen, if I were you, I would maintain the loch system and make sure the moat never dries up."

Lucas nodded. "I won't let that happen. I understand. Nothing will change here. Now, tell me how you revived Nikolas?"

Seppo rubbed his eyes with his long-fingered fists. "Right here. It's this water. The golden water. From here, it heals."

Lucas stared. "Here? Only here?"

Seppo nodded. "Some. But not all. This water doesn't heal everyone. Brigit will add it to her potions. So, we'll see." He handed

Lucas a cup and gestured for him to drink. Lucas did and passed the cup to Alina.

"And the Blue Gate Tavern, is there any connection?" Lucas asked.

Seppo shook his head. "Everything is connected as you know. I can't explain that barmaid and what you noticed in that well. Often a messenger arrives when needed."

Lucas ran his hands through the velvety water. "When I feel this water, it's as if I almost remember."

Seppo smiled. "Here, you have found the source from whence you came. I was pleased when you and Alina discovered this place on your own. There is great power here, Lucas, and I am leaving it to the two of you to protect. You can see, I am truly ancient. And I'm tired. I waited ages and ages for your mother. When she finally appeared, I understood only her blood mixed with mine could fulfill our prophecy."

Alina sat silently listening. She trailed her hand in the water as well and watched the look in the eyes of Lucas as he heard the words spoken from his father. Someday she would bring Lucas' children into the world in this very place. A shiver of apprehension and delight ran through her.

"You are one of the original monks who left the hilltop city, Seppo."

"I am the slender one."

"This grotto was made by your hands."

"And that of the others."

"Are there other monks here, Seppo?"

"Not in such a long, long time." He sighed. "You have seen their gravestones. Their souls accompany me."

Lucas went to Seppo and took both of his hands. "You are haunted."

Seppo nodded, his dark eyes filling as he blinked and swiped at his hollow cheeks with thin-skinned fingers.

Lucas waited wondering if he hadn't noticed lately how worn-out Seppo looked or if this was a recent situation. "How can you have lived so very long?"

"My companions and I, we sought redemption from our misdeeds. We were given this shimmering gift of water, it taught us that the only true treasure is life. I am the one who needed to learn this most of all. On this ledge I sleep. Sometimes forever it seems." He chuckled. "You understand, passing from here to the other side." He gazed at Lucas then, and then at Alina, as if he expected a nod of understanding. When they sat there in confused silence, he went on. "My old companions and I, we meet at the brink of deep sleep between the two worlds. When I awaken I'm very thirsty." He indicated the water.

Lucas shook his head. "I can't grasp it. What you're telling me. How can something like this be? How long can one person stay alive?"

"As long as he must to relight the candles. And if not candles, then to welcome the stars. A man must live as long as he finds it necessary, even if he must survive the pierce of an arrow and shed bloody wounds as you have, or in one extraordinary event spiral through an underground river. If only my lost monk companions could have witnessed your friend Nikolas!

"Lucas, a man must live long enough to pass on a legacy to his son. By the choice of a man or the spirit of a woman, the will to live makes its own path as does the water." Seppo smiled contentedly. He got up and served them each another ladle of water. "It's an endless story, the nature of life. Understand and remember this; . . . there are many things preserved beneath the surface. The water, the stones, the minerals, the soil, the hearts and souls of banished men."

He waved a deep sleeve around the grotto, "This is alchemy, Lucas. All of it. But most of all you are. Your mother and I had more than our love in common; we had the ability to create a man as unique as you. She could not survive the arrow passing through her and save you as well. That is why you're here. Now, because of you, the monastery and this precious water will remain alive. Use the gifts wisely. Mind my secret, son."

Lucas returned his father's steady gaze. "Until the end of my days, I promise."

Seppo turned to Alina and took her small hands in his. "You are strong and brave. As will your children be. Let your heart rest easy, lass. There is naught to fear."

* * *

Late that night reclining in their bedchamber at the Boulevard house, Alina curled around Lucas and said, "They are the only two who could have created you, your mother Linnea, and Seppo."

"I believe so. Like us, Alina, the connection of my mother and father was foresworn. My love, there is untold beauty in the world. It's always there, hidden beneath the surface."

"Why did he whisper to you, as we took our leave, that you would find him in the sanctuary soon?"

Lucas exhaled, long and slow. "He was letting me know that he is finished. He will not sleep on the ledge in the grotto and drink that water anymore. He's ready to go."

"I don't want him to go."

"Nor do I." Lucas stroked her cheek. But who am I to stop him? He has lived a long time without my mother."

"Your mother was also of a rare blood, Lucas."

"She was. I always felt that. All I know now is that so many things in this life cannot be explained, but they are not fearful." Lucas smiled softly.

Alina sighed. "I believe the story of Seppo waiting for, and finally finding your mother, and your remarkable gifts, Lucas, makes the unique nature of Brigit more understandable. Doesn't it?"

"I believe it does. Brigit didn't trust Seppo, and it turns out they both have extraordinary gifts. Her distinctive blood. It's the same as mine and that of my mother. And she and Nikolas, and you and I, and our children we will continue to fulfill my father's legacy."

Alina's eyes shone. "Can you even begin to imagine our children, Lucas?"

"Yes, I can, my love." Lucas gathered her under him. "Enough talking for now," he murmured "Our children await."

The End

Glossary of Names

Alina: Graceful and Noble

Arcana, the Country Town: A deep secret, a mystery

Bernard: Bear

Brigit: Celtic Goddess of Fire

Camille: Free born, honorable

Campbell: Twisted Mouth, *City of Dreams*

Carissa: Grace

Daria: Trustworthy person, *City of Dreams*

Drusilla: Strong, sturdy

Dugald: Dark Stranger, *City of Dreams*

Gacheru: Spy

Ikarus: To have come to be present

Igmus: Unlearned

Irene: Peace

Linnea: Flower

Lucas: Light Giving

Marion: Rebellious, *City of Dreams*

Nikolas: People's Triumph

Pagett (Mr.): Dependable, traditional

Perina: Generous, optimistic
Ragbone: Rag gatherer, bone picker
Vasil: Imperial, *City of Dreams*
Wentworth: From a farm near woods

About the Author

Suzanne Burkett lives in Incline Village, Nevada with her family. As well as writing, she enjoys skiing, hiking, and mountain biking.

Hidden Beneath is the sequel to *City of Dreams* and available everywhere.

Suzanne's other books:
How to Get Along with Yourself and Others, and *Life is a Piece of Pie in Your Eye* are available on Amazon in print and on Kindle.
Love Poems, Journey of the Raindrop and *Still Waters* are available on Kindle.